"*The Calling* is that rare unplug-the-phone, skip-all-meals, ignore-your-bedtime thriller. It's twisty, sharp and very, very creepy — and Det. Hazel Micallef is a perfectly original charmer." — Gillian Flynn, author of *Sharp Objects*

"A clever serial/ritual-murderer tale. . . . Hazel Micallef is a splendid recruit to the ranks of fictional detectives."
— *Literary Review*

"You have to read it. If you are a fan of detective stories you will want to read *The Calling*. If you are a fan of good fiction you will want to read *The Calling*."
— Metapsychology Online Review

"Fans of mystery thrillers by Jeffrey Deaver and James Patterson will likely enjoy [*The Calling*]. . . . A solid and stunningly effective read. . . . You won't be disappointed."
— *Western Star*

"The most enthralling, creepiest, grizzliest book I've read in years." — Chelsea Cain, author of *Heartsick*

"Terrifying, moving and complex. . . . *The Calling* is truly compelling, giving the reader a terrifying insight into the mind of a depraved killer, who still has a capacity for love. It is a thrilling psychological tale which ratchets up the pace from the intriguing opening scene to the heart-in-the-mouth finale." — *Peterborough Evening Telegraph*

"If you're tired of *same old, same old* procedurals and looking for something new and different in a mystery, you won't go wrong by reading Inger Ash Wolfe's highly recommended chiller, *The Calling*." — Bookloons.com

INGER ASH WOLFE

THE CALLING

A HAZEL MICALLEF MYSTERY

McCLELLAND & STEWART

Cloth edition published 2008
Mass-market paperback edition published 2009

Library and Archives Canada Cataloguing in Publication

Wolfe, Inger Ash
The calling / Inger Ash Wolfe.

ISBN 978-0-7710-8896-4 (pbk.).–ISBN 978-0-7710-8897-1 (bound)
I. Title.

PS8645.O442C34 2008   C813'.6   C2007-905842-6

We acknowledge the financial support of the Government of Canada
through the Book Publishing Industry Development Program and
that of the Government of Ontario through the Ontario Media
Development Corporation's Ontario Book Initiative. We further
acknowledge the support of the Canada Council for the Arts and the
Ontario Arts Council for our publishing program.

Typeset in Van Dijck by M&S, Toronto
Printed and bound in the United States of America

McClelland & Stewart Ltd.
75 Sherbourne Street
Toronto, Ontario
M5A 2P9
www.mcclelland.com

I   2   3   4   5   13   12   11   10   09

For Margaret, David, and Alice, with love and thanks

Friday, November 12, 3 p.m.

He was precisely on time.

For most of the afternoon, Delia Chandler had busied herself with small tasks around the house. She had already vacuumed the upstairs and downstairs that week, but she did it again, taking care to move tables and chairs to ensure she got the head of the vacuum everywhere that dust could hide. One of Simon's tenets was cleanliness: she did not want to meet him for the first time with so much as a speck of dirt anywhere in the house.

She ran the dishwasher and cleaned the dish tray. She even washed the bar of soap in the bathroom. In his communications with her, Simon had said that the key to health was to take care of your environment as you took care of yourself. She had followed his advice very closely indeed, preparing the teas exactly as he detailed, drinking them at the prescribed times of day, taking gentle exercise at exactly 6 a.m., and getting into bed at 9 p.m. to make sure she got nine full hours of sleep every night.

His ministrations – however long-distance they were – had been invaluable in keeping her strength up until he could come. The cancer was in her bones now, and it had spread like a moss through her pelvis and into the surrounding tissues. Dr. Lewiston had laid out for her the palliative options: once the pain got too intense, she would be moved into the hospice where it would be "managed." She imagined herself being put to sleep like a dog. Her sons, Robert and Dennis, had said they would pay whatever costs were involved to ensure her comfort. Sweet boys. She agreed to whatever they proposed, knowing that, when the time came, she would not need their help at all.

At two-thirty, Delia went upstairs and changed into something befitting the guest she was about to receive. She pulled on a new pair of pantyhose, and then stepped into a blue wool dress. Any movement of her arms above shoulder level shot a scatter of pain throughout her body, as if a tiny grenade had gone off in her hips. She eased the dress up over her chest and shoulders, and she sat down to catch her breath. Then she stood and looked at herself in the mirror. She was quite presentable for an eighty-one-year-old, dying woman. She put on a pair of black low-heeled shoes, but thought better of them, and put the orthotics back on. Simon would not want her to be in pain for the sake of looking good for him. No, he would not approve of that kind of vanity.

The doorbell rang at three o'clock on the button. She even saw the second hand hit twelve at that very moment. She took a deep breath, smoothed the dress over her stomach, and opened the door.

Simon stood on her doorstep, bearing a heavy valise. He was terribly thin, perhaps one of the thinnest human beings she had ever seen. It gave him the appearance of height. He wore a long black coat and a black derby on his head, and his face was deeply lined. He had the aspect of a gentle elder, even though she knew he was younger than she was, by at least thirty years. His was a face with all the blows of life nesting in it. Her heart went out to him, even though it was she he had come to succour.

"Mrs. Chandler," he said. "Thank you for inviting me to your home."

She drew the door wide and gestured into the house. "Simon, I am honoured to welcome you."

He entered and removed his hat, placing it silently on the hall table. He undid a black silk sash from under his chin, and slid out of his caped coat, and handed it to Delia. The outside of the coat was cold from the fall air without, but inside, where his body had been, it was warm. She went down the hall a little and hung it for him. When she came back, he was sitting on the couch, eyes scanning the room, and his long hands clasping his knees. "I imagined your house would be just like this, Mrs. Chandler."

"Please call me Delia."

"Delia, then. This house is as if I'd dreamed it. Come and sit near me." She did, lowering herself uncomfortably into the chair beside the couch. When she was seated, he lifted his valise onto the table and opened it. A smell of camphor emerged from inside. "We needn't truck in chit-chat," he said. "It's as if we are already old friends, no?" She smiled at him and nodded once in assent. It delighted her that his demeanour in person was entirely of a piece with how he was in his emails: grave, but not humourless, and quietly authoritative. He drew out half a dozen vials from the valise. They were filled with dried plant matter and powders. He lined them up neatly on the coffee table. "How have you been?" he asked. "How's your pain?"

"It's manageable," she said. "I take the lantana for the pain in my bones, and it works for a couple of hours. But I don't mind. A little respite is all I need while waiting for you."

He smiled at this, and reached out to take her hand. He clasped it gently. "I choose very carefully, Delia, who I come to see. Only those who are completely committed will do. Are you still completely committed?"

"I am."

"And you are not frightened?"

She hesitated here and looked away from him. "I have told myself to be truthful with you, so I will say that I have been scared, yes. A little. But not now, not at this moment."

"Good," he said, and his voice told her that it was all right to have experienced some trepidation. It meant she had faced it and moved past it. "We should get started then."

"Yes," she said.

"I do have to ask you to do one thing for me first, however. It will make you somewhat uncomfortable." Delia looked at his eyes and waited for him to explain. "I must look at your body, Delia. I need to see your skin before proceeding."

She blanched at this, and thought of herself picking through the few dresses in her closet for one that would make her look the most presentable. Now he wanted her to stand exposed before him? But she did not question him, rather she rose and faced him in front of the low coffee table. She reached behind herself with one hand and drew the zipper on the back of her dress down, wincing in pain.

"Hold on," he said. "I don't want this to be difficult for you." He stood and came to her, went behind her and unzipped her the rest of the way. The dress fell to the floor in a pool of blue wool. She felt him unsnap her bra, and she shook it off down her arms, and then her hands travelled down the puckered, pale flesh over her belly and she pushed her underwear and pantyhose down. "Thank you, Delia. I'm sorry for the discomfort. Are you cold?"

"No," she said. She felt his finger tracing her spine, and she imagined he was pulsing energy into her, burning away the wild cells under her skin that were eating her life. Simon held her shoulder and gently turned her. She half-expected to catch his eyes, as if this could be a romantic moment blooming – and what would she do if it were? If the last person to show her real compassion also wanted to show her love? But no, all of that kind of love was gone from her life forever. The last time she'd stood before a man naked she had ruined lives. She wondered how far into the past her own purity had to extend for Simon's purposes, and she debated whether she should tell him. Then, selfishly, so she thought, she decided to keep it to herself. There was only this now, no past, only this. He lifted her arms and looked into her armpits, then lifted each breast, one at a time. He touched his fingertip to a shiny coin of skin beneath one breast. "This was a mole, I'm presuming?"

"I had it removed when I was forty," she said. "Vain of me."

"It's all right," he said.

When he reached her abdomen, he laid his hand on a scar below her navel. "My birthsmile," she said, looking down. "Caesarean. Just Dennis. There'd been no problem with Robert." She shook her head. "Fifty-four years ago now, if you can believe it."

"Did they do a hysterectomy? Take out your uterus?"

"No."

He patted the scar. "Good. What about your appendix? You still have that?" She nodded. "But not your tonsils, I imagine."

"No," she said. "Who at my age has their tonsils any more?"

"It's always a bonus if someone does. But I don't expect it." He picked her dress up off the floor and slid it down over her head, then put her hand in his and held it there, in his palm. "I put you at a hundred and thirty-five pounds," he said. "Forgive me for saying."

"One hundred and thirty-seven," she said, trying to sound impressed. "Did you once work on the midway?"

He smiled kindly. "It's only to help me with my measurements. Dosages and that sort of thing."

"Is there anything else?"

"No . . . that's all, Delia. Thank you. You can put the rest of it on and sit down now. Sit on the couch if you will." She pulled her underthings on, feeling more shy than she had when she'd stood naked before him. He leaned over to pick up a piece of thread that had come off her dress. He rolled it into a ball between his thumb and forefinger, and slid it into his pocket. She watched him turn and go into her kitchen and put the kettle on the stove. She saw him inspecting the countertops and the kitchen table. A couple of times, he went out of view, and she heard the lid of her garbage can open and close. She did feel frightened now. She wanted to tell him, but she did not want him to change his mind. He had told her she was special. She had impressed him. After everything he had done for her, now he was asking for *her* help. She could not refuse him, and she would not fail him. What he asked for, what he asked of her, was so insignificant in the face of what she would reap from her courage. She heard the kettle begin to whistle, and Simon brought it back, a plume of white steam trailing behind him, and he laid a trivet on the table. He took a small white teacup out of his valise and put it on the table beside the six vials. He opened them one at a time and held them out to her, to smell. Valerian to calm her, belladonna and hops to help her sleep, herbal sedatives. In higher doses, they acted as anaesthetics. He tipped out a half-thimbleful of each and dropped it into the teacup, then poured hot water over it. Immediately, the air filled with an earthy smell, a smell of the forest floor and bark and roots. He swirled the cup in his hands.

"Are you ready?"

"Will it taste bad, Simon?"

"It will taste absolutely dreadful," he said, and he smiled for her. She took the cup and looked into it. It looked like a miniature swamp, swimming with bracken and bits of matter. "Drink it all. Including the solid bits. Try to chew them a little if you can bear to."

She tilted the cup into her mouth. The herbal stew poured into her like a caustic, burning her tongue and the back of her throat. She pitched forward instinctively to spit the brew out, but he caught her with one hand against her clavicle and the other over her mouth.

"That's it, Delia. You can do this."

She swallowed in fits, her eyes watering. "God," she said, her voice choked. "Is this poison?"

"No, Delia. The tea is not going to kill you. Swallow it . . . that's it, let it go down."

He watched her settle as the last of the tea went down her esophagus. She clamped a hand over her stomach. "My God, Simon. That was the worst one yet."

"Can you feel it in you? Spreading?"

She looked around, as if to check that her reality was as she remembered it. She was in her living room. In the house she had lived in since her wedding day. Her sons had been born in this house, and had grown into men against the backdrop of its walls. Eric had died here. She had grown old here. She would not make it to *ripe* old age.

pushed aside. Its metal head clinked against glass. Finally, his eye fell on a leather knife-sheath, and he took it out and held the weight of it in the palm of his hand. He wrapped his fingers around the handle, and the sound as he drew the blade from its hiding place was like a voice, like a word whispered: an utterance. It said *taketh*, and he did.

] 2 [

Saturday, November 13, 7 a.m.

"Hazel! Hazel Pedersen, are you out of bed?"

Detective Inspector Hazel Micallef opened her bedroom door. She could hear a low chuckle emanating from the bottom of the stairs. "Mother, don't use my married name. Especially this early in the bloody morning."

"Sorry, Miss Micallef. Your breakfast is ready."

"Keep it up, Mother."

That low chuckle again.

Hazel closed the bedroom door and hobbled back to stand in front of the mirror. She was still hunched over, the pain in her lower back radiating around to her hips. She watched herself in the mirror lean forward to brace herself against the dresser. It sometimes took up to ten minutes before she could stand upright in the mornings. If it still hurt after fifteen, she took a Percocet, although she tried to save the painkillers until the evening, when it wouldn't matter if she could think straight or not. She tried to push her pelvis forward, but a bolt of electricity rushed down through her rear end and into the back of her leg. She shook her head at herself, ruefully. "You goddamned old cow." Her grey hair was standing out on the sides of her head and she leaned across the dresser, separated the comb and brush and pulled the brush through her hair. Two bobby pins tucked in tight behind her ears would keep it all in place. She ran her hand over her forehead and her hair, and her other hand followed with her cap. She tugged it down. Every morning, this transformation: a sixty-one-year-old divorcée under the covers, a detective inspector with the Ontario Police Services Port Dundas detachment in front of the mirror. She straightened her name tag and pulled her jacket tighter around her shoulders, trying to stand tall. Then she took the cap off and shook her hair out. "Christ," she said. The Percocet was in the top drawer, between the underwear and the bras. She looked at it, respite tucked between underthings, almost erotic, a promise of release. She closed the drawer.

Downstairs, there was an egg-white omelette with a single piece of sprouted wholegrain flax and kamut toast sitting on a plate. The bread that made this toast was so dangerously high in fibre it had to be kept in the freezer lest it cause bowel movements in passersby. There was a cup of steaming black coffee beside it. "You need a haircut," her mother said.

Hazel Micallef took her seat and put her cap down beside the plate. "No one sees my hair."

"I see it."

"Are you going to eat with me, or are you just going to torment me?"

"I ate." Her mother – either Mrs. Micallef or Your Honour to the entire town – was still dressed in her quilted blue-and-pink housedress. She kept her back to Hazel, moving something around in the frying pan. Hazel smelled bacon. "Eat," said her mother.

"I'll wait for the bacon."

"No meat for you, my girl. This is for me."

Hazel stared down at the anemic omelette on the plate. "This isn't food for a grown woman, Mother," she said.

"Protein. And fibre. That's your breakfast. Eat it." She stared at her daughter until she picked up a fork. "How's your back?"

"The usual."

"Every morning your back tells you to start eating right. You should listen."

Her mother had been back in the house for almost three years. After Hazel's divorce from Andrew, she had taken her mother out of The Poplars and brought her home. She'd never cared for that place, and having her "underfoot" (as Hazel put it to her, to get the old goat's goat) provided them both with company. Her mother was the sort of elderly lady that younger people called "spry," but to Hazel, Emily Micallef was a force of nature, and not to be trifled with. She had seen her mother, on more than one occasion, react to an offer of help – to carry a bag, to cross a street – with a tart "piss off, I'm not crippled," followed by a semi-lunatic smile. She was the only woman Hazel had ever met who loved being old. At sixty-one, Hazel herself was not entirely enamoured of old age, but at eighty-seven, her mother was in her element. Thin and rangy, with skinny red-mottled arms, and long blue-veined fingers, her mother sometimes seemed a clever old rat. Her eyes, still clear but rimmed with faint pink lids, were vigilant: she missed nothing. In her younger years, before she entered civic politics, she and Hazel's father had owned Port Dundas's largest clothing store, Micallef's. It was legend in the town that no one ever stole anything out from under Emily. She could smell unpaid-for merchandise going out the door, and after catching a dozen or so would-be thieves, it was widely assumed that no one ever tried again. It was only after Burt Levitt bought the store, in 1988, that Micallef's even had a theft-detection system.

Her mother brought a plate of crispy bacon to the table. Hazel had choked down half the flavourless omelette (it had a sliver of waxy "Swiss cheese" in it that she suspected was made of soy protein) and watched her mother snap off a piece of bacon between her front teeth. She chewed it savouringly, watching Hazel the entire time. "I need the fat," she said.

"And the salt?"

"Salt preserves," said her mother, and Hazel laughed.

"Are you Lot's wife?"

"I'm nobody's wife," she said. "And neither are you. Which is why I need to put on weight, and you need to take it off. Or the only man who'll ever come into this house again will be here to read the meter."

"What would you do with a man, Mother? You'd kill anyone your age."

"But I'd have fun doing it," said Emily Micallef with a grin. She finished off a second slice of bacon, then flicked a piece onto Hazel's plate. "Eat up and go. My shows are coming on."

Hazel and Andrew had bought the house in Pember Lake in 1971, when Emilia, their first daughter, was eighteen months. It meant a ten-minute drive back into Port Dundas to get to Micallef's for Andrew (whose father-in-law had hired him on), but both he and Hazel preferred being at least a little outside of the town's grasp. Later, when Hazel had been promoted back to the town after paying her dues at a community policing office in the valley, the house served double sanctuary. Both born in places where dropping-in was *de rigueur*, they'd opted for privacy in their adulthoods, raising children in a town outside of the "big smoke" (as they called Port Dundas), in a place with a population of less than two hundred. People knew not to come knocking – with a job that saw her knowing many hundreds of men, women, and children by their first names, Hazel Micallef was a woman entitled to her time off. You didn't come to the house in Pember Lake unless you were invited, or it was an emergency.

Hazel got into the Crown Victoria she'd inherited when Inspector Gord Drury, the detachment's CO since 1975, had retired in 1999. Central Division of the Ontario Police Services had been promising a replacement for Drury ever since, but it was an open secret that the commander of Central OPS, Ian Mason, wanted to roll the Port Dundas detachment, and five other so-called rural stations, into Mayfair Township's catchment. Mayfair was one hundred kilometres to the south, in a different area code. It was a long-distance call to Mayfair. Hazel, the only detective inspector in the entire province acting as a detachment commander, was holding her ground: she reminded Mason on a regular basis that Central owed her a CO, but she was despairing of ever getting one.

She remembered the look on Commander Mason's face at her swearing-in as interim when Drury had dropped the Crown Victoria's keys into her hand, like the passing of a torch. It had been fairly close to a sneer. A female skip. A female skip whose *mother* had once been mayor, and who herself was a mere detective inspector. Drury had been superintendent material, but he chose fishing over it. Hazel knew what Mason thought of her: she'd made DI by the skin of her teeth and now she was in charge of a detachment that represented a savings of over nine million dollars a year to the OPS if they could get the clearance to merge services with Mayfair. She'd been entitled to a new car, one that didn't smell so much of Gord's cigarettes, but she knew the car would air out eventually, and it was still running. Plus, the frugality would look good on her, she thought. Let Mason deny her anything: she was driving someone else's junker. But deny her he did. It was sport to him. Extra men, travel allowances, computer upgrades. He lived to say no, mumbling across the line from the HQ in Barrie, "Goodness, Hazel, what need have you up there for colour screens?" And here she was, six years on, driving the same car. Two hundred and fifty thousand kilometres on it, but it was her vehicle like it or no, and she was going to drive it until the engine fell out. Then, she suspected, Mason would give her a horse if she begged enough for it. She backed out of the driveway and onto Highway 117.

It was fall in Westmuir County. A carpet of leaves had accumulated at the edges of fields, on lawns, in parks. Still red and yellow, but within a couple of weeks, the trees would be entirely bare, and the leaves on the ground brown and brittle. The air was changing, the moisture leaving it, and in its place was a wire-thin thread of cold that would expand, leading deeper into November and December, to become sheets of frigid wind. Hazel could already hear the branches rattling with it.

She took the bridge over the Kilmartin River and noted a torrent of leaves flowing down the middle of it. In three of the last four years, the river had spilled over its banks, eating away at the base of the high shale walls and destabilizing the road above. There had already been one tragedy, across the way from where she now drove, when a car carrying four teenagers back from a prom in Hillschurch had driven off the blacktop by two or three feet and hit a fissure. In a panic (so investigators later said), the girl behind the wheel had hit the accelerator rather than the brake, and the crack in the earth had directed them right over the edge, like a rail. All four were killed. There was not a shop or service within forty kilometres open for business on the day of the burials.

She rolled down the window, coming into town, and the scent of the fall air swirled around her head. She followed the road down to the right and then up into Main Street rising in front of her, its far end a full eight hundred feet higher above sea level than its bottom. On either side of the street were arrayed the buildings and names she had known her whole life: Crispin's Barbershop; Port Dundas Confectionery; The Ladyman Café; Carl Pollack Shoes (Carl himself dead now almost twenty years); The Matthews Funeral Home; Cadman's Music Shop; The Freshwater Grille (the "e" was new); Micallef's, of course; the Opera House and the bowling alley behind it; the Luxe Cinema; Roncelli's Pizza and Canadian Food (which everyone called "the Italians"), and the newer businesses, like the computer shop owned by the guy from Toronto; a bookstore that actually sold more than suspense and horror paperbacks, called Riverrun Books; and a mom-and-pop store beside the gas station, called Stop 'N' Go. All of it serviced a population of 13,500 in the town; Hoxley, Hillschurch, and Pember Lake made it 19,000.

It was strange to have spent all of one's life in or close to a single place. But every time Detective Inspector Micallef drove this strip, her heart sang. This was where she belonged; there was no other place for her. Mayfair was more than a one-hour drive (forty-five minutes if it was an emergency), and Mason, in Barrie, was a further thirty kilometres to the south. She kept that world at a mental arm's-length as much as she could. *This* was her world. Every doorway framed a story for her – some good, some not so good – and the faces that peered out of those doors, or walked the sidewalks, were her intimates. When she and Andrew split up, she felt lonesome and bereft, but the feeling only lasted a while. And then, as if the marriage had been a caul in her eye, she saw her true life-partner in front of her, and it was this place.

She pulled up to the curb beside Ladyman's and put her cap back on. Inside the café, the counterman, Dale Varney, turned the moment he saw her and poured a cup of coffee. "Your mother still starving you?"

"To death," she replied.

"Toasted western?"

"Please, Dale."

She pulled a copy of the *Toronto Sun* toward her along the countertop and took in the front page. Some giant baseball player had admitted to using steroids. *Really – you mean you don't look like a firetruck from guzzling raw eggs, pal?* She sipped the coffee and leafed through the paper. Nothing of interest, and of course, nothing local. You needed a gruesome murder in the middle of Main Street to make it into the Toronto papers. In these parts, the paper came out only twice a week, but everything in it counted. Who was born, who had died, what happened in the county courts, what shocking speeds certain cars on certain country roads were caught going. Her name and the names of her officers were standard fare in the pages of the *Westmuir Record*; it came with the territory. Any crime reported in the county had her imprimatur on it (or her deputy Ray Greene's), and a quote from the Port Dundas OPS meant that what you were reading was true, was vetted.

It was as much a responsibility as policing was, but it had different rules. Hazel had made it clear to her corps that any media requests came through her, and once she agreed to speak, or to let someone speak, to a reporter, she got final cut on the quotes. It wasn't exactly tampering, but her office was the only outlet for the bona fides. So the *Record* played by the rules. And when she asked the paper – as she did from time to time – to hold back something of what they'd learned about a certain situation, or to delay publishing a detail or two, they complied. Because they were neighbours and friends to everyone who walked the streets of the various townships their newspaper covered, they knew everyone affected by a crime, or involved in one. Their first vested interest was their own community, the second was newspaper sales. Hazel liked living in a place where certain priorities still held.

Dale brought her sandwich, and she tore into it. It was hot and salty, with sweet red pepper hidden in the folds. Her mother would kill her if she knew, but at least now, she would have the energy to get to lunch. Her mother was giving her protein and fibre. That's what they put into kibble, she thought.

She paid Dale and got back into the car, drove halfway up the rest of Main Street to Porter Street and turned right. There, set back from the corner a little, was the Port Dundas police detachment. Her men and women covered the front line from Dublin in the south to Fort Leonard in the north, and from Georgian Bay to Temakamig – in other words, the entirety of Westmuir County, an area totalling 1,100 square kilometres.

There were community policing bureaus in many of the larger towns of the county, but for anything major — murder, armed robbery, aggravated assault — the Port Dundas PD was called in. Her officers could make it to most parts of their catchment in under an hour, although many of the larger communities of Westmuir County were within a half-hour drive. They were well situated even if they weren't well staffed: she had only twelve front-liners — eight provincial constables and four sergeants leading the platoons — and two detectives including herself. (They'd been three, but DC Hunter had retired in the summer. She knew how hopeless it would be to try and get *him* replaced.) The Port Dundas detachment was generally regarded the best-run station in the region, despite its lack of an official CO. The phrase "copes admirably" was frequently used in connection with them.

She went around the back and parked in her spot. The sign said, Parking for Inspector of Police Only, not her name, like some of the other signs. Six years in the role, but she was still (and still thought of herself as) the interim commanding.

Detective Sergeant Raymond Greene was standing in her doorway the moment she went into her office. Greene liked to dress the part: beige mackintosh, shiny black shoes, a black homburg. He pushed himself off the frame and came toward her. He looked tense. "Why can't you get a cellphone, Skip?"

"I don't like cellphones, Ray. It means people can reach me whenever they want."

"Exactly," he said.

Melanie Cartwright, her assistant, came out of her office farther down the hall. "Detective Inspector, I have a message for you from the community office in Kehoe."

"River or Glen?"

"River."

"Can this wait?" asked Greene. "I think I have dibs." He gave them both a toothy smile.

"I'm touched, Ray. Is it Ken Lonergan again?"

Cartwright nodded. She turned to Greene. "He wants permission to shoot a cougar."

He smiled at Hazel. "He's not talking about you, is he?"

"Watch it, Ray."

"Sorry."

"Melanie, tell him to talk to someone in Parks and Rec, please. I can't authorize a posse to kill a cat. He knows that." Cartwright nodded and disappeared back into her office. "What is it, Ray?"

"Jamieson got a call from Bob Chandler out in Hoxley. He told him he'd been calling his mother all morning and there's no answer."

"So why is he still in Hoxley? It's only twenty minutes." Ray shrugged. "Fine, then why is PC Jamieson still here?"

"Well, you've known Mrs. Chandler for . . . and I just thought —"

"Fine." She strode partway down the hall. "Melanie, I'm going back out. If Ken calls again, you tell him that shooting cats is a felony today. I don't want him wandering down the middle of Kehoe River with a pistol like some cockeyed Wyatt Earp, okay?"

"Got it," said Cartwright.

"We'll take your car," said Hazel.

"You have diced ham on your name tag."

She plucked the offending meat off her chest and put it in her mouth. "Go," she said.

Saturday, November 13, 10:45 a.m.

Robert Chandler sat slumped forward onto his mother's kitchen table, his head in his arms. Detective Inspector Micallef laid her hand on his forearm and squeezed it. In the room just beyond, she heard the hiss and squawk of police radios and the opening and closing of the front door. It was the morning shift and constables Cassie Jenner and Adrian Ashton had come to the call. Sergeant Renald and Provincial Constable Kraut Fraser, two of their three trained Scene of Crime Officers, were also present.

"You say you spoke with her around lunchtime yesterday, Bob?"

"I was going to come by in the evening, but I called to cancel. I had too much work to do last night."

"Did she say she had any plans herself?"

He lifted his head off the table and ran the side of his face against his shoulder. "When did you know my mother to have plans, Hazel? If she was out of this house, it was with me or Gail. Otherwise she was here, watching the television or reading her magazines. That was her life."

"Do you think she might have come into contact with someone you don't know? Maybe even over the phone? Maybe in a waiting room somewhere?"

"If she did," said Robert Chandler, "then she didn't say anything to me about it." His eyes were wild, moving back and forth over the table as if the blank surface could reveal something to him. "She was just a peaceful lady, you know that. Biding her time, trying not to be trouble to anyone. I can't believe this," he said, laying his arms out on the tabletop. "Who would want to hurt my mother? Who would do this?"

"Do you want to go, Bob? One of the guys can take you home."

He stood, as if she'd told him it was time to leave, but when he did, he rose above the level of the kitchen-wall cut-out, and could see into the living room where his mother sat surrounded by policemen. He dropped back into the chair as if his legs had been kicked out from under him. "I'd like to go out the back way, I think."

"Of course," said Hazel. She put her hand on his neck and kept it there a moment, and then went out into the scene. She took PC Jenner aside and asked her to take Chandler around the back. "Stay with him at his house for a while, okay? Even if he says he'll be fine. I'd like someone to be with him." She led the young constable back into the kitchen. "Bob, this is Cassie Jenner. She went to high school with your Diane, remember?"

"Yes, yes. Hi, Cassie."

"I'm so sorry, Mr. Chandler."

"She's going to run you back up home, Bob. She'll take care of you." He rose and Jenner collected him against her, wrapping her arm over his shoulder. He was shrunken, like an old man. "I'll come and see you and Gail tonight. I'll tell you everything we find out."

She watched them leave, and as soon as the door was shut, she heard Greene's voice behind her. "He gone?"

"Yeah," she said.

"Spere's here. The rest of his SOCO team's ten minutes back. You want to hear this, I think."

Hazel went back into the living room. Howard Spere had made it up from Mayfair in just over thirty minutes. She calculated he must have been doing 180. He was a heavy-set man in his forties with bad body odour and a habit of chewing his nails. She'd remarked to herself on more than one occasion that Detective Spere must have ingested a fair proportion of crime scenes in his career: having an oral fixation wasn't the best vice to have if your job was poking dead things. Port Dundas didn't have its own Ident unit, just three SOCO officers who hadn't had cause to use their training since they took it, and of course no forensic investigator either. The detachment processed an average of fifteen deaths a year, and it was a rare year that one of them was a homicide. The last time there'd been a murder anywhere in Westmuir was four years earlier, a barfight that turned into a stabbing. Up in Hants. Nothing else. Heart attacks, cancer, strokes, a suicide every other year, car crashes: these were death's stock in trade in the county. Spere spent most of his time in Mayfair and Barrie sticking his fingers into bullet holes and pouring plaster of Paris into footprint impressions. The last time they'd seen him in Port Dundas was 2003, and that was to interpret some tire tracks left in the mud at the scene of a restaurant supply warehouse robbery. (It had turned out to be a 2001 Chevy Malibu. They'd found it in East Milverton still full of silverware.)

She brought herself to look at poor Delia Chandler again. Sitting tall against the back of her floral-patterned couch, a fine blue wool dress on, with a bib of nearly black blood down the front of it. Her throat had been cut in a straight line so deep that her head had stayed on only because it rested against the cushion behind it. There were epaulettes of blood on each shoulder.

But it was not the gore that was most upsetting to Hazel. It was the look on Delia's face. Her eyes were closed, as if she were taking a pleasant nap, but her mouth was rent open in a silent cry, the tip of her tongue behind her upper teeth, its underside a pale lavender streaked with livid white lines.

Spere was bent over, swabbing the oral cavity. Hazel's officers stood behind him awkwardly, letting him work. "This is unusual, to say the least," he said. "She's upright, no signs of trauma except for the throat, nothing under her fingernails, no marks anywhere in the room, and yet she looks like she died in the middle of calling out. You gotta wonder how that happens." He turned to take in the room. "This exactly how you found her?"

"I took some pictures," said PC Fraser, the one they called "Kraut." His real name was Dietrich. He tolerated his nickname as a gesture of goodwill. "But this is exactly how she was when I got here."

"Who got here first?"

"I did," said Ashton. "With Jenner. We didn't touch a thing."

Seemingly satisfied, Spere turned back to the victim. "So how do you talk with your throat cut?"

"A good question," said Greene.

"Should she be that pale?" asked Hazel. "Even if she's dead?"

Spere stood up and took a long look at Delia Chandler's body. He snapped his latex gloves off and put them into his pocket. "Well, that's the other thing. There's not enough blood here."

"What?"

Spere telescoped his pointer and touched it to the blood on Delia Chandler's clothing. "The blood patterns are wrong. You cut a person's carotids and you expect to see a burst pattern out vertically and laterally. There's no jetting here at all." Hazel and Ray Greene leaned in. "You know those old water fountains with the spigot in the middle that always had a burble of water flowing out of it? This is what happened here. Almost no pressure at all."

"She had cancer," said Hazel.

"Cancer doesn't explain this. Bleeding gums wouldn't explain this. There's almost six litres of blood in a human being. A little old lady like this, somewhat less, like five, but in any case, it tends to shoot out when you slice a person's throat." He used the pointer to stroke the insides of Delia's arms. "There are no cuts here, none on her wrists, and no blood anywhere else. So we won't know exactly what happened here until they unzip her in Barrie."

Hazel stared at the wreck of her father's old friend. What would he have said at this sight? She looked at the dead woman's feet, clad in beige hose. She wore no shoes. "Lift her dress," she said. Both men turned to look at her. "Pull her dress up, Detective Spere."

Spere tugged a latex glove back onto his right hand and crouched down for the hem of the dress. His discoloured mackintosh pooled over the dead woman's feet. He folded the blue material upward, into Delia Chandler's lap. Her legs were still covered in her pantyhose, but after a moment, Spere noticed a small tear at the very top of her right stocking, at her pantyline.

"What is that?" said Greene.

Spere leaned in between Delia's legs, and carefully pushed the fabric open. Her skin was bruised purple under it, a concentrated little bruise, like an insect bite. "It's a needle site," he said.

"So she's been injected?" asked Hazel.

"It's hard to tell if she's been stuck in the saphenous vein or the femoral artery, so I don't know if the killer was putting something in or taking something out. But given that she looks like a sheet, I'm going to guess femoral." He ran his hands lightly down her legs. "I want to take these hose off."

"Do what you have to do, Howard." She had the impulse to turn around, to give Delia Chandler her privacy. Spere gestured for help and two officers stepped forward and lifted Delia slightly off the couch so he could unroll her pantyhose and reveal the woman's legs. The skin was almost translucent.

"What do you notice about her feet?" said Spere, touching his pointer to one of Delia's arches.

They stared at the pale, bluish foot. "There's almost no lividity," said Sergeant Renald.

"Two points, officer. You'd expect pooling along the whole perimeter of this woman's foot. But there's nothing here." With his index finger, he traced back up to the needle site. "This is a venipuncture, like when you donate blood." He looked up at them again. "He's bled her."

Greene was shaking his head. "She *let* him do this?"

Spere lowered the dead woman's dress. "It's impossible to say what she permitted or not at this stage. But from the look of things, there certainly appears to have been *some* co-operation." He pulled off his glove and stuck a finger into his mouth, chewing the nail thoughtfully. "We'll know more when she gets to Barrie."

"I don't want her taken away from here," said Hazel sharply. "She was a citizen of this town for every minute of her eighty-odd years, and she'll be treated that way. Not like any old victim to be stuck in a fridge."

"This is a homicide, Inspector. I don't know how much say we'll have in it."

"When the scene is locked down, you take her to Mayfair Grace. Your people can come up here for a change."

Spere's Ident team arrived then and came in wearing their green latex gloves. One of them started dusting, while the other bagged the cushions from the couch. "Leave the one holding her up for now," said Spere. He turned to Greene and Detective Inspector Micallef. "It took me forever to find a body bag at your station house. I'll go get it from the car."

Hazel called the station house to assign three officers to a canvass and sent them out immediately. By the middle of the afternoon, they had covered both sides of Maitland Avenue and had nothing. A call to the office just after lunch had reported a late-model Buick parked on Taylor the night before, three streets over from Delia's house, but the caller had not taken down the licence plate number and couldn't remember whether the car was silver, blue, or black. In a peaceful town like Port Dundas, the notion of a car being "strange" wouldn't be common. The news of a special on Folgers Coffee at the No Frills went around town like wildfire, but an unknown car on Maitland or Taylor or any of the streets around Delia Chandler's house would never cause any concern.

Hazel and Ray stayed on through the afternoon as the SOCO team dusted, bagged, and photographed the scene and the rest of the house. There was almost nothing to bag but the couch cushions, the meagre contents of the fridge, and the slightly sticky bar of soap at the kitchen sink. They took two hundred pictures of the scene, pictures that, later, would tell them nothing about the killer. There was no sense at all, despite the thoroughness of the search, that anything had been disturbed in or stolen from Delia Chandler's house. Phone records showed no calls in or out after Robert Chandler's at lunchtime, and because she was on a cable modem, there was no way to tell whether or not Delia had been on the Internet at any specific time, as the connection was permanent. Her web history would show where she'd visited at least, and when. Hazel had hooked her own house up with DSL, which was much the same, as her mother had bought a laptop and insisted that they get connected. "What do you want with the bloody Internet, Mother?" she'd asked her. "It's nothing but filth and collectibles. And chat rooms – what do you need with a chat room?"

"You sound like *my* mother," Emily Micallef said. "I need more in my day than cooking you meals and *Oprah*. You should lose your hatred of technology, Hazel. You might learn something."

She'd acquiesced and hooked the house up, but she insisted her mother cancel her credit cards just in case. "Whatever you want, I can get you in town. I don't want you buying garbage on the Internet."

Ident had taken Delia's computer with them, but it would be a while before they reported. There had been no more calls during the day – not even to get a cat out of a tree – and when Hazel and Greene drove back to the station at six o'clock, she saw why: the streets were busy with people, people standing at street corners, smoking cigarettes and talking, people driving slowly by in their cars. She knew there was no way of keeping the news of Delia Chandler's murder under wraps, but still, she was surprised to see this many people out in the early evening air. "What a day," she said. "I don't know what to do with myself right now."

"I've got a bottle of rye back at my desk."

"Are you 'enabling' me, Ray?"

"There are times that call for a drink, Hazel, and then there are times that demand a drink. But I'll take no for an answer, too."

"I wouldn't want you to drink alone," she said.

"Come on then." They turned and drove through one of the delivery alleys behind the road toward the station. "I can guess what the topic of conversation is back on Main Street."

"I doubt there's a person out there on the sidewalks who didn't somehow know Delia. She worked in the funeral home until she was sixty-five. There wasn't a death in any family in this town that she wasn't a part of."

"Now the town's part of her death."

He held the station's back door open for her and went to his desk. The moment Greene appeared in the pen, though, Hazel could hear a cacophony of questions erupting from behind the counter – the station house was the last place they should have gone for peace and quiet: it was the most logical place for the local reporters to go. Hazel had an instinct that the standard arrangements with the Westmuir press were not going to hold here. The shouted questions were variations on a theme: did they have a suspect; what was the murder weapon; what was the cause of death. Greene stood empty-handed behind his open desk drawer with a blank look on his face and pushed it shut with his knee. He took a moment to collect himself and then she saw him step forward out of view. "Detective Inspector Micallef will be making a statement here Monday morning at nine a.m. Until then, we have no comment."

Please act like small-town reporters, Hazel said to herself. She stepped back into the doorway of her office to avoid being seen in case any of the reporters (who knew they had that many reporters in the whole county?) had parked in back. After a couple of minutes, the footfalls in the foyer died down. Greene knocked on her door. She saw through the frosted glass that he was holding up a bottle and she told him to come in. She ran her finger around the inside of a coffee cup before putting it down on her desk.

"Double or triple," he said, unscrewing the cap.

"I just want enough to keep my hands from shaking."

He poured her four capfuls, which she drained into the back of her throat. "I better call my mother."

"You want me to go?"

"No. Stay there. If I'm still on the line in three minutes, get up and knock on the door like it's some-thing important." She dialled and her mother answered on the third ring, which meant she'd made her get up and cross to the kitchen. Hazel had already told her mother to take the cordless phone with her wherever she was in the house, but the elder Micallef didn't want to be stalked by a phone. She'd already heard the news. "Delia Chandler," she said, as if she were trying to place the name. "That took a long time."

"Don't be like that."

"You should be seriously considering that the killer is a woman."

Hazel blinked a couple of times and wrote "killer = woman?" on a piece of paper and turned it to Greene. He looked at it and mouthed, *no way*.

"You know she never apologized. Not even at your dad's funeral."

"Well, that would have been great timing." Hazel heard tapping. "What are you doing?"

"Just writing an email."

"To who?"

"I have friends, Hazel. I write to them. Don't worry about me spreading state secrets."

My eighty-seven-year-old mother has electronic penpals, Hazel thought. What kind of world is this? "Is the door locked?"

"Did you lock it?"

"Did you unlock it, Mum?"

"No. When will you be wanting supper?" Hazel heard a faint gonging in the background – email arriving or being sent. "Hazel?"

"I'll be eating here tonight. Then I'm going out to see Bob and Gail."

"Poor things," said her mother. "Eat some greens then, dear. And say hello to Raymond."

She hung up and held her hand up to Greene, who'd

risen and was getting ready to rap on the door. "It's fine." He lowered his arm. "Why 'no way'?"

"Women who kill usually do it out of passion. The crime scenes are horror-shows."

She realized there was a gap in Greene's knowledge of the town's secret life – somehow he didn't know what Delia Chandler had done thirty years ago when it seemed to Hazel that even the town's children were aware of it. But she thought better of mentioning it to him now lest it somehow convince him to start liking her mother for the crime. And no matter what her training told her about what kinds of people were capable of which kinds of crimes, she just couldn't see a woman doing what had been done to Delia.

"We'll keep an open mind for now," she said. "But I guess I agree with you." The phone rang again. "Hold that position," she said to Greene.

It was her assistant, Melanie Cartwright, calling from her desk. "Do you know a Carl Stratton?"

"Must be Sandra Stratton's son."

"Well, he called," said Cartwright. "He said he was up from Toronto for the weekend and that his mother was scared and wanted to come back to the city with him."

"So?"

"He wants you to call her and tell her she's got nothing to worry about."

"I've got my own crone to worry about, Melanie."

"Do you want me to tell him that?"

"In your own words, please." There was a long pause on the other end of the line. "Melanie?"

"Do you think this guy's still out there? I mean here? In town?"

"No," she said. "He did what he came to do. I'm sure he's long gone."

Cartwright thanked her and hung up. Hazel knew she'd already committed to memory the phrase *He did what he came to do*. She wasn't going to be surprised to see those very words show up eventually in the *Record*. Small-town hotlines.

Greene held up the bottle. "You okay yet?"

"I better not, Ray." He screwed the cap back on. "Do me a favour and call up Bob and Gail Chandler. We should go there now." He nodded and left, closing the door behind him. Hazel looked at the phone and then took it off the hook. The more she tried to hold the thought in her head that there was a procedure to be followed, the more she felt that something uncontainable had happened to her town, something that would resist all protocols. She felt a presence behind her, breathing on her, casting its shadow. Someone had come through town – without being seen, apparently – and carried off Delia Chandler. Who was this person? Why did he kill her the hard way, when it looked as if she'd already agreed to the easy way? Where were they going to begin?

Robert and Gail Chandler's house was out in Hoxley. The entire way Greene stared out the window at the fall scenery and the failing light, and that suited Hazel, lost in her own thoughts. Some of the horror of the morning would have had time to sink in for Bob

Chandler; she dreaded what kind of state they'd find him in.

When they got to the house, Hazel recognized Gord Sunderland's car sitting at the curb. "Gord," she said when he rolled down the window, "we don't have a comment at this time, and neither do the Chandlers. You're just going to have to wait for a statement back at headquarters."

"Is there *going* to be a statement?"

"Not today," she said. "Monday morning, business hours."

"That's for the boys from Hillschurch and Dublin, Hazel," he said. "I'd appreciate a one-on-one."

"I can't make any promises, Gord."

"The *Westmuir Record* is the main source of news for the people of this county, Detective Inspector. They expect a thorough report from us, and the Monday paper was already put to bed Thursday night. If you don't want me speculating aloud, you'll call me at my office when you're done here."

"I'll call you. Will you go now?" He closed his window without another word and she waited for him to drive off. Greene came up behind her.

"What'd you offer him?"

"Knitting tips."

"He's a sucker for the knitting tips," said Greene.

The Chandler house was a nicely appointed second home – after their children, Diane and Grant, had left the childhood house in Port Dundas, Bob and Gail had bought themselves this brand new bungalow, the first in a new subdivision. Now it was surrounded by variations on its theme: where there had once been the Hoxley farm, there were now eighty homes, all built in the last fifteen years, that looked like they'd been assembled out of a builder's Lego kit with eight different window types in it, six roofs, twelve front doors, eight variations on the lintel, a couple of turrets, and a bunch of gables. Mix them all up and they turned into homes with a soupçon of individuality, but to Hazel, they looked like a botched exercise in architectural cloning.

Inside, the prerequisite Robert Bateman and Alex Colville lithographs, laminated posters of different varieties of chilies in the kitchen, and a big abstract over the fireplace. The Chandlers welcomed them into the house sombrely, and now Bob and Gail sat on the couch across from the two chairs occupied by the officers, each of whom held a glass of ice water in their hands. After the offering of regrets and after Gail had dried again a face that had been drenched in tears all day, Hazel put her glass under her chair and took out her notebook.

"I know this isn't easy for you folks," she said. "But we do have to ask you some questions."

"Go ahead," said Bob Chandler.

Hazel flipped open her notebook and turned to a clean page, fixing it down with the black elastic. "First off, Bob, Robert . . . how was your mother's mood recently? Did she seem upset to you about anything?"

"Well, she had cancer, Hazel."

"And how do you think she was coping with it?"

"I guess okay. She was resigned."

Hazel wrote "resigned" in her notebook. "So she wasn't despondent?"

"Did that look like a suicide?"

"No, no, not at all, Bob. And it wasn't. But the thing is . . ." she flipped back a couple of pages in the notebook.

"The thing is," said Ray Greene, "your mother let whoever did this to her into the house. She knew him. It's possible she asked someone to help her . . ."

Bob Chandler's face was changing colour. "To help her *what*?"

"To . . . assist her," Greene said. "I know it's not pleasant to think of, but we have to consider all the possibilities." He continued in a measured way. "What do you think . . . the chances are that, maybe, your mother arranged with someone . . ."

"*Bullshit*," said Chandler. "My mother was a church-going woman. She would never have . . ." He trailed off.

Hazel held her hand up to Greene, who gratefully closed his notebook. "Bob, there was an IV puncture in her upper inner thigh. We found it after Cassie Jenner brought you home. The person who visited your mother put a needle into her vein. We have reason to think he did it with her permission."

"So he, what? He offered to euthanize my mother but then tried to cut her head off? What are you saying?"

"We're saying," came in Greene, "that your mother may have picked the wrong person to ask for help."

Both Bob and Gail stared at him for a moment.

"People do uncharacteristic things when they're facing the unknown," he continued. "Your mother may not have been herself when . . . *if* . . . she made these kinds of arrangements."

Bob Chandler seemed to subside in his chair. "I don't know . . . I just don't know."

"Would it be one of her doctors, maybe?" asked Gail. "Although, I just can't imagine."

"Do you know *all* of her doctors?" said Hazel. "Did she have any homecare? Maybe she took a delivery of something."

"Bob was her delivery boy," said Gail. "He took her to her doctors, he took her shopping, everything. She didn't need a stranger to bring anything to her. Bob once brought her an Aspirin at two in the morning."

Hazel thought about this, and realized she could not remember the last time she'd seen Delia Chandler in town by herself, and she certainly had not visited that house, not since Eric Chandler's wake almost eight years ago. There had been a long period in Delia's life when she had not felt welcome in town, and after that, she had retreated, had closed ranks around herself. Where once she had been a vivacious woman, even beautiful, she had become frightened, closeted. Hazel could not imagine Delia Chandler letting a stranger into her house. "We'll talk to anyone she might have had contact with at the clinic here, Bob. Glen Lewiston was her oncologist, right? She saw him pretty frequently?"

"Yes," said Bob. "I took her at least once a week."

"He'll know anyone she got referred to after she was diagnosed. We'll follow that trail."

"You honestly think my mother was killed by some doctor or nurse?"

"We have no idea yet. We're trying to cover all the bases."

At the door, both officers shook hands in turn with the Chandlers. Hazel held on to Bob's hand a little longer. "I'm sorry to have to follow all this procedure, Robert, when all I want to do is tell you how sorry I am. Do you know, when Andrew and I had Emilia, your mother drove over to the house with a lasagna as soon as we got back from the hospital."

"She made a fantastic lasagna," said Bob Chandler.

"We lived off it for a week. I blame your mother for Emilia's pasta addiction — she had as much of it that week as we did."

"It was the béchamel," he said, laughing, and then, just as suddenly, he was crying. Hazel stood there holding the hand of her friend from childhood, whom she'd dated twice or three times when she was a senior in high school and he was a sophomore, whose mother had had an affair with her father, whose family had gone back with her own family perhaps five generations, and to keep herself from crying in uniform, she stepped back up onto Bob Chandler's stoop and held him.

She asked to be dropped off at the station house. They sat in the idling car. "I can drive you home," Greene said. "You should go home."

"My car's in back."

"I know you. You go in there and you won't come out until tomorrow."

"I just want an hour to think," she said.

He stroked the wheel, looking out the windshield. "There's nothing a CO would be able to tell you right now that you don't already know."

"Don't read my mind, Ray. It's creepy."

"I'm just saying."

She twisted in her seat to face him. "I should be able to lead this investigation without worrying there's no one in there to look after the shop. That's what a commanding is supposed to do. Did Central think this would never happen? That there wouldn't come a day when something would happen in this town that would need my full attention?"

"I wouldn't use the word *think* in connection with Central."

"Six years, Ray. And counting. And if we guff this, Mason will use it as proof that we should be amalgamated."

"So let's not guff it, Skip. You have me and a dozen good men and women in there who will put in the time and effort. And, hey, you have Spere too."

"Don't remind me." She opened the door. "You going home?"

"Eventually."

"Uh-huh," she said. "Thanks for the pep talk."

She watched him drive south toward Main Street. His house was north. South was the Kilmartin Inn and the horse track.

Back in her office, she put a call through to the operator and asked her how to bypass a direct connection to someone's line and get right into their voicemail. She wrote down the method and then dialled into Gord Sunderland's messages. "Oh hi, Gord," she said. "I'm sorry I missed you. In any case, I'll be making a statement on the station house steps Monday morning at nine. I'll see you there." She hung up and grinned at the silent receiver.

] 4 [

Sunday, November 14, 7:00 a.m.

He passed out of Westmuir and into Renfrew County to the east. As the sun was coming up, he was within fifty kilometres of the Linnet County border, the last county before Quebec. The towns in all of the province were much like the ones he'd encountered in British Columbia and the Prairies — outside of the cities, the villages appeared like beads on a string along two-lane country roads, one perhaps every fifteen or twenty kilometres, about the distance between where you might have last rested your horse and where you might want to stop again. The villages were small, tiny even, some with nothing more than a church, a store, and a Victorian post office long since converted to another purpose: a pub now, a bed and breakfast, an antique store. Here, in Humber Cottage, where he pulled over after driving in a mainly easterly direction for three hours, it was a small café. He was tired and in need of something to eat.

He'd sat with Delia until two in the morning, doing his ministrations, cleaning up after himself, and wandering around the house. Just before two, when she was ready, he brushed her hair, sat her up on the couch, and photographed her. He thanked her then, blessing her, and took to the road. He spent the rest of that day, Saturday, November 13, in a roadside forest, praying and resting. At 4 a.m., he'd got back into his car and started east again. At 6 a.m., he'd switched to smaller roads, and now, an hour later, a predawn gloam was spreading a fan of thick orange light over the few buildings that lined this part of Highway 121 – the hamlet of Humber Cottage – where he would breakfast.

As he came to the door of the café, a pretty woman in her mid-thirties unlocked it for him. "Early riser?" she said.

"Just passing through."

"Coffee isn't even on yet. Come in though."

He told her he didn't drink coffee, not to make any on his account, that if she would bring him some hot water, he would make his morning drink. She brought him a little teapot, stained from years of the hard water in this part of the province, and watched him drop a pinch of grey leaf into the pot. He swirled it around and poured it out into a cup.

"Imported stuff, huh?" she said. "I have a cousin who has a teashop in Cottingham, just back twenty or so klicks. You should visit her."

"I grow my own," he said. "This is damiana. A natural tonic." He sipped it. "Have you any fruit?"

"I can make you cottage cheese with berries in it. That's a good breakfast."

"If you don't mind, miss, I'd rather just the berries. Nothing else."

She shrugged her shoulders good-naturedly and turned for the counter. "I don't mind anything, hon, but you look like you could use a proper meal."

"It's early for a full breakfast," he said, "but thanks. Put the hot water on my bill of course."

"Wouldn't think of it," came the reply.

She disappeared into the kitchen, where he presumed she was now slicing his breakfast. He hoped she might bring strawberries with the tops still attached; the greens were rich in astringent, and his gut felt damp and heavy. But it attracted strange looks, a man who ate something destined for compost. We are all destined for compost, he thought, and smiled to himself. We are but clay.

She brought out the fruit – blackberries, strawberries without their greens, raspberries. She had brought a couple of slices of honeydew, which he would not touch, as it broke down in the mouth and caused anything in the stomach to ferment, and he did not touch alcohol. "Nothing else, then?" she said.

"Not for now."

She stood by the side of his table, regarding him with a gentle look. "Are you some kind of a doctor?" she said, her head tilted with curiosity. "You have the look about you of a doctor."

"And what does a doctor look like, my dear?"

"A little tired from saving lives." She laughed at herself. "Have you been saving lives all through the night, Doctor?"

This one was very charming, he thought to himself. Sweet, even-tempered. But very young. "I have, in fact, been saving lives. So you can pat yourself on the back for a good guess, miss."

"What kind of doctor are you?"

He crunched a blackberry between his back teeth. The juice was flat, without its electrics. He was disappointed. "I'm not really the kind of doctor you might be thinking of. I'm more of what you would probably call a naturopath. I treat the soul as well as the body."

"Ohhhh," she said, knowingly. "You're an herbalist."

"I do use herbs," he said. "But I use many things."

"And they work?"

"They do. Usually. If it's not too late." This last statement seemed to sting her, and she laid her hand on the chairback across from him. When he looked up at her face, she was staring past him, out the window and onto the road. "I've upset you somehow," he said.

"No. You haven't. But it's sad to think that it could be too late for anyone."

"You can't unsalt a soup," he said.

She smoothed the back of the chair and then patted it, as if it were an animal she cared for. "I have a niece. They keep her at home now because she has seizures. She stiffens up and falls over, as if she's dead."

"That sounds very serious indeed." He poured more hot water into his cup. They come to me, he thought. I am called. "Has she seen a doctor?"

"A raft of them."

"Bring another cup, Miss . . ."

"MacDonald. Grace MacDonald."

"I'll make you a cup of my tea, and we'll discuss your niece."

She protested mildly – it was impolite of her to harass him like this at 7:20 in the morning – but he insisted, and she went back behind the counter and got herself a cup. He put a tiny amount of the damiana in it and covered it with hot water. "It tastes like camomile," she said.

"Very much like camomile," he replied. "Now tell me about this girl."

When Grace called her sister Terry, it was still before eight in the morning. She told her that she wanted to bring someone over to see Rose. Terry sighed on the other end of the line. Rose was sleeping, at last she was sleeping. But Grace pressed her: she'd had a visitor in the café and she felt he could offer something none of the doctors could. "He gave me a tea that makes you feel like Wonder Woman," said Grace. "You should meet him. He's like a shaman." She could hear the exhaustion in Terry's voice – Rose's attacks happened around the clock. She would shriek in surprise while in bed, and Terry would rush into the child's room to find her stretched out stiffly on the floor, quaking, or standing in the corner, a look of stark terror on her face. It was like having a newborn in the house again, a haunted newborn.

"I don't want a visitor right now, Grace. I look like hell."

"He won't care, Terry. I have a feeling. Let us come over."

She came back to the table with a look of elation on her face. "You are such a good man to do this," she said. "You have no idea what my sister has been through. First her divorce and now this. She and Rose go back and forth to Toronto for tests – they stick her inside of every machine you can think of. Can you imagine?"

"I can."

She lowered her voice. "She lives in that house as if her daughter is already dead. As if she's already mourning her. They need some hope."

"Let's see what we can do," he said.

The house was only two blocks from the café. He took his valise out of the back of his car, and tugged on the bar fridge door, a habit. He checked the cable from the fridge to the lighter outlet. Then they walked together under the fall sun, now fully up over the horizon and casting a lemony light over the road. Terry greeted them at the door with a tired smile. "It's very kind of you to come, sir."

"I was just passing through. It's pure coincidence, if you believe in such a thing."

"Do you?"

"No, I don't. Is she awake?"

"She is now."

Terry led her sister and the stranger into the house, a lovely old building raised more than 150 years ago. Travelling across the country, he'd seen the materials used in houses get older and older. Here, in Ontario, the farther east you went, the greyer and rougher the stone got. Miss MacDonald's sister lived in a house that in the city would have been an estate for a barrister. Here it was common. He cast his eyes around the stale-smelling home. A framed sampler hung on the wall over the piano, a shibboleth. It meant that, in that town, the family went back generations. The television was on, but it was muted. On it, a woman in an apron stirred a white paste in a bowl.

The girl was waiting in her bedroom, still in her nightdress. She looked at him with black-ringed eyes, inured completely to the appearance of doctors and specialists who came to the house to study her, or saw her in their offices, syringes ready for filling with her blood; machines primed to take pictures of her insides; and their hands, always their clasping, palpating, compressing hands. "Are you going to stick me, mister?" she said.

"With a needle you mean?"

"Which arm?" She offered to him the insides of her elbows. Her skin was pitifully white, her veins a pale blue beneath her skin.

"I don't need any of your blood, Rose. I just want to talk to you. Maybe look at your tongue and your eyes."

"Co-operate with this nice man," said her mother from the doorway. "He's agreed to take time out of his busy day to have a look at you."

Rose nodded, resigned, and lowered the sleeves of her nightdress. She sat back down on the edge of her bed. "I probably have a great big stinking brain tumour," she said.

"*Rose . . .*"

"Did a doctor tell you this?" asked Simon.

"No, he told Terry *something*," said the child, looking at her mother. "She won't tell me —"

"You're going to be fine, honey," said Terry Batten.

"— but I know. My head is like a computer that someone has smashed with a rock."

He looked back to the doorway, where both women stood watching them. He smiled at the mother. "I very much doubt that," he said. "Would you be comfortable being alone in your room with me, Rose? Without your mother or your aunt?"

"Alone?" said Terry. "I'm not sure if I —"

"I don't care, Terry," said the girl. Neither woman reacted to this odd familiarity.

"We can bring you some hot water, Doctor. If you think you'll need any."

"I'm not a doctor," he said, turning sharply to Grace in the door. "I told you that."

"I'm sorry."

"I want hot water, but not scalding."

The two women closed the door. He heard them walk to the top of the stairs and start down. He returned his attention to the child. "You fall down," he said.

"One doctor told me I'd be safest in bed, but I fall out of bed too."

"Of course you do," he said. He took one of her little hands in his and ran his fingertips over the thin veins on the inside of her wrist. "Tell me, Rose, what happens before you have an attack? Do you see light? Do you smell or hear anything?"

"I sometimes smell something."

"Hmm," said Simon. He held her chin and gentled her mouth open. "What is the smell?"

"Scrangle eggs."

He released her jaw. "Do you like scrambled eggs, Rose?"

"Not any more."

He laughed, soothingly. "Do you like tea?"

"I'm only eight. I don't drink tea."

"Perhaps today you will."

He looked at the girl's eyes. The eyes of children were usually clear, as if made of polished glass. Rose's brown eyes looked pale, the irises had the aspect of a watercolour painting that had been tainted with a drop of fluid after drying. They were runny.

Grace knocked on the door and he opened it, taking a tray from her. She glanced anxiously at her niece, but Simon stepped in front of her to block her view. He listened again to her footfalls in the corridor. "Think of your body as a garden," he said to Rose. "Does your mother keep a garden?"

"She does."

"What happens if weeds grow?"

"The plants don't get water."

"That's right," he said. He opened his valise and traced his fingers over the vials attached to its sides with elastic ribbons. He pushed the hammer on its side to get to a row near the bottom. Mistletoe. Across from it, powdered yew-berry seed, a poison. He took them both out and unscrewed their lids. "Would you like to smell?"

Rose leaned forward and put her nose into the mouth of one of the vials. She screwed up her face. "Horrid," she said. "I'm not drinking any tea made from that."

"I will adulterate it – *slightly* – with honey. Just for you."

"I don't want it," she said, and he simply smiled at her, a smile from the world of adults, saying your disobedience will be allowed in theory, but not in practice. She watched him crush a couple of tiny green leaves between his thumb and forefinger, and sprinkle it into the cup her aunt had brought up on the tray. Then he dropped in a minuscule pinch of the white yew-berry powder. He poured steaming water on it.

"The leaves are mistletoe, like you have at Christmas. Do you know it, Rose?"

"You kiss because of it."

"Indeed. But that is a silly application of mistletoe. It is a much more noble plant than that. The Druids practically worshipped it." She shrugged. "It grows on the bark of certain trees – a true parasite deriving one hundred per cent of its nutrient from living flesh. The Druids would climb an oak tree under the first full moon of the new year, and cut a piece of mistletoe from the bark with a golden knife. It was considered a protective herb. If so much as a leaf fell on the ground during the ceremony, they would wail and cry out that their great nation would become victim to misfortune. You can imagine how tightly the man in the tree held it."

"Were they elves?"

"No."

"They sound like elves."

"Your seizures are a symptom, rather than the illness itself. The mistletoe will establish a beachhead in your nervous system and prevent the communication of the wrong signals from your brain to your muscles."

"So I do have a tumour?"

"You may. If you do, the yew-berry powder I've put in here will deal with it." She looked at the cup of steaming liquid in his hands, less now with fear than with curiosity. "Honey, then?" he said.

"Yes," she replied. "If I have to."

"You don't want to have got out of bed for nothing." He went to the door and called down for a jar of honey and a teaspoon. Grace came up with it.

"Have you diagnosed her?" she asked.

"Yes," said Simon. "She has seizures and falls over. Leave us now."

He poured a tiny dram of honey into the tea and passed it to the girl. She stared at the mixture with contempt. "Do you know how to sing, Rose?" he asked her. "This is a cup of tea that tastes nicer when you sing to it."

Before nine, he was on his way again, having performed his ministrations and said his blessings. The MacDonald house was quiet when he left it. Very peaceful, indeed.

He was less than forty kilometres from Ottawa when he next stopped. This was Chamberlain, at the dividing line between Renfrew and Linnet counties. Population 2,100, said the sign. He checked the map that he had printed off the web. The house he was looking for appeared to be near the centre of town. He parked in the municipal lot, and walked with his valise to the address.

When he rang, he had to wait a long two minutes before he heard the clunk and shuffle of Michael Ulmer's walker coming to the door. At last it opened, and Simon considered the kind, slack face of his host. "You're right on time," said the man. He was not yet thirty, although he had wasted so considerably that his body was that of a man three times his age. Simon's heart went out to him – to have your youth stolen so brazenly by a disease, that you should wear it on your skin like the mark of Cain.

"I am. I'm grateful to be welcomed into your home."

"I'm not sure you're welcomed," said the man. "But you're needed. Come in."

Simon closed the door behind him, locking it with the chain. At eleven-thirty, he heard a knock on the door and he froze in silence. After a minute, he heard footsteps moving down the walk away from the house. He went to one of the living-room windows and pulled the curtain back slightly to see a man in a black parka walking along the sidewalk. He was carrying a little black kitbag, a miniature of his own. A Jehovah's Witness, perhaps. Imagine building a church out of whomever wanted to join it, Simon thought. He and his brother had always been more discriminating than that. At noon, he searched Mr. Ulmer's fridge and found a bunch of parsley, which he moistened with the juice of a lemon and ate. At two-thirty, Mr. Ulmer was ready. Simon photographed him and thanked him. As luck would have it, the house was already so immaculate – but for the faint, hanging odour of cigarette smoke – that there was nothing for him to do.

He was pleased when he found that the ones he visited had taken his directives seriously, although he imagined in Mr. Ulmer's case that the cleanliness of his house was a result of hired help. Just the same, it confirmed for him that he had not made a mistake in choosing Mr. Ulmer, or indeed any of them, and it deepened his joy that he was there with them to give succour, to save them. As he had been saved in his own life. He was repaying his debt, and it filled his heart with happiness. And for this reason especially, his entire morning and early afternoon, both with the MacDonalds and with Mr. Ulmer, twenty-nine, had been very agreeable indeed.

Sunday, November 14, 8:15 a.m.

Detective Howard Spere slapped an envelope down on Micallef's desk. "I *was* planning on spending today watching football with my sons, but you know what I do when you say jump, Hazel."

"Yeah, Howard, you say it can wait until Monday."

"She's still going to be dead tomorrow."

"And you can tape your football game."

"You're welcome."

She unwound the string on the back of the envelope and pulled out the post-mortem report. She scanned the summary. "Hyoscyamine? Humulene? These are drugs?"

"Sort of," said Spere, wedging a thumbnail between two of his front teeth. "They're compounds found in belladonna and ps."

"She was drinking?"

"No . . . this was medicinal hops. In plant form. They found bits of matter in her stomach that she'd ingested just prior to death. Both plants are sedatives."

"How strong?"

"In the quantity of belladonna they found in her, probably very."

"So you're telling me she was *anaesthetized*?"

"I'm saying she probably didn't feel a thing. She was as high as a kite. But neither of these compounds killed her. This did." He put his finger on a word at the bottom of the report.

"Amatoxin."

"You ever heard of the destroying angel?"

"No."

"It's a mushroom. *Amanita bisporigera*. The most poisonous mushroom on the planet: the amount that would cover the surface of a dime one-tenth of a millimetre thick would be enough to kill her three times over. It's a hepatotoxin."

"English, Howard."

"Shuts down the liver and kidneys almost instantly."

Hazel cast her eyes over the report again and her mouth turned down. "Are you telling me that Delia didn't die of blood loss?"

"The amatoxin is fully metabolized. He bled her after she was dead."

Hazel closed the folder and sat back down in her chair. "How do you get the blood out of a person's body when their heart isn't pumping it any more?"

"You suck it out."

"Jesus, Howard. Who is this guy?"

"There's more. She'd been fasting, too. There was nothing in the bowel, clean as a whistle. I gave her to Jack Deacon at Mayfair Grace. He said she probably hadn't eaten in three days."

Hazel lifted the pages of the report, noting the pathologist's charts with the measures, the weights of Delia Chandler's internal organs, and she thought, it comes down to this: the body in its constituents with their poorly kept secrets. Only a living person can refuse to tell the truth. Delia's heart was a little smaller than average, she noted. She'd make sure not to mention that to her mother.

"So she arranges with the killer in advance?" she said, thinking out loud. "And according to *his* instructions, she begins to fast. He arrives, prepares this anaesthetic cocktail, and knocks her out. He delivers the death blow with the amatoxin, then he drains the blood from her body to remove as much trace of the poison as possible, and then slits her throat to make it look like a murder."

"Because it's *not* a murder?"

"Well, at the very least it's not the murder it appears to be, is it? A corpse with a slit throat but the cause of death *isn't* blood loss . . ."

"He tries to hide what he's done."

"Maybe," she said.

"You think maybe this *is* an assisted suicide?"

"No. I can't get to that."

"So it *is* a murder. Whether he slits her throat or not."

"I know, Howard. But why kill her and *then* do her violence? Why would he want it to look like he attacked her? Maybe we come up with the profile for a psychopath and that's what we start looking for. But he's not a psy-chopath, is he? He's something else."

Spere had leaned back in the chair on the other side of Hazel's desk. He stared at the ceiling. She thought she could smell onions. "I don't know. On one hand, no one who *isn't* a wack-job could have done this. But on the other, he knows what he's doing. He's skilled enough to put her under with two powerful sedatives and then kill her with *mushroom* powder. He drains her blood, but he's got to know he's not covering his tracks. He knows the *Amanita* is going to turn her kidneys into raisins. So he's in control. Maybe he *is* a doctor." He fell silent a second and Hazel, knowing there were times it was wise to let Spere keep talking, waited him out. "Someone with an urge to kill, but he can't do anyone who just walks into his office. He's going to get caught that way. But he can make arrangements —"

"— how though?"

"I don't know. But say he's promised her that he can cure her, or maybe just relieve her pain, and she goes for it. She doesn't know what belladonna is. And once she's under, he has a romp. Maybe he doesn't like to fight with them, or hear their screams."

"I don't think so. I think she knew everything that was going to happen to her. I think she agreed."

"You think she agreed to *die*?"

"She was already terminal, Howard."

"Yeah, but no one agrees to die like this. Unless they're as nuts as their killer."

"No forced entry, no struggle, the place is immacu-late. Explain any of that to me."

"So is this a murder or not, Hazel? At the very least, can we decide what we *think* it is?"

"It's a murder. It doesn't matter what he calls it or what she thinks she's agreed to, if she's agreed to anything. It's what it looks like to us. Don't you think?"

"Do you really care what I think, Hazel?"

"Yes, Howard. I care. You feel better now?"

Spere shrugged deeply – his head almost disappeared into his shirt – and pushed his way out of the chair. The effort triggered a fit of wet smoker's cough. She was always glad when it was time to say goodbye to him. He held his hand out for the report. "I gotta make a copy of this. I'll bring it back."

"Make one for Greene." Spere shut the door behind him, and she picked up her phone. "Melanie? Tell Jack Deacon at Mayfair Grace I want to see him. I'm going to drive down there now."

"Got it, Inspector."

"Did you do your cougar homework?"

"I did."

"And?"

She heard a shuffling of paper. "Cougars or pumas – *Puma concolor* – are large, tawny or greyish brown carnivores –"

"Just the part I need to know, Mel."

"Okay. They *are* indigenous to Ontario. But they see them mostly north of here."

"How north?"

"Two, three hundred kilometres."

Hazel tapped her pencil tip on her blotter. Little dashes like knife-marks appeared under the nib. "Fine.

Send two officers down to Kehoe River then, okay? Find out who's lost their pet kitty, and make sure Ken Lonergan behaves himself. But call Deacon first."

She pulled her jacket off the back of the chair and went out into the pen. Greene wasn't in yet, but there was a uniformed cop she didn't recognize, sitting at the desk beside Ray's, tapping on the keyboard. She went and stood behind him, and after a moment, he stopped typing and put on his cap. He stood up and faced her, hands at his sides.

"Do I know you, officer?"

"DC Wingate. Ma'am," he said. He changed his mind about his cap and took it off again. "Inspector."

"DC who?"

He coughed into his hand. He looked like an elongated boy scout to her—a six foot one boy scout, mussed yellow hair and freckles, in the wrong uniform. She saw Ray Greene enter through the front of the station. "Just stay there," she said to the young officer. She met Greene at the counter. "Does the name Wingate ring a bell for you?"

Greene squinted at her. "Wingate. His name come up on something?"

"Not exactly," she said. "But he's standing over there with his cap glued to his chest."

He looked past her. "Oh God," he said. "*Wingate*. He's here? I thought he was coming next week."

"For *what*, Ray? Are we having a jamboree?"

"From Fifty-two. Downtown Toronto. He's replacing Hunter."

The officer had sidled up to the counter. "Yes," he said. "Fifty-two Division."

"We got a *replacement* for Hunter?" said Hazel in complete disbelief. "Now how the hell did that happen? I thought Mason was waiting for us all to die off."

"We put in the paperwork," said Greene. "I guess he didn't notice."

"Thank God for the right hand's relationship with the left. So you're actually here to work for us?" Wingate smiled, and Greene held his hand out to shake. Hazel looked the officer over. How did a kid this young get made detective? She offered her hand, and he put a cool, ever-so-slightly clammy palm into hers. Looking at his name tag, she asked, "Is it James or Jim, then?"

"James is fine."

They walked back toward Greene's desk. "You picked a hell of a day to start," she said. "Has anyone caught you up?"

"I heard on the way. I'm not supposed to begin until tomorrow, but I thought I'd come in and see if I could be useful."

"You psychic?" said Greene.

"No, sir."

"Then you're in about the same boat as the rest of us." They stood there behind the front desk, awkward now that introductions were over, and Wingate cast a glance back toward the safety of his desk, but stayed screwed to the spot.

"What were you up to at your desk, DC Wingate?" she said.

"I hope you don't mind, but I asked Miss Cartwright over there for Dr. Deacon's email. I had a question for him."

"I don't mind at all." She smiled. "God, I'm going to call you 'son' if I'm not careful. Did he write you back?"

"I hadn't finished my email. I wanted to ask him his opinion on which of the injuries killed her. I glanced at Detective Spere's report, which said there was *some* blood on her. So it occurred to me that, maybe, she —"

"None of her injuries killed her, officer," said Hazel.

Wingate slowly closed his mouth to a thin line. "Sorry," he said. "I didn't mean to get ahead of myself."

Greene had opened his copy of the report and was scanning it. "What do you mean she didn't die of her injuries?" he said.

"She was already dead before he did any of that violence to her. From a mushroom."

"A mushroom," repeated Ray Greene.

They followed Wingate back to his desk. The message had been started *Dear Sir*. Hazel saw a toothbrush beside the keyboard. "Have you got a place to stay, James?"

"My landlady isn't expecting me until tonight."

"So you came here to work?"

"Is that all right?"

"I can't possibly promote you until at least Thursday."

"Ma'am?"

"She has a rather dry sense of humour," said Ray Greene, leaning over Wingate's keyboard to erase his salutation, "which is to say it's hard to know when to laugh." He stood straight again and gestured at the computer screen. "Jack Deacon works for us, so there's no need to kowtow. Just say, 'Jack.'"

"I think I'll write him later," said Wingate.

He'd put his cap down on the desk beside the keyboard, and Hazel picked it up and handed it to him. "You feel like a drive?"

"Sure. Yes."

"Let's go for a drive then." She strode away from him, and he followed, but quickly doubled back to toss his toothbrush into the desk drawer.

"I'm not invited?" said Greene.

She called back to him over her shoulder. "Do some work. Set an example. I'm taking the new guy to Mayfair."

They drove south on 41, farmers' fields on either side of them, the brown cornstalks knocked over. Detective Constable Wingate sat stiffly in the passenger seat, looking straight ahead down the highway. Silence had never bothered Hazel, but she suspected Wingate was being polite, so she asked him where he was from.

"Toronto born and bred," said Wingate. "You know the city?"

"Certain buildings."

"It's not easy to like unless you were brought up there."

"You hoping to work your way back?"

"I just want to be wherever I can do the most good."

She glanced over at him. "Okay. And what's the real answer?"

He met her eyes, and she saw confusion in his. "That is the real answer."

"You have scout badges, DC Wingate, don't you?"

He laughed. "You want to guess where I keep them?"

"In a cigar box underneath your bed?"

"My mother has them. In an envelope in her sock drawer."

She remembered one of the questions they asked applicants at the academy. *What kind of relationship do you have with your mother?* they asked the men. Because good sons made fine cops. Ray Greene had brunch with his mother every Sunday. Drove out to the Poplars to get her, and took her to Riverside House for mimosas and pancakes. That was the only other woman in his life, she realized, apart from Michelle Greene, who had nothing to worry about, if you didn't count the boredom of being married to a cop whose dull vice was playing the ponies. She tried to remember the question that had given her pause at her own interview. Thirty-two years ago now. Yes: did she want to have a family? She'd said she did, and one of the interviewers had written it down.

"There are hardly any women your age in Port Dundas," she said. "Hard place for a young man to settle down."

"I'm not thinking about that right now," Wingate said. "I have enough on my plate."

"Did you leave a girl in Toronto?"

"No," he said. "There's no one right now."

At the hospital, they were given their visitor tags, and Dr. Jack Deacon came to collect them from the registration office. He was a man of quick gestures whose physicality communicated that at any given moment he might have to be somewhere else. But in fact he was a patient, likeable man. Hazel trusted him. "Spere caught you up?" he asked.

"Bare bones," said Micallef. "I want the whole tour."

Deacon brought them down to the basement and into the morgue. Wingate wiped his forefinger under his nose. "You can put on a face mask, son, but it won't help." The place smelled of industrial detergents and rotting meat, rather accurately. Deacon passed them each a pair of thin blue gloves.

Delia Chandler was lying in a white body bag in a steel drawer. Deacon pulled the drawer open with a chunk and rolled a steel trolley underneath her, slid her onto it, and brought her under some lights. He unzipped her and they saw the Y of heavy stitching holding her trunk closed. The wound in her neck had also been roughly stitched shut and lathered over with surgical glue. The three of them leaned into her, and Hazel shot a look at Wingate, who seemed to be holding it together.

"Okay, a couple of things," said Deacon. "We took a sample of vitreous fluid and put the time of death at five p.m. yesterday afternoon, give or take. Cause of death was acute blood poisoning. She was already dead by the time he tried to cut her head off."

"Do you think he was trying to remove her head?" said Wingate. "To take it?"

Deacon tapped the slit in Delia Chandler's throat with the back of a gloved finger. "The cut on her throat is surgical — it goes through her windpipe and esophagus on the first cut; he goes back in a second time to deepen it all the way to the spinal cord. I think if he wanted a trophy he could have had it. Anyway, he had all the time in the world, and he didn't cut it off. Look at this." He tapped his pointer to Delia's mouth. Wingate and Micallef shifted up the table. "Rigor mortis has resolved now, but at the scene, her tongue was lifted up against the back of her teeth. Howard said it looked like she was hollering or something."

"God," said Wingate.

"You want to see the pictures?" Wingate nodded, and Jack Deacon opened a folder on a table beside him and drew out a sheaf of photographs. He pulled one out and handed it to Wingate. "Rigor mortis sets in about three or four hours after death. It starts in the small muscles of the face and moves down the body and it takes about twelve hours before it's done. Then the process reverses itself and the rigor dissolves. In rare cases you might see muscles that seized up at the moment of death, but that's usually in the case of a violent death – then you get these cadaveric spasms and people gripping onto things like railings, or their killer's hair, that kind of thing. But this" – he tapped the photo repeatedly with the pointer – "this isn't really possible. Even if you're screaming when somebody shoots you through the heart, you still fall down and your tongue tumbles out of your mouth, and three hours later, everything starts to harden up."

"So how did this happen?" said Hazel.

"The only place you find faces frozen in looks of terror are in horror movies. Mostly, the dead wear expressions of drunken stupor. They don't open their mouths and touch their tongues to the back of their teeth."

Hazel found herself mimicking Delia's mouth. "So what's happening here?"

"To get her mouth to look like this, the person who killed her would have had to wait at least three hours and then hold her mouth and tongue in this position until the muscle set. He would have been standing there about forty minutes with his fingers in her mouth."

Hazel pulled off her gloves and Wingate did the same. "There's one more thing," said Jack Deacon, and he lifted one of the corpse's arms from the slab. He held the hand up for them to see. Delia Chandler's left pinkie finger was broken.

"She put up a fight?" said Wingate.

"There's no evidence that this is a defensive wound. And he does it before he bleeds her. There's evidence of edema – swelling."

Hazel looked closely at the other hand. "Just one."

"Just the one."

"The easiest one to break," she said, and Deacon nodded.

The three of them stared at the hand for almost a full ten seconds.

"Maybe he didn't want her to feel any pain," said Wingate.

"So he breaks her finger?"

"To make sure she's asleep," he said. "Then he poisons her, puts the port in her leg and he begins." Deacon lowered Delia's arm and Wingate looked up at his new boss.

"So he *cares*?" she said to him.

The doctor began rolling the body back toward its hole in the wall.

—

They drove back to Port Dundas with the radio playing quietly under their silence. Mercy was one thing, thought Hazel, but DC Wingate's suggestion that there was actual *thoughtfulness* in the killer's actions disturbed her. If it were true, it meant the killer was not angry, he was not fuelled by a sense of injustice, or overripe with hatred. Those kinds of killers slipped up: their passions led them. What was he doing by making it appear as if he'd killed Delia Chandler in a rage? Delia was already being killed by cancer. Was a more overt act of murder a comment on her disease? A critique of its silent, creeping methods? And the mouth, what did this disguise?

"What kind of 'caring' are we talking about here, do you think?" Hazel said.

Wingate took his eyes off the road for the first time. The turnoff for Port Dundas was coming up on their right. "I shouldn't have said anything," he said. "I don't know anything about this case yet."

"You know about as much as any of us, Detective. It's okay to think aloud."

"He might have broken her finger by accident."

"Do you really think that?"

He sat, seemingly unwilling to reply, as she took the turnoff. "No," he said at last. "My guess is he was in complete control of the whole situation."

"That's where I'm at too," she said.

"It's hard to know what we're supposed to be paying attention to," said Wingate. "Is he there to take her blood? To murder her? To desecrate her in some way?"

"Maybe all of it," said Hazel. She was taking the last turn before the bridge over the Kilmartin River.

"We're not going to know anything until we have another body. To see if he's being consistent with his victims." Hazel shot a look at her new detective constable. He shifted uncomfortably. "You don't get this good on your first try," he said.

"You think there are other victims? Where are they?"

"Nearby." He cleared his throat. "Most serial killers stake out a territory and work it methodically."

Her jaw seemed to be stuck in a half-open position. She consciously closed her mouth and put her attention back on the road. "There's thinking out loud and then there's thinking out loud, James. I wish you hadn't said any of that."

"I'm sorry," he muttered.

"What I mean is, I hope you're wrong."

They pulled into the station house at 3 p.m. Shift change. Ray Greene was standing at the back door with a plastic bag at his feet and his arms crossed over his chest. "What's that?" said Hazel as she locked the car.

"Gift," said Ray. "For you." She took the bag from him and pulled out a box. It was a cellphone. She stared at it like it was a moonrock. "You buy twenty bucks' worth of time at a go. I'm the only one with the number."

"I don't want a cellphone, Ray."

"I know. But you need one. If you'd had a cell this afternoon, I could have called you on your way back and told you to meet me up in Chamberlain. The community police there are shitting themselves."

"They called *us* in? That's East Central. We've got no jurisdiction there."

"It's just a little office, something like three cops. I asked them why they hadn't called the Ottawa OPS, but they'd heard about Delia Chandler and they were pretty insistent on us coming out there. They have a crime scene they described to me as 'creative.'"

Hazel looked over at Wingate, who was keeping his expression neutral. She wanted to tell him to be careful what he wished for. "Well, we can't," she said to Greene. "Tell them to call Ottawa."

"It's him, Hazel."

"You don't know that."

"I don't," he said, and he left it at that, but the three of them stood there staring at each other. "It's about three hundred kilometres from here to Chamberlain. We could be there in two and a half hours."

Hazel had passed the bag with the cellphone in it to Wingate and started walking back to her car. "What about the mouth?" Wingate asked.

"You know that old saying, The dead don't tell tales?" said Greene. "Well, even if they did, this guy would be telling one with a considerable speech impediment." He followed Hazel to her car and held open a back-seat door for Wingate. "Spere's already on his way," he said.

"They called Howard, too?" she said in disbelief.

"I called him." She was staring at him. "He knows the Chandler scene better than anyone. I figured . . ."

"Imagine needing Howard twice in forty-eight hours," Hazel said.

Greene clicked his seat belt as she pulled out of the lot. "There's a guy who loves his job again."

—

Chamberlain, 315 kilometres to the east, was at the edge of Renfrew County, an old milltown converted into a village of quaint B&Bs and knitshops. Sleepy was a good word for it. The last police event of any significance there that Hazel could remember involved a delivery van with a snapped brake cable that had crashed through the wall of the Chamberlain Opera House in 1986. It had been delivering ice cream and the Opera House stank of chocolate and strawberry for the whole season. Local playwrights revised their plays to include the odours, and the director of *You're a Good Man, Charlie Brown* had taken the liberty of bringing his actors onstage actually licking cones.

A murder in Chamberlain?

Michael Ulmer's house was on a side street off the main drag, a street of well-kept lawns and freshly painted dormers. Yellow tape encircled the house. Howard Spere was standing behind a pile of leaves, smoking a cigarette. It was seven o'clock in the evening. "Those'll kill you," said Greene.

"At least I'll get to choose my death."

Hazel introduced him to James Wingate. "How many dead bodies you seen, Jim?" asked Spere, shaking the young man's hand.

"I've seen a few. But never two in one day."

"And you're from *Toronto*."

"Fancy that," said Greene, taking his homburg off his head. "Let's stop breaking balls and go see the victim."

"Ray's a master at small talk," said Spere, handing the three of them latex gloves. He nodded at one of his SOCO officers, and the man opened the door.

The house was dark and close, the main floor cluttered with Salvation Army–style furniture: no two pieces matched. There was a cot against the dining-room wall, the stale sheets pulled back, the pillow stained almost brown. A fug of old cigarette smoke laced the air. A folding TV-dinner table stood in front of a La-Z-Boy chair, its surface colonized by pill bottles and moisturizing products. An extra-large box of two-ply tissues was balanced on the arm of the chair. "Do I want to know what the tissues and the lotions have to do with each other?" said Greene.

Hazel shot him a look. "Dry skin and sniffles, Ray. Don't think too much."

They went up the stairs. A knot of Ident guys were milling about in the hallway labelling ziplock bags, packing up various bits of equipment, generally trying to stay out of one of the bedrooms. They could see camera flashes going off, and hear the high-pitched report of battery cells. "In here, detectives," called one of the men. They followed his voice into the master bedroom. It was much cleaner up here, the air more breathable. The blinds were drawn. There was a figure in the bed dimly lit by a bedside lamp casting a feeble yellow light.

"What's your name, officer?"

"Matthiessen."

"Do we need it so dark in here, Officer Matthiessen?" said Hazel. The man took it as an order and turned the overhead light on. Light flooded the room and the body burst into view.

"Fucking hell," said Greene. He stepped back instinctively.

Wingate was the only one of the three of them who approached the bed. In it lay the ruined body of Michael Ulmer. "What was wrong with him?"

"Less than there is now," said Matthiessen. "He was taking something called Avonex, plus other things for his muscles and stuff. Detective Spere says he probably had MS." Ray Greene finally stepped forward. "Poor bastard."

"I wonder how he got up the stairs. His walker's still on the main floor," said Wingate.

"He carried him up the stairs?" said Greene, his brows raised. "That's a pretty thoughtful killer." Hazel shot a look at her new detective, and Wingate said nothing else. His theories were going to have to wait for a better moment.

Ulmer was covered with blankets, as if he were sleeping, and there was a rise where his arms were crossed over his chest. Two huge circles of blood drenched the sheet atop his hands. "Can you pull those back?" asked Hazel, and the officer drew away the heavy blankets. "*God.*"

Ulmer's hands were like two balloons of blood. Just with the movement of the sheets being drawn away, they shook like jellies: the killer had taken a hammer to them. But the violence done to Ulmer's hands was nothing compared to his head. His mouth had been smashed in so thoroughly that the upper half of his jaw hovered like a dome over a soupy mass of teeth and tissue. The killer had hacked at each of the victim's eyes and torn through the sockets laterally, opening up his head like a box-top on both sides of his face. Then he'd staved the man's skull in. "He's not exactly subtle, is he?"

"Has Ident finished?" Hazel asked PC Matthiessen.

"I don't know if they could ever finish, but yeah, it's been photographed and swept. We were just waiting for you to bag him."

"Bag him then and get him out of here. Where's the ambulance?"

"There's a guy in the alley. We figured we'd probably want to take him out through the back."

"Good idea."

Greene snapped off his gloves with disgust and tossed them into the hall. "Dare I ask if anyone saw anything?"

"We spoke to some of the neighbours, and no one knows anything. But we haven't done a canvass yet."

"And who notified you guys?"

"PC Degraaf took a call before lunch. He says Ulmer had a homecare appointment at eleven, but he didn't answer the door."

"Who was the caller?"

"We could find that out for you."

"You didn't ask?" said Greene, incredulously.

"He said Ulmer sometimes slept through his appointments."

"But he called the police, this man? If this was a normal occurrence, why would he call you?"

Matthiessen shuffled his feet a little. "I don't know. Maybe he didn't want to have to circle back and check on Ulmer again. We sent a car out at three."

Greene was shaking his head in disbelief. "You didn't want to interrupt his nap, I guess."

"Do we have a recording of this call?" said Hazel.

The officer looked down. "Sorry, Chief. We're not in the habit of doing that. And it was so fast . . ."

"Who's your commanding?"

Matthiessen leaned back a little and looked through the door. They all turned, but there was no one there. "We're between commandings," he said. "Our skip retired last year. Seventy-four years old. East Central promised us a new guy by the end of the summer, but you know how things are."

She certainly did. Was the OPS planning on leaving every detachment north of Toronto rudderless? There were great savings to be had in places where the population wasn't large enough to make a noise. "So it's you and Degraaf."

"We have a couple of volunteers."

"Good Lord," said Hazel. "You couldn't break up a barfight here."

Matthiessen looked sheepish. "Luckily, things are mainly peaceful hereabouts. This isn't Ottawa, y'know."

"Well, whatever, let's get this guy out of here now."

"Yes, ma'am." He seemed to be happy to leave the room. She turned to Wingate, who was still standing over the bed. Greene had already gone downstairs.

"So where's the love in this one, Wingate?"

"Appearances are misleading."

"Uh-huh."

DC Wingate leaned in closer. "Do you think the blood's different colours?"

Hazel looked from where she was. "Do you?"

"Arterial and venous blood look different. The oxygen in arterial blood makes it look redder. Venous blood is darker. Compare the blood on his head to the blood on his hands."

She looked closely. It did appear as if the blood on Ulmer's hands was brighter. "It's one for Spere. Mention it to him." Two officers with a black body bag appeared in the doorway. Hazel ushered them in, and Wingate stood back as they laid the bag beside the body.

"What do you think he doesn't want us to notice?" he said.

"Why do you think he's trying to communicate with anyone?"

"He's trying to make these killings look like something they aren't."

One of the baggers started pulling the zipper up. "One last look?" he asked. Ulmer lay in it stiffly, his chest nearly blue and a line of blood under his skin where it had pooled. It was like a chalk outline in purple.

"I think we're done here," said Hazel.

The officer closed the bag over Ulmer's destroyed head. "No one asked me," he said, "but this guy, whoever did this, was pretty fucking angry. Psycho or not, he wasn't in any kind of control of himself."

"I'm pretty sure you're wrong about that," said DC Wingate.

They found Greene on the front lawn, sucking on one of Spere's cigarettes. The streetlights had come on since they'd gone into the house. Glowing circles lay over the road. "Ten years without a smoke," Greene said, turning the burning ember to himself and staring at it. Spere held out the pack to them and they declined.

"So, again," said Hazel, "the victim opens the door, lets the killer in. Right? No sign of a struggle. The killer probably *carries* the victim upstairs and puts him in bed. Ulmer lets him."

"Maybe these people are signing on for one kind of death, but they're getting another," said Greene. "Or getting the one they want, and then the killer is either letting loose because he can, or because he thinks he won't get caught if the murders aren't connectable."

"Two violent murders two days apart within three hundred kilometres of each other?"

"Maybe he knows something about the state of policing in this part of the province," said Greene. "Such as it is." He crushed his cigarette underfoot. "Christ, they've got two rooks here playing house and writing parking tickets."

Hazel cast a glance at Wingate, whose eyes were directed straight into the grass. "Well, you've got your proximity now, James."

"What does that mean?" said Spere.

"Serial killers," said Wingate quietly, as if he was in pain, "they work territories."

"So do milkmen," said Greene. "Anyway, I'll tell you one thing we do know. If this is the same guy, he's heading east."

] 6 [

Simon climbed out of the river and onto the bank, reaching for a white towel he'd draped over a boulder. The sun in its oblique angle didn't offer much heat, but after he'd towelled off, he stood on the sandy riverside and with his eyes closed faced the light until he could feel it reach inside him and scour what the rushing water could not reach.

He'd pitched camp near the eastern border of Quebec the previous morning. Here, in these forests, he could replenish some of his supplies, despite the lateness of the season. The eastern provinces were a better source for some of the mosses and lichens he could not find in such abundance out west. Club moss and Asclepias. He scoured the forest floor for seedpods, herbs, and fungus. The evening before he'd had the marvellous luck of discovering a cluster of *Laetiporus cincinnatus*, the mushroom foolishly called "chicken of the woods" by those who could not liken a food to itself, and although he did not usually eat fungi, he had been losing weight lately from his exertions, and needed to give his stomach something to work on. He'd cooked the huge bracket of mushrooms on an open fire, and delighted in the firm flesh redolent of the forest.

Soon he would be close to the ocean again – it had been nearly two months since he'd left the Pacific on his journey – and he would allow himself the indulgence of fish once he reached the shores of the Atlantic. He ate flesh once a year (secretly, as his brother would not approve), and in the time he'd spent in the wilds outside of Port Hardy, high up on Vancouver Island, he had allowed himself to indulge only during the coho migration, capturing a sow partway to her breeding grounds and eating her raw, bones, eggs, and all, on the riverbank. He liked to feel the power of the animal in him at these times, ravishing himself on the blind, unquestioning faith these creatures showed in the cycles of their lives, returning to die where they were born, not conscious of their paths but committed to them, the way the ocean is magnetized to the moon. In the week after these feasts, he could feel their flesh coursing through his, leaping in his blood, tidal.

He'd passed through to this part of Quebec without stopping. He'd had requests in French from various parts of the province, but despite his grounding in the romantic tongues, his French was poor. Clear communication was of the utmost importance in this endeavour, and he could not risk misspeaking, or failing to understand.

So he had ignored all but one request from Quebec, this one from a small town high up on the St. Lawrence River called Havre-Saint-Pierre. It had taken him a day and a half to drive through Quebec, keeping to the 117 and the 113 through Chibougamau until the highway brought him back down toward the St. Lawrence. He'd had a premonition of being sighted somehow, knowing that his stop in Humber Cottage was perhaps not a wise one: he'd been called to attend to his willing supplicants, not to those in random need, and God knew there were many who would benefit from his ministrations. Still, he was a man on a merciful mission, and if God should send him a child in need of transformation, he could not refuse. He was glad of his opportunities, but he did not want to be stopped before his work was done.

And his Great Work was nearly complete. There were four men and women at the end of this mighty chain waiting to play their small role in it. How he loved them for their patience, their willingness. He would not fail any of them; had not failed to this point.

He looked back on his and his brother's years in Port Hardy, and although they seemed at the time to be years of turmoil and doubt, now that time in his life seemed encased in something. Its shape was crystalline, light-catching, and the kernel of himself that had been made by those years glowed within it, something whole. He realized this crystal was his battery: this image of himself, which contained the force of his brother's being, powered him now, allowed him to move forward across the country nearly sleepless and barely provended, a starving, wide-awake prophet. When he came to the end of his path, in Newfoundland less than ten days from now, he would make the final gesture of his quest and that crystal would burst open and spread his light among the stars.

He prayed beside his tent in the thick forest north of Havre-Saint-Pierre. He laid out his photographs on the flamelit grass, putting them in order, fifteen figures, with four to go. Nineteen in all, the particles of a wholeness that could not be made without these orisons, these petitioners. He thanked the Almighty for allowing him to reach this day.

He worried that these last men and women might have weakened during their wait. He had already lost two on the way, an elderly man in Canmore, and a woman in Wawa. These he had replaced with the only two people on his waiting list.

He spent a full day and night in the woods, replenishing his strength and resting. In the days, he ate, bathed, and prayed. At night, he could hear the life of the forest around him, creatures aware of his presence, but not frightened of him, not threatened. He listened to the myriad scurryings around his tent, the sound of a watchful stillness from the branches above him, and he felt contained in it, another animal in a sanctuary of its own making.

After dressing and taking down his tent, he went into Havre-Saint-Pierre and checked for mail at the main postal station. It was Wednesday, November 17, at eight o'clock in the morning. He found a letter of confirmation from Mrs. Iagnemma, saying that she would like to see him as arranged. But *not* as arranged, as she stated that her daughter, a Miss Cecilia Iagnemma, would be present to assist him and to give him her support. Simon had been especially careful to choose his hosts from among the many men and women who fit a certain profile. First and foremost, they would live alone. Second, they were to understand that the process they were involved in was to take place in utmost secrecy. It was no secret between himself and his hosts that what they were engaged in was illegal in every lawbook but God's: if he were to be stopped, their participation would be for nothing. Telling anyone about him, or worse, involving anyone else in his plans, was grounds for dissolving the arrangement. Once, at the very beginning (it had been his third appointment), he'd arrived at an apartment and seen two sets of shoes of different sizes on the mat outside the door. He'd simply turned on his heel and left (although he returned later, unannounced and somewhat displeased, and proceeded without ceremony). But now at least Mrs. Iagnemma had prepared him. She had not really asked permission, but she had told him honestly what she was planning. It allowed him to consider his options. And given that he had only three more stops after this one, it struck him as wise to go with what was being given him.

He was to see the woman in six hours, but however much he disliked deviating from his plans, he would go now. He followed the directions to her house on a hillside beyond the town. It was a humble cabin surrounded by Jack pine, and as he approached it, a thin finger of woodsmoke came from the chimney.

"I'm early," he said when she came to the door, and she looked behind him to see if anyone had accompanied him. Seeing no one, she opened the door for him anyway. She was a woman of about sixty, her entire aspect a wash of white: white hair, white terrycloth robe, the skin of her face like onionskin. She bent over to write something down on a pad she was carrying.

You got my letter?

"I did. And I've come out to ask you to reconsider," he said, standing in her hallway, his hat in his hand. He had left his kit in the car. "I cannot do what you ask of me; there can't be a witness."

Mrs. Iagnemma gestured for him to come into the house proper. Throat cancer had left her without a larynx or much of her tongue. There was a semi-permanent port in the base of her throat where liquid nourishment could be taken. She was a borderline case for him: her disease had violated her so profoundly that her doctors had removed her speaking parts, and she was no longer complete. He'd justified his visit to her by considering that her voice would be raised in a different way than medicine could imagine. Her tongue-lessness was prelude to a miracle. But he'd known he was tempting fate by coming to this woman, and his fears had been grounded: she'd broken their agreement and forced him off his schedule. He was not happy. She brought him into the kitchen and put a kettle on to boil. The house was not as tidy as he liked; he would have very little time to clean once she was finished, and he had to ensure he was well out of the area before her daughter arrived at two o'clock. However, if Cecilia

Iagnemma showed before he was finished, he'd already decided what he would have to do. Gladys Iagnemma sat across from him at the table and began writing on one of the pads of paper that seemed to litter every flat surface in the house.

You look as I thought you would.

"A little severe?"

Kind, she wrote. She pulled the pad back and continued. *I don't want to be alone when this happens. My daughter understands. You will be safe even if she's here.*

"I can't, Gladys. This is a private thing. Between you, me, and the Lord. No one else is invited. I'll understand if you don't want to go ahead. I can find someone else."

She seemed to collapse into herself a little. From the looks of her, had she lived a little farther away and been his second-last, or last visit, she'd already be dead.

Okay, she wrote. *But I want to write her a note. I'll write it, and then we can start.*

He reached across the table and gripped her writing hand, and she looked up at him and smiled wanly. "You do that, then," he said, keeping his expression steady. "I'll get my things, and you can put down what you want to say."

She nodded gratefully and tears fell down her cheeks. She lowered her head and began writing; he saw her write the words *My beloved Cecilia,* and he left her to it. Out in the car, he opened the hatch and took his bag out. His movements were abrupt. He tugged on the fridge door and checked the cable.

He had not been pressed for time during any of his

visits before now, and he would need the better part of two hours after Mrs. Iagnemma gave herself to him to finish up. The arrangement was quite unsatisfactory, and if the daughter showed early, he would have a mess on his hands. He went back into the house and saw the woman crouched over her writing. The kettle was steaming now. Never had he foregone mercy, but if any of his supplicants had earned a rough dispatch, Gladys Iagnemma was the one. "I must ask you again, Gladys: do you wish to go forward?"

She pushed what she was doing aside and wrote *Yes*, then pulled the unfinished letter back toward her. "You can consider yourself fortunate that I'm willing to go through with this at all," he said. The kettle whistled and Simon lifted it off the element and raised it over Mrs. Iagnemma's head. She'd turned at the sound of the water boiling and lifted her eyes upward in time to witness the stream of boiling water coming down over her. In panic, she ducked forward and Simon poured the steaming liquid into the woman's white hair and down the back of her neck. Her scalp went instantly livid, as if a nest of eels had burst to life on her head, and Mrs. Iagnemma reared up and flew over the back of her chair. She hit the floor with a bang – he could hear the hoarse susurrations emanating from her broken mouth – and he kicked her over onto her back and held her down against the cupboards with a foot on her chest. He poured the water over the port at the base of her throat. "Do you know what an agreement is, Gladys?" She writhed beneath his foot, a pink, steaming foam cascading out of her mouth and nostrils. Within a minute, she was dead. The flesh around the circular port was cooked to a translucent pink.

He was going to need ice now if he was going to get his work done. He replaced the kettle on the stovetop and struggled to get Mrs. Iagnemma's body back into the chair. Her eyes were still open and would not close: the thin muscles already hardening. There was a single tray of ice in the freezer, and he cracked and freed the twelve cubes from it and packed five of them into her mouth. The heat there began to melt the ice instantly, and he replaced the shrinking cubes with fresh ones until he could feel her jaw begin to stiffen. He scrabbled around in his kit and took out a piece of paper and consulted it. Her mouth was already rounded a little: he put his thumb behind her lower teeth and drew her jaw downward. Cool water coursed over his knuckles. Her jaw wanted to spring up, but he held it firmly until the muscles in her mandible accommodated him. With his other hand, he pushed the stub of her tongue back and upward in her mouth. He could feel the muscles firming up beneath his hands, as if he were sculpting her, and indeed he *was*, he was changing her at the moment of her death into a work of art.

It took ninety minutes, but at last she stayed in the position he'd placed her in. He photographed her with the Polaroid and waited to see her face emerge from the vague darkness within the white frame, her frightened, egg-white eyes drifting through the fog toward him. Fixed now, forever, in his gaze.

Back in the car, after quickly cleaning up and drawing her blood, he keyed the lock on the little bar fridge and opened its door. He'd lined one of the shelves with camphor pucks to mask the smell – even refrigerated, blood began to reek after a while. Just the same, he'd learned not to hold his breath: the priest does not look away at the moment of supreme sacrifice. He brought out one of the jars, opened it, and filled his nose and lungs with the scent of decay. He dipped his chalice into it. He took the cup into the house, where Mrs. Iagnemma sat in permanent peace, and he tipped the contents of the chalice over her burned head. "I bless you," he said to her. Black, brackish blood coated her face and slowly trickled down the front of her terrycloth robe. "You are in the choir now, Gladys Iagnemma, welcome."

He swept her letter to her daughter from the table-top and quickly searched the house for his letters to her. He had instructed all of his hosts to keep his correspondence in one place, where he could retrieve it at the end, and here, in this house, as in all the others, he found the letters just where he had told Mrs. Iagnemma to keep them: in a small box in a clothing drawer in her room, weighted with a long, rough black stone on its top. With the bundle of paper, he got back into the car and continued driving east.

Monday, November 15, 7:30 a.m.

Hazel Micallef stared into her All-Bran. It stared back. Resigned, she picked up her spoon and began eating. Food for horses, she thought. Her mother sat across from her in her petit-point-adorned housedress, her short grey hair sticking up from sleep. It was seven-thirty in the morning under grey November clouds. Hazel wanted to go back to bed.

"Do you think you're losing weight?" said her mother.

"I'm losing sleep."

"I think you are." She went back to her paper. The *Toronto Star*. After a moment, she said, "So this other man – you're certain he was killed by the same guy?"

"I'm not certain of anything, Mother. All we know is that we have two bodies within three hundred kilometres of each other. And up here, that's a pattern."

Her mother held up the front section of the *Star*. "Down there, it's a weekend."

"Ray thinks he's travelling. The killer. West to east."

"You need a third body to prove that."

"I know."

"We had one murder the whole time I was mayor. A man killed his wife."

"Gerald Clipshaw."

"You remember." Her mother was smiling as if Hazel had recalled her birthday. "He stabbed her in the heart and then showed up at the station with the knife. Crying. The whole thing took an hour to solve."

"Ah, things were so much simpler in the olden days." She took another spoonful of the soggy cereal. Already she was imagining what she would order at Ladyman's. She dreaded showing up to work this morning. Word of the Ulmer murder had made it to Port Dundas, and she was certain she'd be hearing from Gord Sunderland today. She'd had a phone call the night before from a TV station in Mayfair – if the news had already made it halfway to Toronto, she had to wonder if it wouldn't make it the rest of the way soon, and that was something to be delayed as long as possible. She'd already had the instinct that the outcome in this case depended upon the police protecting the killer's privacy and therefore upholding his sense of invincibility. She was certain that he would vanish at the first sign of danger. His touchstones were patience and preparation. Just the same, another body would mean bedlam. She feared its inevitability. "I better go," she said. "Try not to answer the phone today."

"You want me to lock the doors and stay in bed with the covers up to my chin?"

"No. Just don't talk to anyone you don't know."

"I'm playing rummy with Clara and Margaret this morning. We'll cower together under the table if you like."

Hazel sat on the deacon's bench in the front hall and leaned over to put on her boots. She felt the familiar twinge in her lower back, the pain radiating in a sharp electrical shock around the front of her hip. Her mother could probably still pole-vault, if she wanted to, and here I am, thought Hazel, falling apart at sixty-one.

Her mother came down the hallway with something wrapped in wax paper. "What's this," said Hazel, taking it from her.

"Something to cheer you up, love." Hazel held the little package up. There was a piece of toast inside. She could smell butter.

"You're a nice old lady," she said. She kissed her mother on the forehead – that smell of rosewater – and went out to the car.

Monday was the news conference. The editorial staff of the *Westmuir Record* would have been hard at work all weekend resetting today's edition of the paper, and she had no doubt that Sunderland was not going to be pleased he'd been shut out of a personal audience with her. Hazel had to smile inwardly at her mild deception. *Misdirection* is how she liked to put it. But who was Gord Sunderland to think he was entitled to anything? She was interested in knowing what the paper was going to say about Delia Chandler. She pulled over by the Stop 'N' Go and bought a copy of it. The front page and the two inside local news pages had been reset to deal with Delia's murder. Spelling bees and Christmas wreaths were going to have to wait for a quiet newsday now, she thought. A picture of Delia, taken sometime in the last three or four years, was on the front page under the headline PORT DUNDAS LOCAL MURDERED IN HER OWN HOME. The front page advertised full coverage of the murder within, plus an editorial. There were no specifics about Delia's death, which meant the station house was still sealed tight, but the witness who had seen a "strange car" on Taylor Street was now claiming it was a black, late-model Ford sedan. Interesting what a microphone can do for a faulty memory, Hazel thought. On the inside pages there was a picture of Delia from the 1960s. She'd been quite beautiful then, her lips painted darkly. Old photographs could make you feel bad for anyone: those innocent faces with no knowledge of the future. There was Delia, not knowing that forty-odd years from that moment, she'd be lying dead on her sofa, her head almost completely sawn off. Best not to know, Hazel said to herself, and she shuddered, realizing that the mystery of her own future contained first her mother's death, and then her own.

At the station house, she slipped in through the back door where she could avoid the small gathering of local press she expected had already begun to assemble out on the front steps. She gestured to Melanie to follow her into her office. She shut the door once her assistant entered and stood in the middle of the room with her. "I have a cellphone now," she said.

"I know," said Cartwright. "That's really excellent."

"You and Ray Greene will have the number. No one else, though. No reporters, no mothers, no one. Is that clear?"

There was a brief silence. "Is there anything else?" asked Cartwright.

Hazel brought the phone out of her vest pocket. "I'd like you to show me how to place a call on this thing." Cartwright smiled faintly. "I'd wipe that look off your face, missy."

"You have to turn it on."

"Take me through it." Melanie Cartwright took the phone from her and pushed the power button.

Everyone at the station house had the newspaper. Hazel walked into the pen and one of the duty officers, PC Ashton, held up his copy and said, "Apparently, we're still at square one."

Hazel took the paper away from him and held it at her side. "All of you may be as shocked as the rest of the readers of the *Westmuir Record* that a murder has happened in our sleepy little town. But unlike those people, we don't get our news from the *Westmuir Record*, no matter how tempting it may be. Now, how many of you in this room spoke to reporters at this newspaper?" No one raised their hand, but all looked around; they took her question to indicate that someone had broken rank. But instead, Hazel smiled at them. "Right. None of you did. And none of you will. And that's why I want to see every copy of the *Westmuir Record* in this room in the recycling bin immediately. It has nothing to say to us, and I don't want you getting your facts mixed up with other people's speculation."

"Um, Inspector," said Ashton, whose paper she'd taken. "I was actually looking for a used fridge. Mine's on the fritz."

She handed Ashton his paper back. "Adrian can buy a new fridge, but the rest of you . . ." The room seemed to rise as one. "Greene, Wingate: I'd like to see you in the conference room when I'm done with the hordes. Howard Spere will be here any minute." Both detectives nodded at her. "I'll be back in ten."

She recognized Paul Garland from the weekly *Dublin Ledger*, Patricia Warren from the *Beaton Advertiser* (monthly), and two younger reporters from parts unknown. She suspected they might be from the cable access station in Mayfair. But there was no Gord Sunderland. "We're going to wait a minute," she said, and Garland put his hand up.

"Any chance we can go inside? It's the middle of November out here."

"It's the middle of November inside too."

"But it's warmer inside."

"This won't take long," she said, "and my people are pretty busy with this investigation, as you can imagine."

"Do you have any leads on the Chandler murder?" asked one of the two kids.

"Who are you? I've never seen you before."

"Alex Finch and Janet Turner" — Janet waved sheepishly — "CKBF Mayfair. I hear that there was a strange black car spotted on Taylor the day of the killing."

"First off," said Detective Inspector Micallef, "I'm here to make a statement, not to answer questions. Secondly, if you're getting your facts from the paper of record, you should know that nothing you've read in today's issue of the *Westmuir Record* is based on statements made by the Port Dundas PD."

"So there's no car?"

"Here's the statement." She took a single sheet of paper out of a folder and held it out in front of her. The wind caught the corner and folded the paper over on itself. "'On Saturday, November 13, the body of Delia Chandler, age eighty-one, was discovered in her home. At this time, the Port Dundas police, in co-operation with personnel from Mayfair, and under the direction of Central Region of the OPS, have embarked on a full-scale investigation. In the interest of the investigation, we are unable to enlarge on the particulars of the case; however, we will update the public with pertinent details when they become available and thank you all in advance for your understanding.' Our community liaison officer, PC Eileen Bail, will be out shortly with copies of this statement should you like to have one." She looked around the small gathering. Their eyes seemed to have glazed over. Patricia Warren looked down at her notes.

"Um, Inspector?"

"Yes?"

"Can you confirm that Delia Chandler was murdered?"

"Can I confirm that?"

"Yes, can you confirm that?"

"Don't you read the *Westmuir Record*?"

"I do, but you said —"

"Yes," said Hazel Micallef. "She was murdered." She turned, ignoring the three other hands in the air and went through the door. PC Bail was waiting with a thin sheaf of photocopies in her hand. "They're all ready for you, Eileen. Positively rabid with anticipation."

"Thanks, Chief."

"Anytime."

"Um, Skip?" Hazel stopped and faced her. "They're just doing their jobs, you know."

"They're cannibals in slacks, Eileen. Ask my mother about it sometime." PC Bail looked down at the floor. "Anything else?"

"Not right now."

Hazel turned a sheet over the top of the easel. Ray Greene, James Wingate, and Howard Spere were sitting with their coffees at the table in front of her. "We're going to go over what we know and then figure out what our best move is. Ray, you start."

Greene opened his notebook and flipped back a couple of pages. "We have two bodies. One here in Port Dundas, the other in Chamberlain, three hundred and fifteen kilometres away. The first, Delia Chandler, was murdered sometime after four o'clock on Friday, November 12. White female aged eighty-one. She was heavily sedated, murdered, and then partially drained of blood. After she was dead, the killer cut her throat. According to Dr. Deacon's report, her mouth was interfered with post mortem. She also had a broken finger."

"DC Wingate has a theory about that," said Hazel, who had been writing the details down hurriedly on the easel, "which, for the time being, he is going to keep to himself." Wingate smiled in a pained fashion. "Forensics, Howard?"

"We found fingerprints on the door that belong to the victim, as well as to Bob Chandler. We have to presume that the killer wore gloves, because there are no fingerprints inside the house that don't match the victim or her son. There was a scuff in the carpet inside the door with a partial impression of a shoeprint in it, and it suggests the killer is a size eleven, but it's inconclusive. No forced entry, as has been previously established. No struggle is evident —"

"Although let's keep in mind that the place was spotless," said Hazel. "Either Delia cleaned it top to bottom before her visitor arrived, or the killer himself cleaned up. Jack Deacon says he would have had to be in the house a minimum of three hours after her death. If there was a struggle, there would have been plenty of time to erase all evidence of it."

"Okay," said Detective Spere, "so maybe there was a struggle, but I think Jack would have been able to back it up with defensive wounds on the victim's body, so for now, we're going to go with no struggle, and I think we'll find the Ulmer murder backs that up."

"No, it doesn't," said Greene.

"Can we finish with Mrs. Chandler before we move on?" said Hazel, and Greene gestured to her to carry on.

"Okay," said Hazel, taking out Jack Deacon's report. "The time frame of the murder, according to Jack, is that a heavily sedating agent is introduced to the victim at around four o'clock in the afternoon, and takes effect shortly afterward. Between four and five, the killer breaks the victim's finger and then introduces a trace amount of amatoxin, this being the agent that causes death. Then he puts a wide-bore needle into the victim's femoral artery and *sucks* most of the blood out of her body, either by using a large syringe or pump of some kind."

"They have pumps for that?" said Greene.

Hazel ignored him. "Deacon puts death at five in the afternoon, according to the potassium levels in the victim's vitreous humour. He had three hours after that to cut her head nearly off, clean – if he cleaned – and to do what he did to her mouth."

"What do you think that means?" asked Greene.

"It could mean that it doesn't matter to the killer whether we see that sign or not," said Spere.

"Great," said Greene, and he made a gesture as if to throw his notebook over his shoulder.

"All right, that's Delia, unless anyone has anything else to add." Hazel drew a circle around the facts as she'd written them down in short form on the easel. No one spoke as she wrote "Michael Ulmer" on the other half of the sheet. "Ray?"

"Okay, so Ulmer. Less than forty-eight hours later, most likely around noon on Sunday, November 14. A call was placed to the Chamberlain Community Policing office around eleven. The caller identified himself as a homecare nurse. We're going to have to go with Chamberlain's superior policing skills on that one and take it at face value unless anyone wants to propose a reason the killer called in his own crime."

"Forty-five minutes before the time of death?" said Spere. "Sounds a little daring."

"That's what I think," said Greene. "So: white male, twenty-nine, multiple sclerosis sufferer. Was apparently killed by blunt-force trauma to the head, emphasis on *force*. Forensics found teeth embedded in the victim's pillow. Both hands were severely traumatized in a similar fashion, but there was no evidence of venipuncture, and it would seem, from what we saw at the crime scene, that there was no shortage of blood supply in the victim's body. East Central OPS is sharing jurisdiction with us on this one, and we sent Ulmer to Mayfair to keep Jack Deacon in the loop. We're waiting for pathology to be faxed up to see if there was anything in his stomach similar to what was in Mrs. Chandler's. The victim here was almost certainly carried upstairs to a master bedroom that, apart from the murder, appeared to be unused."

"Forensics?"

"Same as the Chandler murder," said Spere, "but without the carpet scuff. One item of interest is that despite the amount of blood, it's limited to the murder site. The killer would have had to clean himself up, but there's no blood on the carpet in the master bedroom, or in the closest bathroom. He's very meticulous. I think he's only *appearing* to make a mess."

"Deacon isn't done with the body, but we know what we know about its physical condition. Let's sum up." Hazel circled Ulmer's column and now she drew a line under it all. "Ident practically bagged both houses, but nothing points anywhere conclusive so far, correct, Howard?"

"My guys brought Mrs. Chandler's computer in this morning," said Spere. "There's nothing. Some emails to and from an old girl in Florida — weather and gardens, that sort of thing. A couple of web receipts from the drugstore — she knew how to renew her prescriptions online. Very little else. There was virtually nothing of interest in her web history."

"What would that be, Howard? A web history."

"Just a way to go back over the places you've visited on the Internet over a period of time. What we found out was that she learned how to make parmesan rice last Monday on a recipe site, on Tuesday she Googled 'Merle Haggard,' and *As the World Turns*, and two Wednesdays before her death, she bought a duvet cover on Bidnow.com."

Wingate seemed surprised. "So was this an assisted suicide or not?"

Spere cast him a look. "You think buying a duvet cover is evidence one way or the other?"

"I think so," said the young detective. "If she knew this person was coming to visit her with the purpose of helping her to end her life, then why would she be buying *anything* online?"

"Good point," said Hazel. "She lets this man in, but she has no idea what's going to happen to her?"

"Or she's actually not expecting him," said Spere.

"Let's reiterate: no signs of a struggle," said Greene.

"Right. But he's sedated her with belladonna."

"He broke her finger," said Wingate. They all looked at him, and then at Hazel.

"Go on, James," she said.

"Okay," he said nervously. He directed his comments at the others. "He broke Delia Chandler's finger to ensure she was anaesthetized. It was snapped cleanly in two, and it wasn't an accident. Deacon says in his report that it had definitely happened while she was still alive because there was swelling around the break, and that means that her heart was still beating. So the killer used it to test if she was ready. There was an agreement between them, and this was part of it. He's invited, and the victims know what will happen to them when he arrives."

"Then what about Ulmer?" said Spere. "What was it with breaking every bone in that man's hand? He just wanted to be ultra-certain?"

"I don't know," said Wingate.

Ray Greene was drawing an invisible circle on the tabletop with his forefinger. "I think maybe we're being a little fast out of the blocks with all this. On the *surface*, nothing really connects these two killings except for the fact that they've happened within a three-hour drive of each other. And right now, all we have are surfaces to work with."

"But Ulmer wasn't killed three hours after Delia," said Wingate. "It was almost two days later."

"So what?" said Greene. "Listen, kid, I appreciate that

you'd like to make a good first impression, but you've been here all of, what, twenty-one hours, and frankly, I'm not sure I want to factor in all your cubscout wild guesses about this guy's *agreements* with the people he's slicing and bludgeoning to death." Hazel was staring at him. "Okay?" he said to her.

"Detective Constable Wingate, what was the point you were going to make about the delay between the killings?"

Wingate turned to her. "He's not just showing up out of the blue, Inspector. He's keeping appointments."

There was a knock at the door and Cartwright stuck her head in. "I have Jack Deacon on the phone. He wants to talk to you before he faxes his report. That okay?"

"Conference him in," said Hazel. She switched on the receiver on the tabletop. It looked like a black starfish with three arms. Presently, they heard Deacon's voice.

"Let me guess — you guys are desperately trying to find the connection between Ulmer and Chandler."

Greene leaned toward the device. "You should be a detective, Jack."

"Well, you can relax. Kind of. It *is* the same guy. Ulmer's stomach was full of belladonna. I doubt he felt a thing."

"I guess that's good," said Hazel. "So what killed him? Amatoxin?"

"No. None of that here. My guess is that it was the blow to the head. Is Wingate there?"

"Here, sir."

"That was a good notion you had about the blood, son. It was Ulmer's blood on his head and neck, but the fresher blood, the blood on his hands, it wasn't his. Ulmer was B positive, but the blood on his hands was mainly O."

A chorus of voices called out to the doctor at once.

"Do I still have your attention?" he said, and they fell silent. "It's a mixture of blood. I mean, from more than one person. So I don't know whose it is."

"What the hell," said Greene. "Are you certain?"

"I am."

"Can you find out whose blood it is?"

"It's going to take a few days to unravel, I think. I sent a sample down to the Toronto lab. They can separate out the types and the DNA."

"I want all the physical evidence associated with the first scene taken down to Mayfair," said Hazel. "Jack?"

"Ma'am?"

"You're going to test all the bloodstains from the Chandler site again."

"I'll be waiting." He rang off. Hazel stood over the conferencing device, rubbing her forehead.

"What is it?" asked Greene.

She sighed heavily. "I'm going to have to call Mason now."

"How's that going to go?"

"My guess is not well." She shook the cobwebs away and stood straight. "James, you go to Mayfair and get Delia's clothes out of evidence and take them right to Jack Deacon. Ray, we need to talk to Bob Chandler again. Unless you'd like to go with DC Wingate to Mayfair."

"No," said Greene, quietly. "I'll go see Bob."

—

Mason's secretary kept her on hold for twelve minutes. The average was fifteen. It failed to make her feel optimistic. "I have Commander Mason for you," said the secretary when she came back on. He was one for pomp.

"Hazel?"

"Hello, Ian," she said. "I won't keep you long. I need some more manpower up here. Maybe for a month, maybe less."

"Manpower?"

"A minimum of two detectives."

"I thought you folks said 'personpower' these days. How's your mother?"

"She's well, thank you. Beth?"

"Terrific. Two detectives. Didn't I just send you one?"

"Yes. And thank you. But it's not enough right now."

"See?" said Mason. "Give an inch?" Ian Mason was the worst kind of police bureaucrat: capricious and jolly about it. In the early days, he seemed to delight in denying any and all requests. His standard rejoinder was *is it really a rainy day?* If you could prove there was a need that could not be dealt with in any other way but by spending money, you had a chance. But the best way to deal with Mason, Hazel had found over the years, was to appeal to his vanity. If his name could, in some way, be attached to a positive outcome, he was much more likely to acquiesce. Although "likely" was a relative term.

"You've got twenty people up there already, Hazel."

"Twelve, Ian, and only two detectives, not including myself, and I have the whole detachment to look after."

"That's plenty. What on earth could you need two *more* good men for?"

"Commander, have you not heard what's happened up here?"

"Yes, of course I have. A nice lady with terminal cancer died."

"Was murdered."

"Yes."

"And now there's a second one. In Chamberlain."

She heard him moving some paper around. Probably he was signing something without reading it. "Chamberlain's in Renfrew, Hazel. You're in Westmuir. Are you asking me to staff you so you can go digging in another county's dirt?"

"We believe these murders are connected. In fact, we have growing proof that they are, and that the killer . . ."

She heard him breathing into the pause. "Oh, *do* say it, Detective Inspector."

"We have reason to believe we have a serial killer on our hands."

Now Mason laughed. "I love it," he said. "In a land without murder, two deaths within a thousand kilometres is obviously the work of a serial killer. You know what they call two murders close together in Toronto? The morning shift."

She counted to five in her head. "You could take control of this, Ian," she said quietly. "You're retiring in a year. You could put your mark on something like this; leave on a high note. Help us crack an important case."

"Are you going to use the stick next?"

"Please, Ian. I wouldn't ask if —"

"Ah, the mantra of the small-town police chief. You wouldn't ask if you could think of another way." She remained silent. If she said anything else now, his answer would be an instant no. But she knew, even though her reference to his ego needs was a craven one, he'd heard the upside. Playing Mason well was no guarantee of success, but playing him poorly ensured that you'd leave empty-handed. "My retirement is actually six months away, Hazel. But I think you know that."

"I must have forgotten."

"I'm going to fly my plane and hunt moose. That's the plan."

"It sounds great, Ian. Are we going to go ahead with this? A couple more hands?"

"Hazel," he said, "you've got a serial killer up there like I have a tail." Her heart sank. "But I'll see what I can do."

Greene drove to Bob Chandler's office on Pearl Street. His law firm was in one of the offices at the back of the new strip mall behind the town. Everyone hated this development: box stores and sprawling parking lots lurking behind the main strip. At least it wasn't visible from town. He pulled up in front of the squat building where Chandler's small firm did business and buzzed him. Chandler said he'd come down.

The two of them sat on the side veranda of Alma May's, a stately old house on the main drag turned into a greasy spoon. It was almost too cold to sit outside, but Bob Chandler didn't want people listening in on any conversation he was having with the police. He looked at the name on the piece of paper Greene had passed him and said he didn't recognize it.

"She never told you about a friend in Florida?"

"I didn't even know she was on the Internet. I mean, me and Gail hooked her up because we thought if she was interested . . . but she never mentioned it. I figured she was using the computer as a paperweight."

"No, she was set up," said Greene. "She knew email and she could surf the web."

"First your kids are a mystery to you, and then your parents," he said.

"There are early adopters and late adopters, and then there's us. Hazel's done the same thing for her mother. She could spend the whole day on her laptop."

Bob put his spoon back into his coffee and stirred it needlessly. "How is Mrs. Micallef?"

"She's fine."

"I guess she probably wasn't totally heartbroken to hear. About what happened."

"You'd have to ask Hazel." He stirred his coffee. "So you don't know how your mum might have known this Rhonda woman in Hallandale, huh?"

"She's never been to Florida," Bob Chandler said. "She must have met her online somehow." He looked at the name again. "Can I see the emails?"

"Not yet," said Greene. "But there's nothing in them, really. Unless they're all in code."

"I think you can safely assume my mother wasn't writing some strange woman in Florida in code. She could barely remember a phone number."

"I know, Bob. The emails were along the lines of gardening tips. It's probably just like you say."

"Was there anything else?" Chandler asked.

"I don't think so," said Greene, and the two men stood. Greene held out his hand and they shook. But he didn't release Chandler's hand.

"What?"

"I was just thinking. Did your mum talk about wanting new bedclothes or anything like that?"

"Bedclothes?"

"No, I'm just wondering. What did she sleep with?"

"About eight blankets," Chandler said.

"She didn't have a duvet?" said Greene.

Chandler wore an expression of complete bafflement. "I don't have a full list of all my mother's linens, Ray, but as far as I know, she didn't own one. Anyway, what does this have to do with anything?"

"It's nothing," said Greene, and he patted Chandler on the shoulder and started back to his cruiser. Back in the car, he called Spere. "You're needed," he said. "Talk to your computer guys again." He told Spere what he wanted.

Back at the station, Hazel was waiting for him in the parking lot.

"Well?"

"He has no idea," said Greene. "He told me she didn't own a duvet." He shook a cigarette out of a brand new pack.

"Spere gives you one cigarette and suddenly you're buying packs?"

"They help me think."

"Give me one," she said. He looked at her with his eyebrows raised. "Maybe I'll have a new thought myself."

He lit a second cigarette off the end of his and passed it to her. They stood together in the parking lot, smoking like two kids outside of school.

"Don't inhale."

She took a deep drag and inhaled the smoke. "If you want to admit you're scared shitless, Ray, I will too."

"I've never seen anything like it," he said.

"We had two murders in the four years I was in Kehoe Glen, and in all the time I've been back in Port Dundas, I've had five more, and all seven of them were open and shut. Christ, six of them were domestics. Now two in one week, and we have no idea where this guy is right now. He could be in Texas for all we know."

"He could be anywhere."

"I get the feeling he's not thinking of getting caught."

He flicked the spent cigarette onto the asphalt. "How far along is he? What's your guess?"

He'd put into words the thought she'd been dreading: that Delia Chandler and Michael Ulmer were not this person's first two victims. But which ones were they? The fifth and sixth? The twentieth and twenty-first? She ran her hand through her hair. "Any number you say could be right. And he could be beginning or ending or right in the middle, and we're exactly nowhere. This woman in Florida is probably some knitting champion Delia met online somehow. But just the same, if Spere can figure out where she lives, maybe we can get in touch with her."

She crushed the cigarette under her foot.

"I had a question for you." She waited. "Bob said something about your mother not being heartbroken about Delia's death. What did that mean?"

The last uninformed soul in town. "My father and Delia," she said. "It went on for about five years." Before Greene could reply, she walked straight into the station.

] 8 [

Monday, November 15, 9 p.m.

The house was dark when Hazel got home. She could hear her mother's music coming from upstairs – she couldn't sleep without CBC Two playing, and Hazel made out the sounds of a Bach sonata wafting out from under the closed bedroom door. The kitchen was spotless, and a plate of cold chicken was wrapped in the fridge. She sat alone at the small table and ate it with her fingers.

Her head was swimming with details. Everything they knew now had a relationship with everything they did not know. What they'd learned stood like a range of trees on a lakeshore, reflected in reverse on the water below. Hazel dreaded the journey it would require to get to those dark shapes. A dead woman, a dead man. A pact of some kind. Was it being kept? Were these deaths, at least, part of something longed for? As she got older and acclimatized herself to her own failures, she had begun to understand death's draw. At the worst of times, even those who were not inclined to consider death an escape could still look at it as a point beyond which they could do no more wrong, would suffer no more. Death brought with it more than just the mere cessation of cellular life: it meant the end of action, and on days like this, Hazel felt that it would be a welcome change – sometime in the future – to be permitted to stop thinking and making choices and waiting for their outcomes.

Her back was killing her. She pushed herself out of the chair and went upstairs to get a Percocet. She was almost out and she took the cap off to leave on her bedside table as a reminder. The drugstore could call in a renewal to Dr. Pass in the morning – it bothered her that she could only get fourteen pills at a time; it meant nuisancing Pass twice a month, but she understood that such a dangerous substance as one that could rid you of pain had to be carefully monitored. She went back downstairs and took the pill with a glass of milk. *Go now, little pill*, she thought. *Go find those knives and blunt them.*

Wingate had come back from Mayfair after lunch with the bewildering news that *none* of the blood on Delia's clothes had been hers. He'd described Deacon's face as "blanched" when he'd emerged from the downstairs lab at Mayfair Grace. The clothes had gone to Toronto to be tested further, but Deacon had said that there was more than one person's blood on the victim's dress. Whoever had killed Delia Chandler had enacted something so precise that he'd been capable of painting a pattern on his victim's body, clothes, and furniture with another person's blood. This killer's attentiveness and creativity were beginning to give them all a sense that he could see them in his audience, was aware of their growing amazement. Greene had said that the killer was making it impossible for them to categorize any of their evidence as purposive behaviour on his part, or, alternatively, accidental. Because everything that looked like mayhem was turning out to have been carefully planned. *Made* was the word Wingate used. The killer was *making* the crime scenes. So even if they lucked out now and found a hair or a fingerprint, they wouldn't know if they had been meant to find it, or if the killer had made a mistake.

They didn't even know if these bloody tableaux they'd found in Port Dundas and Chamberlain were even meant for them. The most terrifying possibility was not that the killer was leaving complicated clues behind to taunt the police, but that he was not talking to them at all.

In the afternoon, Hazel had put the new kid on a national canvass, asking him to look into killings elsewhere in the country that had any of these hallmarks, specifically terminally ill victims who had been murdered in their own homes. Anything that fit this description would be worth following up. By five o'clock, Wingate had completed his calls to all the major centres in the country, and none of them were surprised to learn that nothing fitting the MO of their guy had shown up. This confirmed one supposition: that this killer was staying out of cities, even the small ones. He was taking advantage of the state of police affairs in smaller communities: a single murder in a minor municipality – even if it were referred to a larger jurisdiction – was unlikely to appear as a pattern to anyone. If Delia Chandler had lived in Toronto and Michael Ulmer in Ottawa, it would not be long before the lines between the two police services would light up. As it was, the Renfrew County cops had called them not only to share information, but because two cops accustomed to fishing in the afternoon needed serious backup.

"We have to call him something," Greene had said. "Make him more real so we can hold him in *some* way in our minds."

"How's 'Satan' hit you?" said Howard Spere.

"What about Destroying Angel?" said Wingate, and Greene had almost sneered.

"Sure: *Look out! It's Destroying Angel!*"

"Fine," said Wingate. "It was only a suggestion."

They'd finally settled on calling him the Belladonna Killer, and before the end of the day, they were calling him, simply, the Belladonna.

The Percocet was starting to work. Hazel poured herself a shot of Bushmills and turned on the television in the living room. There was a report on the news out of Mayfair that a killer had "struck" in the "small town" of Port Dundas. They had shots of both Delia's house and Bob's. There was nothing on the Chamberlain killing. At least that was still under wraps. Hazel was pleased to have confirmation that the information dikes were still holding at the station house. They'd got the officers in Chamberlain to agree on a story for the time being: people stopping by on the sidewalk in front of Ulmer's house had been told that there'd been a break-in, and the canvass on Ulmer's street was conducted with a burglary as a cover story. Again, no one had seen a thing.

There was nothing on the Toronto news except some folderol about how much time a waterfront revitalization program was going to take. Maybe it would make more sense to build condos. The phrase "income-per-vertical-square-metre" was used by an expert. She pictured people – maybe old women like herself – piled up practically to the sky on the edge of Lake Ontario, pacing the rest of their lives to the rate of vertical acreage going up on all sides. Penned in, hemmed in, like animals. Maybe people like her mother were going to be the very last generation in history to have any chance of growing old with dignity. Most of her mother's friends were either dead or living in retirement homes in towns like Port Dundas and Kehoe Glen, playing cards and making crafts in little gingerbread houses quietly staffed by bored nurses. Suddenly, she felt terribly lonely.

She dialled Andrew's number. Glynnis, his new wife, answered. "Hi, Hazel," she said. "He's just gone to bed."

"Is he asleep?"

"You want me to check?"

"Do you mind?"

She waited on the line for longer than a minute. A call this time of night meant a drunken Hazel; she knew this was the content of the conversation Glynnis was having with Andrew. She hated being seen as a kind of occupational hazard, the occupation being married to Andrew. "I'm not drunk, for Chrissake," she said when she heard Andrew pick up the phone.

"Who said you were drunk?"

"You've been married three years and already you go to bed before your bride?"

"At least she's home at bedtime." Hazel laughed into her glass. "You said you weren't drunk."

"I'm having a nightcap, Andrew."

"How's your back?"

She knew what that meant. The first warning on the pharmacy fact sheet was not to mix alcohol with oxycodone. "It's much better now, actually," she said. "Although I guess you're aware that I'm spending a great deal of my time running pillar to post to catch a murderer."

She heard Glynnis's voice in the background, and for a moment, the mouthpiece on the other end was muffled. "It's terrible about Delia," Andrew said. "It's a real shock."

"I think it was to everyone but her."

"How do you mean?"

"We think she let the killer in. That she knew what was going to happen."

"Should you be telling me this?"

"I can trust you."

There was silence on the other end for a moment. "It's late, Hazel."

"I know it's late, Andrew. But I figure thirty-six years of marriage entitles me to a late-night phone call once in a while. On days like this."

"Okay," he said. "Just a second." He put the phone down on a hard surface, and Hazel strained to hear the brief conversation her ex-husband was having with his second wife, a woman he'd met two years before their marriage ended. At the time, and to this day, she could not begrudge the fact that her husband had cheated on her. It was so completely out of his character that she had been forced to see it as a necessity. By 2000, with Drury gone and all the new responsibility fallen to her, her drinking was out of hand. She'd had to shift her hours forward to accommodate her difficult mornings, and when he finally saw her in the evenings, she'd already put away a couple at the Thirsty Goose and had left him to eat dinner on his own. She'd cleaned up by 2002, the year they divorced, but by then it was too late; he'd fallen in love with a new lawyer at his company. The firm was called McMaster Pedersen Crombie – Glynnis, née Crombie, had made partner the year after the divorce – and now this Glynnis Pedersen sported what used to be her last name. She hadn't felt an ounce of anger. The sadness had never given way to it. "We can talk now," he said, coming back to the phone. She pictured him sitting on the bed, shirtless, his fine head of curly grey hair framing his face. She'd sometimes slept with her fingers in that hair.

"You know, I don't think Glynnis likes me."

"She doesn't know you, dear. To know you is to love you."

"Thank you for that."

"So, how much have you had tonight?"

"I'm not drunk, Andrew. I'm Percocet."

"Ah. So dangerously relaxed?"

She finished the finger of Bushmills and cast a glance over at the bottle. She knew if she had one more, she'd be stepping over an edge. She looked away from it. "Did Marty tell you she and Scott broke up?"

"She did. I think it's a good thing. I wasn't crazy about him."

"I wasn't either. But she's heartbroken."

"Martha's strong, Hazel. She's her mother's daughter."

"How old is Glynnis?"

"For God's sake." He was laughing. "Why don't you date, Hazel? Just go out with someone nice and have supper. Get back out there."

"Where am I going to find someone to date me, for the love of Pete? Should I just go out and cuff someone? Toss them into a banquette at Silvio's and hold a gun on them until they order a carafe of the house red?"

"You can make it sound impossible, Hazel, and then it will be. There are ways."

"Single white divorcée, sixty-one, arresting, seeking man with clean record."

"It would be a start."

"I'd like to see you sometime. For dinner."

"I'd like that, too," he said.

"I suppose Perky couldn't complain if you saw your ex-wife behind her back."

"I would tell her, Hazel. It wouldn't be behind her back."

"It was behind my back."

He sighed. This was territory that was well worth staying out of. But she knew that Andrew could not suppress his penchant for truthfulness, and he said, "It could have been on the front lawn, dear. You wouldn't have noticed. For the top cop of a major township, you had your blind spots."

"I guess I did."

"I'm going to go," he said. "Call me during the day at my office and we'll figure out a time to have a nice lunch, okay?"

"You're talking to me the way I talk to my mother."

"How is Her Honour?"

"Trying to slim me down for some future altar. Maybe a sacrificial one, I haven't figured that out yet."

"Call me, Hazel."

"Fine."

"And go to bed now."

She hung up and stared at the phone, silenced in its cradle. That old voice there, which used to ring in this house. Her glass was empty. She got up from the couch and picked up the bottle, pretended to read the label – *DISTILLED THREE TIMES* it read (imagine being capable of such purity) – and then put the bottle back on top of the fridge.

She opened the door to her mother's room and stepped in quietly to turn off the radio. In the fresh silence, she listened to her mother's soft breathing. She remembered the profound pleasure of sleeping in her parents' bed as a child, escaping a nightmare to the safety of their warmth. She'd once woken between them in the middle of the night and watched the curtains in their bedroom transform into a carousel full of children. The sensation of this sanctuary came back to her as if she had just sat up in that bed of fifty-five years ago. She smoothed the covers over her mother's back and closed the door behind her. As she turned, she saw a wave of light swim through the window of the front door and move off down the street, the sound of its source humming past. It was late to be out, but she had the urge to go back down to the main floor and look outside. The car had already vanished down the street and turned another corner. She looked across the street at the Edwardhses house — all the lights were off, although she sensed the thin glow from a light left on in an upstairs bathroom.

She had her coat on now, although she could not remember slipping it on, and the car keys were in her hand. The night air was sweet and cool, like riverwater. Hazel got into the Crown Victoria and turned right out of her driveway. The 117 between Pember Lake and Port Dundas was not lit, and she snapped the brights up and drove the empty road. The twin cones of light drenched the trees on either side in a wash of brilliance and the leafless birches glowed in her headlights like bones standing in the earth. And then, as if her mind had wandered, she was making the turn onto the main street of Port Dundas, drifting down it under the lonesome streetlamps. A few people were still out, leaving bars or walking their dogs once more before turning in. Although what time was it? The dashboard clock said it was half past two in the morning; no one should be out with their dog now, she thought.

She went up the hill past the station house and saw a man and a woman walking hand-in-hand past the funeral home. Her father and Delia Chandler. They gazed calmly through Hazel's windshield, and she thought she saw her father's hand rise faintly in greeting. A long thin tube trailed from under Delia's dress and skittered on the sidewalk behind her. Hazel passed them and continued to the top of the hill, where she turned left and descended again into the side streets. The one she drove down was packed on either side with black Ford Cougars, their yellow headlights steadily burning. She pulled over beside Delia's house and got out, ducked under the police tape lining the front lawn, and rang the doorbell. Delia answered and let her into the lemon tea–scented house. She was wearing a blue wool dress and stood in the living room waiting in front of Hazel with her hands folded over her belly. She passed a teacup on a saucer to Hazel, but Hazel declined. She asked if she could look around, and Delia gestured with her hand in a broad sweep. The place was spotless. She opened a couple of cupboards in the living room and kitchen. The ones in the living room were empty, but the one in the kitchen had a small campfire silently burning on the floor within. Hazel held her hands over it, but a cold draught of air lifted off the yellow flame. She closed the door on it. When she turned around, Delia was standing behind her under the single light in the kitchen ceiling, hands at her sides. Her eyes were translucent white, like raw albumen, and the damp cut across her throat hung loose. Hazel heard the susurration of air from inside the gash and then the edges of the cut began to move like a mouth. She stared at the huge wound as it stretched and pursed and thinned itself and the air behind it hissed. *Shhaassahhm nuhhhh*, said the tear in Delia's throat, and Hazel stepped toward the dead woman to hear better. She turned her ear in. *Hazel*, she heard, *Hazel* and then the voice began choking and Hazel righted herself to the vision of blood gushing from Delia Chandler's neck, the wound smacking and spitting.

She woke to the sound of her own cries and lay in the bed, wet with sweat and tears pouring down her face. She sat up and switched on her bedside light and began writing her dream down around the edge of a page from the *Westmuir Record*. *Delia*, she wrote, *what are you trying to tell me?*

Ray Greene and James Wingate stood in front of her as she pushed two of the crime-scene photos across her desk toward them. "Everything but the mouths is a distraction. We have to focus on the mouths."

Greene spun the photo of Ulmer's destroyed face toward her. "If the mouths are so important, then why did he do this?"

"I thought about that. I think the rest of the Belladonna's killings are farther apart than Delia and Ulmer. Nothing he's done hasn't been thought through completely – he must have been worried that the same people would be investigating both of these killings. So he broke the link." She put her finger on Delia Chandler's mouth. "But he did this to Ulmer too – changed his mouth. Then he covered his tracks, as it were, with a hammer." The detectives stood staring at the pictures of the two victims. "We have to find the ones who came before now," she said, "the ones far enough apart that no one has linked them." She swept the pictures back into a folder. "James, I want you back on the phone. Find me an unsolved murder less than two weeks old in a town no bigger than Port Dundas. It should be between five and nine hundred kilometres from here." She brought her eyes up from Delia's mouth and saw Wingate was staring at her, lost. "Where's it eight a.m. right now?" she said.

Greene looked at his watch. "Uh, here Hazel."

"Fine. Wait an hour and start calling some stations in the western part of the province and in Manitoba."

Wingate left and Greene stepped back to shut the door. He turned and stood with his arms crossed, watching Hazel lower herself gingerly into her chair. "You okay?"

"I'm fine."

"You don't sleep much."

"I lie awake and try to figure things out."

"Fatigue isn't the key to unlocking the whereabouts of a serial murderer."

She put her hands flat on the desk and stared at her second-in-command. "You want me to take the day off? Wander the streets and reassure people? Go find something to do, Ray. Call Howard or go through yesterday's sheets and find out if there's anything we should be following up on apart from this bastard. Okay?"

"It's been four days, you know, Hazel. It's still early. I'm just saying –"

"Go check the day sheets, Ray! Leave me alone."

—

Greene went out into the pen and closed Hazel's door behind him. Cartwright had heard Hazel raise her voice and eyed him as he went past. "I'm fine," he said.

"Can I ask you something?" He stopped beside her desk. "I don't think I should be bothering the chief with this right now."

"So you want to bother me with it?"

"They saw the cougar again in Kehoe River, and I don't know what to tell them down there."

Greene shook his head. "What do they think we're going to be able to do? Tell Lonergan or whoever it is that's calling you that we're not the frigging Wildlife Services here!"

Cartwright blinked at him. "All right, Detective. And in your opinion, is that who they should be calling?"

"That would be my opinion, Melanie. Unless that cat can ring doorbells and slit people's throats, maybe you should be referring them elsewhere."

"Okay. Then I'll tell Ken Lonergan it's okay with you to keep his gun at the ready just in case." He stared at her. Sometimes Melanie was cowed by Hazel, but she wouldn't be pushed around by him he saw, and it struck him then why Hazel had hired her. She said, "He feels it incumbent on him to protect the citizens of his town."

"Ken Lonergan said *incumbent*."

"He's the only one in Kehoe River with a rifle."

"Fine, Melanie. Give me yesterday's log. I'll kill two birds with one stone."

She passed him the call binder without taking her eyes off him.

—

Howard Spere arrived at the station house an hour later. "Fourteen at Delia Chandler's," he said, tossing the sheaf of lab reports onto the conference-room table, "and then fifteen from the sample taken from Michael Ulmer's hands. Neither aggregate blood sample actually contained the blood of the victim it was found on." He fanned the lab tests out across the table. The Toronto lab had separated out fifteen separate DNA signatures from the Ulmer site. Fourteen of them matched the bloodstains on Delia Chandler's clothing; the fifteenth signature was Delia's. Ray Greene was still in Kehoe River, but Wingate and Hazel cast their eyes over the papers spread on the table.

She picked up the lab report closest to her and pushed another one across the table to Wingate. The one she held told of an unnamed human being whose unique DNA was being painted like an autograph in a scrapbook of the dead. It was a chain, a message being passed down a wire. "So this is it, then," she said. "We really have a serial killer here."

"It would look that way," said Spere.

"Before he got to Port Dundas, he managed to kill fourteen people without attracting any suspicion that anything more significant was going on than garden-variety murder," she said. "There are fourteen little station houses or police outposts throughout this country asking themselves why anyone would want to hurt Uncle Bob or Granny Faye. They don't know the body in their morgue has something in common with the ones in ours." She paused for a moment. "When we find where these other people were killed, we can't say why we're interested."

"Why?" said Wingate.

"Because he's getting close to the end of his task. He's at least in Quebec, and if he's been able, to this point, to spread sixteen murders across this country without setting off alarm bells, then they've been spread widely. He must know Delia and Ulmer were too close. Like I said, that's why there's no mouth on Michael Ulmer to solidify the connection for us."

"Surely if he's this smart he knows we'd notice there were fifteen different blood samples on his latest victim."

"Then this is his first mistake," said Hazel. "Let's hope he makes another one."

She flicked an arm out toward Wingate. "What have you found out?"

"So far, a body in Pikangikum, north of Dryden," he said, opening his notebook. "It was last Tuesday, the ninth."

"Three days before Chandler," said Howard Spere. Hazel pushed aside the easel from the previous afternoon and tugged down the provincial map on the wall behind the table. Pikangikum was about one hundred kilometres northwest of Red Lake, close to the Manitoba border. It was a First Nations reserve.

"Is this the Ontario Police Services up there, or does the reserve have its own police?"

"They've got four native officers." Wingate looked down at his notes. "I spoke to the senior constable there, Gordon Chencillor. The victim was an elderly band member named Joseph Atlookan . . . eighty-three years old. They've ruled it a suicide now, said the victim had cut his own throat."

"That's what it must have looked like," said Hazel. "Was he dying of something before he was killed?"

"Whoa," said Spere. "It's possible to cut your own throat, you know. I don't want to sound insensitive or anything, but let's say this old guy *was* dying of something – he *is* an old man living on an Indian reserve."

Hazel ignored him. "What about the coroner's report, James? Are there any pictures?"

"I'll ask. They're going to want to know why, though."

"Say you're investigating an apparent suicide down here on the M'njikaning Reserve. You want to check out the Atlookan death to rule out foul play."

"These places have their own police, Inspector – why would I be calling from Port Dundas?"

"Use your imagination, Detective. Maybe there's been a spate of suicides on reserves close to Port Dundas and you're looking for a pattern. Just get me some details on this old man. And get Jack a blood or a tissue sample. Do whatever it takes. I bet this guy is on Delia Chandler's dress." She picked up the phone on the table and dialled Melanie's extension. She used her other hand to wave the two men out of her room and off to work. "Hold on," she said to Cartwright, and covered the receiver. "Howard, where are we on Delia's computer?"

"Nowhere. It's a dead end. She wanted a new duvet cover, but I guess she changed her mind and chose death instead."

"You're a model of compassion, Howard. Keep them looking." He went out and she put the phone back to her ear. "Where's Ray?" She listened a moment, then hung up and got her cell out. She stared at the buttons for a moment and then dialled. It worked. "Ray?" she said, "I thought you were supposed to be going over the logs."

"Yeah, thanks for the promotion, boss. I'm in Kehoe River trying to disarm Ken Lonergan. I was going to look over the logs on lunch."

"Get back here. I'm putting you in charge of all the Belladonna's movements east of Renfrew County."

"The rest of the country is east of Renfrew, Hazel."

"You'll understand in a minute. James found a dead native man about twelve hundred kilometres from here, on the Manitoba border. He's been dead exactly one week."

"This is the only small-town murder Wingate could find in the province?"

"He was eighty-three, with his throat cut, Ray. Delia was on Friday, Ulmer on Sunday. The next one's going to be farther away. I want you to find it as soon as it happens. The next victim is going to be number seventeen."

There was no sound from the other end of the line. Then, "*What?*"

"Seventeen, Ray. And counting. The lab found fifteen different sets of genes in the blood on Ulmer's hands, and none of them were Ulmer's. But one of them was Delia's. Her clothes had the blood of fourteen people on it. But not hers. Are you getting any of this?"

"God," said Ray Greene, then, "hold on." She heard his voice from an arm's-length distance: "Hey!" he said, and his voice sounded curious and frightened at once. "What the Christ —" he said, and then Hazel heard the sharp report of a gunshot.

"Ray!" she shouted. She could hear a commotion on the other end of the line, but the voices were indistinct. In the middle distance, there was the sound of another gunshot and someone roaring in pain. Her cellphone skittered across the conference-room table, and she rushed out into the pen. "I need cars! Whoever's closest to Kehoe River!" She rushed through the bewildered room, pulling on her jacket. "Someone get on dispatch and get to Kehoe River right now! Ray Greene's been shot —"

9

Wednesday, November 17, 6 p.m.

Simon was in a place called Matapédia, on the southern border of Quebec, and night had fallen. He'd been noting, on his long drives from the west, how much shorter the days were now. It was dark at six in the evening here.

He was due in Doaktown, in the middle of New Brunswick, the next afternoon. He was wearying now — the length of his journey was weighing on him as he came close to completing it. He recalled his stops in Quesnel, in Grimshaw, in Creighton, and the joy of meeting the people he had encountered in this country, a country he had only imagined could feel this vast. He had been on rivers, in towns of fewer than three hundred souls, on Indian reserves, on farms. He had been welcomed graciously everywhere he went, and he had conducted himself with ceaseless love. It felt to him as if his heart had tripled in size inside of him, a heart through which it seemed the blood of seventeen souls now pulsed.

He readied a tincture of foxglove in his tent. Earlier on, the herb had rendered startling, fortifying effects, and he could see why those with illnesses of the heart depended on it. It had eventually failed his brother, but Simon took it in tribute, and he revelled in the small explosions of energy it gave. But now, the herb seemed to be failing him. His body was fighting it. He thought sometimes that he could feel air passing through his heart and he wondered if, in sympathy, his own heart was refusing the foxglove's balm. It occasionally made him feel weak. He prayed to God to spare the men and women under his care by letting him go on. He needed so little time now. After he was done, he would be like so much dust whether he was alive or not.

He took out five foxglove leaves from a sleeve and macerated them. He made the tincture with chloroform water and sodium carbonate, then titrated it. The herb's bitter scent filled the inside of the tent. He took his time. It was pleasurable to do even the smallest tasks with complete attention. He loved to move slowly and watch himself work, the way the drippings of the freshly made drug fell into the glass through the cheese-cloth. He recalled his brother's eyes patiently watching the drug being made. *You are a blessing to me*, he'd say, holding Simon's hand in his, that cold hand. Simon would try not to show his brother his deepening grief. He'd say to him, *You will return to strength. You will walk among us again*, and his brother would put his hand behind Simon's neck and draw him down to him, bestow a kiss on his mouth. Simon would smell the stale air leaking from his brother's body and try to take it into himself, to drink those poisons away. But his brother had died. No matter their ministrations, his own or those of his followers. And then they drifted away, those men and women with their false hearts, and Simon was alone. Thinking of their perfidy, he regretted his haste in Havre-Saint-Pierre. Mrs. Iagnemma deserved better than he had time to give her, even if she had tried to meddle. She had, at least, given of herself. He'd had such fine ideas for her, his tongueless songbird. Instead he rushed her, gave her so little of the grace she had earned. His anger had been replaced by shame, but at the same time, he knew he could have done nothing else. The situation demanded dispatch, and dispatch he did.

The tincture was ready after standing for an hour. He diluted it slightly with spring water, but not enough to mask the pain of the bitterness in the leaf. The Saxons had called the plant "folke's glove" – the faerie's glove – and the spots on the foxglove blossoms were said to be the places where these small creatures of the forest had touched the flower with their tiny fingers. Without it, his brother would have left this world sooner than he did.

His brother, Peter, was his only family. They'd never known their mother, and it had been hard for their father raising two sons alone. His father had been a quiet man, happier with books than with people. He'd grieved their mother for years after she'd left him, grieved her as if she'd died, and for all they knew, she had. And when he died, there was no one willing to take them. There were foster homes on the mainland, and they placed the brothers with the priests. No one wanted brothers. Eventually, a childless couple took in Peter, the docile child, the weak child, and took him away to another province. Simon, in his rage, had grown strong, and no one would have him. He took down the crucifix above his bed and replaced it with a picture of Peter. The priests didn't like it. "Christ was meek in his faith, but not feeble," said one of them angrily. "Your brother's as helpless as a kitten. He couldn't save a penny." Simon wrote his brother and begged him to hold on. When he reached sixteen, the priests released him. He heard his brother calling him. He found him in the middle of the country, chained like an animal to a bed, his adoptive parents cashing the government cheques. He smashed in their skulls like he was grinding meal and brought his brother home. He'd saved Peter. Peter never forgot it. But now he was gone and all that was left was Simon: Simon the survivor, Simon the saviour.

He poured the drug into the back of his throat and he gagged, but held his mouth closed and made sure the tincture went down. He stretched out on the floor of the tent. It was important to take the herb on an empty stomach, but he had not eaten for a day now, and his entire system cried out for nourishment. He knew he would be nourished soon enough. He would make his meeting in Doaktown, then on Sunday he would be in Pictou and he would be on the ocean. He would celebrate his arrival on the other coast. Then there would be one left, and that one would be the most joyous of all.

—

In the morning, he drove the two hours into the village of Doaktown. It was on the Miramichi, and driving down the main street, he could see the river flashing between houses and down the few side streets. He had purchased three organic eggs from a farm outside of Bathurst and stopped by a lake partway through his drive to eat them. There was now very little in the way of greenery that he could trust was still nutritious – he would have to eat foods that did not agree with him until he could get to the Atlantic and reward himself with meat. He pierced each egg with a hypodermic needle and drew out the insides. It was pleasantly comic to see an egg transmitted from one shell to another: inside the syringe, the egg was transformed into a column of swirling yellow and grey. It looked like a broken tiger eye. He squirted the contents of three syringes into his mouth and swallowed. Then he crushed one of the empty eggshells and ate it for the calcium.

It was the end of the work week in Doaktown, and the town was fairly quiet. He found Prospect Street easily and parked at the end of it. It was ten in the morning; he was precisely on time. The house where the priest lived was halfway down the street, set back on a large yard. He knocked on the door and the old man opened it a crack. "Simon?"

"Father," he said. "I'm pleased to find you looking so well."

The priest admitted his guest. Simon stepped in and looked around the cedar-scented house. It was almost empty of furniture, a stark place, with varnished wooden floors. "I've given most of my belongings away. The church has most of the furniture."

"Did they think it strange?"

"Perhaps they think I'm planning on spending the last of my days in the church, surrounded by my own things. A right nuisance to everyone. I've earned it though, so let them complain."

"Let's find a place to sit down, Father," said Simon. The old priest led him into the bare living room, where there still remained a set of chairs and a modest wooden table. The man sat with difficulty: there was cancer throughout his spine. "How much pain do you have?"

"Enough to remind me that I'm still here." He watched Simon lower his heavy black bag onto the tabletop. "How do we do this, then?"

"Slowly, and with care. You're not expecting anyone?"

"People drop in all the time. But I've drawn the curtains, and we can choose not to answer the door. I'd like to ask you for a favour, though."

"Anything."

"I'd like to pray."

"We will pray, Father."

"Not your way, Simon. I'd like to commend myself before committing what is, you must acknowledge, a sin."

"I'm sure God will allow you a transgression in honour of a great deed, Father."

"I'd like to be certain." Simon thought for a moment, then took his bag off the table and lowered it to the floor. He lay his arms on the table, palms up, and the priest lay his hands in Simon's and closed his eyes. "Our Father, who art in heaven, hallowed be thy Name. Thy kingdom come, thy will be done, on earth as it is in heaven. Give us this day our daily bread. And forgive us our trespasses, as we forgive those who trespass against us. And lead us not into temptation, but deliver us from evil. Amen." He opened his eyes and looked up. "'Trespass' is an interesting concept, isn't it, Simon?"

"It is."

"It was 'debt' in the Old English. But 'trespass' is more interesting to me. It suggests territory. The soul as a territory onto which someone might tread without leave. But we forgive them these trespasses."

"Are you afraid, Father Price?"

"No." The priest drew his hands off the table. "Only that I am allowing you to trespass, and God must forgive us both."

"God is going to hear our call, Father. We will be made whole again; we will form a righteous council."

"'Sit at my right hand until I make thine enemies a footstool for your feet.'"

Simon pulled his bag up to the tabletop again. He spread the mouth of the bag. "We have no enemies, Father. Those who think they are against us will simply be left behind in the end. They'll live bereft of our truth. I pity them." He took out his vials and laid them on the table. Father Price stared at them.

"These are the agencies of my death, are they? Little bottles of dust and powder."

"This is belladonna," said Simon. "It will make you sleep."

"And then what will you do to me?"

Simon got up from the table, taking the vials in his

hand. In the priest's kitchen, there were two cups and a kettle already set out. Simon turned on the stove and boiled water. Through the kitchen door, he looked at the old man sitting slightly hunched at his table, and it came to him anew what cruelty it was to give a man a body only to make him witness its decline, its failure. When he and Peter were young, they would lie under their covers and compare their bodies. The taut muscle coming down over the shoulder and under the collarbone, the wreath-work of thin flesh below the eye, the blind moles of their penises. Each detail logged in the other, a repetition of life. He saw himself age in Peter, saw his life passing through his brother's, as a charge does through a wire, both of their lives a coil glowing in an airless glass, des-tined to burn out. That God had chosen for them their burdens was a blessing for them both, as through their weakness, Simon had found their calling.

"I will break you in twain," he said to the priest. "Like crushing a seed to draw the oil out."

Father Price turned in his seat to look at Simon. "Will I feel it?"

"I promise you won't."

"Then let's begin, son."

The kettle boiled and Simon prepared Father Price's tea. The priest drank it slowly, smiling over the rim of his cup at his visitor, his saviour. His eyes began to droop. "This morning," Father Price said slowly, "I dis-patched a small bottle of Holy Water to your brother. I hope he will receive it soon."

"My brother appreciates your kindness, Father, as do I."

"I did wonder, when I took it to the post office, what he would do with it. It's a strange gift. Have all your . . . friends sent religious articles?"

"Oh, no," said Simon. "It doesn't matter what it is. I just ask that it be something from the heart. A tribute as it were. Also, these gifts tell him how far along I am. For instance, now he will know I've been to see you. He'll know how close we all are to our goal." Simon smiled at Father Price. "Have I answered you well?"

"Of course. I didn't mean to question your —"

"Not at all," said Simon. "Now tell me: are you strong enough to stand?"

The priest stood carefully, and Simon, apologizing, undressed him. The older man stood, shivering slightly, under his guest's gaze. "You've been left almost untouched by the storm of life," said Simon. "I'm very pleased." He helped Father Price back into his clothes, and then pulled his chair out for him to sit again.

"I will have another small dram of that," said the old man, his arm almost too weak to lift his cup. "But doesn't it have a wee kick, now?"

"It does," said the one who called himself Simon, and he filled the priest's cup. "Let us pray."

10

Tuesday, November 16, 12 p.m.

Greene came in triumph with Ken Lonergan in cuffs in his passenger seat. "Christ," said Hazel, throwing her arms around him, "I thought you were dead."

"He's got no right to arrest me!" said Lonergan through the open window. "Take these cuffs off me, Hazel."

She released Ray Greene and pressed her face into Lonergan's. "You're damn right you're cuffed, you bloody fool. You discharged a firearm in a street full of people!"

"Twice," said Greene. "I wouldn't have arrested you, Ken, if you'd laid it down when I told you to."

Lonergan muttered something and kicked the dash under the glove compartment. "Just write him up and let him go," said Hazel. "Let me see this poor thing now."

Greene unlocked his trunk and the two of them stared at the sad, dead form of the cougar lying on its side.

"Imagine having your life ended by Ken-fucking-Lonergan," Greene said. "What a beautiful animal. I've called Wildlife Services. They're going to come and take it away." He opened the passenger door and Lonergan stepped out, ignoring Greene's hand. "Be grateful I went for a live capture in your case, Ken."

"Shut up, Ray. That thing ate three dogs before I stopped it. What do you think it was going to go after when all the dogs were gone?"

"I'm sure you were safe, Ken. I get the feeling it didn't like its meat stringy."

"Get done with him," said Hazel, "then come and see me."

Greene pushed his prisoner in through the doors of the station house, and after one last look at the cougar, Hazel closed the trunk on its motionless form.

When Greene was caught up on the DNA reporting from Toronto, he sat back in the chair opposite Hazel and tried to figure out the answer to her question. It was beginning to look like they had worked out the Belladonna's modus operandi. Wingate had located what looked like a fourth victim after lunch, in Gimli, Manitoba. Here, too, the victim was terminally ill, a woman in her forties named Ruth Maris dying of ALS. They found her headless body lying under the covers in her bed. The head they found in Maris's freezer, split in half down the middle and turned around so the victim was looking herself in the eye. The crime scene was so gruesome that it had made the news in Regina, more than five hundred kilometres away. This was November 3, and if the death in Pikangikum six days later was the next killing, then of course no one would ever have linked the two deaths. It was still uncertain if the Atlookan killing in Pikangikum was his – the reserve police were being uncooperative with Wingate, asking for a warrant for release before they showed Port Dundas anything. They were still stuck in second gear.

Hazel's question had been this: Given that they had no way to predict where the killer was going to strike next, was it a good idea to put out an APB for all points east of Ontario? It could warn the killer that the law was aware of his presence, but it might also cause him to make another mistake. And they needed him to make more mistakes. The argument against it was simply that they didn't have enough pieces of the puzzle to know, exactly, what to warn people against. The side effect that many thousands of terminally ill people east of Ontario might begin doubly fearing for their lives wasn't worth the exercise in awareness. And what, exactly, should people and law enforcement be on the lookout for? A man driving the countryside with a bucket of blood in his trunk?

Ray Greene was staring at the ceiling. "Well, I know the RCMP would have had a bulletin out by now."

"If they'd ever clued into the fact that a serial killer was at large."

"We could clue them in," he said.

She laughed softly. "You want to take a back seat to

the Mounties in your own town, Ray? They've had four-teen chances to pick up this guy's scent. They have a deeper network than we do and, clearly, they don't have any idea what's going on in any of their jurisdictions."

"How can you be sure of that?"

"I thought we were talking about our next move here."

"Anyway," said Greene, "an APB is the same as alert-ing the RCMP."

She thought about that for a moment. "Then we don't do it."

"Someone's going to say this stinks of Central Canadian arrogance. The OPS going it alone."

She looked him in the eye. "This is a big case, Ray. And I've got the RCMP asleep at the switch on one side of me and Ian Mason on the other, so unless you're absolutely sure we can't handle our own shit, maybe you should get onside. We're the last thing standing between this guy and his remaining victims, and if Central Canadian arrogance gets the job done, I'm all for it."

Greene had come to complete stillness, lost in thought. *With me or agin' me?* she wondered. She'd never made Ray Greene for anything but an ally, but for a moment here, her faith was being tested. Then he ran his hand through his hair and put his cap back on. "So no RCMP and no APB," he said. "For now."

She felt her shoulders fall back into place. "Right. For now. We have to think like hunters in a blind here. We don't show ourselves until we absolutely have to. We're going to get one chance to catch this guy. We have to find who his other victims were, figure out how he found them, and get to him before he's finished what he's doing. Because if he finishes, he's done. He'll disappear."

"Fine." He looked at his palms. "You said this guy had to get to Pikangikum by boat, right?"

"That's right."

"So he's an unfamiliar non-native face crossing over twice in one day."

"We presume. Maybe he crossed at two places, though. If I was as smart as he seems to be, that's what I'd do. And anyway, who says he *isn't* native?"

"Do *you* think he's native?"

"No, but any assumption that cancels out another possibility is a dangerous one."

"We have to start somewhere, Hazel, and if you're not prepared to put out an APB, then a fair assumption is a good thing to hang your hat on. At least for a day."

She mulled the idea a moment. "Who's less likely to piss off the natives, you or Wingate?"

Greene held his palms up in a gesture of supplication. "God, don't send me. I'll have my foot in my mouth the second I step onto the riverbank."

Hazel picked up her phone. A moment later, Wingate knocked. "Any luck with the PD in Pikangikum?"

"I'm waiting for a callback."

"Don't wait any more," she said. "Go see Melanie and tell her to call Great Shield Air. You're flying to Red Lake this afternoon."

"I'm not good on airplanes."

"You'll love it. You get to sit beside the pilot. Go."

———

Hazel zipped up the back of her mother's dress and looked over her shoulder at the two of them in the mirror.

"Do you think it'll cause a stir? My going to Delia's funeral?"

"It would cause more of one if you didn't, Mother. You're just being a good citizen."

"There's not a man, woman, or child in this town who doesn't know what Delia did."

"Don't be ridiculous. Not everyone knows. Ray didn't know."

"Oh, but you told him?"

"Look, Mum, Dad did it too. And you went to his funeral."

Emily Micallef leaned forward to open her jewellery box. She had never been one for jewellery and pushed around the few trinkets she had before selecting a modest pearl necklace Hazel's father had given her when Hazel was still a child. "Help me with this," she said, baring her neck to her daughter. Hazel attached the two ends of the necklace together. "You think the papers will be there?"

"I don't know, Mum. You don't have to worry about them."

"They hounded me out of office only eight years ago, Hazel. You think they've forgotten how to sell papers?" Hazel thought of the Monday edition of the *Westmuir Record* and chose not to answer.

On the road leading to St. George's Church, cars were parked in both directions – Hazel estimated more than two hundred cars, with their passengers, had descended on the church to hear Father Glendinning deliver his eulogy. Inside, Ray Greene had held a few seats in his pew, and the two Micallef women went to sit with him. He was dressed in a proper suit, but Hazel had decided that she would be expected to appear in the official capacity of Inspector Micallef, and so she had worn her dress uniform, a getup she had not put on since she'd become interim CO in 1999. The uniform made her feel powerful, and although she was the top-ranking officer in the Port Dundas OPS only by default, this was a moment in which she felt she was the real thing.

She shook hands as she walked down the central aisle, but behind these handshakes, and in the eyes of her fellow Port Dundasians, she saw the expectation that she would provide an answer to the dread mystery that had brought them all together on this day.

Father Glendinning cast his eyes over the congregation. "Come in," he said to those at the back, pressing against those standing. "There is room for anyone who would be here. Come fill the sides." He waited as people shyly filtered down the edges of the nave. "*Sed et si ambulavero in valle mortis non timebo malum.* 'Yea, though I walk through the valley of the shadow of death,'" he said, "'I will fear no evil.' What cold comfort that is to those of us who gather here today to mourn the death of Delia Chandler. For you may not fear evil, but it is afoot, and it has walked among us. The manner in which Delia was carried off is too well known to us, and I will not speak of it, my friends." He looked down at the casket that lay below the dais. "She was too modest a woman to suffer the additional indignity of having the horror of her dying bruited amongst the townfolk like so much gossip." Hazel had squeezed her mother's hand in warning when the priest had said *modest*. "But let us talk of evil. What is our responsibility when faced with evil? Is it to avert our eyes and hope that God will protect us? No, for God protects us only when we stand up to evil; when we allow it no purchase in our lives. Our police tell us that Delia opened the door to her killer, and in so many ways, we open our doors to evil. We make our homes welcoming to Satan. We must batten our doors against evil, lest it seek us out."

"What an idiot," said Greene at the gravesite an hour later. Hazel stood alone behind the crowd with her fellow detective. Before coming out to the cemetery, she'd driven her mother home when Emily said she'd had enough of mourning Delia Chandler. Greene was scuffing the dirt with his shoe. "He has a chance to give these poor people some comfort, and instead he incites them. We'll have ten more Ken Lonergans waving their guns behind their peepholes before long."

"Do you think that's what they heard?" said Hazel, watching the congregants surround the grave ten-deep. "I thought they heard they were safe if they were clean. He said Delia had it coming to her."

Greene thought for a moment. "Is it possible that's what our guy is doing? Was this her sentence? But what did Ulmer do? The man could barely walk."

"I doubt our guy is crossing the country punishing sinners. Surely there aren't people out there effectively committing suicide to expiate their sins."

"Just a thought."

"No, I think Father Glendinning just told us all that nothing bad will happen if we live our lives under God. He hasn't seen what people in our line of work see. If he did, he'd hang up his cassock."

"We rarely see it ourselves, Hazel. I'm about as unfamiliar with murder as Glendinning is."

"But you don't have a cassock to hang up, Ray."

Glendinning was standing at the head of Delia's grave with his Bible open. "Ashes to ashes," he began, and the crowd of townsfolk pressed in and crossed themselves. Hazel looked through their numbers, hoping to see an unfamiliar face, but there was a sea of faces she knew too well — men and women whose houses she'd been to, whose children she'd warned and even arrested, whose neighbours she'd calmed. The whole town was here. She saw a couple of people standing in the back with notebooks. There was little enough to go on from an investigative perspective, and she was relieved to think that there was nothing to tell the press, such as it was here in Westmuir County.

Bob and Gail stood beside Father Glendinning holding hands, and Hazel tried not to look at Bob, who was weeping. Delia's other son, Dennis, had come in from Calgary, but Hazel hadn't seen him for almost thirty years. She recalled him as a reedy-looking jock, a shy kid known for how far he could hit a fastball. If she was remembering correctly, he'd gone off to Michigan on a sports scholarship, but she had no idea how he'd ended up in Calgary. She wasn't entirely sure which of the four or five adults standing near the priest he was.

Presently, Glendinning nodded to Bob Chandler, and he, as well as another, larger, man, stepped forward and each took a handful of dirt and threw it into the grave. The second man turned to look at the mourners, and she saw the hint of that young man's face she'd been trying to remember. He'd gone to seed.

Afterward, Hazel made a point of seeking out Dennis Chandler. She introduced herself, and Bob's brother took her hand. "I almost didn't recognize you," she said.

"I tried to stay away as much as I could," he said. "Have you made any progress?"

"It's slow," she admitted. "He was very careful."

"I appreciate everything you're doing here, Inspector."

She didn't correct him. He released her hand, and Hazel found herself staring into the man's eyes. He was in his early fifties, younger than his brother, but he'd thickened. Thirty years was enough time for a person to change completely. In the mid-seventies, when she'd last seen this man, she was thirty pounds lighter herself. And married. "Were you in touch with her very much?" she asked.

"We kept in touch through email," he said. "Once a week, or so. And before you ask: no. There was nothing in her emails last week or the week before to even suggest she knew her time was running out. Or that she was planning anything like this, if it was actually planned."

"Can you see your mother asking someone for help ending her life?"

"I don't know what any person might become capable of once they know they're dying, Inspector. I suppose it's possible. It doesn't *feel* like her to me, but I haven't lived near my mother for fifteen years."

"Did you see her much?"

Dennis Chandler lowered his head slightly. "No," he said. "It was emails and a package a few times a year. I hate to say it, but it was enough. For me."

Hazel saw Howard Spere standing in the grass near the road talking with Ray Greene. The two men started toward her. "What would she send you? Birthday gifts?"

"Christmas too. The usual. I have a six-year-old daughter. She'd buy something here in town and wrap it up in butcher paper and send it out. Although the last couple of years, we'd get something from whatever online store she'd shopped at with her credit card. There wouldn't even be her handwriting on the package. And a computer-generated card in the box with her message." He leaned in a little, and Hazel held her hand out behind her to warn Spere and Greene not to come any closer. "You want to know the truth? My mother was lazy. She took the easy way out. That's why she could convince herself it was okay to do what she did with your father – she would have told herself it was preferable to suffering alone. And so, yes, maybe my mother turned into the kind of person who would have asked someone to help her end her life. I don't know."

"May I ask you another question?"

"Sure."

"Did your mother send you anything recently? A gift?"

"If she did, I haven't got it yet. But there's no birthdays in our household after October, and Christmas is still a month and a half away . . ."

"I'm sorry for your loss," she said, and she put her hand on his shoulder. "I'm glad we talked."

Dennis Chandler nodded to her, and passed on his way. Her two colleagues were standing right behind her. "Who was that?" said Ray Greene.

"Delia's younger son."

"*That's* Dennis Chandler?"

"Yeah."

"That kid could skin a hardball. What did he tell you?"

"He wasn't her biggest fan. He said she was lazy around birthdays and Christmas. That she had her gifts shipped directly off the web."

"I'd call that convenience, not laziness," said Spere.

"Howard, will you think in a straight line for once? That duvet cover Delia bought on Bidnow . . ."

Spere blinked a couple of times. A stream of people flowed past on either side of them, like water around a stone. "I'll have one of my guys find out who the seller was. I presume he'll know where the item was shipped."

"You 'presume'?" sneered Greene.

The big man picked a fleck of something out of the corner of his mouth. He fixed Ray with a hooded gaze. "Beg your pardon, Ray?"

"I'm just saying. I thought you guys weren't supposed to presume anything."

"It's a figure of speech, Ray."

"Fine."

"Are you boys done?" said Hazel. They turned to her. "What were you loping over here to tell me?"

"Good news, sort of," said Spere. "The RCMP up in Gimli sent me some digital images of the Maris murder. It's our guy for sure. He did her mouth."

"But he cut her head in half."

"He did, but they took the crime-scene pics and put her back together digitally. She looked like she was whistling."

Hazel unconsciously pursed her lips. "Whistling."

"Or blowing a kiss."

"Good Christ," said Greene. The three of them began walking back to Hazel's car.

"We have to find the rest of these victims *now*," she said. "Gimli makes four in eleven days."

"He's working quickly," said Greene. "If Gimli is November 3, the Atlookan murder November 9, Delia the twelfth, and Michael Ulmer November 14, then he's killing almost every three days."

"If you're right, then we've missed one between Gimli and Pikangikum," said Spere.

"So you presume."

Spere ignored him. He'd taken out his notebook and was writing dates furiously. "There'll be another one within five hundred kilometres east of Chamberlain, anytime now."

Hazel stopped beside her car. "Howard, I want some spare personnel from Mayfair. Quietly. I want everyone we can get on this – phones, email, police frequencies." She tapped Greene's notebook. "Ray, get a map and start triangulating towns around these times and distances. If he's killing every three days or so, and he's coming from the west, we should be able to figure out how many more visits he's planning on making. We have to get to him before he's done."

"I'll do it right away."

He began sprinting for his car. Spere was standing in front of her, unused to action. "As for you, get someone in to Delia's Bidnow.com account. That duvet cover was not for her."

Lake Superior looked like the ocean from twelve thousand feet. "It's about the size of Nova Scotia," said the pilot into her microphone. Wingate picked her up in his headphones. "It's a biii-iig cuppa water," she said.

Wingate had stopped gripping the armrest sometime back around the northern shore of Manitoulin Island, but he wasn't getting used to it. The plane was an old Cessna 180 and it had room for the pilot, Wingate, and a briefcase, although the pilot claimed she could carry five people in the craft, if she had to. Her name was Brenna. "Luckily, it's just the two of us, or I might have trouble getting all the way there on one tank," she'd said. "Red Lake's just on the edge of my range."

"But we'll get there."

"Even if we have to glide down to the runway, I'll getcha there."

He had to admit it was occasionally pleasant being in a plane the size of a minivan, although he could feel the bumps as if he were riding a bicycle down a potholed road. And Brenna kept him fairly distracted, pointing out towns like Wawa and Rossport as they passed over them. "You can make out the geese down there," she'd said over Wawa.

"What?"

"They've got a couple huge goose statues down there. You can see 'em from up here." He couldn't see that far, but he took her word for it. It was going to end up being a four-hour flight, and he needed all the distraction he could get. There was no talking but through the intercom system wired into their headsets. The plane was so loud he couldn't hear himself sneeze. They were approaching a town called Marathon.

"How much longer?"

"You gettin' bored of my stories, hon?"

"Not at all."

"Check this out," she said, and she put the plane into a sudden dive and then pulled it up again. Wingate almost vomited.

"God," he said.

"You can drive this little shitbox like a race car. It'll do anything."

"Please don't do that again," he said.

She put her hand on his knee. "Oh, come on – I could crash this thing, and we'd jump up and throw the pieces over our shoulders."

"Well, I'd just the same –"

"– rather not, I know. Everyone says the same thing. Don't worry, Officer Wingate, this thing is safe as houses. I'll have you into Red Lake in one piece, I promise."

11

Tuesday, November 16, 3 p.m.

The ferry from Berens Landing to the reserve went over three times a day: once in the morning, once in the mid-afternoon, and once around suppertime. Wingate bought a newspaper and a bag of chips and waited inside the small, sour-smelling terminal. His pilot had been instructed to stay in a motel in Red Lake and wait for him to come back. DI Micallef was going to have him in the air twice in one day; there was no time to wait. The date on the newspaper he was reading was November 13, the day after they found Delia Chandler; the locality was too small to support a newspaper that came out more frequently than once a week. He opened it and scanned the news pages, knowing he would find nothing about what had happened in Port Dundas. Next week's paper would have nothing on it either. As Hazel had said, the Belladonna was ensuring that none of those who mourned his victims would have cause to know each other.

He'd been driven here in a squad car out of Red Lake. A surly constable named Jackman had been assigned to him, and he whipped along the highway at 140 kilometres an hour just to limit the amount of time he'd have to spend with a cop from "Toronto-way." That Port Dundas was a full three and a half hours north of Toronto made no difference to this guy, and Wingate kept his mouth shut about the fact that he'd only just been transferred from the city. Jackman kept his transmitter on the whole time, listening in on his station's frequency but not commenting to Wingate on anything they both heard. The only thing the constable said of any note to Wingate was to watch his wallet once he got to the reserve. "No compunction on these guys," he said, "cop or no." He told Wingate to call his dispatch when he was heading back to this side and someone would be there to meet him. Some lucky person, no doubt, thought Wingate.

There was nothing in the paper to keep his attention, so he went out to where the ferry would tie up. He and two other men were the only people waiting. He noticed them noticing him. It was cold by the Berens River, a hard slant wind driving the water up against the pilings. It made him think of Lake Ontario in late fall, the way the wind over the lake could push you down the boardwalk. That was a place he didn't think he'd be able to walk again anytime soon.

"You being posted?" said a voice behind him. It was the younger of the two men. "You coming to live with us?"

Wingate turned to face the man. The second one was still standing over by the door to the terminal, smoking. "I thought the reserve had its own police service."

"It does, but they always send us one solid citizen from Red Lake or Sioux Lookout. Keep an eye on us."

"I'm from Port Dundas. I'm visiting."

"You're in costume for a visit, officer." He leaned in to look at Wingate's badge. "*Detective*, I should say."

Wingate debated how much he should tell this man, then thought if he gave anyone cause to doubt his honesty, this whole trip could be for nothing. The cover story Detective Inspector Micallef had suggested he use seemed particularly ill-advised. He told the man he'd come to learn a couple of things about Joseph Atlookan. There'd been a suicide on a reserve near Port Dundas, and they wanted to rule out foul play.

"You talking M'njikaning?" said the man. Wingate nodded. "Nobody died in that community by their own hand for over a year. And if they did, what would it have to do with us?"

"My superior just asked me to come and ask a couple of questions."

"You came fifteen hundred kilometres to ask some questions about a sad old dead Indian, huh? You think he killed himself because someone drank Lysol out in M'njikaning last Christmas?" Wingate scuffed his feet. The man had his hands on his hips. "We got a right to know what's going on in our own house, you know?"

"I understand," said Wingate.

The man fell to silence, looking at Wingate without looking away. It seemed to him then that the best move might be just to head back to Red Lake and figure out another way to get the information they needed about Atlookan. A morgue photo would do if they could get their hands on one. The man interrupted his thoughts. "Joe was my uncle on my mum's side," he said. "What do you know about him that I don't?"

"I don't know anything," said Wingate quickly. "I honestly don't."

"But you think there's something on the other side of this river you should look at."

"I guess I do." He offered his hand and the man took it. "I'm Detective Constable James Wingate. I don't mean to give you the impression that I'm skulking around. And if you're his nephew, then maybe I should be talking to you anyway."

"I'm one of his nephews," said the man. "Joe had five brothers, four sisters, and nine kids of his own. There's no shortage of Atlookans on the reserve and every one of them knew him."

"He was sick," said Wingate.

"For years," said the man. "He had cancer. My uncle used to get up every hour all night to smoke. We figure he smoked two packs a day and the best part of a third when he should have been sleeping. But he made it to eighty-three. Then he'd had enough."

"Why do you think he'd had enough? Why did he kill himself now?"

The man shrugged. "He'd tried everything, I guess. Wife was dead, thought he was turning into a burden for his kids. He was in pain."

Wingate had taken out his notebook and shown it to the man, and the man had nodded. Wingate wrote down "tried everything." The man standing behind them whistled.

"Ferry's coming. I'm going to get a cup of tea for the crossing. If you want, we can talk more on the boat. But I don't want to be snowed by any of your cover stories, officer. If I talk to you and it leads you somewhere, I want to know."

"Agreed," said Wingate. "I might not be able to tell you everything I know right away, but I'll try to keep my promise." The man turned with his hands in his pockets and started back toward the terminal building. "I didn't get your name," said Wingate.

"I'm Joe Atlookan," said the man. "And there's six more of me on the other side of the river."

By the time the boat left the dock, twenty-five more people had shown up. The ferry was so regular that there was no reason to get there early unless someone had dropped you off. It was a small vessel, with room for perhaps fifty. The reserve had all the services and amenities the community needed, including a school and a clinic, so the ferry wasn't used as a daily conveyance for more than a handful of people who worked off the reserve.

Wingate was much more conscious of his conspicuous presence now than when only two people had been looking at him. Getting on, he'd proposed to Joe Atlookan that they talk in a more private setting once they'd got to the reserve, and Atlookan had nodded and left him sitting more or less alone at the back of the ferry.

Halfway across the river, the other passengers began to lose interest in him, and Wingate allowed himself to raise his head and observe the people around him. He didn't know a lot of native people, and like a lot of city folk, his experience of natives was limited to poverty and addiction. There were community centres and native health centres in Toronto, and on occasion, he'd had a reason to go to them while on the job. But the atmosphere in these places was so sad that he'd found he couldn't look people in their eyes. He wondered if he'd feel the same ugly pity in Pikangikum as he did in Toronto. He'd soon find out.

The reserve was a collection of about four hundred houses and some larger buildings, surrounded by trees. Joe Atlookan waited for him to get off the ferry and took him to his mother's house, a small wooden structure with a wood-burning stove in the middle of the main room. The small house was redolent of roasting meat. Wingate sat at the woman's kitchen table clutching the cup of tea she'd insisted he take when he came through the door. He listened to the son explain to the mother in Ojibway what Wingate presumed were the main points of the reason he'd come all this way. As she listened, she kept her eyes on Wingate, who felt compelled to sip the too-hot tea.

When Joe was finished talking, his mother came and sat beside Wingate. "Are you hungry?" she asked.

"I'm okay, thank you."

Her son said a couple more phrases to her and she got up, opened the oven door, and removed a roaster. She ladled out a couple of shallow dishes of stew and put them both on the table. "My son says it's an hour out here from Red Lake, an hour's wait at the landing, and then forty minutes by ferry, so you must be hungry even though you say you are not. So first you eat."

"Your son has a talent for catching me in untruths."

She cast a look behind her as her son came to the table. "He means he is a police officer and he is careful, Ma. He's fine." Joe reached into a cloth-covered basket and took out a slice of white bread and passed a second one to Wingate. "Her name's Mary," he said. "You catching on to the naming trend here? I got a mother and two aunts named Mary. My mum's the only one who kept it, the others went by their middle names. All four of my remaining uncles are called Joe something. They all go by the *something*. The man you came here to ask questions about, he was the last Joseph Atlookan of his generation."

Wingate turned to Mary, who stood in the middle of the kitchen folding and refolding a handcloth. "Were you close with your brother?"

"I was very close with him."

"Your son told me that he'd 'tried' everything. To help with the cancer. What kinds of things did he do?"

"Joseph tried any medicine he could get his hands on, but he put no faith in giving up his poison. A smoke in one hand, a pill in the other. There was no medicine could help my brother."

"So you think he just gave up?"

"You want more stew?"

Wingate looked into his plate and saw he'd wolfed down the portion she'd given him. He hadn't had a home-cooked meal in more than a month. "It's absolutely incredible. What is it?"

"Caribou," she said. "I have a freezerful of it."

"I'd love some more," he said.

She gave him another serving, and this time Joe Atlookan just passed him the bread basket with a half-smile. He slowly pulled away the cloth covering the bread for Wingate like he was drawing aside a curtain. He was looking Wingate in the eyes. "I guess he gave up," Mary Atlookan said. "I don't know. They just came and took him away."

"Who did?"

"Some men from the band council."

"There's nothing unusual about that," said Joe.

"Was anyone with him the day he died?"

Mary considered the question for a moment. "He lived alone. But he still has two daughters here in town. You could try one of them."

After the meal, Joe placed a phone call to one of his cousins. Fifteen minutes later, they were holding fresh cups of tea in an identical house on the other side of the reserve. Wingate wrote the woman's name in his pad: Wineva Atlookan, an unmarried daughter of the dead man. She was in her fifties. She'd been with her father the morning of his death. "Did anyone visit him that day?" Wingate asked.

"One of his doctors from over the river," she answered.

"One of his doctors?"

Joe put his tea down with a dull clunk on the kitchen counter. "My uncle was addicted to New Age crap as much as he was to his cigarettes. I think there was a new quack in town every three days."

"Did you meet this man?"

Wineva shook her head. "Not really. Dad said he was coming and he would not make medicine with him unless he was alone. So I waited until there was a knock at the door. Dad insisted I go out the back, but I caught a glimpse of the guy."

Wingate turned to a new page. "What can you tell me about him?"

"He was thin as a rail," said Wineva. "He had on a long black coat with a cape that was tied around his throat. He might have been holding a hat. I didn't really see his face, though."

"Did you hear him say anything?"

"Just 'Hello Joseph,' like he knew my dad from somewhere."

Wingate's hand was shaking. First contact, no matter how remote, was a huge step forward. Their man had just begun to emerge from the mist. "Anything else? Rack your mind, Miss Atlookan, this could be important."

"*Now* there's something you're not telling me," said Joe. "What is it?"

Wingate closed his notebook instinctively. "I'll keep my promise," he said. "But I need you to trust me now."

"You think my uncle was murdered."

He looked back and forth between the dead man's two relatives. The danger of the truth was this: he could offer it as a sign of fellowship, but if word spread, it could scupper their advantage. "I don't know what happened to him," he said at last.

"Do *you* think he was murdered?" repeated Joe Atlookan, holding Wingate's gaze. "That's all I want to know."

"I think it's a possibility."

Wineva Atlookan stumbled back into one of the kitchen chairs and sat down. "Why? Who would murder an old, dying man?"

He pulled out the chair beside hers and took her hand in his. "Do you think the men who came to take your father's body might have photographed the scene?"

"And who cuts their own throat?" she said to herself.

"Have you been back to your father's house?" said Wingate.

She was still staring down at the tabletop, then she seemed to notice her hand in the officer's and she removed it. "My father didn't pay this man, whoever he was," she said. "Not in cash. When we went back into the house, my father's Bible was gone. I didn't think anything of it — it's not uncommon here to barter for services. I thought to myself, he's given up. He paid for his last doctor with something he thought he wouldn't need any more. But now, if you say he was killed, did this man steal my father's Bible?" She stood, agitated. "What kind of person is this? Who would come to our home and do such a thing?"

Wingate watched her pacing the room, her hands suddenly alive. She shook them as if there were water on her fingers. She still had not answered his question about the photo, so he came at it from another angle. "Miss Atlookan, I'm sorry I've upset you. Your father's death has been hard enough on you, but may I please ask you one more thing?"

She stopped in the middle of the room, stranded in her worry and grief.

"Did you see your father's body?" Wingate asked.

"My God," said Joe, "is that really necessary to ask her?"

"Of course I saw it. I found him."

He proceeded carefully. "It must have been awful."

"It *was* awful. There was blood everywhere. On the walls. On the ceiling."

"I'm sorry you had to see that," he said. "It's not the kind of thing anyone who loves a person should ever see." In the back of his mind, he wondered how many people's blood must have been dripping from the old man's ceiling. He watched some of the tension draining from her body. She would cry any moment now. He went to her. "Wineva," he said, "if there's anything else you think I should know, please do tell me."

She shot a glance at her cousin and then brought her face back around to Wingate. "He was *singing*," she said in a low, dread-filled voice. "There was no sound, but his lips . . . he was singing when he died."

And then she shook as if she were freezing cold and burst into helpless tears.

"He's posing as a healer!" he shouted over the sound of the rain. He was standing between the beds in the hotel back in Red Lake, the phone pressed to his cheek. "He's somehow making contact with people who are terminally ill and then visiting them, perhaps with a promise of a cure. Then he's murdering them."

Hazel listened carefully on the other end of the line. She pictured her young detective jumping up and down in a hotel room. "Are there any crime-scene pictures?"

"I still don't know. I couldn't get a straight answer out of anyone. But this is our guy for sure. He did his thing with the mouth – the victim's daughter showed me what it looked like."

"How?"

"She drew a couple pictures for me in my notebook. The shape of her father's mouth. And she tried to draw her father's visitor, but she didn't see a face. Just drew a man in a black coat. She said her father was *singing* – his mouth was pursed like he was hooting or something, but obviously whatever he was doing, it fits the Belladonna's MO. And it supports your theory that he destroyed Michael Ulmer's mouth because he thought there was a possibility someone would link that killing to Delia Chandler's. So I agree with you. The mouths are the most important thing here."

"You have to get some pictures, James. Did you talk to the band police?"

"I didn't. I got in through the back door, as it was. But the guy I met here, I think he might be willing to talk to the band detachment for me."

"Find out," Hazel said. She finished writing her notes. "Well, now here's our big question: how is he finding these people?"

"Or how are they finding him?"

She thought about it for a moment. "That's good, James. They might be seeking him out. Let's put that into the mix when you return and we'll see what we come up with. Call your contact and find some pictures, then get back into your little airplane."

"It's coming down here in buckets, Inspector. And it's getting dark. It *is* dark."

"It's the rain, James. If your pilot says you can fly, then you're going to have to suck it up. We need you home and ready to go first thing tomorrow."

He hung up and sat on the bed. The rain was a grey curtain beyond the window; it came down with the kind of ferocity he associated with the countryside, as if the man-made obstacles in cities somehow broke up storms like this and reduced them to a simulacrum of bad weather. Here it was awesome; it felt as if the lightning could pierce the building and pick him out of his supposed safety.

This thought led somewhere painful for him, and he pushed himself off the bed. There were many presumed sanctuaries in one's life, and none of them were completely impermeable. He'd learned this and he'd come to think that this lesson was one that delivered you into permanent adulthood. It could turn you cynical if you let it. He hadn't let it, this far.

The phone rang again, and he ran his palm upward against his cheek and picked it up. It was Brenna, the fun-loving pilot. He braced himself for the news that the flight home was going to be an *adventure*. He was sure she was going to use that word. But she surprised him by telling him that not even sparrows could take off in this weather. They were grounded, and would he like to have dinner downstairs in an hour? He gratefully agreed, then called Port Dundas again to give them the bad news that he wouldn't be home on time after all.

She was wearing a red dress. Why had she packed a red dress for what she surely presumed was going to be a single-day gig? She stood up when he came in and shook his hand. The waiter came by with two whiskey sours. "Sorry," she said. "I decided the first round was on me, so I ordered something I like. You can pick next."

"That's great," he said, holding his drink out to her. They clinked glasses smartly. "To the weather."

"Absolutely!" she said. She threw most of the drink back without grimacing.

They ordered hamburgers with cheddar and bacon and had seconds of whiskey sours, and James felt pleased to have landed here, with this woman who turned out to be better company on the ground than in the air. She was a merry creature, twice divorced, the last time, he learned, from a man who couldn't take all her energy, as she put it. "I'm a handful," she said, spearing a french fry from his plate. "You have to keep up with me."

"I can see that," he said. She held her empty glass up to the waiter. Wingate tried to refuse a third drink.

"You're not on duty, Noah's building another ark, and it's rude to let a woman drink alone. So you'll have that third sour, young man."

"Can I have a beer?" he said, laughing.

"Oh, would you like a *light* beer, you boy scout? You're a frigging policeman, James! Now stop wriggling, or I'll order you a double."

She told him about the little town she lived in now — it wasn't all that far from Port Dundas. Apparently, the age of the average citizen was 108. She was the company's only female pilot and, as she put it, the only upward mobility possible was on takeoff. Otherwise, she was stuck. "It's a good job," she said, "although I've always dreamed of flying jets. But listen to me, yammering. You must have had an interesting day."

He tried to negotiate her interest wisely; he already knew she wasn't the kind of person to be put off with vagueness. He made up something one-quarter true and she did some nodding, pushing the ice around in her drink with her forefinger. Then, when he was in the middle of connecting the true detail about the caribou stew with something he made up about looking to recruit a new officer for M'njikaning, she interrupted him and said, "Whaddya say we continue this conversation somewhere else?"

He smiled at her, then the smile went away, and then he tried to put it back on and failed. He centred his water glass at the top of his plate.

"Come on now," she said. "Don't go all Opie on me, officer."

"I'm sorry, Brenna, I can't."

"You're off-duty, aren't you?"

"I am," he said.

"So you can't, or you don't want to?"

"If I could, I'd be honoured. But I can't."

She considered him for a moment with the knowing look of an experienced dater. "That can only mean one of two things, Detective. Either you're married or you're gay. Or both. Both is a possibility." She watched him carefully for a reaction. He said nothing. Her eyebrows went up. "Not both," she said. "And not married."

"I'm sorry," he said.

"So . . . you're invited to dinner in the middle of nowhere by a fairly attractive woman who shows up in a red dress. What about that is unclear to you? You don't have three whiskey sours with me and a meal and then announce you don't play on my team. You walk in, see the girl in the red dress and you say, 'I hear the banquet burgers here are great and by the way, I don't sleep with women.'"

"Can you please keep your voice down?"

"Or you could have sent back the whiskey sour and ordered a white wine spritzer instead. That would have done it."

He laughed despite the look on her face, or maybe because of it. Her mouth was twisted up in a ferocious scowl. "I had no idea what was going on, Brenna, honest."

"But you're a *detective*."

"There's no crime here."

"I disagree. Look at you. You're yummy. And you're afraid of flying, how sexy is that? I'd been praying for rain all afternoon just so I'd have the chance to invite you to dinner, get you drunk, and see if you wear boxers or briefs. Now that I know you're gay —"

"Please," he said in a stage whisper.

"– I'm guessing briefs."

He reached over and grabbed her hand, figuring it was going to be the best way to quiet her down. He didn't realize until that moment that he was drunk: his hand punched her water glass clear off the table. It crashed to the ground and shattered. "Brenna, please. You can fly loop-the-loops tomorrow. Just let me off the hook."

She looked at him, shaking her head slowly. Her long brown hair fell over her mouth. "Your secret's safe with me."

"It's not a secret. Not in general."

"Well, it's still safe," she said. "Although if you were a *real* gentleman . . ." He squeezed her hand, just a little too hard. "Okay," she said.

] 12 [

Ray Greene walked in through the front door of the station house, stopped, looked around, and for a moment thought he was in the wrong place. Almost every desk in the pen was full; there had to be an additional fifteen officers with their heads down, phones cradled against their shoulders, or their eyes fixed on a glowing screen. Detective Inspector Micallef came out of her office and saw him standing there, transfixed by the activity. She came down and held the gate open for him. "We're a secondment factory now, Ray. If Ian Mason isn't going to send me what I need, I'll beg, borrow, and steal it. Come meet some of the troops."

He went through, still shaking his head. She pointed out rough clusters of new staff. "These folks are from Mayfair — they're on police frequencies and scanners from here to St. John's." She turned him by the elbow and pulled him toward two tables that had been pushed together. There were six officers arrayed around it. "These folks are calling every town in this country with a population of less than fifteen thousand and making inquiries about unsolved murders in the last eight weeks."

"Nice gig," Greene said to the officers. "Welcome to the big time." Hazel led him to the back of the pen, and they stood there looking at the buzz of activity. "Someone should tell Mason that for what it's going to cost him in unwritten parking tickets in Mayfair, he could have given us one good man for two weeks."

"Would you really try to talk that kind of sense to Ian Mason?"

"If I thought I had a chance . . ."

"You think it's bad having him for commander? Wait until he runs for premier. We'll be fighting the bad guys with wooden swords."

Greene laughed. "Until then, why don't we focus on the task at hand."

"Let's go in the back."

In Hazel's office, Greene produced an old folding map with the logo of a local gas station on it. He opened it and tried to smooth it down on her desk. There were small, round yellow stickers on the towns of Gimli, Pikangikum, Port Dundas, and Chamberlain. Then he'd put little blue dots on a series of towns to the east of Chamberlain, and red dots to the west of Gimli. "I did some math. Chandler and Ulmer break a pattern, like we're saying, but we're still talking four if not five murders between the towns of Gimli and Chamberlain in ten days. That's two thousand kilometres, or a killing about every four to five hundred kilometres."

"There better not be any cube roots here, Ray."

He put his finger on the map. "These red dots show distances from Gimli westward to the most distant part of Vancouver Island. It represents over three thousand kilometres. There could be at least eight more bodies."

"We're up to sixteen according to our lab results. Maximum five, let's say, between Gimli and Chamberlain, plus your eight, only gets us to thirteen. So you're missing three dots on this half of the map. And what about these —" She counted the blue stickers heading east. "Six more?"

"If he's doing the same math, at least."

Hazel Micallef leaned on her forearms against the edge of the desk. "So twenty-two victims. At least. Sixteen of whom he's already killed. And all these little dots are what? Four hundred and fifty kilometres apart?"

He turned the map to face himself. "I accounted for proximity to large centres and factored in how accessible these towns are. They're best guesses."

"He got into Pikangikum."

"I know."

She stared at the map another moment and then pushed herself upright. "Okay, let's get back out there." She swept the map off the desk and he followed her into the pen. The sound of the map crackling caused a general raising of heads. "Listen up people," Hazel said, "we're trying to narrow down likely landing spots for our man." She spiked the map on the back wall of the pen. "Any of you assigned to calling small municipalities west and north of Gimli, Manitoba, start consulting this map. Start calling the red dots and then move out in a spiral from them. We're looking for at least eight more victims now." The six men and women at the desk near the back stood up nearly in unison. "I want results, people. Five dead bodies – minimum – by the end of today." She turned to Ray. "You and I are going to hole up in my office and call the blue dots until we find our next victim."

They were about to close the door when one of their own, PC Windemere, put her hand against it. "Sorry," she said, pushing a stray hair back up under her cap. "I was assigned to electronic bulletins. I found something I think you're going to want to look at."

"Where?"

"Eastern border of Quebec."

Now Cartwright was standing in the doorway too. "And I have Mason for you on line one."

Ray and Hazel traded a look. "Everything's heating up all at once, huh?" she said.

She shook his hand and passed him his pack. "Nice flying with you, sailor," she said and winked at him.

The solid ground beneath him felt slightly unstable. They'd flown clear blue skies, but the entire way it had seemed to him that the air was full of invisible medicine balls, buffeting the tiny craft.

"I guess I don't have to say 'call me.'"

"Don't take it personally."

"Is it about my airplane or my X chromosome?"

He smiled for her and hoisted his pack over his shoulder. There was a payphone beside the hangar and he called the station from it. "Find a chair," said Ray Greene. "We're sending you a Frenchman."

"Just what I need," said Wingate.

"Hard day, James? Wait till you get back here."

"Who's the Frenchman?"

"A gift from Commander Mason. Son-of-a-bitch actually came through. The French guy's a detective out of Sudbury. Name's Sevigny."

"How long do we have him?"

"Skip didn't say. He should be to you in about an hour."

Wingate hung up and watched Brenna circle on the tarmac and take off for some point west. The craft shrank against the clear sky in an agonizing slow fade. Wingate hadn't been propositioned by a member of either sex in well over seven years. For the last five, it would have been entirely unwelcome, but even now, he wondered if he'd know what to do if someone eligible came along. He told himself to view Brenna's invitation as a form of kindness, but instead he felt troubled by the fact that someone had found him out. Not his sexuality, but just *him*. He'd had to act like a person for a few moments, rather than the Job. His uniform and badge could stand in for a lot if he wanted them to. He could even mask a personal reaction with these trappings, as he had with the young Joe Atlookan. It was possible that Joe was accepted for who he was on the reservation, but then again, maybe no one knew. When Atlookan had pushed the bread basket toward him that second time and looked him in the eyes, Wingate's suspicions were confirmed. It had made Brenna's advances seem even sadder. What a lonesome night it had been.

Wingate stayed lost in these thoughts for another half-hour, his mind turning down into the dark cul-de-sac where the worst memories were, and when he was next aware of the outside world, it was because a plane identical to Brenna's was touching down. For a moment, he worried it was Brenna herself, come back to take another crack at him, but a towering man came out of the plane, stooped over. "Detective Sergeant Sevigny?" he asked.

"Se-vin-yee," said the man, offering his hand.

"Welcome to the Port Dundas Police."

The man almost didn't fit in the car – his knees pressed up against the glove compartment. It was as if Wingate had bagged a moose and instead of tying it to the grille, he'd put it in the passenger seat. There was very little conversation on the way; Sevigny told him only that if he never saw Sudbury again it would be fine with him. "A toilet," is what he said. He sat in the passenger seat with a neat pile of folders on his lap, details of the case had already been faxed to him. Wingate was tempted to try his French – he'd been nearly fluent by grade eleven – but he intuited that the behemoth in his passenger seat probably wasn't going to be interested in a Berlitz moment.

They got into Port Dundas at two in the afternoon. Driving down the main street, it felt to James as if he'd been away for a month. He'd only been in the town for four days, but his relief made him feel like he was coming home. The station house was overflowing with men and women on phones. Ray Greene waved off his questions: all would be explained. There was a kind of neighbourliness to the whole place, Wingate thought, like it had been transformed into some kind of telethon headquarters. There was a map at the back of the room, and beside the map a white board had a series of place names written on it. He read *Milk River*, *Grimshaw*, and *Quesnel* before he had to catch up with Greene and the French officer. DI Micallef was waiting in one of the meeting rooms. There was a laptop in front of her. She turned the screen to Sevigny. There was a picture on it of a sickly looking woman with blood all over her face. It was a frontal view, and Wingate could see the wooden handle of a hammer sticking up behind her head. The woman's mouth was cast in a huge, thin grimace. "Her name is Gladys Iagnemma. The daughter – Cecilia – spoke to her this morning in anticipation of seeing her with a friend of hers. When she went over, this is what she found. Spere is waiting in Mayfair for a courier delivery of her clothing."

"Although we already know what's on it," said Greene.

"What is that?" said Sevigny.

Hazel pulled out a chair for the man, who fit himself into it, and she began to slowly lay out the facts of the case as they understood them. Sevigny was a quick study. "This guy," he said, "he thinks no one is paying attention."

"That's right," Hazel said.

Sevigny jerked his chin toward the door. "Now a lot of people are paying attention."

Greene crossed his arms. "We're being careful, Detective Sergeant."

The French policeman unfolded himself from his chair. "A lot of little jugs, eh?" The three others stared at him, uncomprehending. "Is my English so bad? They have big ears, little jugs."

Hazel was staring at him like he was changing colour. "I've never understood that saying."

Wingate was amused to see this massive man lose his composure a little. He held his hands up like he was surrendering. "The more people talking about your case, the more ears to hear. We don't want this man to hear anything we are saying."

"Well, you're not saying anything yet, officer," said Greene, and he came forward to shut the laptop where Gladys Iagnemma's face continued to leer out at them. "You're getting caught up, then you're pitching in, and then you're going home."

"I'm not going anywhere," said Sevigny, and he took a tiny step forward, toward Ray Greene. Greene instinctively stepped back before he could tell himself to stand his ground.

"Boys?" said Hazel, and Sevigny thrust his hand out toward Greene. Everyone flinched.

"Detective Sergeant Adjutor Sevigny," he said. "I will be at your service until I decide I am no longer needed."

"What the hell's an 'adjutor'?" said Greene, refusing the man's hand. Sevigny kept it out.

"That is my name, Raymond," he said. "Now shake my hand, and let us all work together."

—

Hazel Micallef sat alone at the back of The Laughing Crow, toying with the plastic swizzle stick in her bourbon. This was Andrew's local, and she'd deliberately chosen a table near the back where she would not be seen by any of his colleagues. But it entailed turning around in her chair in an obvious manner to see if he'd come in and failed to see her. Twenty minutes after the time he'd agreed to meet her she was still sitting alone. The bartender leaned over the bar to hand her a second bourbon. "You can sit at the bar with me, Chief," he said, gesturing to the countertop. "I can keep 'em coming."

"I'm waiting for someone," she said. "But thank you." She wondered if he believed her, and then decided she didn't care. If she was going to be tonight's story, so be it. It was impossible to go for a drink anywhere within two hundred kilometres of Port Dundas without being spotted. In uniform or not, it was like a sign was hanging around her neck. She pushed the ice down with her finger and at that moment felt Andrew's hand on her shoulder. This was one of the ways he'd touched her; that spot on her shoulder could mould itself to his hand from memory.

"Do you want my excuse?" he said.

"Whatever it is, I forgive you."

"Okay," he said, "thanks." He gave the bartender a thumbs-up and then reached behind her to receive his drink: a gin and tonic.

"Aren't you worried about the bartender across the street stealing your signs?" she asked Andrew.

"It's just a shorthand we've developed over the years." He sipped his drink and held it up in front of him. "Thumbs-up is this, anything else, I have to go up and order."

"I don't know if I'm relieved or sickened," she said.

"I come here almost every day after work, Hazel. There's nothing sinister about it."

"With Glynnis?"

"With my wife? Yes, Hazel. I go out for a drink with my wife quite frequently."

She reached across the table and put her hand on his. "Please don't," she said. "I didn't mean to start anything."

He gave her a soft look, but pulled his hand away out from under hers. "Okay. Meter's reset. Let's toast to something neutral."

Hazel laughed without smiling and lifted her glass to him. "To fog."

"Uhh, okay. Fog, Hazel. To fog." They clinked and drank and Andrew's gaze fell on the swizzle stick lying at the base of the ketchup bottle. "What fog are we drinking to?"

"The one that's coming in about an hour, dear."

This caused the light to go out of his eyes. "I don't want to be part of some kind of masochistic ritual, Hazel. I've seen enough of that for this lifetime. If that's why you wanted to see me, I don't think I'm okay with it."

She wiggled her drink at him. "It won't be from this," she said. "In an hour, when I go home, I have to take three pills to counteract the pain I've been in all day. They turn out my lights."

"Doesn't sound like something you feel neutral

about," he said. He stirred his drink. "I didn't know it was that bad."

"If it gets any worse, they're going to cut me. I'll be in bed for ten weeks. Or more."

"Your mother'll love that."

"Maybe." The ice melting into the liquor looked like smoke. She suddenly remembered some homework Emilia had brought home in grade eight or nine that purported to show hidden messages in an advertisement for Canadian Club. Someone had carefully outlined the word SEX about fifty times in the ice cubes. This was the difference between policework and other fields that called for interpretive powers: in her line of work, what you saw had to actually be there.

"I didn't mean to be flip," said Andrew. "About your problems."

"Nothing's happened. They're not real problems yet."

"But the pain is real."

"It is."

He held his hands steepled over his glass. "What was it you wanted to talk about, Hazel?"

"I just wanted to see you. See how you were."

"Uh-huh. Are we eating tonight?"

"You're willing to spend an entire meal with me?"

"I put in thirty-six years. Dinner is nothing."

She waved down a waiter and took a menu, then passed it to him. "Order me whatever's good." He asked for two New York strips, medium rare. "Mother'll kill you," she said.

"She got you eating alfalfa?"

She hung her tongue out of her mouth. "My God, I'd kill for a bowl of alfalfa. It's just little pebbles and dehydrated water for me, Andy. I gotta get me a husband."

He smiled, recognizing her. She saw it in his face and a swell of raw fear went through her that felt like someone had jumped out at her. The base of her tongue was throbbing with it. She lived most of her days and nights now unaware of the kind of need that once animated her; the need for touch, for comfort. Her mind was home now, not her body.

"Andrew . . ."

"Oh-oh."

"We're out of practice. It used to be you could read my mind. But you can't now."

"Certain skillsets fade, Haze."

"You wanted to know why we were here, and I told you, but then we went past it."

He lowered his drink from in front of his mouth to his throat. "I don't remember that part of the conversation."

"And it even happened when you were here."

"Give me a hint."

"It was the part that should have triggered images in your mind of my eighty-seven-year-old mother carrying me to the bathroom."

The drink went the rest of the way down to the table. He made a little sound in the back of his throat. "Right," he said. "I did miss that part."

"But now I hear the sound of a coin rolling down a ramp."

His mouth, which had fallen open into a soft O, slowly closed. "God, Hazel. How can you even ask me this?"

"We don't have the money for live-in help, Andrew."

"And what about Marty?"

"Are you serious?"

He breathed out heavily. "Christ."

"I have another test coming up in two weeks. After that, they'll schedule me for surgery if I'm a candidate."

"I wish you'd told me it was this bad."

"Andrew, it's this bad."

"And what do I tell Glynnis when she says you're a manipulative witch who'd submit to surgery if she thought it would get me back under your roof?"

"Tell her you'll see her in ten weeks."

He laughed, but his eyes were not smiling.

On the way home, the pain was so intense that she drove with her fist balled up under her right buttock. There was a point there a chiropractor had shown her that was supposed to relieve some of the pain in her leg, but if anything, it only gave respite because it meant she wasn't sitting all the way down on the seat. She was a shade away from drunk now, probably over the limit, but still alert enough to drive. The surging pain in her back and leg counteracted some of the effects of the liquor.

They'd left the topic alone when the steaks came, but Hazel still had the impression that it had been left open. Before any final decisions were made on either side, she knew she was going to be sitting down alone with Glynnis, and she also knew what the suggested compromise was going to be. This appealed to her about exactly as much as having to manage on her own, but managing on her own after surgery was going to be impossible as opposed to unbearable, and unbearable was subjective. She already knew that if Glynnis agreed to her husband nursing his ex-wife, there was no way it was happening under the ex-wife's roof.

When she pulled into her driveway, she was in a black funk. She tried to think of a single part of her life that was in complete working order, a part she had control of, where she was actually exercising that control in a measured, intelligent way. Ahead of her: pills, bed, morning. Days scattered across a landscape of weeks and months.

"How's the one that got away?" said her mother, looking up from the television.

"Four decades of marriage is not 'getting away,' Mum."

"The *escapee*, then."

"He was fine."

Emily Micallef twisted away from the television to see her daughter better. Hazel recalled herself turning in the chair at the Laughing Crow, nervously looking around for her ex. "I'm having a moral dilemma right now," her mother said. "You need to take your medicine and go to bed. Your day needs to be over right now."

Hazel stepped into the living room. "What happened?"

"See, this is what I'm struggling with right now."

"Mother." Hazel followed her mother's sightline to the portable handset on the sideboard.

"You have a message."

"*Thank* you." She picked up the phone and dialled into the voicemail. "I'm the chief of police, Mother, not the president of the glee club."

"How come I'm the one who doesn't get your cell number?" said the voice of Howard Spere. "It's nine o'clock. In case you've ever been worried about how safe your personal details are on Bidnow.com, you may shop with confidence. They wouldn't give out your shoe size without a notarized release from your podiatrist." She pushed the 3 button to fast forward. Howard said, "Practically had to send them a blood sample before they'd —" and she pushed the button again until, at last, he informed her that the website's management had given in. The shipping address Delia Chandler had intended to use for the duvet cover she was bidding on the day she was murdered definitely was not Maitland Avenue in Port Dundas, Ontario. It was for a post-office box in Port Hardy, the last town before the Pacific, high up in the northern wilds of Vancouver Island.

13

Saturday, November 20, 3 a.m.

He continued driving through the night after resting at the roadside. His hunger pangs had turned into cramps, and every couple of hours, in the static dark through the countryside of central New Brunswick, he'd pull over and squat in the brush to push out a hot stream of shit into the dirt. It stank of bile. His body was starting to eat itself.

He drove the highway crouched over the steering wheel, his stomach tortioning inside his gut. He could smell his breath bouncing off the inside of the windshield: a combination of wet dog and tooth rot. An undertone of acid. He was very sick, he knew this now. He knew it could become an obstacle.

The headlights pushed along the road surface, the cracks in the old asphalt rolling toward him, an ever-changing, wild line moving like an endless branch under the car. He fought his exhaustion and reached inside his mind to find his brother, and he spoke to him. *Be with me now, my brother. Sit with me and look at this night with me, this beautiful, empty night.* He saw his brother lying racked in his bed. The flower of his beloved body, sudden in death's preawakening, ready to seed. *We are drawing the spore of your soul from one ocean to another, like a lace cinching us together.*

He pulled his head up suddenly and saw the road again, forced the car hard back onto the flattop, his breath as thin as the buzzing of a fly. He saw the pale, blinking light of the gas station that marked the halfway point of this road that slid through the dark between the two main highways. There lay the promise of a few empty calories, perhaps a toilet with a light, but he blew past it, pushing his foot down on the accelerator. He would be in Pictou by mid-morning as he'd promised. He'd emailed Tamara Laurence from a library in Quesnel to say he would arrive on November 20 at one o'clock in the afternoon, and he had been late only once in his travels, and early just once. He tried to keep his appointments to the minute. He had even waited in his car on the streets of Port Dundas for half an hour the afternoon he'd arrived to take Delia in order to be at her door precisely at three. He could not ask for the trust it entailed to join him in this profound chain if his first gesture was to break his word.

His stomach folded over on itself and he had to stop again. He stumbled out of the car and hurriedly pulled his black pants down around his ankles and shat into the gravel, heard the explosion of pebbles underneath him. He cleaned himself, and in the rising steam he smelled meat and he carried the soiled tissue around to the front of the car and held it up in front of his headlights. It was drenched with blood.

He drove through the rest of the dark in a stew of dreams and agony, but when he saw the ocean at eleven o'clock in the morning, his stomach settled like a storm lifting and he was able to sit up straighter behind the wheel. There was the compulsion to take any one of the little dirt roads that led north to the shoreline now, but by the map he saw that he would arrive at Pictou with only minutes to spare and he kept his eyes forward. Back in Amherst, a tang of salt had suddenly manifested in the air, an Atlantic salt, though, lighter and more acrid than the smell of the ocean from back home. Still, it woke him, thrilled him to the root. From a well he knew he could draw on when he had to, strength returned to his muscles. The sunlight processing through the windshield went into him like sugar.

He followed the curving road through the shore towns, their houses stacked up on the hillsides like loose teeth. Finally, he saw the signs for Pictou and went through the town to the other side, just where the forest began again. He passed a golf course and went right, bearing down toward the harbour. A huge plume of white smoke hung over the trees from the paper plant across the water, puffing out its scrubbed toxins over the inlet. Sulphur and salt in the air. He saw

Tamara's house as she'd described it in her message to him and he pulled over.

A hard surface, a sensation of rope. Gullivered. His eyes would not open. There was an irregular surface beneath him. Wood or straw. He pushed his eyelids together to moisten them and then forced them open and he was looking up at a stucco ceiling inlaid with rough planks. The air was cold on his face. Someone had tucked a heavy blanket around his body and the weight of it was somehow immobilizing him. His mouth was crusted, and he lifted his hand to wipe his lips and heard the dull clack of a tangle of tubing that, to his great surprise, he had pulled up with his arm. He was attached to something; he turned his head slightly upward and saw a metal stand behind him. Two bags, one with a clear liquid, the other containing blood. A transfusion. Someone was saving his life, a great transgression: the blood of strangers. He managed to lift his shoulders and he craned his neck forward to see it was not the blankets that were holding him in place, but cloth straps over his shins and his pelvis. They were ratcheted tight by means of belt clasps cinched against the surface of the bed.

This was not a hospital, however. A house. He was in a basement. The lights were dimmed, but through a doorway halfway down the wall on his right, he saw a quiet yellow glow. He called out and something blocked the light momentarily and the door opened. A woman stood in it with a burning cigarette in one hand

and his gun in the other. The room was warm, but she was wearing a sweater and a thick burgundy shawl lay over her shoulders. She was as thin as a crack in a wall. "You're a dangerous man, aren't you, Simon?" she said.

"Where am I?"

"You drive up right on time. I watch you from the window, you go to the back of your car, open the hatch, and drop like someone's cut the legs out from under you. Half-dead behind your own car. You were hunched over a leather kitbag *full* of neat things." She held the gun up. "This for one. Although I found the hatchet and the hammer interesting backup. I guess hatchets don't jam."

She came farther into the room and sat at the foot of the bed. She moved with great difficulty and when she sat, her knees and hips crackled. "You're Tamara," he said.

"You'd better call me Dr. Laurence for now. I could get into a lot of trouble for doing what I'm doing. But I'm already in a lot of trouble, so what the hell. Death removes your hospital privileges anyway, doesn't it?"

"Why am I restrained?"

She tugged on one of the straps. It barely moved. "Who knows what you might do to me if you weren't restrained, Simon."

"You're frightened of *me*?"

"I wasn't until I found your medicine bag. Then I started to wonder what I'd signed up for."

He struggled against the ties until he was almost sitting up. He felt a tugging under the covers in his groin. "You shouldn't be smoking, Tamara."

She laughed in disbelief. "I know. It's bad for me. Look, I want to know what you were planning to do once you got here."

"I was going to kill you. You know that. That's why you invited me here."

She shifted on the bed to face him. Her eyes were set back in her head and the smoke drove them farther away from him, as if she were wearing a veil. He was finding the farther east he went, the closer his suppli-cants were to the edge. He was arriving in the nick of time. "I signed up for mercy. Or at least I thought I did. What is all that shit in your bag?"

"Medicine."

"Since when did the healing arts include hand-to-hand combat?" She coughed heavily.

"Release me, Tamara."

"I thought that was *your* job."

"Tamara."

"You're not wearing any pants," she said. "You've got a tube up your prick. A catheter. Didn't want you wetting my rattan."

He lay back down to take the strain out of his lower back, looked at the tubes in his arm again. The one in his hand delivered the clear liquid. The blood was flowing into a port on the inside of his arm. "I gather you're having second thoughts," he said.

He heard her get up and leave the room, then re-enter. She put his medicine bag down on the floor beside him and opened it. "Take me through this," she said, remov-ing a couple of glass vials from within. "Foxglove?"

"I've done nothing to deserve being held prisoner."

"This is like, herbal digitalis, right?"

"It's for my heart."

"Or someone else's. This stuff can stop you like a clock." She tossed it back into the bag with a clink and took out a vial of powder. "What's this?"

He strained over his shoulder to look at it. "It's a fungus."

"Shrooms, huh? What's it do?"

"It sedates."

"How much of this to kill a person?"

"Not a lot. Look . . ."

"No, *you* look, you fucking sicko." She stood up with his kit and tossed it into the corner of the room. He heard something inside the bag shatter. "I thought you were some kind of shaman. But obviously you're a right fucking lunatic and I don't know how many people have fallen for your –"

"TAMARA." His voice filled the room and covered her up. She fell silent. "If you'd like to stand there speculating on the evil I represent, then go right ahead. But given that I can't pose much of a threat in the position I'm in, perhaps you'd be willing to let me address your issues."

"*Address my issues?* I'm a bag of cancer, Simon. A tumour with a face on it. What's to address?"

"You can't go about killing people even if you have their permission," he said. "It's a crime. And given that I'm committing crimes, I think it best to at least hide my purpose. I deliver a painless death in the name of something quite profound, Tamara, and then, if I think it advisable, I cover it up another way. I leave no trail but the one I am laying down and the one that you've asked to follow."

She laughed now. "Do you give this speech to all your victims?"

"None of them seem to require it. But you, in witnessing my weakness now believe me to be capable of a great insult. You invited me here, Tamara. To be a part of something. What is it to you that my methods seem strange? Either you want to join us, or you don't. Whichever, you'll still die. I only offer an alternative."

"An alternative to death."

"An alternative meaning."

She was silent a moment. He remained on his back, looking upward. He had the desire to pull the tubes out of his arm, but he wanted to bring her back. He had no one else in this area to call on: it was Tamara followed by Carl Smotes in Trinity Bay and then he was done. She said, "So just let me get this straight. You've been showing up at people's homes, gently euthanizing them, and then, let's see, committing unspeakable desecrations to their dead bodies. Is that right?"

"Sometimes," he said. "I would be breaking my word to all of you if I got caught. Would that not be worse?"

She thought about it. He was aware that she was shuttling from anger and disbelief back toward where he had met her. She was almost with him again. "So what were you going to do to me?"

He raised himself back on his elbows so he could look at her. She was sitting in a chair on the other side of the room, her shawl pulled tight across her chest now. "I would have made you some tea. Something to settle you.

Then I would have examined you to ensure your physical body was complete —"

"Complete."

"Yes. As I said in my messages to you, only those who are whole in body can be a part of this. Whole as God made you."

"I've had about fifteen pounds of tumour removed from my body."

"I'm more concerned with surgeries of vanity, Tamara. Stomach tucks, breast enlargements. I want a body as God intended it to be. I make room for some things: tonsils . . . tumours."

"What about a new heart valve?"

His own heart sank. "Have you had a valve replaced, Tamara?"

"No. I'm just asking."

"It would probably be too much. Is there something you want me to know?"

She shifted in the chair. It seemed to creak as much as her body did. "After the tea, then what?"

"I'd make a tincture of some kind. It's always different. An opiate in your case, to help you deal with your pain, followed by something to stop your heart."

"And then what."

He stared at her, willing her to tell him she didn't need to know, but she calmly returned his gaze. "In your case, Tamara, I was going to remove your arms and legs."

She blinked at him a couple of times and then broke into a broad, if nervous, grin. "Really? How were you going to do that?"

"I have a flensing knife in the car. I don't keep it in my kit. The blade's too long." He watched her face. She wanted it all. "Before rigor mortis sets in, I'd take your limbs in my hands and pull hard to loosen the joints. It's easier to cut through the ligaments and cartilage if the joints are pulled apart manually. Then I'd slice through your arms just below your shoulder sockets and your legs just below your pelvis."

She swallowed. "And what are you going to do with my arms and legs?"

"I'm going to put them in the oven, Tamara. It's going to look like a madman was here. Just like you said."

She pushed herself up to standing with difficulty and approached the bed. "But you're telling me you're not a madman."

"I'm no madder than you. I'm suffering the pains of death, but they have not made me mad." She stood at the side of the bed, her hand playing over one of the cloth straps. She slipped a forefinger under the steel latch that locked the clasp beside his shin and flipped it. He felt the belt loosen and she tugged on the cloth to pull it through the clasp. Then she loosened and removed the one on his pelvis. "I'd like to be taken off your medicines," he said.

"You took four pints, you know. I had to steal them from the hospital's blood bank. Luckily I'm not afraid of being fired." She screwed closed the port on his arm and tied off the saline going into his hand. "You were practically hollow when I found you."

He grieved the thought of having taken sustenance from unknown bodies. "I'm not supposed to take aid. I'm to go forth on my own strength."

"You'd be dead, then," she said. He felt the plastic stent slide out of the vein in his hand. "This last one is going to be a bit uncomfortable." She reached down below the sheets and he felt her hand, warm, on the inside of his leg. With a sudden motion, she ripped tape from his inner thigh and then he felt the painful sensation of the catheter being drawn out of his urethra. He felt as if he were pissing fire. "Sorry," she said.

Like most of the houses he entered, Tamara Laurence's was spotless. He could never be sure if these houses had been cleaned for his benefit, or if a terminal illness naturally made people want to simplify their lives. He appreciated the respect it showed, whether for him, or for the coming of these many ends.

Her home was modest. Furnished in a spartan manner, with a couple of adornments about: an antique clock, a painting over the fireplace. No mirrors anywhere. He sat at her bare dining-room table as she put her kettle on and then came to join him. The hair she'd lost over a failed course of chemotherapy had grown in again, although it was new hair rather than old growth: it was soft and loose and thin. It had grown long enough that she could tie it back into a short ponytail that came down only to the nape of her neck.

At the table, he put his medicines down in a row and explained in what order he would apply them; what effect she would feel, and how long it would take for these compounds to go to work. When she'd thrown his bag, she'd smashed the bottles of slippery elm and henbane, the latter of which he used quite a bit, and he told her he was improvising now. She handled the individual jars with care, turning them in her hands. "Do you find people are ready when you come to them?"

"Most are," he said.

"Are they frightened?"

"They have different reactions. Some are scared, but most of them are resigned. Or even relieved."

"I'm not relieved." She set the vials back down on the table in the order of their use and regarded them. "I liked being alive. I was good at it. I loved well and I worked well. I was good at my job."

"You helped a lot of people."

"An oncologist with cancer," she said. "*That's* not ironic. Good thing I didn't choose a career in explosives." She laughed and drew the first vial back toward herself. "So, this one for tea, then?"

"Yes," he said.

She brought it into the kitchen with her and he told her how much of it to put into a cup and how much water. She stood in the doorway of the kitchen with the cup cradled in her hand.

"I'd like to die in bed. Is that okay?"

He followed her down the hall to her room. She put the tea down and undressed with her back to him. He had intended to release her from this obligation, in return for allowing him to continue. However, here she was, standing beside the bed, her body giving off a greyish glow, like a stone lit from within. She turned to face him, and he took in the bones pushing out from under her flesh. There were patches of liverish marks pocked over the surface of her belly and chest. She sipped her tea.

"I can't tell if you're examining a patient now or actually looking at a woman."

"When I ask people to undress, I look for scars."

"You didn't ask me. But I did it anyway."

"I had thought twice of it," he said. His palms were buzzing. "But here you are."

"I want to be seen. I want to be lit up in my last seconds on this planet."

She had answered her own question – he was looking at a woman – and in doing so, he was reminded of all the things he had once been, when he'd been merely a man. He'd had no mission at all then, and life had been a series of tasks that he fulfilled with passion or without. Now it felt as if he were bodiless; he had lost his corporeality when his brother had fallen ill. He was a memory of his brother's body that had been projected into the world.

But this woman reminded him that he had once wanted to express himself differently.

"I'm guessing you're not the kind of guy who'd go to bed at a time like this," she said.

"I'm sorry."

"You'll hold me at least. Right?"

He said he would. He collected the two remaining vials off the dining-room table and returned to her with them. "This is just pulverized ginger," he said, holding up his right hand. "It's a natural antiemetic."

"I guess the other one is pretty nasty, then?"

"This is ground amanita. It's a fungus."

"My ex was an avid mushroomer. I know it."

"Destroying Angel, some people call it."

"Another exciting Sunday night in Pictou," she said, and she sat down on the edge of the mattress, naked and shrunken, and looked up at him with her ruined face. He felt suddenly uneasy, but he was too focused to understand what it was that had distressed him. It was a cloud passing over the sun. "Let's get going," she said.

He sat with her and administered the belladonna. She grimaced at the taste of it. He started to mix the amanita into what remained of her tea, but she grabbed his wrist to stop him and began to weep. He held her against him, anxious now to be done, to be separated from her love of life and her agony at leaving. "I never prayed," she said. "I don't believe in any of that. What's that going to mean when you try me out on your God, Simon? He's not going to be happy."

"You can come home whenever you're ready, Tamara, even now."

She released her grip on his wrist. The belladonna was already flowing through her – in a dose that high, it was almost enough to put her under. She took the amanita from his hand and walked back into her kitchen, where she poured a dram of the remaining hot water out of the kettle and into a glass. "How much?" she asked him.

"The equivalent of one grain is enough." He watched her take twice that and mix it into the water. She took his hand and drew him down the hallway. In the bathroom, she cracked a syringe and filled it.

"Let's not fool around now," she said back in the bedroom. He tied her off and she expertly found the vein in the crook of her elbow and put the needle in. They both watched the milk-coloured liquid vanish into her arm. "You said you'd hold me. I want you to get out of your clothes."

"Tamara —"

"You'll never have to do anything I ask ever again."

She reached for the button at the top of his shirt and he pulled away from her. "Get in," he told her, and she drew back the covers and lay down. He undressed. In the bed, she folded herself around him.

"Tell me how long."

"Minutes."

They lay there in silence. "Turn off the lamp." In the dark, he listened to her breathe.

He remembered what had disturbed him ten minutes ago. "It's not Sunday night," he whispered to her.

"You got here yesterday, Simon. You were out for more than a day. You almost died."

He tried to sit up, but she held him there against the bed. She said, "I'm still here." And then, "Still here," and ten seconds later, she was dead in his arms and it was Sunday night and his plans were destroyed.

He was furious with himself. He carried her form down the hall, cooling against his nakedness, and to the stairs and brought her into the room where he'd lain insensate for twenty-four hours, hours during which he was supposed to have been making the final leg of his journey. He was meant to be in Trinity Bay tomorrow afternoon, celebrating completion, but now he was nowhere.

He'd followed his own rules, but instead of consecrating himself, he'd woken up to find himself fallen. He had not been right about his own strength.

He laid her on the bed in the basement, her body as light as air, this very body that had pressed itself to him, held him back, spoken to him, begged him. He dressed and went to the car and got his flensing knife out from under the back seat and dragged the tin cup through the stinking fluid he'd driven across the country. In the house, he tilted her head back and poured his brother's blood into her, the blood of Victor Wente out of Oyen, Alberta, the blood of Elizabeth Reightmeyer from Norway House in Manitoba. Robert Fortnum, dead in Hinton, spread in her. Delia Chandler, Port Dundas, graced her. Father Price blessed her. He filled her with the congregation.

He could not cut her, though. She'd transited through human in his presence. She'd been too much with him. His weakness had brought him here and he could not bear it. He knelt by the edge of the bed she lay on and brought up the curving blade of the flensing knife, seeing the little light that was there in that now-silent place glint in the steel. He gave a cry of anger and brought the blade down hard against the bottom knuckle of his right thumb. With two levered sawing motions he had the thumb off and the digit, as if possessed of its own life, sprang free from him and bounced across the floor. He cried out in agony and doubled over onto Tamara Laurence's cold belly, cradling the ruined hand between them.

14

Thursday, November 18, 6 a.m.

ADDICT RAMPAGES THROUGH WESTMUIR
COUNTY screamed the headline of the *Westmuir Record*
Thursday morning. Ray Greene was on Hazel's doorstep
first thing, the proof that all hell had broken loose
drooping in his hand. "I thought I'd better be the one to
show you this," he said. Hazel held the door open for
him as she stared at the newspaper. She couldn't move.

"What the good Christ do they think they're doing?"
she said.

Her mother was descending the stairs behind them.
"What who is doing?"

"Your Honour," said Greene, not joking, and bowing
ever so slightly. "The *Record* has decided to try out
investigative journalism."

"I can't believe this," Hazel said. "There's going to
be a fucking riot at the station."

"I'm Mrs. Micallef to you, Ray," said Emily, heading into the kitchen. "Or Emily, if you must. Let's put on some coffee."

Hazel didn't look up once as she walked down the hall behind Ray Greene. "I guess I really pissed off Sunderland," she murmured. Greene said nothing. The entire paper was devoted to the murders of Delia Chandler and Michael Ulmer. All their sources were "unnamed," but the facts, such as they were, were correct. It was their conclusions that were going to cause all the trouble. "Ray, they think the Belladonna is killing for drugs."

"Yeah, I know. Because who has better drugs than the dying? Painkillers, sedatives, hallucinogens, you name it."

She fell into a kitchen chair, her forehead in her hand. There were pictures of both houses. Someone had even got a photo of Ulmer being loaded into the morgue van. "I thought we took Ulmer out a back door."

"It's not that easy to disguise an icewagon driving down a side street, Hazel. Someone followed it. These guys did their homework."

She leaned in closer to an item on the second page. It had a picture of her cellphone box lying in a garbage can with the caption "Second Murder Jolts Chief into Twenty-first Century," and below it: "Questions? Call her on . . ." and there was her cell number for every last reader in the county to see. She shoved the paper violently across the table. "Great! Now they're infiltrating our bloody offices! They're supposed to be covering giant pumpkin contests for Christ's sake!"

Emily put down two cups of instant. "I don't under-stand how you can be surprised, Hazel."

"I suppose I'm not."

"After I left your father, they asked the good people of this town if I was the kind of role model they wanted in city hall. They asked that question all the way to the polls the following year. 'Will she abandon you next?' they asked. And you're surprised they took a picture of your garbage can?"

Hazel pulled one of the coffee cups toward herself, still holding the paper in the other hand. "What is it about this place that inspires such vindictiveness? Everything about Westmuir County is a little pastoral dream except for the fucking newspaper."

"Don't forget the guy butchering the terminally ill," said Greene. "He's not so nice either."

Emily opened the fridge door. "You hungry, Ray? I can make you a couple of fried eggs."

"Actually, I am kind of hungry. Thank you, Your Honour."

Emily shook her head, smiling, and turned to the stove. "Can I make a suggestion, officers?" They waited. "Hold a press conference. Now. This morning. Not a statement on the station-house steps, Hazel, a press conference. Eat and get into the station house and act like public officials who care. Grant an interview to Gordon Sunderland. Let him sit down with you."

"The son of a bitch."

She turned from the stove with an egg in the palm of her hand. "Take control of the story. Don't make the mistake I made." They heard the crack and sizzle in the pan. "They'll ambush you if you don't invite them in first," she said.

"It's too late for that," said Hazel.

Her mother swirled the pan on the stove. "It's *almost* too late," she said.

The station house was full when they got there, but it was ruled by a fearful silence. Hazel walked out into the pen and held the paper up. "It's eight o'clock right now, people. At nine, we're having a press conference. Set this place up and get anyone in here who wants to hear what I have to say." She checked to make sure her cell-phone was still off and retired to her office, surrounded by the only people she was certain hadn't betrayed her.

"I have to sit down," she said when the door was closed. She couldn't make it behind the desk and sat down in the visitor's chair in front of it. Greene, Wingate, and Sevigny tried to arrange themselves in front of her. "We've lost complete control of this thing."

Greene reached toward her and gingerly slipped the paper from her grasp. He folded it and put it down on the side table. "What are you planning to say at this press thing?"

"I'm going to remind them what community service means."

"Should we maybe get Eileen in here? Go over some talking points?"

"Eileen knows how to lead school trips, Ray. I know what needs to be said."

"She *is* the community liaison officer."

She squared to him from where she was sitting, her

head tilted to one side to take the sting out of her middle back. "I was using the term *community* euphemistically, you know? When the local paper decides to cash in by printing the results of their own investigation, the concept of neighbourliness is not one that interests me all that much. Just make sure Sunderland is here in one hour."

Greene went back into the hallway to organize the conference. Hazel hoped he wasn't going to warn Community Liaison Officer Eileen. She turned to the other two men in her office.

"Do you need an aspirin, Skip?" said Wingate.

"I need a bottle of Scotch and a long blade, Detective," she said. "But let's focus on what's possible. Catch me up on what's going on out there."

"Crime scene and morgue photos are coming in. We're getting a lot of digital images, and Detective Spere is calling in some favours out west anywhere we're getting resistance."

"We're getting resistance?"

Sevigny spoke up. "Little jugs," he said. "I spoke to some of your people and told them to keep the details of the investigation as vague as possible." He made *vague* rhyme with *bag*. Hazel pushed herself up from her chair, ignoring the shooting pain that went down through the back of her thigh and into her foot. She felt she had better be behind her desk now.

"Who gave you permission to talk to 'my' people, Detective?"

"I offer my apologies. But I felt it was important."

"You're a guest here. You don't give orders."

"I apologize. However —"

She waved her hand at him to stop him from speaking, and lowered her head. She hoped it appeared as if she was thinking, but sitting in the padded chair behind her desk had introduced a pain so exquisite that she was worried she would cry out. She raised herself minutely out of the chair and then slowly lowered herself back down. She breathed out slowly. "The both of you know what Howard's people found on Delia Chandler's computer, yes?"

They both nodded.

"Then what do we do about it?"

Sevigny came forward tentatively and pulled one of the file folders on Hazel's desk toward himself. He flipped it open and removed a sheet. "The delivery address is a post-office box which is part of a rural array about five kilometres out of Port Hardy," he said. "It's registered to a 'Jane Buck.'"

"That's clever," said Wingate.

"I don't care who it's registered to," said Hazel. "What do we do about it? I'm presuming, Detective Sevigny, that you'd advise against deputizing someone in the Port Hardy PD to go and look into it for us."

"If you want to maintain control . . ."

"Someone has to look into it." She turned her eyes on Wingate, who visibly shrank back.

"Oh no," he said. "You can't ask me to do that."

"I *would* if we had the budget for it. But I doubt Ian Mason will spring for four flights in the same month." She flipped her fingers out at the paper in Sevigny's hand. "James, you take that and go lock yourself in an empty office – if you can find one – and track down this Buck woman."

"She doesn't exist," said Wingate. "This is the Belladonna's idea of a joke."

"He's not killing John and Jane Does, however, is he? So go find out. And if it's a dead end, I expect you to push through into the woods. Find out who's checking that mailbox."

Wingate left with the sheet in his hand. Sevigny watched him go and then turned back to the desk. Hazel's fist was balled up on the blotter. He stepped to the file cabinets on his left and opened the bottom drawer. "That's a cliché, Detective," said Hazel. Sevigny hesitated, then lifted his hand to the drawer above, opened it, and took out a bottle of Jack Daniel's. He brought it over to the desk. "Can you guess where I keep the knife now?"

"When you talk to your newspaper men," he said, "remember that you are really talking to your staff. Tell them that nothing can get in their way now. They will find him. They will win."

She opened her hand to accept the bottle as he slid it to her. "They make you guys pretty confident where you come from, huh?"

"My mother had eleven children, *Chef*. I learn to make myself heard." He looked at his watch. "I'll be in the audience listening."

"I'll try to impress you, sir," said Hazel with a crooked smile.

She sat with the bottle in her hand. The palpable sensation that things were truly coming apart was upon her now. Perhaps at one time in her life, when she was just starting out, a case this big would have been a dream come true. Eager people all around her, the puzzle pieces dropping into place. But the most pressing thought she was having right now was that here a person she'd known her whole life was dead. Underneath the grandeur of the crimes they were now confronting, under the cipher of this man's intentions, was the simple thought that Delia Chandler had been murdered. Dead bodies were the coin of the realm for every entertainment she knew of: television mysteries, Hollywood bloodlettings, celebrity magazines, pocketbooks (what her father would have called "dime-store" novels) – all of it was so general that it was as if everyone lived in the midst of a bloodbath. But here she was, so-called chief of police of a small-town police detachment, a woman who'd seen bodies, the profoundly unentertaining facts of death, and she still couldn't wrap her mind around the fact that someone had passed through *her* town and drained a woman she'd known her whole life of almost every drop of blood in her body.

She twisted the cap off the bottle and poured a full inch into her coffee cup. She thought twice of making her desk drawer the new hiding place, but if Sevigny ever thought of bartending out of that drawer, it would look even worse than if the bottle *had* been in the bottom drawer of the file cabinet. She got up and hobbled over to the file cabinet and put the bottle into the bottom drawer. He'd look there last. But, she felt quite certain, he'd look there eventually.

Exactly one week ago, November 11, she'd been on the phone in this very office arguing with Patti Roncelli, who with her husband, Steve, was the owner of the town's main pizza joint, and she had been telling Patti if she didn't want kids congregating in the parking lot in front of the pizzeria at midnight, revving their engines and smoking, that she should consider closing earlier. Patti had wanted her to come down and issue some warnings, but apart from annoying the hell out of Patti Roncelli, these kids weren't doing anything wrong.

It had been the height of excitement the week of November 8. When she'd hung up the phone that Thursday one week earlier, the Belladonna was completing his drive from Pikangikum and was almost in central Ontario. The next day, he'd keep his appointment with Delia Chandler, and the present would change shape for them all. Hazel doubted that there were many kids cluttering the Roncellis' parking lot this week.

She drained her coffee and looked down at her notes. She was going to remind these people what their supposed jobs were. There was a knock at the door. "Come," she said.

PC Eileen Bail popped her head in. "Can I have just a moment?"

Hazel sighed. "What is it, Bail?"

Her community liaison officer crept around the door and closed it behind her. "Inspector? Listen, I know you're awfully mad about the paper this morning —"

"Are they here?"

"Yes, but —"

"Is Sunderland here?" Bail, one finger in the air, paused and said nothing. "Fine. What were you going to say, Eileen?"

"We have a slightly larger crowd than you did on Monday, but Sunderland is not here. Not yet. I just wanted to say, Detective Inspector, that you have every reason to be upset, but I don't *feel*, necessarily, that you need, that this press conference, which I think is a very good idea, that you need —"

"That I need *what*?"

"It's not the right place to make your feelings known."

"I see," said Hazel. "And what is it the right place for, Eileen? If I were to ask you?"

"Well, ma'am, maybe you should give them something. A bit of information. How the investigation is coming."

"Why would I compromise our investigation by telling that pack of dogs what we're doing?"

"If you told them something that wasn't entirely untrue, I think they might go away and write something less damaging than what was in today's *Record*. That's all I'm thinking."

"Well, thank you, Eileen. I'll take your views into consideration."

PC Bail seemed to bow slightly and then she walked backward to the door and left. Hazel looked down at her notes again. She counted nine exclamation points and there were six words underlined. With a grunt of disgust, she swept the papers off the desk and into the garbage can.

—

At nine o'clock, she stood at the front of the conference room. They'd taken away all but the table she stood behind for the purpose of meeting the press. About thirty people had piled into the room. She saw most of her staff, including the officers seconded from Mayfair, as well as a number of faces she didn't recognize, which she presumed were members of the Westmuir County's fifth estate, if not beyond. She scanned the room for Gord Sunderland's face, but he had not yet arrived. Coward.

She nodded to Eileen to close the door at the back of the room, and then Hazel brought up that morning's edition of the *Westmuir Record* and held the front page up for all to see. Eileen locked eyes with her, and then Hazel put the paper down on the podium in front of her. "Good morning, everyone," she said. "I'm sorry it's taken this long to have a proper Q&A, but judging from this morning's paper, the time would seem right to correct some misperceptions. First off, we don't know what the person who perpetrated these two crimes wants. It's not drugs, however. He left a bathroom full of sedatives and painkillers in Michael Ulmer's house. I'll tell you a few things we *do* know." Several of the reporters opened their notebooks. "The victims are not related in any way. We don't know why the killer chose either of them. And we don't know where the killer is or where he or she is headed."

A reporter from the Hoxley monthly raised his hand. She thought his name was Aaron. "Excuse me, Inspector, but is there anything you do know? I mean, was the cause of death the same in both murders?" There was a low murmur from the rest of the room and Hazel shot a glance at Eileen.

"Well, Aaron —"

"Actually, it's Geoffrey. The *Hoxley News*."

"I apologize. Michael Ulmer was attacked with a hammer, but the killer cut Delia Chandler's throat. So in both cases, the victims were violently assaulted, but not the same way."

"Were the injuries the victims sustained from these assaults the cause of death in both cases?"

"We're still investigating these matters, Geoffrey. I can't comment any further about that."

"Well," continued the reporter, "is it true that both victims admitted the killer, and that there was no sign of a struggle at either scene?"

They'd done at least some of their homework, she thought. It was impossible to tell what this one already knew and what was based on hearsay. She cleared her throat. "As you all know, crime scenes are complex. We collect a lot of information, not all of which is pertinent, and it can take time to figure out what happened. It may seem as if there wasn't a struggle in a crime scene, for instance, but then you have to consider did the perpetrator clean up after himself? Did he attack the victim too quickly for a struggle to take place? Was the victim restrained in some way? At this stage, we still can't say what happened in these two houses." She saw Bail nodding imperceptibly.

Patricia Warren put her hand up. "Is it true that Delia Chandler was sexually assaulted?"

Hazel's attention snapped back to the room. "What? Who told you that? That isn't true." She watched the young woman writing. "Miss Warren?"

"Yes?"

"I don't want to see in the *Beaton Examiner* that *DI Micallef denied the victim had been sexually assaulted.*"

"Of course not," said the young woman.

"Who told you that Delia Chandler had been sexually assaulted?"

"No one. I wanted to see what you would say."

Hazel laid her hands on the podium. "This press conference is over, ladies and gentlemen. Thank you for coming." More hands shot up, but Bail and Jamieson began to herd the dozen or so reporters out of the room. As the crowd was filing out, Hazel noticed Gord Sunderland trying to get into the room. "Let him in," she said. "He can stay."

In a moment, the room was empty and Sunderland turned to watch Bail close the door silently behind him.

"I missed the festivities."

"Just some of your future scriveners airing their brilliant theories."

"I have a couple of my own."

"Oh, I know," she said, coming out from behind the podium with the paper in her hand. She gave it to him. "If you suffer from pain," she said, "lock your doors. Bar them, too. Depression? Anxiety? Board up your windows: there's a killer on the loose. Are you an elderly person suffering from arthritis? Keep your phone handy to call for help. And if you have cancer? Maybe a brain tumour? If you're dying and already in fear? Arm yourself. If you hear someone at your door, shoot first and ask questions later. He might be after your Vicodin."

"It's nice to talk at last," said Sunderland.

"Where do you get the balls to call yourself a newsman, Gord? You're just an old lady talking over a fence."

Sunderland folded his paper in half and tucked it under his arm. "Let's see now. Delia Chandler was killed in the morning or afternoon of November 12. Michael Ulmer two days later. It is now November 18. In the intervening week – probably the most terrifying week in living memory for the citizens of this county – not only have you failed to address the public once, but you have conducted an investigation that falls well outside of your jurisdiction entirely on your own, and in secret. It's not me you're going to have to answer to, Inspector, it's the East Central OPS and probably the RCMP, but I'll get to write about it. I'm not worried about the future of my institution."

She walked out around the front of the table. "If you publish a word on Monday that isn't about pie-eating contests or the best way to deep-fry a turkey, I'm going to have you charged with interfering with police business. Anyway, shouldn't you people be hard at work on your annual Christmas story? Everything you published in today's paper was wrong except for my bloody phone number."

"Have you checked your messages yet?"

"There's a switchboard here. People know how to reach me if they need to."

"If you *want* to be reached, you mean." She stared daggers at him. "You don't get to tell me what I can publish, Hazel."

She took a step toward him. "Let me fill in some of the numerous blanks for you, Gordon. He's a serial killer. Port Dundas and Chamberlain were just two stops on the tour. He's killed at least sixteen people from British Columbia to Quebec, and he's smart. He's put space between his bodies, and he's chosen his victims carefully. Or I should say, they've chosen him." She reached out and snatched his notebook out of his hand. "He doesn't give a shit about their drugs, Gordon. He has all the drugs he wants. He's after something much harder to get."

"What?" said Sunderland quietly.

"I'm not telling you that." He flicked a look at his notebook, and she tossed it over her shoulder. It flapped like brief applause and hit the ground behind the table. "There's no one to warn. He's issued some kind of invitation and they've accepted it. The only person who's going to benefit from your shots in the dark is *him*. All it's going to take is one red flag, and this guy goes to ground. Do you want to be responsible for that?"

"You can't run this thing alone, Hazel. Not from a frigging station house in the middle of nowhere."

"We're getting help."

"From where?"

She dug her cellphone out of her vest pocket and turned it on. It sang its hello and then went into a cacophony of alarms. She had fifty-eight messages. She dialled a number. "Can you come to the conference room, please," she said and put the phone away, then limped behind the desk and retrieved Sunderland's notebook. Sevigny entered the room. "Here's some of my help," she said. She handed Sevigny the notebook and watched the reporter take in all two hundred and ninety pounds of the newest member of her temporary force. "Doesn't 'Adjutor' mean 'judge,' Detective?"

"Yes," said Sevigny.

"I was just giving Mr. Sunderland an exclusive. And I wanted a witness to hear me say that if he publishes a word of it, he can expect to hear *your* rebuttal."

Sunderland's eyes were shuttling back and forth between the two cops. "You can't threaten me, Hazel."

"I'm not threatening you, Gord. Publish whatever you want. Detective Sevigny, show Mr. Sunderland out, please."

Sevigny held the door open and Sunderland left, casting a look over his shoulder.

When Hazel was sure Sevigny had frogmarched Sunderland out of the station house, she went back down the hall toward her office. Wingate was waiting at her door. "Jane Buck is real."

"You're kidding me."

"No."

"Come in."

He closed the door behind him and consulted a couple of sheets of paper in his hand. "She's a housecleaner. She lives in Port Hardy, but she's on a local route. Which means she gets her mail delivered to her house. This postal box is nearly ten kilometres from where she lives."

Hazel thought about it for a moment. "Well, that would fit. Whatever these people are shipping to her, she doesn't want her neighbours seeing it."

"But who is she, then?"

"That's the million-dollar question." Sevigny knocked at the door. "Come," she said. "Did you take our friend back to his offices?"

"He is not scared of you," said Sevigny.

"How about you?"

"He is scared of me very much." He smiled, faintly. Sometimes complex threats didn't work at all. She was liking this Sevigny more and more every minute. "Can I just say, *Chef*, of your press conference –"

"No, you may not," she said. "Jane Buck is real. Let's focus on her."

"She exists?"

"Fancy that: a real clue," said Hazel.

James repeated to Sevigny what he'd told her. Sevigny nodded, listening. "Then we have to go out there," he said.

"How fast do you walk, Detective?"

"I will fly," he said.

"I have no budget."

"Thank God," said Wingate.

Sevigny was holding up his hand to show he would brook no debate. "My mother goes to Fort Lauderdale every winter for the past twenty years," he said. "She gives me the flight points every Christmas. I have two hundred and ninety thousand air miles."

Hazel whistled. "It sounds like she could use them."

"She flies Boxing Day every year. They accept only cash or credit on Boxing Day. I will use the points. I will fly to British Columbia."

Hazel was shaking her head in wonder. "You're far from home, son. This is a hell of a thing to offer another jurisdiction, you know."

"I am in no hurry to return to my hometown of Sudbury."

She traded a look with Wingate. "Well, thank God for blackout periods, then," said Hazel, and she rose to shake his hand. "How quickly can you set this up?"

"I'm going back to my hotel to pack now. I'll call you from Vancouver Island."

They watched him turn on his heel and leave the room smartly. Wingate was still watching when the door clicked shut.

"*He's* not afraid of flying," she said to him.

"He's not afraid of anything," said Wingate.

Hazel lowered herself carefully into her chair. "We're about to turn the corner on this thing, James. I can feel it."

There were thirteen crime-scene pictures. Dead faces set in grimaces and shouts. Faces howling, whistling, moaning, crying, hissing. They pinned them to the wall and stood back. It was a silent opera of ghosts.

"Let's start talking about these faces," Hazel said to the room. Her assembled forces stood before her, looking from one terrible image to the next. "What is happening in these pictures?"

One of the officers from Mayfair raised her hand. "They just seem scared to me. Rigor mortis sets in faster when people are frightened at the time of death."

"Jack Deacon says these people didn't die with their mouths like this. The killer did it after the fact."

"Is it possible the perp has put something in their mouths?" said PC Forbes. He shrugged after he said it, worried about being wrong. "I mean, to hold their mouths in these positions?"

"It's possible," said Hazel, "but I'm not sure the method is as important as the meaning of his actions. These mouth shapes are the only thing that links these killings, except for the fact that everyone he killed was terminally ill. And we know these people *invited* him to their homes."

"How?" said the same man.

"We don't know that yet, but –" Wingate had entered the room. She returned her attention to the force. "James Wingate went to a reserve near Dryden and got confirmation that the victim knew the Belladonna somehow, but until we know how the killer communicated with his victims, all we have are these pictures."

"Communicating," said Ray Greene. He was standing behind her, beside the pictures. "Whatever is happening in these pictures, it's obvious these people are making a sound."

"If they are, then most of them are making different sounds," said Hazel. She went over and pointed to the victim from Fort St. John in British Columbia. His mouth was in a loose, open O. "This is Gary Dewar, discovered by his son on October 11. He was hanging from a chandelier with a plastic bag over his head. Look at him. Then look at this woman" – she pointed at the victim from Wells, B.C., named Adrienne Grunwald – "her mouth is puckered, like she's blowing a kiss. These two were killed four days apart. And then, this man, Morton Halfe, he was killed on the twenty-eighth or twenty-ninth of October in Eston, Saskatchewan, and his mouth is identical to Dewar's. Why? What do these two victims have in common? *Do* they have anything in common? Is this a code? Come on, people, think out loud!"

There was silence from the room.

"If they are sounds, Inspector," said the dispatcher, PC Peter MacTier, "then how do we find out what they are?"

She looked out onto a small sea of faces unconsciously making the puckers and dead grins on the wall behind her, and a thought came to her.

] 15 [

Her name was Marlene Turnbull and Howard Spere had driven her from Upper Watertown. He brought her into the conference room against her will, it seemed, and she hung back, looking behind herself, an ankle-length green parka swirling around her boots. She'd done nothing wrong, but some people act guilty in the presence of the law, and Hazel marked it. Howard pulled a chair out for the girl, and she sat at a table with the pictures of the Belladonna's victims splayed over the tabletop. Her black hair covered her face so they couldn't see what she was thinking, but she had one hand over her mouth and the other wrapped around the Styrofoam cup of coffee she'd been given when she came in.

"These are thirteen pictures we've been able to track down over the last couple of days," said Hazel.

"These people were all killed in the last six weeks or so all over the country."

"My God," said the girl behind her hand. With the other, she was gingerly pushing the pile of pictures apart with a single fingertip, trying not to touch them. She was no older than twenty-five, her round, open face pinched at the temples where her tiny glassframes fit too tightly. "Who did this?"

"We don't know. But I think you may be able to help us," Spere said. Turnbull looked up, her face white. Whatever she was feeling culpable for, Hazel thought, this was the moment she thought it was going to be named. She hated Howard for pausing. "You work with the deaf," he said at last. "We think these people are making sounds with their mouths." The young woman nodded absently at the pictures. "Can you figure out what they are?"

She looked bewildered to be told that her expertise and these pictures might have anything in common. "No."

"Shit," said Spere.

"I mean, I could give you some possibilities, but you can't get a positive phoneme out of a picture. I'm not the person you want for this."

Hazel came forward. "Marlene? Do you deal drugs?"

"What?"

"Maybe you have unpaid parking tickets? Or you drive a stolen car."

"God no!"

"We didn't bring you in to accuse you of anything. I don't care if you smoke pot at an expired parking meter, not right now. We looked you up because you lipread. That's all. Whatever else you've done, it doesn't exist in this room, not right now." Marlene considered her for a moment, blinking. Her eyes seemed huge behind the tiny lenses. "We good?"

Marlene jutted her chin forward minutely. Hazel took it for a nod that didn't want to look like assent. The girl turned back to the pictures. "We call ourselves 'speechreaders' now," she said. "Not lipreaders. There's more to talking than lips, that's why." She turned one of the pictures to herself. It was the morgue photo taken of a woman named Elizabeth Reightmeyer. The Belladonna had driven a twelve-inch spike through her ears. The bulge in her facial structures made it look as if a train were travelling through her head, just beneath her cheekbones. Reightmeyer's lips were rounded into a loose pucker. "Like I was saying, it's hard to make a phoneme positively from just a picture. Take this lady, okay? She could be making a plosive here –"

"A what?"

"A hard sound. A *puh* sound or a *buh*. Or she could be going *mmm*. It's impossible to be sure. And these ones, with their mouths closed . . ." She stopped for a second and looked away. "Sorry. It's hard just to look at their faces."

"Take your time," said Hazel.

"If you can't see the oral cavity, it's more difficult. People use all the parts of their mouths to make sounds. There are eighteen distinct parts." She looked to Spere to see if this was useless information to him, but he was expressionless. "Um, there's the tongue and the teeth and different parts of the palate and the throat – it's a lot more complicated than you'd think." She studied some of the images more closely, her face a mask of horror. "Okay, like this lady. See her tongue?" She was pointing at Delia Chandler's chalk-white face. "Her jaw is slightly open, the back of her tongue is pressing against her upper teeth and the tip of her tongue is against the roof of her mouth. So she's probably making a *luh* sound."

Spere looked closely at the picture. "Could it be a word, though?"

"If the word is *luh*," she said.

"What about *the*? Could she be saying *the*? Or *then*?"

Marlene put her fingertip against the image of Delia's tongue. Her hand was shaking, as if she were touching the dead woman's actual face. "You see how the tip of her tongue is behind her teeth?" They looked. "This is an alveolar lateral approximant. I mean, that's what it's called. It's nothing like the *thuh* sound."

"English."

"It just means that the *luh* is made with the air flowing over the sides of the tongue with the tongue touching a zone directly behind the teeth. The *thuh* sound – it's completely different. The tongue's lower against the back of the teeth. And the air goes over the middle of the tongue." She touched another picture, this one of Robert Fortnum, from Hinton, Alberta. "You can see this guy's tongue is curved a little at the edges, but this lady's tongue is flat. You can try it."

"I'll take your word for it," said Howard Spere, but Hazel was quietly making the two sounds.

"I see your point," she said. "One makes a rumble, the other a hiss."

"Sort of," said Marlene. "The bottom line is you can't see air in a picture." She pushed her chair back, relieved to have been no help at all. "I'm sorry I can't —"

"Well, hold on," said Spere. "So there's nothing you can give us at all?"

"What these people are doing, if they're doing *anything*, could be any number of sounds, and sounds are not what I'm trained in. I'm trained in speech, and speech is made up of movement, sounds running together. To me, these are just scary faces. Can I go now?"

Hazel had been staring at the face of Morton Halfe (sixty-six, Eston, Saskatchewan, Lou Gehrig's disease, shot through the heart); she was certain he was saying *wuh*. "Hold on, hold on," she said. "Speech."

"Yeah. Like I said, what I do is called speechreading."

"Oh my God," Hazel said. She grabbed Spere's arm. "Don't let her go anywhere."

She burst out of the office and into the hallway. The entire pen stood as one. "Wingate. Greene. The French guy —"

"He went to B.C.," someone shouted.

"Fine, Wingate and Greene, where are they? Get them for me. Now!" A flurry of motion, and within ten seconds both men appeared.

"What is it?" said Greene.

"Come with me."

Back in the conference room, Marlene Turnbull already had her parka on. "Tell them what you told me."

"About what?"

"About what speech is made of." The young woman looked around uncomfortably – she was certainly not pleased to see the number of policemen in the room double – but before she could recall what she'd said, Hazel was rotating her hands in front of her chest as if she was trying to catch her breath. "Speech," she said, "sounds. Two things. She said that sounds, individual sounds, are made with your tongue and your teeth and your lips and all kinds of things, right?"

"Yeah . . ."

"But speech, listen, speech is these sounds put together."

"Very good, Skip," said Greene, "you've invented talking."

"*No* . . . listen! These faces: they're not just making sounds. They are, on their own, making a sound, each of them. But that's not what the Belladonna is doing. He's making them say something. One thing. All together."

They looked to her and then to the pictures, and as if magnetized, they moved toward the table where the images still lay.

"A word," said Hazel, "or a phrase. They're each contributing a sound to it."

Marlene reached down and straightened the pictures into a line. She took her parka off and laid it over the back of the chair and sat down again.

"Are they?" said Spere.

"Could be."

"Can you see what it is?"

Wingate was leaning over Howard Spere's shoulder. "How would we even know what order to put them in?"

Marlene Turnbull suddenly swept the pictures back up into a pile. "I need a phone," she said.

Hazel pawed at the various piles of forms and papers that had built up on her desk during the week. The last thing she wanted to do was explore the varied misdemeanours, complaints, regulatory conflicts, licensing queries, and job applications that made up a normal week in Port Dundas. She doubted her ability to make sense of any of it in this state. It was as if the agglomeration of meaningless things that comprised a life in policing were merely the stuff of distraction while something truly awful made its way toward you — perhaps over the distance of many years. The one case that made you, that destroyed you. This was it. I'm retiring after this, she thought, and then remembered that her mother had been mayor of Port Dundas until she was seventy-nine, and would have been mayor longer if not for the newspapers. Sixty-one was going to look like early retirement. But then she could blame her back for it if she had to.

She'd got Ray to silence the ringer and the alarm on her phone, but nothing could stop it from its endless blinking. It lay at the corner of the desk signalling her like a madman in a crowd — *Over here! Over here!* — and she picked it up and flipped it open. She had seventy-one messages now. She somehow navigated her way to the voicemail function and the voice said "You have . . . seventy . . . one . . . new messages. Press one to –"

She started listening.

"Officer Micallef," said seventy-one. *Detective Inspector* she said to herself, "I was in Matthews Funeral Home on Tuesday, and there was a guy standing alone at the back, and I –" Erase.

"I'd like to know when we can expect to be able to –" Erase.

"Inspector, it's Paul Varley from Kehoe. My brother-in-law is a policeman in Owen Sound, and if you guys need any –" Erase.

Sixty-four: a man wondering if the municipality would reimburse him for extra locks he felt he had to put on his door.

Fifty-five: A spiritualist.

Fifty-one: "This would never happen in Winnipeg." *No, but Norway House and Gimli, sir, try those places.*

She'd erased down to twenty-two, writing down three numbers she felt she had to call back, and then she heard an anxious voice: "Inspector, I'm sorry to keep calling – I'm sure you've turned off your phone by now, but please do call us."

This same voice had left five messages. Hazel skipped down to the first one. It was from a woman named Terry Batten. She lived in Humber Cottage. Hazel listened to the message and took notes. Three minutes later, she was in her car with Wingate in the passenger seat. "When was this?" he asked.

"This Batten woman says it was the fourteenth of November. Early in the morning. Ulmer was killed around noon that day. It's only twenty-five kilometres to Chamberlain from Humber Cottage."

She was driving a hundred and sixty with the lights flashing. When they went through the small towns that dotted the 121, she turned on the siren. The towns went by like identical siblings lining a parade route. They were there in just under two hours.

Wingate knocked. "You guys are allowed to speed, I guess," said Terry Batten.

"It's the only reason to become a policeman," Wingate said.

She opened the door wide and they entered. There were sandwiches on a tray and coffee, for which they were grateful. Terry's sister Grace was there, but she wouldn't look them in the eye. Terry called the child in from the yard.

"This is my daughter, Rose," she said.

She shook hands with both of them. The girl's cheeks were red from running around. "How do you feel, Rose?" said Hazel.

"I'm excellent."

The two sisters traded a look.

"Should she not feel 'excellent'?"

"She started having seizures back in February. They didn't know what was causing them. By June, she was having them almost every hour."

"How old are you, Rose?"

"Eight." The girl took one of the egg sandwiches. "Those are for our guests, Rose."

"But I'm hungry, Terry."

"Let her eat," said Hazel, casting a glance at the girl's mother. "Come sit with me, sweetie." Rose hopped up onto the couch beside her, her legs almost reaching the floor. She ate through the middle of her sandwich and put the crust down on the sidetable. "Your mother tells me you were a very sick girl."

"Terry worries a lot."

Hazel looked up at the girl's mother. "It's a phase," said Terry. "I ask myself, would I rather have a sick child, or a disrespectful one?"

"It's your name," said Rose.

"I know."

Hazel patted the girl on the knee. "How did you get better, Rose?"

"Auntie Grace brought me a witch doctor."

"He told me he was an *herbalist*," said Grace MacDonald. "Or a naturopath or something like that."

"Maybe he said *psycho*path," said Terry.

"Anyway," continued Grace, "he came into the diner at sunrise that morning and we got to talking. I had no idea . . ."

"We're not saying he's our guy, you understand," said Hazel. "And even if it is, you've done nothing wrong. Rose," she said, turning back to the child, "this is James Wingate. He works for me. He's going to show you a drawing someone made, and I want you to tell us if you think it's the same man."

"Jim is short for James," said Rose.

"You can call me Jim if you want." Wingate opened his notebook to the sketch Wineva Atlookan had made of her father's visitor. "Take your time."

"That's a terrible drawing," the child said. "You people sit tight." She bounded off the couch and ran upstairs. Hazel put her mug down.

"She hasn't had a seizure since . . . since that man was here," said Terry Batten, opening her hands in wonder. "She'd have ten or twelve a day, but since last Sunday morning . . ."

"That's remarkable," said Hazel.

"It is."

"Do either of you know what this man did with Rose when he was here that morning?"

"He wouldn't let us into the room with her. He asked for hot water —"

"Hot but not scalding, please," said Grace, as if she were having a simultaneous conversation with someone none of them could see.

"And he closed the door. We heard them talking. Rose was talking about elves at one point, but I have no idea what went on in there. He came out after about forty minutes, and she was asleep in her bed. He shook our hands. She didn't wake up for about nine hours, and when she did, she was as sick as a dog."

"She threw up for thirty hours!" said Grace, coming back to them, and Hazel could see this woman was on the verge of cracking up.

"It's okay," she said.

"No, it isn't!" shouted Grace MacDonald. "We thought she was going to die! She had a fever of a hundred and seven. No one lives through that! I brought him here," she said, looking wildly at her sister. "He tried to kill her."

"Grace –"

"He could have killed us all." She put her face in her hands, and Wingate got up from the couch to guide her into a chair. "I invited a murderer into this house."

"You people are hysterical," said Rose Batten from the stairs. She held a hardbound scrapbook in her hands. "Honestly. He was a nice man, he just dressed funny." She went to her aunt and pulled her hands from her face, then folded herself into Grace's lap. "You stop that," the girl said to her quietly. She passed Wingate the book. "Jim, you can look at these if you want." He sat down again, opening Rose's scrapbook between himself and Hazel.

"She was always an artistic child," said her mother.

They flipped the pages. The girl had rendered her visitor in a number of poses. The drawings were stellar: she'd made images of the man in black ink and then coloured them. "Is it him?" asked Grace.

"Absolutely," said Wingate. "It's him." He held Atlookan's drawing of a long, thin man in dark clothing up against Rose's scrapbook. What had been a ghostly remembrance of a visitor seen from afar in the Pikangikum drawing was here a series of living portraits. Rose had drawn the Belladonna standing in her doorway, a phantom in a dark coat, his hands leaking from his sleeves. In another image, he was crouched down holding a weed in his hand. "That's mistletoe," said Rose.

Hazel touched her finger to that drawing. "Did he kiss you?"

"Uck, no," said the child. "Anyway, that's a silly application of a very important herb. The droods worshipped it."

"Who?"

"I think she means Druids," said Wingate.

"Droods," said Rose.

"He told you all this?"

"He made me tea out of it. It made me barf." The girl leaned forward and flipped the page. It was a closeup of the Belladonna's face. His eyes were set back in his skull, like little black beads. There were lines all over his face, in all directions.

"Did he really look like this?"

She waved her hands side-to-side over the drawing. "These are wrinkles," she said. She waved her hands up and down. "This is steam. He's holding tea."

"Can we take this, Rose? Just for a while?"

"*No . . .*"

"Honey, these people are trying to solve a very serious crime."

"They're not taking my precious significant drawing journal, Terry."

"I understand," said Hazel. "Maybe you could make one just for us, then. A drawing of the man who helped you get better. So we can see his face. Could you do that?" She saw the girl staring at the tray of sandwiches, and Hazel picked it up and passed it to her. Rose took two sandwich quarters.

"It'll take me at least fourteen minutes," she said. "Do you have that kind of time?"

Hazel could not help it: she laughed. "Honey, I have all day for you."

"Then I'd better get started," she said.

"What a fantastic creature you are."

The girl attempted a curtsy. "Thank you!"

She ran up the stairs. The four adults watched her in a bewildered silence. "I'm not going to say I preferred it when she was sick, because, Christ, I really don't," said Terry.

"I hear you," said Hazel. "Where's her father?"

"Long gone."

"Dead?"

Terry Batten narrowed her eyes. "I wish."

They raced home, lights and sirens, a blue, red, yellow, and white streak. Wingate sat with the girl's drawing in his lap, staring at it. She'd drawn him face front, his legs planted slightly apart, his arms slack at his sides. The coat was done up to his neck, and above it, the killer's pale, creased face stared out. His expression was one of calm expectation, as if he were waiting to hear the answer to a question. He did not look a danger to anyone. Wingate ran his finger lightly over the coat. At one point, he tapped a spot over the Belladonna's heart. "Did you notice this in her other drawings?"

Hazel tried to look at what he was pointing at. "What is it?"

"Just a couple of white scratches against the black of the fabric. I didn't really think anything of it until now. Do you think it's a tear?"

"We have his face now, James. I don't think a tear in a coat is going to be an identifying characteristic, do you?"

"No . . . but it's just odd she would notice it."

"She noticed everything. She was completely alive. *He* brought her back to life." She tapped the paper in

Wingate's lap. "What do you think of that? He's on a murder rampage and he stops to save a life."

"Yeah, I know. But maybe . . . maybe he *was* trying to kill her, and he botched it."

"James, do you really think this guy is capable of botching anything? If he wanted this girl dead, she would be dead, her mouth twisted into some alien hoot, and her mother and aunt chopped into catfood. No: he stopped and saved this girl. He knows how to do such a thing." She looked out over the road, shaking her head. "My God, he's magnificent."

"Magnificent?"

"I think you were right about him," she said. "That he 'cares.' He's motivated by love. He is. He believes he's doing something good. This trail of dead bodies is a monument to something. And those mouths, those mouths, James, they're going to tell us what they're a monument to."

"I want to thank all of you for your hard work, and especially for your discretion," said Detective Inspector Hazel Micallef. The entire force, local and seconded, was standing in the pen. "I know a lot of you feel the way I do about this case: you've never seen anything like it in your lives. We've seen how something this disturbing can change a place. People are frightened. People we've known our whole lives seem different to us. Accept that, but try not to change yourselves. You were here to do a job, and you've done it brilliantly. Now I ask you to do the hardest thing: go back to your regular lives. All you men and women who came to us from Mayfair, it's time to go home. Your aid was indispensable. But I ask you not to speak. The time to tell of what you saw will come. But you've seen how irresponsible speculation can be a major setback in an operation like this. Keep your own counsel. And as for those of you who were taken off your desks to assist this week: please go back to your dockets. There's a week of catching up to do.

"We now have fifteen pictures, including the Atlookan images, which I understand came in this afternoon, right, James?" Wingate nodded. "Good, now, judging from the blood samples we have, we're short two victims. But we can work with what we have, and what we have is all due to your hard work. So again, I thank you. As you were."

The Mayfair cops gathered their things and began to file out. Many shook her hand as they went and thanked her for letting them be a part of the investigation. *Thank me,* she thought, *for putting pictures in your heads that will give you nightmares for years to come.*

When the place was cleared out, it looked empty. The nighttime shift began to filter in. She tried to dismiss Greene and Wingate, but they weren't hearing any of it. Greene was eating an Oh Henry! for supper. "Where's Sevigny?" she asked him.

He peeled the candy like a banana and spoke without looking at her. "He left on a four o'clock flight out of Toronto. He had to take the dog down to the airport."

"You speak to him?"

"Yeah, we traded recipes."

In her office, she took Rose's drawing out of a file folder and put it down on her desk. "A kid did this?" said Greene. "Maybe we should hire her."

"What's your problem, Ray!"

He stared at her for almost five full seconds, his eyes dead. "Nothing."

Wingate stepped between them. "When are we going to hear from Sevigny?"

Hazel looked at her watch. "He won't be in Port Hardy until late tonight at the earliest. He's got to get a car and then he could be up north for days. By now, the Belladonna's at his next stop, or even the one after. Ray's chart shows at least two more killings after Havre-Saint-Pierre. One somewhere in Nova Scotia, and one in PEI, Newfoundland, or both. We don't have time."

"*Anyway*," said Ray Greene. He sat in Hazel's chair to find the garbage can under her desk. He threw his candy wrapper at it. "I don't think we can tip our hand now." He was looking at Rose's drawing again. "I don't think these eyes miss a lot," he said.

"When does Ms. Turnbull's friend get here?"

"She's getting on a bus first thing tomorrow," Hazel said.

"Buffet-style policing," said Greene, leaning back in Hazel's chair. "I like it. A little bit of this, a little bit of that. All four policing food groups."

"Get out of my chair, Ray."

He took his time standing up. She felt like she was going to grab him by the shirt and wrench him out of it. "This is what I'm saying: don't you think it's time to stop accepting the kindness of strangers and catch this guy?"

"You're the one who wanted me to be open to 'the new.'"

"I meant cellphones," he said.

"Well, you'll be thrilled with me then," said Hazel. "Because our lipreader's friend is coming here with some kind of supercomputer that makes instant cartoons. Miss Turnbull even said it was *cool*. So show me some respect."

"Cartoons," said Ray Greene, his mouth pursed into mock wonder. "Well then, we must be close."

"Sorry," said Wingate. "Cartoons?"

"What kind of state is your apartment in, James?"

"*My* apartment?" She waited him out. "I'm still in boxes."

"Stash 'em," she said. "When our guest arrives, we'll be working from your place."

Wingate gave Ray Greene a look. "Hey, I didn't know anything about this," Greene said. "It's a whole new world for me, too."

"That's my home, Skip. I like to go there *after* work."

"Look," said Hazel, "I don't want to be a bear about this, but Sevigny is right. You weren't here for my press conference, but you wouldn't have liked it. Only God knows what kind of shit people are going to think up. It's star-chamber time now. I want privacy with this woman, and you live alone, James, so it's got to be you. When her bus gets here, I want you to pick her up at the station, call us, and we'll all meet you at your apartment."

"You do things differently here," he said.

"I'm making it up as I go along, James." Greene made a huffing sound. Hazel held the door open for Wingate, but stood in it when Greene started to leave. "What the hell is your problem, Ray?"

"I don't have a problem, Hazel. And if I did, I'm sure it wouldn't be anything a few dozen extra people couldn't solve."

"You think this was a job for you and me and a couple of duty officers?"

"No," he said, "it was a problem for the RCMP. But since we took a pass on —"

"Don't start with that again, okay?" He shrugged, like he couldn't be bothered to get into it with her, but this gesture upset her even more. "You let me know when you want to sit behind this desk, with no commanding to help keep you out of the soup, and a whole county scared out of its wits, okay?"

He squared to her, the look of sarcastic defiance gone from his eyes, replaced with a glint of real anger. "When did you lose faith in your own abilities, Hazel? Huh? When did you lose faith in mine? Because I don't recall a time when we couldn't handle what happened in our own town."

"This isn't just in our own town any more."

He flung his hands into the air. "Yeah, and now I got fucking Howard Spere in my rearview mirror all day long, a rookie with theories, appointments with lipreaders and comp-sci grads, and about twenty strangers in uniform stalking the halls of my station house. I haven't had a drink out of my own coffee mug in three days —"

"I'll get you a new mug, Ray —"

"But the thing is," he said, running over her, "is that any of it would be bearable if not for that wild goddamned look in your eyes. You look like someone who heard her name called from a tree."

She'd never seen him this pissed off. At anyone. They'd had disagreements in the past, but she could always joke her way out of it. Ray Greene was one of the easy parts of her life, one she could always predict. She stepped toward him and he backed up to the door, and she found herself raising her hands and showing him her palms, as if to demonstrate she was unarmed.

"You're angry."

"Sure . . ." he said uncertainly, aware of her proximity.

"I understand," she said. "But the thing is, you and me, we could never have done all this on our own. We needed the help. Which is not to say that I could have got through any of this without you."

"Well, thanks for that."

"No," she said. "Listen. You're the one I don't worry about, Ray. I know that might sound a little callous right now, but I keep an eye on a lot of things here. Not you, though. I tell myself *you're* okay, and usually you are." He was looking away from her now. "I thought it was trust, Ray, but if you're telling me it was neglect, I'm sorry for that."

He put his hand on the doorknob. "All right," he said. "I appreciate you saying that." He wouldn't look at her. She'd embarrassed him. "I should get home for dinner. I'll see you at James's."

She let him go and went back to her desk. The chocolate wrapper was on the floor beside the garbage can.

Had he done that on purpose? She knew after today that she'd be searching for the truth behind everything he said. She stared at the desktop, lost. Had he accepted her apology? She knew for certain he wasn't going home. They simulcast the trots out of Fleetwood down at the track at seven o'clock.

She looked at her watch: it was almost six. She needed a drink and a big serving of starch. She dialled the house to negotiate a meal with her mother that might include a potato, but then she remembered that it was Friday, Emily's regular poker night. She was on her own.

The next morning, at nine, her mother was still asleep. She didn't know what to think about the fact that her mother had more exciting Friday nights than she did, but there it was. Emily Micallef still knew how to party. Hazel knew these poker nights were rye-soaked affairs, and on the last Saturday morning of every month, her mother got up well after she did.

This was going to be a day off if it killed her. The girl from Ottawa wasn't going to be in town until late in the day, and there was nothing worth doing but being alone. She put the coffee on and changed into a tracksuit. She couldn't run any more; her back would not allow it. But she had to get the air moving through her or she would bog down in everything that was closing in on her now. She drove the road leading to Little Bass Lake and walked down Stott's Lane toward the water in brisk, short steps. Wet leaves lined the roadway, great heaps of them piled up in gleaming, orange mounds. It smelled of the end of fall: no longer crisp or sharp, just wormy, dank, and heavy. Winter on its way to bring it all to stillness. Only a month earlier, it had all looked like it was about to burst into flame. Now it had guttered.

It was an unpaved road with only a few houses on it. No one had any neighbours here, and there wasn't a window between the main road and the lake that offered a view of anything but trees. The sun was already strong, but the air was frigid. She kept her hands in the pouch of her sweatshirt and pulled her cap down over her eyes. She could hear a motor around the next bend.

It had been more than three weeks since she'd spoken to either of her daughters. Emilia was in Delta, B.C., occupied with her new husband, a man she'd actually said *thrilled* her. Hazel couldn't imagine. She was not close to her eldest; she had the feeling Emilia sided with Andrew, and it wasn't something she wanted confirmed. Being happily married to a thrilling man probably predisposed her to think of Andrew as the victim here. Probably he was, she thought, she just didn't need her first child underlining it for her.

As for Martha, she hadn't spoken to her since she'd called in tears to say Scott had broken up with her. Hazel didn't know what kind of advice to offer a broken-hearted girl of thirty-three. She didn't believe in "other fish," and right now wasn't sure she believed in the sea, either. But she was certain her silence was hurting the girl. She was a fragile plant, that one. In need of just the right amount of water and light. She believed, without knowing for certain, that Andrew was staying in regular touch with her.

Her own mother had never wavered from tough love, and it was all Hazel knew. It had worked with her, or so she thought; she presumed the person she'd become was satisfactory. No doubt others would disagree. She saw in her mind's eye her youngest daughter's weeping face, the blue veins under her fair skin like shadows of those wet streaks.

She made her way around the curve and saw a woman wielding a leaf blower. Clumps of dead leaves shot into the air as if alive. The woman was aiming everything at a huge orange tarp. Hazel waved as she strode by. Her own yard was spotless; she realized she didn't know if her mother had raked the yard, or if she'd hired someone. It wasn't just the distractions of the previous week that left these strange lacunae in her mind: she'd been this way since the divorce. As if a thin line of light shot out from her and illuminated only the near view of things. It was a good quality if your job was to solve problems. It didn't lend itself so well to living, however, which came at you from all directions.

The road sloped downward past the last house. She leaned back a little, and as she did, small sparkles of pain burst in her sacral area. Sometimes it felt as if someone had cut out her lower back and replaced it with a steel plate. She slowed. The lake lay behind the trees at the bottom of the road, constantly moving, shape-catching, and redistributing light. It looked alive. If she'd wanted to live in the midst of murder and suffering, she could have had a job in Toronto, she thought. She'd stayed here in Westmuir County because it promised an ordered life. It had kept this promise until a week ago, but even so, she felt tricked. She'd undergone almost forty years of marriage only to have it come apart, and maybe the events of this November were meant to send her off at the end of her career under a similar cloud.

She walked out onto one of the docks at lake edge. But for the soft lapping of the water, there was silence here. Martha was almost certainly still abed in her apartment in Toronto. There was no work to keep Hazel's mind off what had happened to her daughter. Hazel imagined her wandering the rooms of her apartment in her pajamas for an entire day. Emilia was probably still in bed too, but Hazel turned her mind from that thought and walked back up the dock to the road.

When she got home, her elderly party animal of a mother was still in bed. The house smelled of coffee. Hazel poured a deep mug of it and checked the time: it was almost nine-thirty. She dialled Martha's number and let it ring until her heartsick daughter picked up.

Her day off effectively ended at three that afternoon.

"We got another one," said James Wingate on the phone. "A priest in New Brunswick."

She'd been making soup. Her mother had eyed the concoction with suspicion and said, "How much eye of newt have you got in there?" It was minestrone. Hazel hadn't cooked a thing in nearly a month.

"He's one of ours?" she asked Wingate.

"PC Ashton has a digital photo. It's the Belladonna."

"We should get that picture to Marlene Turnbull right away."

"I took the liberty of sending it to her already, Skip. I hope that was okay."

She was pleased but said nothing.

"Apparently . . ." continued Wingate, who seemed to be consulting some notes, "the victim, Father Price, is an 'obvious voiceless palatal fricative.'"

She scraped something off the bottom of the pot. Her mother called from in front of the television: "Smells burnt!"

"I know, Mother!"

"Should I call back?" said Wingate.

"No. Where's Marlene's friend?"

"She's due in at five."

"Fine, call me then." She put the phone down.

"You know what they say about a woman who burns soup," said Emily Micallef from behind the kitchen wall.

"I don't want to hear it, Mother."

"They say that woman doesn't know the first thing about making soup."

Hazel had an instinct that she might want to save some energy for the evening. She turned off the ruined soup and went upstairs to bed and curled up under the layers of blankets. No matter how many blankets were on the bed, though, she still had to wear socks. She dropped off almost immediately but within moments, her mother was knocking at the door. "Good Christ," she said.

"Officer Wingate wants to know when they can expect you," her mother said, opening the door.

"I told him five. Go away."

"It's six-thirty, Hazel."

She threw the covers off and grabbed the alarm clock off the bedside table. Three and a half hours had passed. She did not feel rested in the least.

James Wingate opened his door and offered her a look that said *You are going to make this up to me.* The room behind him was dark, but she could hear Ray's voice and another one, a high, excited voice twittering on about something she couldn't make out. Like any room where police business is happening, this one smelled of coffee.

Wingate's place looked like he was selling it, rather than moving into it. Although the lights had been dimmed, she could see there was nothing on the walls and nothing on the floors. A bookshelf stood beside the living-room window with only one shelf filled. The door to the bedroom was closed. Greene and their guest were sitting at the kitchen table behind an L-shaped counter that extended off the wall beside the stove and defined the cooking and eating area as a rough, square horseshoe. The table was littered with metal boxes and wires, all of which led to an open laptop casting its bluey light against the wall behind them. How her world had gone from rotary phones and two eight-year-old computers in the pen to this glossy high-tech litter on James Wingate's kitchen table . . . she was never going to make sense of it. She tossed her jacket over a chair and squeezed Greene on the shoulder, passing him a paper bag. "I brought you some flowers," she said, and he slid a bottle of bourbon out of the bag. "You know how I love flowers," he said.

She held her hand out to the woman sitting behind the computer. "I'm Jill," said the woman, extending an impossibly long hand to Hazel. "Jill Yoon." She was a tiny woman, small enough to be folded into a suitcase. "This is very exciting," she said.

"We're talking about a serial killer," said Hazel.

Yoon racheted her energy down a rad or two, as if Hazel were messing with her high. "Okay, that part is pretty sad. But I think I can help you guys."

"I hope so," said Hazel, moving around to look at the machinery. Was this stuff even machinery? Is that what they called *information technology*? It still looked like a pile of machines to her, but she was aware, faintly, that these steel boxes and gleaming windows could form an opinion about her. Maybe that's why she didn't like any of it.

A shimmering green light emanated from a box placed there. It was a projector of some sort, and they'd taped a large white linen napkin to the fridge to catch its light. "What is that?" She was looking at an image of a human head made out of green, criss-crossing lines. It was hollow. The lines sizzled against the linen like something unstable.

"We call this a ligature," said Jill Yoon. "It's like an electronic mannequin or something like that."

"Wingate, maybe get her a beer for this part," said Greene, and Wingate reluctantly opened the fridge. The green light tracked across its contents, lines shooting over his milk cartons and condiment bottles. He took out a beer and handed it to Hazel.

"Where's Spere, by the way?" he said. "Wouldn't he want to see this?"

"Howard works for Mayfair," said Hazel.

"Ah," he said, nodding approvingly. "Members only?"

"He'll know when he needs to know."

Wingate shut the fridge, and the head contracted back onto the frame of the napkin. "Why do I think he's not going to like that very much?"

"Because he won't," said Hazel. "But he's my problem, not yours."

"Forget Spere, come sit," said Greene, patting the seat beside him. "You gotta get a load of what this lady can do."

Hazel screwed the cap off the beer and, glancing around with a look of suspicion, she sat in the chair. Jill Yoon picked up a digital camera from the tabletop. "I need three pictures of you, Inspector. One with your mouth closed, one with your mouth open wide, and one of your tongue."

"Just do it," said Greene. Hazel self-consciously did as she was told. When the pictures were taken – three quick flashes – Yoon connected the camera to her laptop. "Now we read a little," she said. She handed Hazel a thick book and a microphone.

"You want me to read poetry?"

"The computer needs to know how you make sounds," said Yoon.

Hazel read:

"I, who erewhile the happy Garden sung
By one man's disobedience lost, now sing
Recovered Paradise to all mankind,
By one man's firm obedience fully tried

Through all temptation, and the Tempter foiled
In all his wiles, defeated and repulsed,
And Eden raised in the waste Wilderness."

Ray clapped robotically. Hazel put the book down. "We're going to catch this guy with poetry?" Wingate swept the book off the table and went to put it back on his shelf. "That's *yours*, James?"

"Previous tenant must have left it here," said Wingate.

Jill Yoon sat down at the computer. She typed something into her keyboard. There was a kind of high tension in the room. "You ready?" she asked Hazel.

"She's not," said Greene, "but show her anyway."

Hazel turned to face the fridge and as she did, an image of her own mouth blinked into existence on the hollow green head, across its eyes. It was almost as wide as the head. She heard Yoon clicking behind her, and the mouth shrank and began to move down the ligature until it reached the zone where a human mouth would normally be seen. It seemed to snap into place. Yoon stabbed a button on the keyboard and the head with Hazel's mouth breathed in. She narrowed her eyes at it. "What the hell?"

"Watch."

"Today is the twentieth of November, a Saturday," said Hazel's mouth in her own voice. Her lips had moved as if she'd been filmed speaking the words. Her own mouth fell open. Jill clicked a few more keys and Hazel's mouth breathed in again. "*Aujourd'hui, c'est le vingtième novembre, un samedi.*"

"Holy shit!"

"That's just a silly computer trick," she said, "the French. I can borrow the English phonemes for it."

"How did you do that?"

"The three pictures I took establish tongue-size, lip-width and -length, and the volume of your oral cavity."

"Yuck," said Greene.

"The program works out all the other measurements." Yoon got up and flipped on the kitchen lights. "It's called digital visetics. The program translates phonetic units of speech into visual ones: visemes. Usually we use it to train the deaf for speechreading. But it can go the other way, too."

"You can take our victims . . ." said Hazel.

Jill Yoon nodded. "Come," she said.

Hazel went to stand behind Yoon. On her computer screen was an array of characters, beside which was a rudimentary mouth shape. She explained that each symbol corresponded to an English phoneme, and that each phoneme had its own viseme. Yoon clicked on a series of these characters, and they appeared in a window at the top of the screen. "Look on the fridge again," she told Hazel, and Hazel turned. She heard a click, and her computerized mouth went into a silent spasm.

"What was that?"

"I typed in a random collection of phonemes and uploaded them to the ligature as visemes. Do you want to hear what you said?"

"Sure," said Hazel.

The face on the screen breathed in. Then it said, "Aah-haay rrrrr lemmbebepp gyuh." Yoon fiddled with her settings, and then the face said, "Aah-haay? Lemmbe*bepp* GYUH!"

"That's the most sensible thing she's said all week," said Greene.

Hazel turned back to Jill Yoon. "How long do you need?"

"A while. I presume your pictures aren't lit for the kinds of measurements I need. I have to scan and clean them to make sure I get accurate readings. And then it's going to take time for me to make sense of the results. The computer knows about fifty thousand words in English, so I can get it to search for words that use those visemes in some order. But the program doesn't have any use for grammar. It knows words, not sentences."

"But I just spoke a sentence," said Hazel. "In English and in French."

"The program didn't know it was a sentence. It thinks it's just a series of sounds. You're going to give me some pictures, correct?" Hazel looked over at Wingate and he nodded. The pictures were in the room. "As Marlene told you I'm sure, a lot of visemes could be more than a single phoneme. Like, if you say, 'Where there's life, there's hope,' to a deaf person, he might think you said, 'Where's the lavender soap?' There's context in real life, so that a person should know if you're talking about taking a shower or taking your life, but my program is going to translate your fifteen pictures into a lot more than fifteen phonemes, and then it's going to have to strip them for possible word units, and then after that, someone's going to have to figure what kind of order they should go in."

"How's twenty-four hours?" said Hazel.

"It's a start."

"It's probably all the time you're going to get. James, give her what she needs."

Wingate came forward with a thick departmental envelope. "We just added Winston Price. The priest from Doaktown. So that's sixteen in total now." Yoon took the envelope in her hand and unwound the string. She pulled the pictures out and laid them on the table. Already all three officers were getting their coats. "Take whatever you need for food," said Wingate. "The fridge is full."

Yoon was shaking her head.

"You shoulda saved your money," said Greene. "She just lost her appetite."

] 16 [

Sunday, November 21, 3 p.m.

Sevigny had spent the last of Saturday afternoon in a rented car parked at the side of Sewatin Road on the outskirts of Port Hardy. He'd flown there from Vancouver and spent the entire flight over the water in a state of bliss. The whitecaps below had appeared as dustings of sugar from that height, and it had put his mind off what could lie ahead of him.

In Port Hardy, he rented a car and went to his motel, a tiny wooden structure off the main drag. His accent seemed to prove to the lady at the desk there that he'd come a long way for some sportfishing, and he let her believe that. He was in plainclothes to keep the curiosity factor at a bare minimum.

He showered and went into town to buy some food, and then drove north out of the townsite. Four kilometres down Sewatin Road, he pulled over and watched, choosing a spot about a hundred metres away from a bank of gleaming postboxes that lined the road like a scale model of an industrial warehouse. He was unlikely to catch anyone checking their mail on a Saturday afternoon, but there was no point in delaying. He'd likely be in this spot all day tomorrow and Monday as well. The box assigned to "Jane Buck" was one of the ten oversized ones along the bottom of the array, and in the five hours he sat in the car sipping coffee and eating apples out of a paper bag, he saw all of two people come and go. Every half hour he turned on the motor for ten minutes to reheat the car; it was six degrees outside. No one unlocked box number 31290. When it got dark, he went back to the motel, ate two large garden salads, and went to bed.

He returned to his spot at six the following morning. By two in the afternoon, not a soul had come by the postal array. He was freezing and running out of fruit. Then, at three, just as he was beginning to think he was wasting his time, someone came and unlocked 31290. It *was* a woman. There were two packages in her mailbox. She took them to her car and drove off farther down Sewatin Road. He followed at a comfortable distance, and she eventually turned north onto an unpaved road, followed that for four kilometres, and then turned onto a private lane where the grass had grown up through the carpath. From the road, he could see a small structure in the trees, a rough shack no bigger than a hunting cabin. He pulled his car over and got out in time to see her go behind the house. He went into a crouch and ran through the brush beside the driveway and up over the still-thick lawn to the side of the house. His heart was pounding.

He pressed the side of his gun against his leg as he side-stepped the length of the house. When he reached the end of the wall he could see the woman was keying the door to a small shed at the back of the property. She entered the dark space with the two packages and a moment later reappeared empty-handed. He twisted around into the open and drew a bead on her. "*Arrête!*" he shouted, forgetting himself, and the woman screamed. "Stop!" he said. "Step away! Keep your hands up front!"

The woman's hands flew into the air, and he rushed to her and spun her around, pushing her back against the shed wall, where he kicked her legs apart. "Don't hurt me! Don't hurt me!" she cried over and over as he patted her down.

"I'm the police!" he said. He'd forgotten in the midst of his anxiety that he was in plainclothes.

She was clean. He spun her to face him. "Please! What have I done?"

"What's your name?"

"Jane! My name is Jane! My ID's in the car –"

"You show me."

She walked in front of him, looking over her shoulder, and when she lowered one of her arms, he reached forward and slapped her under the elbow and she put the arm back over her head. At the car, he saw her purse sitting on the passenger seat and, keeping his gun level on her, he opened the door and took it out. "Show me," he said, handing her the purse. She fumbled in it and removed a cloth wallet. Her driver's licence was registered to Jane Buck. He looked at her and then at the picture. "This is really your name?"

"Who are you?"

"I'm asking the questions."

"But who are you? Why are you doing this?"

"Jesus Christ," he said and he noticed her wince. He dug his badge out of his back pocket and flipped it to her. She examined it and then looked up at him again and she seemed even more frightened of him. "Okay?" he said. "Now tell me who lives here."

"I just bring him his mail," she said, her whole body shaking.

"*Who?*"

"His name is . . . his name is Peter."

"Goddammit!" Sevigny shouted, throwing her things to the ground, "I'm not playing twenty questions, woman. Who lives here, and what have you got to do with them?"

"Peter Mallick! His name is Peter Mallick! I bring him whatever's in the mailbox. That's all."

"The mailbox is registered to you."

She narrowed her eyes at him. "How do you know that?"

"I'm the police, lady, I showed you my badge. I know what I know. Open that shed again."

She hesitated but started back toward the rear of the house. "He'll be very upset if we wake him," she said. "He's sick. He needs his rest." She put the key back in the door and opened it on a shallow, dark space. Despite the cold, he could smell the sourness of the little shack. It took a moment for his eyes to adjust, and then he could see that there were upward of twenty unopened packages on the floor. He leaped at the nearest one. It had been sent on the seventh of October from Wells, British Columbia, from a woman named Adrienne Grunwald. The one beside it had the name of Morton Halfe and a return address in Eston, Saskatchewan. Then his eye fell on a small box with Gladys Iagnemma's name on it. It had been sent two days before her death. None of them had been opened. "*Fucking hell,*" he said under his breath. "Why are all these packages here?"

"I told you, I just —"

"Do you speak to this man? To Peter?"

"He mustn't be disturbed."

"Says who?"

"His brother."

He couldn't help it; he shook her violently. "Give me a name!" She stared at him in terror, and Sevigny turned her by the shoulder and pushed her back out into the daylight. The back door to the house was twenty metres away. The two windows on either side of it were obscured by curtains. He pulled Buck by her purse strap toward the house.

"No," she said in a hoarse, frightened voice. "We're not to go in the house."

"What is the name of the man whose brother lives here?"

"Please."

"Then I will ask the man inside this house."

"I don't have a key to the house."

"You have a key. Open the door."

"Please —" she said, and she opened her arms. He tried the door. "Simon," she said, "his name is Simon. If he knew we were here —"

"What? He would kill us?"

"Please," she said. "I vowed —" He didn't wait for her to finish. He took a step back and smashed the door open with the flat of his boot. The door exploded against the wall on the other side. There was the smell of dust, and then, gusting in under it, a sickening death reek. They both recoiled from it.

"When was the last time you saw the man who lives here?" said Adjutor Sevigny.

"Peter must not . . . be disturbed," she said, her voice suddenly querulous as she stepped back from the broken door. Then she turned suddenly and puked on the step. He grabbed her under the armpit and muscled her back out onto the grass.

"Stand up straight."

"You don't know what you've done —"

"Give me your car keys," he said. She meekly put them into his hand. "Sit down and don't move." He got out his cell and flipped it open. There was no signal. "Goddammit. You have a phone?"

"In my purse." He grabbed the purse off her shoulder and rooted around in it for her phone. He flipped it open. There was a signal. He dialled Port Dundas. Someone answered in the station house. "Get me Hazel Micallef right away."

"She's not here," said the voice. "Who is this?"

"Detective Adjutor Sevigny! I'm calling from the fucking Pacific!"

"Hold on, hold on, I'll forward you to her cell, hold on." He waited through a series of clicks, and then Detective Inspector Micallef picked up before it even rang.

"Hello?" she said, sounding bewildered. "Sevigny, is that you?"

He could hear voices behind her. "I'm here," he said. He was short of breath. "There is something bad happened here . . ."

"Where's 'here'?"

"I follow the woman after she pick up the mail. After she *picked* up the mail. I mean, I followed her. I'm at a cabin in the woods, maybe it's ten kilometres from the town site. There is a man here, she says, Jane Buck."

"You're with her right now?"

"I broke the door."

"Hold on, Detective, just slow down. Where are you exactly?"

"I told you! North of Port Hardy. In the woods. I followed her, I followed Jane Buck here. There is a house. A shack. If there is someone in there, they are not alive."

"How do you know?"

"I can smell it."

"Have you been in?"

"Not yet. But there is absolutely for certain something dead in this house."

She said nothing for a moment. "Do you have something you can soak with water? A cloth or something?" He opened Buck's purse; there was no Kleenex or hankie, but he saw something he thought would work and reluctantly took it out of its plastic wrap. There was a connector for a garden hose beside the back door, and he turned it on and ran water over the thing and pressed it to his nose and mouth.

"What are you doing?" said Jane Buck, looking at him in disgust.

"Shut up," he said.

"Now go back in," said Hazel. "Stay on the line."

He looked at the frightened woman squatting in the grass and unsnapped his flashlight from his belt. The moment he crossed the threshold to the house, the smell penetrated his makeshift mask. "Shit," he said.

"What is it?" said Hazel.

"I'm in . . . a small . . . it is a small room," he whispered, choking on the air and taking shallow little breaths. He was trying to hold the cellphone to his head and the mask to his mouth with one hand. "There is nothing here. Cold and dark. Two chairs and a table." His feet crunched on grit. He lifted his flashlight and swung the beam over the room. "One door in the wall. Over there," he said.

"Open it. I'm here with you, Sevigny. Open the door."

He crossed the room, the smell driving at him, and put his hand on the knob. It was cold, stiff. He forced it to the right and the door opened. He lifted his flashlight. "*Christi tabernac —*"

"Adjutor . . ."

"My God."

There was a small bed against the wall across the room, nothing more than a pallet of straw. On top of it, his face a maze of maggots, lay the body of a man, his arms hanging down. A black, roughhewn stone pillar was standing on his crushed chest, as if it had fallen out of the sky. Sevigny looked up, expecting to see a hole in the roof, but it was solid. He looked back down at the ruined body. It was a man who, in life, would have weighed well over three hundred pounds. The body was suppurating a thick black fluid.

"Detective?"

"I find a body," said Sevigny hoarsely. He tried to describe what he was looking at. His voice seemed to issue out into a huge silence. "I am going to be sick," he said.

"Hang in there, talk to Ray." She passed Greene her phone.

"Whose body is it?" said Greene.

"Peter Mallick. Jane Buck says Peter Mallick. Brother of Simon Mallick. I find an unopen package in a shed in back of the house with the date of October seven on it. There are others. He has been dead . . . a long time." He turned and ran, unable to contain himself any longer, and heaved violently onto the floor beyond the doorway. "I have never . . . in my –"

"Easy, Detective."

"I have a woman on the back lawn . . . there is something I don't like about this woman –"

"You better call in the locals," said Greene.

"I know what to do," he snapped. He tried to settle himself, and he stepped back into the room and approached the bed. He could only imagine the smell in here had it been ten degrees warmer. "I am trying to look at his mouth." He leaned down, overwhelmed by the stinking cloud of decay that hung over the body, and used the edge of the flashlight lens to brush the lace of maggots away from Mallick's mouth. The light turned the inside of the body's head a sickly dark orange. Sevigny spun and vomited again, then turned back. The mouth was closed in a thin line.

"Try not to soil the crime scene too much," said Greene.

"There is nothing. His mout' is just closed."

"You have an accent when you're terrified, Sevigny."

"If you was 'ere, Raymond, I bet you don't be able to talk English at all."

He heard a rustle and Hazel's voice telling Greene off. "Take some pictures for us," she said, "and get out of there. There's an RCMP detachment up there?"

"I don't know."

"Find out and get back here. Try not to tell them anything they don't need to know."

"Hold on," he said. "There is a desk in the corner. I didn't see it from the doorway." He crossed the room to the desk and shone his flashlight onto its surface. "There is a laptop here —"

"A laptop?"

"There's a computer in that shithole?" said Greene in the background.

"And some books. Old books." He opened one. "This one is in Italian . . ." he said. He pressed the cold pad to his face for a moment. "No, Latin. I recognize it from the nuns."

"Take it all with you, Detective," said Hazel. "Do what you have to do and call us from your hotel."

They heard him helplessly puking.

He'd muscled her into the front seat of his rental and on the way back to town she neither protested her treatment nor made reference to her rights. He hadn't arrested her and he took her meekness as a sign that she thought herself in enough trouble that co-operation was her only option. That or she wasn't clever enough to know that he had no right to take her with him unless he was going to charge her with a crime. And he had no intention of leaving a paper trail in that town. Port Hardy would barely know he'd been there.

He told her to direct him back to her house and she complied. Her place was just off the main drag, in an old wooden house painted light blue. "Am I going to get my car back?" she asked.

"What do you think?" She stared out the windshield at her house. "Are you guilty of a crime?"

"No."

"Are you sure?"

She absently nudged a paper bag on the floor by her feet. An apple core rolled out of it. At last she said, "I didn't know Peter was dead. All I did was bring his mail."

"Sure you did," Sevigny said, "because you knew nothing." He threw open his door. She waited for him on the other side and got out when he opened her door.

"What are we doing?"

"We're going into your house."

She cast a frightened glance over the top of the car, as if she were worried someone might be watching them. "Don't you need a warrant for that?"

"I could get a warrant. Do you want me to get a warrant?" Another look up the street. "Are you expecting someone?"

"They don't like attention. Simon and Peter. They would be upset if they knew I was talking to you."

"Well at least one of them will never find out."

"I'm the secretary, okay? That's all. I volunteer my time."

"Why?"

She shook her head slowly, her upper lip in her teeth. "Look. I have nothing. I have the church and my government cheque and that's it. And my car."

He reached for his wallet in his back pocket, and she followed it with her eyes as he brought it up between them and opened it to take out two twenties. She made no sign of being disappointed that money was about to change hands. He folded the bills in his hands and held them out, then pulled them back just a little. "How does a woman with nothing have a house?"

"It's not my house," she said. "It's the church's." He kept the money in the air. "It's theirs, okay? They own the house."

He gave her the cash and led the way to the front door. "When we're done here, if I think you've been helpful, I'll drive you back to your car," he said.

He got back to the motel just after 4 p.m. A low, dusky light was lying across the harbour and the die-hard pleasure-boaters were heading out in the cool fall air to fish or take in the sunset. The only thing between them and the giant evening sun was an imperceptible line separating the earth from everything else. He'd taken a small folder of paper from Jane Buck's house. Nothing that would incriminate anyone, but he had a sense that some of the information in that folder, at the right time, would cast a little light in the right direction. More pressing, however, was the laptop. He placed it on the little wooden desk in the motel room along with the books. The books were old; some were bound in leather. His mother had once had high hopes for him entering the priesthood, but even given his years in the seminary, his Latin was worse than poor. The only book in English was an old formulary, a guide to the uses of various plants. This made sense: it was clear by now to them all that the Belladonna was a self-taught pharmacist of some kind, except his specialization ran to the lethal. He checked all of the books for markings, but they were clean.

The computer had been used for a single purpose: apart from the operating system, the only program was a web browser about five years out of date. It had even been stripped of the games that came with it. Sevigny clicked the open browser, but there was no signal here. The browser returned a grey screen with the news that the "server was not found." He was fairly certain the killer wasn't getting a signal out in the death shack either, so where was he hooking up to the Internet? There were no bookmarks in the browser, but when he pulled down the history, he saw links for an online email service and links to a site called Gethsemane. He knew what Gethsemane was. He was going to have to get online to find out what it meant to the Belladonna.

He called the front desk, and they were happy to let him use their single computer, but there was no way to connect this laptop to the Internet. They wanted to help him. He told them he was looking for a good place to fish steelhead. "The man in room five caught a lunker this morning just five kilometres out in Bear Cove."

"That's great," said Sevigny. "But I still need the Internet."

There was an Internet café in town, but it closed at four o'clock on Sundays in the winter. He asked the woman if she knew the name of the person who owned the Internet café, and she did. It was Kevin Lawton. "Everyone calls him 'Kev,'" she said. There were five thousand people in Port Hardy. He called directory assistance and got the man's home number. He reached the man's daughter, who gave him her father's cell number. The man was on a boat.

"Who?" said Kevin Lawton.

"Se-vin-yee," said Sevigny. He could hear the wind coming out over the ocean.

"Well, I'm fishing tarpon, buddy," he said. "Not that they're interested in me, I'll tell you that."

"I'm on police business. This is what you would call an emergency."

"Bad connection," said the man, "You sound like a Spaniard."

"Close," said Sevigny. "I'll pay you two hundred dollars to open your café for one hour."

"Oh fer jeez sake," said Lawton, "if it means that much to you, I'll go fishing tomorrow."

Tomorrow was Monday, thought Sevigny. A regular business day, but then again, he didn't have much of a sense of what kind of world he was in now, anyway. Maybe they went fishing here anytime they wanted.

He met the man at his café, and Lawton refused Sevigny's money and let him in. He snapped the lights on, revealing a small establishment done up in a Hawaiian theme. Sevigny was about to ask, but then thought better of it. The man put a pot of coffee on to brew.

The laptop was set up for a wireless connection, and as soon as Lawton had his system running, the browser came to life. Sevigny clicked the link for Gethsemane and the page that came up showed a single image: the rough black stone he'd found standing on Peter Mallick's staved-in chest. He ran the cursor over the image, but there was nothing.

He went back to the history menu and clicked on the Belladonna's webmail link. He got a home page with a login screen. The computer filled in the username. It was "simon." The password window was blank.

Lawton came over with coffee and a thick piece of carrot cake. The smell of it made the back of Sevigny's jaw ache: he hadn't eaten since he'd been sitting in his car on Sewatin Road. Lawton looked over his shoulder, and Sevigny lowered the screen. "This legal?" he asked.

"Let's say the owner of this computer would not be happy to see me doing this." He took a massive forkful of the carrot cake. It was salty-sweet.

"You know the password?"

"Not a clue."

"Sometimes there's a keychain in one of the preferences folders that'll tell you the password, or at least give you a bit of code you can paste in."

"I'll try that," said Sevigny. Lawton began to move away. "Can I ask you a question?"

"Sure," said the man, stopping.

"You know the name Simon Mallick?"

"I heard of him, but it's been a while. He was the pastor of a church up here."

Sevigny got out his notebook. "Where is this church?"

"There wasn't really a 'where' to it, if you get my drift."

"I don't."

"More of a 'what.' It was him and a bunch of back-to-basics types. They were scattered all over Vancouver Island, but the Mallick place was sort of their Mecca. They'd assemble up here once in a while and go baptize a bunch of people in kayaks, that sort of thing. They were harmless . . . there's about a thousand little religions festering in the trees out here, you know? Most of them disappear up their own assholes, excuse my French." Sevigny narrowed his eyes. "Mallick's group called themselves the Western Church of the Messiah. They were vegans, if that tells you anything."

"When's the last time you saw him? Simon?"

"Oh God," said Lawton, and he drew his hand over his mouth. "It's been absolutely years. Him and his brother, Peter, live up in a little shoebox out in the forest. Is all this about the church?"

"No," said Sevigny flatly.

Lawton looked at the empty plate in Sevigny's lap. While talking to Lawton, he'd devoured the entire slice. "I could just put that back into the cupboard. You want another one?"

Sevigny did but said no. He felt he couldn't waste his hands on anything but what was in front of him.

"Dave plows yearly," and "Cube the vibrations."

"Cube the vibrations," said Ray Greene. "That's going to come in handy one day, I feel certain of it."

"How many different things can it say?" asked Hazel.

"Twenty-four hours isn't a lot of time for something like this. I haven't nearly exhausted all of the possibilities."

"But?"

"But I've come up with a vocabulary of sixty-eight words," said Jill Yoon, "and I'm up to a hundred and fifty-five phrases."

"Do we want to hear any more of them?"

Yoon searched down her list. They stared at the bedsheet, where their sixteen dead had been melted down into a living, electronic face. It breathed in and said, "A cute doe saves belief."

"Fuck," said Ray Greene. He walked into the living room and sat heavily on Wingate's couch. "I liked this better when there was a possibility we could have programmed Hazel's lips to promise me a raise."

"We're not going to hit on it right off, Ray. It's not an exact science."

"That's right, it's witchcraft."

Wingate was standing beside the fridge, staring at the inhuman face. "What if it's not in English?" he said. "You made DI Micallef talk French earlier."

"It was a party trick," said Jill Yoon. She'd borrowed one of Wingate's sweaters from the dresser in his bedroom and moved around in it like a clapper inside a bell. She'd raided his bed for its sheet. He'd felt sick when she called them back to his apartment at five in the afternoon and seen that she'd all but moved in. The sink was full of dishes from some kind of pasta meal she'd made herself from shrimp in his freezer, olive oil, fresh peppers, and a sundried tomato pasta he'd hidden at the back of a cupboard and never imagined she'd find. For a tiny thing, she ate like a bear. He wanted her out as soon as possible. "I have high-school French, that's it."

"How does the program know English?" asked Hazel.

"I taught it. I read it *A Midsummer Night's Dream*, half of *Executioner's Song*, and *Snoopy* comics. I still read to it sometimes, like it's my kid. It wants to learn."

"We need Sevigny," she said.

Ray groaned from the couch. "What, we're going to wait until our man in B.C. flies back, then get him to read the collected works of Voltaire into this thing just so it can tell us how to trim raspberry vines in French? Honestly, Skip, I think you were right. We should seriously consider distributing the drawing that girl made. If he's in the Maritimes, then it's only a matter of days before he's finished what he's doing, and by the looks of it, he's the only one who really *knows* what he's doing."

"I'm calling Sevigny," Hazel said, and she pulled her cell out of her pocket. "Damn it, does he even have a cellphone?" As she was saying this, she heard a voice calling to her from her hand. She put the phone back to her ear. "Hello?" she said. "Sevigny, is that you?"

Wingate and Jill Yoon watched her straining to hear Adjutor Sevigny. She covered the phone with her hand and said to them, "He's in a shack somewhere." Wingate could hear the man's clipped voice cutting in and out from the mouthpiece. He was terrified, that much was clear. He watched Hazel's face, then Greene's, for some clue as to what had happened. Sevigny was far away. Hazel had passed the phone to Greene, but grabbed it back from him. He said, "There's a computer in that shithole?" and with that, Wingate knew a door had swung wide.

"Take it all with you, Detective," said Hazel Micallef. "Do what you have to do and call us from your hotel." She snapped the phone shut. "He found a body. He found Jane Buck and she took him to a body."

"Sev was going to give him mouth-to-mouth," said Greene, "but he said he hates the taste of maggots."

"Ray."

"Sorry."

"Strike French," Hazel said to Jill Yoon. "We don't need it. James, go pluck Father Glendinning from his Sunday roast and bring him to me. Tell him to find his oldest Bible. We're going to teach Miss Yoon's computer how to speak Latin."

Sunday, November 21, 8 p.m.

Three hours later, they were huddled over Father Glendinning, who, still in his coat, was telling Jill Yoon's computer about the miracle of the loaves and fishes in Latin. At precisely 8 p.m., Hazel's cellphone rang again. She listened to the voice of Detective Sevigny spill into her ear from the other coast. He was highly agitated. "Hold on," she said after a moment. "Stop." She turned to the room. "James, does your phone have a speaker on it?"

"Why would I have a speaker phone? I don't even have a clock radio."

"I have VoIP," said Yoon, and everyone looked at her at once. "Just give him this number, I can take his call on my computer." She handed Hazel a piece of paper and she read the number out to Sevigny. A minute later, the bridge from "Disco Inferno" erupted out of Yoon's computer speakers, and she connected Sevigny to the room.

"Start from the beginning again," said Hazel. "Go slow."

Sevigny was breathless. His voice manifested on Wingate's fridge as a black bar with a violent line waving down the middle of it. "He is a priest, Simon Mallick. He run some kind of a church out here called" – there was a pause as he consulted his notebook – "Western Church of the Messiah."

"What, like cowboys for Christ?" said Greene.

"Vegans," said Sevigny. "Weird people, it sounds. But for some reason, he kill 'is own brother. And then, after, he begin to search for people who want to die. People had to look hard for him," Sevigny continued, "he has a website, but only people who are really desperate are looking deep to find him. He's linked to other sites, places people would go for alternate t'erapies. His links were buried, but they say things like 'end your suffering,' and 'complete release from pain,' impossible stuffs like this. If you click, you go to a site called Anastasis and you can write to him on a form. This site, it only has the form, he tells you nothing. So you write."

Father Glendinning, who'd been giving of himself in the most stingy manner imaginable, began to pay attention. Hazel marked it.

"Once you filled out the form, you press send and it automatically link you to another site, this one is called Gethsemane. There's nothing there but a big picture of a rock. I find this rock on the man's chest. But if he choose you –"

"For what?" said Hazel.

"If he choose you, he give you the rest of the address for the Gethsemane page. And then the stone moves."

Yoon already had the page up. They were standing behind her, looking at a black rock. "We see it, Adjutor. What's the rest of the address?"

He spelled it out for them and Yoon put it in. The stone moved away and there were words behind it. They all leaned in. "*Mashach* is Hebrew," said Glendinning quietly. "It means to anoint with oil. It's the root for the word *messiah*."

The cold went through Hazel. The space behind the rock said:

The stone releases its oil
He is anointed
In Gethsemane, you are the fruit of the tree
In Gethsemane, your seed will wither
Here, you are ground
His messenger comes
You are joined to Him
His messenger comes to you
You are the stone
His messenger is lashed to you
The stone releases its oil
You are anointed
You are the root and trunk and branch and flower

Yoon clicked throughout the message. Nothing happened. They reread it. It was the first silence any of them had experienced in more than a week. "Anastasis," said Hazel Micallef to Father Glendinning. "You looked at me."

The priest's lips were wet and trembling. "It's Greek for resurrection," he said.

"Are you still there, Adjutor?"

"I'm here."

"What do those emails say?"

"They're contracts, I think," he said. "There are times and places in them. He's made arrangements with these people."

"Jill, can you give him an email address he can forward to? Adjutor, write this down."

Jill Yoon read out her email address. "I'm forwarding all of this as I talk to you," said Sevigny. They saw the emails begin to pop up on Yoon's screen instantly; the names of the dead in a clean blue font. "I am afraid that we have already missed another one."

"Who?"

"Her name is Tamara Laurence. She is in Pictou, Nova Scotia. They arrange for yesterday, the twenty-first. But there is one more to go. Newfoundland. A man named Carl Smotes. Tomorrow, the Belladonna says, he is arriving tomorrow at two in the afternoon. I know it, Trinity Bay, I visit it with my ex-wife some years ago. It's beautiful there." His voice was tailing off.

"Sevigny?"

"I'm here."

"Send us everything. Send us everything you have."

"Yes."

"You okay, Sevigny?"

"I feel sick. *Un vrai malheur de tristesse.*"

"What?" said Greene.

"Heartsick," whispered Wingate and Greene looked at him.

Hazel leaned in toward Yoon's computer. "You did good work, Detective."

"Yes. But they are all dead. All of them."

"You're done there. Do the Mounties know what's going on?"

"I was never here," he said.

Yoon disconnected. The line on the fridge where Adjutor Sevigny's voice had been jumping went flat. They found themselves staring at it. "I bet the Port Hardy RCMP are going to be real grateful to be tossed a bone by the Port Dundas OPS," said Greene.

"They'll get their crime scene," said Hazel. She turned her attention to Glendinning. "What do you make of all this?"

"He's promised to open their graves," he said, his face a mask.

Hazel was scanning the emails as Yoon opened them one by one. She looked behind herself to Greene, who nodded in response to her silent question.

"He was good at keeping his word," he said.

"We need to get someone out to that house in Pictou to confirm the body. He's been and gone, but we can still catch him in Trinity Bay," said Hazel. "We have —"

she looked at her watch. It was just after eight o'clock. "We have less than sixteen hours to intercept the Belladonna, and if we miss him in Newfoundland, he's gone for good. I want every RCMP officer within three hundred kilometres of Trinity Bay to hit the road doing a hundred and eighty. James, you're personally in charge of making sure Carl Smotes gets into protective custody. After that, I want you to rendezvous with Sevigny and put together whatever information you can on this Western Church of the Messiah. Ray, you and I are going back to the station house to coordinate with the Mounties in Nova Scotia. And you –" she turned to Glendinning. He started.

"Yes?"

"You sit with Miss Yoon, and don't go anywhere until you hear that dead mouth say something that makes sense to you."

"Ohh no . . . I don't want any part of this now! I came when summoned, but I've done my bit. And anyway, that French officer, he told you where to find your man."

She sat down beside him and put her hand on his. She'd never liked this priest, had always felt that Port Dundas deserved someone with more forebearance, more warmth. But he was their lot and they were his. "I saw how you looked at me, Father. This scares you."

"You're damned right it scares me."

"We may know where to look for this man, but we still don't know what he wants. If these people have a message for us, you might be the only one who can tell us what it is."

He subsided a little. "I don't want to know, Hazel," he said quietly, ashamed of his fear. "I've been sitting here for nearly ninety minutes reading catechism to a machine. But I don't want to know the results of my actions. I don't want to hear what he wants."

"I can't let you go, Father. I'm sorry." She stood and looked over the computers at Jill Yoon, who nodded at her. She was going to have to handle the reluctant priest. The rest of them had phone calls to make.

"*Lemma*," said the face on Wingate's fridge.

"No," said Glendinning, his eyes in his lap. "Start with *libera*."

There was no one available at the Pictou detachment. It was suppertime on a Sunday. Hazel had to call down to New Glasgow, twenty kilometres away, to find a person who'd answer a phone. The dispatcher there had one guy on the road, a Constable Nevin. "Can you patch me through to him?" she asked, and a moment later, she heard the man's voice. "I'm Detective Inspector Hazel Micallef," she said to him. "I'm calling you from a detachment in central Ontario."

"Good evening, Detective Inspector."

"Constable Nevin, we've had some information that leads us to believe there may have been a murder in Pictou last night."

"All's quiet up here, ma'am," Nevin said. "We had a couple kids driving a stolen golf cart across the Eagle's Nest driving range last night, but nothing else. Not even a DUI to keep us entertained."

"I think the murder might not be discovered yet. The victim lived alone."

"How do you know this, Detective Inspector?"

"We had a tip. Can you go up to Pictou? The address is 61 Mackie Road."

"It'll take me about fifteen minutes," he said. "I'm out by Trenton way."

"I don't know where that is, Constable Nevin, but I'll take your word for it. I'll give you my direct line. Call me when you get there."

"Will do," said the officer.

Two desks over, Greene was arguing with the RCMP. He put his call on hold when she came over. "The detachment in St. John's is willing to send a car."

"We need a regiment."

"I don't know if they *have* a regiment."

"Don't be stupid," she said. "Where's James?"

"You told him to get Carl Smotes."

She stood up and looked around. Wingate wasn't at his desk. Then she saw him standing beside the desk sergeant talking to a cop she didn't recognize. "Hello?" said Greene into the phone. "Listen, we need a minimum of two cars out there. One at the victim's house and at least one — yes, I *know* there's no victim yet. For Christ's sake —"

Hazel took the phone from him. "Good evening, this is Detective Inspector Hazel Micallef. May I ask who I'm speaking to?" The voice on the other end identified itself as Staff Sergeant Power. "By this time tomorrow morning, sir, you're going to have a dead man in Trinity Bay and quite possibly, by this time tomorrow night, the local paper is going to run a story saying you fellows were warned in advance. This is for real, Sergeant; you need to drop everything." James was waving her over to the counter; she held a finger up. "Yes, I understand you have staffing issues, everyone has staffing issues. But you can't take a lead any less seriously because of it. Please," she said, "get some people down there. You need someone on the house, someone roving, and someone watching the exits off the highway. We're faxing you a drawing of the suspect." She listened for a moment. "I'm not telling you how to do your job. I'm telling you that if you catch this guy, you're all going to get medals. I promise you." She passed the phone back to Greene and strode out to the counter, where the strange cop was patiently waiting with his hands in his coat pockets.

"Sorry to interrupt you," said Wingate. "But I thought this was important. This is Sergeant Gary Wharnsby, from Sudbury."

The man stuck out his hand and Hazel shook it. "Is Detective Sevigny here?"

"He's on his way back from British Columbia," she said.

"Can I ask what the hell he's doing in B.C.?"

"What is this about, Sergeant?"

Wharnsby looked back and forth between them. "He was due to make a court appearance yesterday morning. He never showed up."

"I don't know anything about this. He was seconded to us in the middle of the week." She waited for the man to respond, but his face was implacable. He seemed very angry indeed. "I guess someone got off a speeding ticket then."

"He wasn't appearing as a police witness, Detective Inspector. He was being arraigned."

"What?"

"He beat a fellow officer unconscious two weeks ago. He's been suspended from the force."

"Jesus Christ," Hazel murmured. She thought she was going to smash something. "That fucking Mason . . ."

"I beg your pardon?"

She pulled herself together. "Sevigny should be landing in Toronto tomorrow morning. My assistant will have the flight number. I'm sorry, Sergeant, we had no idea of this."

"It's probably not something he elected to tell you."

"No," she said. She noticed Melanie out of the corner of her eye. "This is who you want to speak to," she said. "Melanie, this is Sergeant Wharnsby. Give him whatever information he needs."

"I have Officer Nevin for you on your direct line," she said.

"God, okay." She turned to Wharnsby and shook his hand again. "We're in the midst of something here."

"I can see that."

"Sorry for the confusion with Sevigny."

The man turned to leave. "Just a sec," said Wingate.

"What is it?"

"I'm curious," he said. "About this . . . assault Sevigny committed. Allegedly committed."

"He committed it. I was there."

"The officer, then, the one he beat?"

"What about him?"

"Did he deserve it?"

Hazel couldn't help it: she smiled. "Let the man get down to Toronto, James."

The three of them stood over the speaker phone on the desk in the conference room. Hazel punched the transfer button and spoke down into the microphone. "Detective Inspector Hazel Micallef speaking."

"I'm here," said Constable Harry Nevin. He was turning into Tamara Laurence's driveway from the sideroad that led down from the highway. "Looks quiet from the front."

"I don't suppose you know this woman, Constable?" asked Ray Greene.

"No, sir. I understand from Kevin back at dispatch that she's a doctor."

Hazel leaned in again. "I'd keep your weapon unholstered, officer, and your eyes open."

"Will do, ma'am." They listened to the faint sound of crunching as Nevin crossed toward the house. "Lights are off inside –"

"What time is it there?" said Wingate.

"Nine-thirty. An hour later than you guys." They heard him knocking on Tamara Laurence's front door. Then again. "No answer."

"You've got to get in there, officer," said Hazel.

"I'm sorry, Inspector, but I can't just enter a private residence without a reason. Now, I respect that you have a tip, as you say, but maybe this is the time to tell me more about it."

"I don't have time to fill you in on our whole investigation. This is an extraordinary circumstance – if there's someone inside and there's any chance to save her life, we have to do it, and we have to do it now."

They heard the November wind whistling in his mouthpiece. Greene strained to hear beyond it. "I thought you said she's already been murdered."

Hazel hesitated. "I'll tell you what I know about Tamara Laurence. She's terminally ill. She may have been contacted by someone offering to help her. To end her life. If by some chance she's in there, and she's still alive, it means our guy hasn't gotten there yet. So I need you to get into that house."

There was silence from the star-shaped conference console on the tabletop. "I'm going to need my hands free for a few moments," said Nevin at last. "I'll call you back."

He rang off. "We should call for backup now," Greene said. "There's got to be another detachment within fifteen minutes of this place. I've got a bad feeling about this one kid breaking into a dead woman's house with nothing but a pistol and a cellphone."

"Give him a minute," said Hazel. "If he finds her, he'll radio for backup before he calls us."

Two minutes ticked by in slow motion. Then the phone rang and they all jumped. Hazel grabbed the receiver, "Hazel Micallef here –"

She could barely make him out; he was gasping for air – "Caucasian female! Late forties, five-six, I got a, I got a victim here –"

"Nevin! Nevin, listen to me –"

"What's going on!" said Greene, leaning over the table and trying to catch Hazel's eye. "Put him on speaker phone! Is she there?"

Hazel stabbed the speaker button and laid the receiver down. "Nevin? Can you hear me?"

"There's blood everywhere –"

"Calm down –"

"Have you called for backup?" said Wingate.

"I'm getting into my car," said Nevin, and they could hear the door to his cruiser slam shut.

"You need to call your CO, Nevin . . . Nevin, are you listening to me?"

"I gotta get out of here," he said, and the sounds of his engine rose up to cover his voice for a moment. "Car eleven, car eleven to dispatch?"

Another voice crackled in the background. "Harry?"

"Kevin, I got a situation out on Mackie in Pictou. I need an Ident unit and some backup –"

"What is it?"

"I got a murder out here – hey, what the *fuck* –"

The surprise in the officer's voice sent a wave of cold through Hazel. "Oh God," she said. "Nevin?"

"There's a car blocking the driveway here now." He honked his horn, loud. "Get the fuck out of the way!" He honked again and then they heard him open his door.

"Don't get out of your cruiser!" Greene shouted.

"There's no one in it," said the officer. "This other car's empty."

"Nevin," said Greene, gripping the edge of the table, "get out of there. Get back in your car and get out of there!"

"I think —" he said, but he didn't complete his thought.

"Constable Nevin?" said Hazel.

The line had gone dead. Hazel frantically redialled the number, but there was no answer. "Oh Christ," she said. "Mallick's there. He's there right now."

Father Glendinning shoved the chair back and it smashed against the stove. He stood facing the mechanical dead mouthing the words over and over, his hands white at the ends of his sleeves. "Get your boss," he said, his voice stuck in his chest. "Get her now."

] 18 [

Blood streaked his chest and groin as if he'd been a participant in an ancient sacrifice, the blood of the offering drenching him. He'd wrapped his hand in layers of sheeting from the bed she'd put him in, but his blood soaked through. It would not be a bad thing if he were able to rinse himself of this foreign blood that had saved his life, but he had to accept that without it, he would not have the power to continue. Presently, the flow diminished, but as he went about collecting his things, he left a thin trail of blood running up the stairs and down the hallways of Tamara Laurence's house.

He felt pain, but it was an ecstatic pain. He'd evened things out now; he was back in the light. He hoped his brother would forgive him. He'd drawn the blood chain to this place, but he would be late for Trinity Bay. It was a profound failure, but he could not wallow in his guilt. He had to get moving.

He dressed in her room, using his black socks to mop at the blood that had stained his skin, and once he was dressed, he put his things back into his black kitbag, tucking the glass vials into their elastic holders. Bolts of pain shot up his arm and across his chest. Shards of broken bottles lay at the bottom of the kit, but he would not stop to clean it out now. He thought of the body downstairs, which he'd laid on the bed he'd found himself in like an offering on an altar. He could still feel the warmth of her limbs as they lay across him, and then that warmth beginning to ebb. He'd felt her passing into that line, felt her rise up and stand beside the others. There was no time to wait to sculpt her, however. He'd simply held her mouth with his hands and marked her with his eyes.

He looked around. He'd become less fastidious in these last few days. It felt less urgent now to be careful, but still, he washed out her teacup and placed it back in its cupboard. He made her bed. He left the lights on and went back out to the car. It was full dark now, almost nine-thirty at night. He had two hours to make it to the ferry, but the drive would take him nearly six. Being brought to this day, he had faith another hand would guide him now.

He put his kit in the back of the car and then got in and reversed up Tamara Laurence's driveway. He would head to North Sydney to catch the ferry to St. John's anyway and trust that somehow he would find himself at Carl Smotes's door and Carl Smotes would welcome him. He got to the highway and put his signal on to turn left, and as he made the turn, he saw an RCMP cruiser turning right onto the access road that led down to Mackie. There had been a single man inside the car, and he could have been doing anything on the access road; he could even live down there. But did cops take their cars home for the night? Simon contemplated this as he continued down the road, and then finally, his instincts telling him not to go on, he did a U-turn on the empty, darkened highway. He drove back down the access road, looking for the cruiser parked somewhere, and by the time he got within half a kilometre of Tamara's, he was fairly certain where the car had gone. He turned off his headlights and drifted in toward the trees at the top of her driveway and saw, down to his left, through the bare branches, the headlights of the Mountie's cruiser illuminating the front of Tamara's house. He was trying the door and talking on a cellphone.

Simon tried to figure out who had led the police here. He went over in his mind all of the houses he'd been in over the past two months. There had been no witnesses and he'd left no trace of himself in any of these places. He'd taken from these houses and destroyed any paper correspondence he'd had with his hosts, and he'd meticulously erased any emails to or from himself that he found remaining in their computers. Could Tamara have warned someone? What did she do after she'd discovered him out cold behind his car on Saturday night? Did someone catch her taking blood from the hospital and decide to look into it? Surely she hadn't called anyone; if she had he wouldn't have woken up in her basement with tubes sticking out of him. He was at a total loss to explain what he was seeing. At this moment, the officer was kicking in Laurence's door with the flat of his boot, and the next, he was inside the house. Simon put the car in neutral, got out, and put his shoulder into the open doorframe, pushing the car forward silently. When he'd crossed the open driveway, he jammed his foot against the emergency brake and the car stopped there, blocking the way onto Mackie Road. Then he retreated to the trees beside the driveway and waited.

A minute later, he saw the policeman burst from the doorway of the house and stumble toward his car. Simon heard, "– blood everywhere –" and he crouched down and toed a discarded piece of cinderblock, then felt its heft in his hand. The cop was in his car now; he was coming back up toward the road. Honking. Simon could feel the man's fear and rage. The officer got out of the car, the cellphone pressed to his ear; he said, "There's no one in it," and Simon rose out of the dead scrub and stepped soundlessly onto the verge of Tamara Laurence's driveway. When he struck the officer on the back of the head with the block, the man spun to him, as if his name had been called, and Simon swung the weight into the man's face for good measure, and he fell there, at Simon's feet, like a broken branch.

The cellphone had smashed against the side window of his car, cracking the glass. It lay in the roadway and began ringing. Simon watched it until it fell silent. Then he picked it up, opened it, and checked the call log. The numbers for the incoming call and the one the officer had last dialled were the same: it was in the 705 area code. Somewhere in Ontario. He chose the number, pressed "send," and almost immediately, the phone was answered. An anxious voice said, "DI Micallef here. Nevin? Are you all right?"

"No," said Simon. "He's not." There was backup coming. He returned to his car, hearing the voice in his hand calling to him in a tiny, furious voice. There was no time left at all. He would not be going to North Sydney now, nor Newfoundland. Everything was ruined. He hurled the phone out the window and watched it bust to pieces on the road behind him.

Two hours later, he was out of Nova Scotia, his eyes switching back and forth from the road to the rearview mirror, but there was no one behind him; he was unknown again and going to ground. Whoever this Micallef woman was, he presumed she was massing her energies to the east, where he was expected, if she wasn't already another step ahead of him and had deduced the actions he was undertaking at this very moment. There was no way out of the province but by the coastal highway, but once he reached New Brunswick, it was his intent to abandon the highways altogether and stay on private roads, side highways, and logging roads. New Brunswick was a couple of cities, a handful of towns, and a great deal of forest. December was encroaching and camping was not an option that appealed to him, but until he could think of what he must do next, he was going to have to be invisible.

Outside of Amherst, he veered onto 126 and headed straight up toward the centre of the province.

He quickly switched onto smaller roads and all the little oases of light provided by towns and gas stations vanished and he was in a consuming darkness. The roadway seemed fit for only one car heading in one direction, but even at this time of night, he saw, once or twice an hour, headlights shivering in the distance, light snipped into bits by the trees until they appeared full-force in front of him, and he would have to pull over as far as he could to the right to ensure both he and the oncoming car could pass. It was harrowing driving. Four hours into it, he felt himself descending into grief, imagining that he could have been almost all the way to North Sydney by now, almost to the ferry, and in that other life, he would still be clinging to the faith that he would get to Carl Smotes in time. Now he knew who would get to Carl Smotes. He imagined whoever was sent to collect the dying man would have a warrant to search his place and even if Smotes had gone over his house as carefully as most of his hosts did, the police would still find something, and whatever holes that yet existed in their investigation would begin to fill in. Simon always found something after his men and women were gone: some small correspondence, something missed on a hard drive, and he would erase, or burn, or bury; he would leave these places pristine. But Carl Smotes, crippled with tumours and barely able to walk, would be taken now from his home and brought somewhere for his own safety and it was *his* fault, it was his own fault that this had happened. He had ignored some warning from somewhere and now he was in full flight. He cried out in his car, screaming his anguish, his disgust with himself; he smashed his fists into his skull until the roadway appeared to separate into two paths, two light-strewn paths wending through the forest. He wept and screamed until his throat was raw. And at two in the morning, exhausted by his grief, he finally pulled over and hid the car in among the trees.

He didn't feel like eating or making a fire, but he knew his body could give in now. Stripped of his purpose, he felt he could welcome death, or at least not resist it, but he would not let this strange woman who had found him claim him like this. He built a fire and ate two apples he had taken with him from Tamara's house. He could barely force the second one down. He raised his tent under the thin cover of the bare branches, a hundred feet away from the road where he could still hear the traffic. He faced the door toward the fire. It had begun to mist, a cold, sharp rain that came down in reedy gusts. The tent was exactly as cold as the air outside, and by four in the morning, he knew he would not sleep at all, and he came out and stood in the wet, dark cold.

It was a clear night, the stars spread out over the dome of the sky, distant and unharried. This was the light that had been meant for all of them, this eternity was for the unfinished congregation he had been making. Their mouths open, ready to sing the final note, but waiting. He felt his throat thicken with this heartache and he tried to push the image of these bootless dead away. A faint mist covered everything around him. He felt it slowly building on his skin.

He concentrated on the stars. An uncountable heaven of openings. This gazing occupied him for a while; he was aware of time passing. Soon, he would have to change his dressing. He looked down at the cloth. In the pale firelight, the stain was black. He lifted a strip of soaked bandage up toward the flickering glow. It was black, black as starlessness, black as oil. Then he could smell the oil. He brought the drenched cloth to his mouth and touched his tongue to it. It *was* oil. Dark, heavy, sweet, pungent olive oil.

His brother was there.

He stood in the trees on the other side of the fire, the stars behind him boring their light through his body, needles of light piercing him and holding him, lifting him. His feet hung above the dead ground. Simon wept.

Brother, you are the root and trunk and branch and flower.

"Yes," said Simon.

His brother shone like the word of God. An impossible light. It saw him. *I'm dying.*

Simon walked across the small clearing to where his brother was. He reached up and stroked the sunken cheek. "Tell me what to do."

I'm cold. He took his brother in his arms and carried him to the fire, laid him down in its feeble light. His lips were cracked and dry and his breath came in ragged bursts. *Your drugs aren't working any more. I'm getting worse.*

"It takes time."

No. I can feel it. I'm really dying now. The fire against his face seemed to creep inside his skin, to light his head from within. His eyes glowed in his skull. *What you're doing isn't working any more.*

"I have another preparation."

I can't take any more of your medicines. Take me to town. For the pain.

"*No!*" shouted Simon. "You will not be poisoned by outsiders who know not who you are. Why have we done all this work? Why come to this day if only to give up?" He leaned in and stroked his brother's gleaming brow. "You will not die."

But I must die. We knew I must die.

"We're all going to die. Just not today."

Kill me.

"A little more physick. You'll see. You'll see how it makes you feel." He pushed himself up from his haunches and went into the tent to retrieve his kit. When he returned, it was as if his brother was barely there. He could see the ground beneath him through his pale skin. "Hold on. Stay with me, you've got to stay with me." He prepared the drug and raised him up, held him against his chest. His brother opened his mouth and took the drug and Simon held his mouth closed, pressed his face against his brother's. "There's another way," he said. "You'll see."

The ghost began to fade against him. Simon felt his arms pass through his brother's chest until they were wrapped around his own body, and he was rocking and sobbing in front of the guttering fire.

] 19 [

Hazel convened everyone in the conference room at 8 a.m. Father Glendinning hadn't slept from the look of him, and he shot a fearful glance at each person as they entered the room. There were Greene, Wingate, Spere, and two other officers. Spere had strongly voiced his displeasure at being left out of this part of the investigation, but now he sat silently, waiting. Jill Yoon was sitting behind her projector and her laptop.

"Father," she said. "You can begin anytime."

The priest wearily got to his feet and leaned forward against the tabletop. "First off, I'm here against my will."

"Noted," said Hazel.

"And second, no person should be compelled to engage in activities that run counter to their deepest-held beliefs, which is exactly what —"

"Also noted," said Hazel, an edge of anger creeping into her voice. "I want you to tell everyone here what you told me last night at DC Wingate's place."

Glendinning looked over at Wingate, as if the mere existence of that man's apartment were the cause of all his grief. "I presume some of you are familiar with the contents of the New Testament?" He glanced around the room with barely concealed disgust, and when it was apparent he was waiting for some form of response, a couple of them grunted their acknowledgement. "Fine. Now, there's a long history to the Bible, and some of that figures here, in your investigation. So unlike the way you pay attention in church, when you bother to come, you should pay attention to this."

"Father," started Hazel, but he rolled over her.

"To begin, the scriptures the New Testament are based on were originally in Aramaic, an early Semitic language. It wasn't a Bible then, just a collection of stories and laws and blessings that were copied out from hand to hand. The first Bible was in Greek, and it collected and organized these writings. The Greek Bible was brought over into the vulgate Latin by Jerome around 400 AD. However, it has always been understood that there was an oral component to the scriptures, and that some fragments were subject to a prohibition. They were never written down, nor were they supposed to be. This spoken component consisted mainly of blessings conferred only on the closest of Christ's disciples. These were meant to travel from mouth-to-mouth, as it were, in the keeping of the high priests. Once uttered, the recipient of the blessing became the keeper of it, and the speaker of the blessing was to offer himself up as a sacrifice. Naturally, the later Christians were eager to rid themselves of these pagan rites, and none of the Greek Bibles have any of these so-called *carmina inconcessa* in them. Forbidden songs." He looked about the room to ensure they were following him. Hazel nodded. "In any case, they begin to turn up in Latin commentaries around the year 800 AD, and of course they are suppressed, but after that, from time to time, they reappear. Never in the Old English, or later translations. But some people are aware of them, it would seem."

"You are," said Greene.

"In the seminary, the history of the Bible is taught. There's a great deal of folderol concerning the writing of scripture, a lot of which is very colourful. But most of it is nonsense."

"Most?" said Howard Spere.

The priest continued. "The *carmina inconcessa* have a special power over the imagination of those who know anything about them. Sects have sprung up over them, and the charismatics who founded these sects claim to have access to some terrifying powers."

"Which brings us to the Belladonna," said Hazel.

"He started a church," Greene said. "We already know that."

"Well, this is its congregation," said Glendinning. "And it has only a single prayer in its Mass. One of the *carmina* is known as the *Libera Eos*. When the women went to complete the burial rites at Christ's tomb, they found the tomb empty. And it is said that their holy service, never to be completed, was rewarded by the

Holy Ghost with a consecration against death. It's a prayer of resurrection, and in every instance of resurrection investigated by the Church since the time of Christ, it has been said that this *Libera Eos* has been invoked. The speaker dies instantly, but the blessed are reborn."

Greene was scrubbing his mouth with his hand. "Wow," he said. "So this . . . series of sounds . . . ?"

"Yes," said Glendinning.

"He's *way* crazy, isn't he?" said Greene.

The priest rounded on him, his face red. "Whether he is crazy or not is beside the point, Raymond. He's a believer. This church of his is a serious thing."

"Which is worse than being crazy?"

"That's up to you people," said Glendinning. "All I know is that he mustn't be allowed to finish it."

"Because otherwise . . ." said Greene, trying to get the priest to say it himself. "Because . . . if he does, then the world ends and little red men with pointy sticks come and drag us down to the centre of the earth?"

Glendinning was glaring at him. "Because it's an offence to God, that's why."

"I thought this stuff was 'nonsense,'" said Howard Spere. "Are you telling us now that you believe?"

"There's nonsense and then there's dangerous nonsense. No man should wield such a thing for his own purposes."

"Jill," said Hazel. "Do you want to play us what you have?"

"I've just told you what you have," said Glendinning. "It's not necessary to listen to it."

"There's a division between church and state for a reason, Father," said Greene. "I'd like to hear this zombie prayer for one."

Hazel shook her head at him. "It's okay, Jill. Let's hear it once."

Yoon tapped a couple of keys and the projector fired up. A dart of light hit the screen and the focus resolved into the face that had so frightened Glendinning. He turned away from it. "Ready?" she said.

"Go."

The face breathed in. They heard the voice, intoning. "*Libera . . . eos . . . de vinculis mo —*" it said, and broke off.

"What does it mean?" asked Wingate.

Glendinning kept his face averted. "'Free them from the bonds of death.' Once it's completed. There are two more sounds."

"Tamara Laurence's pictures are coming in," said Hazel. "But Father Glendinning says he knows what the last two phonemes are."

She looked at him, waiting, and finally, with a miserable expression on his face, Glendinning went to the easelboard and pulled on the projection screen. It rattled back up into its frame, and he faced the board and began writing. The digitized face wavered on the back of his coat. When he stepped away, the letters R T I S were on the board. "I'd be grateful if you men and women would be so kind as to keep yourself from profaning my beliefs by pronouncing what I've written here." He turned to Hazel, slapping his hands against each other. His face seemed deeply red in the light. "May I go now?"

She moved silently to open the door, and Father Glendinning was about to hurry out of the room when she put her hand up. "Is there anything else you think we should know about resurrection, Father? Anything that might help us decode this man's behaviour any more?"

"All I know about resurrection is that I've never seen it happen."

"But you must believe in it. Isn't it the cornerstone of your faith?"

"And yours, Hazel?"

"Yes, I'm sorry. Mine as well."

He drew back into the room a little, willing to delay his departure another minute to have a final word on the matter. "Only those of pure spirit and body can be raised from the dead. Their hearts must be pure and their bodies whole."

"Excuse me," said Greene from within the room. "How do these people count as 'whole' when they've been chopped up, cut in half, and drained of blood?"

"I didn't say they had to be in one piece, Mr. Greene. If God can raise you from the dead, he can put you back together. But if you've outraged His gift in some way, you cannot be given it back."

Hazel put her hand on Glendinning's arm. "So despite the states of these murder scenes, Father, our killer is keeping to a set of rules, you think?"

"What does it matter what I think?"

"I just want to know if you think he really believes in what he's doing."

Glendinning gestured with his arm minutely, enough to communicate he didn't intend to be held a moment longer. He looked around the room behind him. "Hazel, he's as serious as cancer," he said, and then, at last, he swept out.

When she closed the door, Wingate gestured to Jill Yoon and she shut off her machines. "So what we know is that he's absolutely compelled to finish this thing," he said.

"And Smotes is out," said Greene. He was staring at the ceiling. "Libera . . . eos . . ."

"*Don't* –" said Wingate sharply.

"You religious, Jim?" Wingate just stared at him, and Greene became aware of another pair of eyes on him. Hazel's. "Are we getting superstitious here, people?"

"We're trying to stay focused, Ray, that's what we're doing." He shrugged, like staying focused was at the front of his mind. Hazel continued. "Sevigny gave us the whole list. But I don't know if there's a backup list or anything. There could be."

"Understudies?" said Spere. "If he's this fastidious, I doubt he'd have a waiting list. These were his people. Wingate's right. He needs someone now."

"What would you do if you were him?" she asked.

After a minute, Greene said, "If you run out of willing victims, there are always . . ."

"Or you take your own life," said Wingate.

Hazel shook her finger at them. "No. Whatever that scene meant, in his shack in Port Hardy, he didn't go to that trouble, to all *this* trouble, just to blow his brains out in the Maritimes." She fell silent a moment. "Do you think he cares if Robert Fortnum enters the Kingdom of God? Or Ruth Maris? Did he go to these people, complete strangers, to give *them* the gift of life?" She looked around the room and could see the penny dropping for all of them. "These people . . . they're like a wire carrying a charge. One end of the wire is in Peter Mallick's dead heart, and the other plugs right into the heart of God. They all wake up, but that's not why he's doing it. He couldn't care less if Delia Chandler rises out of her grave. He just wants to go home and see his brother standing in the door."

"So he's going to finish," said Wingate.

"Yes," she said. "He's in this to be reunited with Peter. And now he has to find someone who will be to him what Smotes was willing to be. He needs a willing victim."

She looked around the room, waiting for someone to say out loud the terrible thing that had just occurred to her. So she wouldn't have to be alone with it.

Once Glendinning was gone, Hazel dismissed everyone but Greene and Wingate. "I actually wanted to talk to you about something else for a couple of minutes," said Greene.

"Can it wait?" said Hazel.

"It shouldn't," he said.

Wingate started to leave the room, but Hazel waved him back in. "I'm sorry, Ray, but we have to push on. Let's talk after lunch. Sit down, both of you." The men sat. "What's the update on Harry Nevin?"

"He's awake, but he's not happy about it," said

Greene. "Massive concussion, and just about every bone in his face is broken. Plus he lost about eight teeth."

"Jesus," she said. "Please tell me we sent flowers."

"You can thank Melanie."

She shook her head in wonder. "Mallick could have killed him."

"I guess one thing went our way then," he said, and he fixed his eyes on her.

"Then there's Carl Smotes," said Wingate to break up the brief silence. "He's too sick to be moved. He's agreed to have someone at the house, though. There's one guy there, and a nurse."

"Well, I don't think it matters, anyway. Simon's not going anywhere near Newfoundland now. Our cover's blown and so is his."

"Do you want me to call off the RCMP then?" asked Greene.

"No," she said. "Keep them on it for now. Just to be safe." She sat down and rested her forearms on the table. "I guess you both know about Sevigny."

"A little," said Wingate. "I hear he clocked his partner."

"Apparently the guy was helping himself to a little extra money and Adjutor called him on it. They were swinging at each other on the station-house steps. Partner's an Anglo though, and Sevigny's CO is Anglo too. It's half-and-half up there, but there are tensions I understand. They're probably going to suspend him."

Greene shrugged his shoulders. "It's not an Anglo thing, Hazel. The guy's obviously a loose cannon. He walked in here telling us what to do with his funny accent. Higher-than-thou prick, is what I say. He's getting what he deserves."

"He's the one who broke this case for us," she said. "I just feel bad for him."

"Maybe Mason'll let you have him when he's served his suspension," said Greene.

She smiled at him. "James, can you go see how the background check on Simon Mallick's coming?"

Wingate stood up quickly and put his cap back on. "I'll be at my desk."

She hadn't taken her eyes off of Greene. "I thought we were past this, Ray."

"I guess we're not."

"You developed new problems with me over the weekend? We're making progress, Ray. Real progress here."

"All you're doing is handing Mason his dynamite. After you're done here taking evidence off-site, failing to share information, claiming jurisdictions, there'll be a crater here where the station house was, with two guys standing in it holding their coffee mugs."

"You want to make up your mind what you're so upset about, Ray? One second there's too much competition for your coffee cup, the next you're accusing me of not reaching out. I asked for support, Raymond; I didn't get it. What would you have done?"

"Shouted," he said. "I would have gone down to Barrie and hammered on Mason's door until he did what I wanted him to."

"You've got that power, do you?"

Greene swept an invisible crumb off the table in front of him. "I don't know what it's like to be a female

CO, Hazel. Or a female mayor, for that matter. Maybe experience teaches you you're not going to be taken seriously, that you're going to get screwed. I'm sorry if it does. But you know, in all the years I've worked with you, you've never acted like that was true. Not until now. I don't like Mason's ways any more than you do, but that wouldn't make me careless. It might make me angry, but I'd still be using the same playbook." She started to speak, but he went on. "I don't like having my name on this investigation, Hazel. I don't like being a part of these methods."

"These methods are getting results, Raymond! Fuck! On Friday, you're telling me to have more faith in myself, and today my methods aren't good enough for you!"

"I didn't realize on Friday what was going on here. I thought you were flailing. I thought you were lost. But I see it more clearly now. Mason gave you licence. He set you free to *really* do it your way."

She lowered her head. He was out of line, by a country mile. She was going to have to discipline him after this, but first, she realized, she had to listen. "I've made mistakes —"

"I'm resigning," he said.

She set her jaw. "You don't have to do that."

"I'm resigning so you don't have to fire me."

"I wasn't going to fire you."

"Yes, you were," he said, and he stood up. "I'm Sunderland's source. I went to him because I thought it was wrong of you to shut him out. He talks to our constituency. At first, I really just wanted to tell him he should write about the way Mason's left us out to dry up here, but the more I talked to him, the more I thought it wasn't about Mason. He's a certain kind of animal, Mason is. You're a different one. But you changed. So I ended up talking to Sunderland about that."

"A week ago."

He said nothing.

"I don't know what to think now."

"I wanted to wait to tell you until after I thought the case was hopeless. Thinking maybe there was something I could do. Now that there isn't, I wanted you to know."

"You could have talked to me," she said quietly.

"No," he said. "No, I couldn't have. There were times when I could work with you, Hazel, but I could never talk to you."

"What were we doing in here Friday night? What was that?"

"We were trying to save a marriage. I think we both know what that's like. It's hard." He watched her absorbing that, watched her expression soften to disbelief. He waited for her to decide what she needed to say, but after a moment, he sensed there was nothing to come. "I'm gonna go," he said.

"I accept your resignation."

He nodded once and turned to leave. He expected something at the door as he opened it, but, again, there was nothing.

She'd told everyone in the station house that she needed time to think, and she'd locked her door. She opened the file cabinet so quickly that the bottle fell over and clinked and rattled against the bottom of the drawer, loud enough that she was certain it could be heard in the pen. But no figure appeared shadowed against the frosted window in her door, and she returned to her desk with the half-empty bottle in her hand. She expected no further twists in the day and told herself she might as well dip into oblivion if she felt like it.

She'd avoided Greene as he cleared out his stuff and said nothing to anyone about what was going on, but she'd made eye contact with Wingate on her way into her office and she knew he was aware of what was happening. For the first time in two weeks, she could not focus on the case. Instead, she saw what lay beyond it: there was going to be an inquiry, and she was not going to come out of it looking at all good. In a way, this comforted her: she couldn't bear the thought of Greene's accusations standing as a private matter. They would have to come out. And then, afterward, as a matter of public record, she would have to accept that she'd been found wanting, or that she'd merely lost a friend. She couldn't think which she preferred right now.

She poured herself a second drink, one eye trained on the door. She wanted to sleep. If possible, she wanted to sleep with someone, and not because she desired to be touched in any way, but because she was tired of being alone. During the day, her staff swarmed close with their questions, with their need to be set on the right path. But this was not human contact, and in the mornings, waking alone, she felt keenly the lack of another body. Even someone who came into her bed in the middle of the night and left before she woke would be enough, she believed. Anything to maintain a connection of some kind. She despaired she'd ever know it again.

Before long, the bottle was empty. She put the last dram away into its hiding place, feeling the welcome but artificial warmth in her limbs. As she closed the drawer, there was a knock, and she went to open the door. It was James Wingate. He wouldn't meet her eye. "I thought you'd want to see these," he said. He passed a small sheaf of paper to her. "Sevigny emailed his pictures of the crime scene. They're pretty disgusting." He seemed to notice she was uncertain on her feet. "Maybe you should sit down," he said. She retreated to the safety of her desk.

She sat and shuffled through the images, her stomach tightening. The man in the pictures was as thick as a felled redwood. He lay on a small dais-like bed and she thought she could smell his half-rotted form right off the digital image. She couldn't imagine the kind of strength it would have taken to lift the stone pillar that lay on his chest. "I don't suppose you've heard any RCMP theories on the body? Cause of death?"

"I thought it would be wise to keep low."

"Probably. You think Simon killed his own brother?"

"It's impossible to say."

"And what about Peter Mallick? Did Sevigny find out anything about him?"

"Not yet. He just sent the pictures. We can't find anything on the church from this end. We did find something, though, at the Pictou scene: there were two distinct trails of blood in Laurence's house."

"What?"

"Two blood trails, in addition to the cocktail of blood they found on Laurence's face. As if she'd been anointed with it, said the forensics guy there. The two clear trails, though, one of them is hers, but the other doesn't check out with anything we have a record of. So I'm thinking she might have tried to hurt him."

"She changed her mind?"

"Maybe," he said. "But then again, she had no defensive marks on her."

"It hardly matters now. We're never going to see him again. We had him for a second there. But he's gone." She watched him fail to think of something that would give her a little hope.

"Inspector," he said, "he's still out there, and what he wants hasn't changed. The way I see it —"

"How do you see it, James?"

"The way I see it, until he feels he's done, we still have a chance to catch him."

"Do you like our chances?"

"No," he said flatly. "But I haven't given up."

She gestured to the chair and he sat. "Ray Greene isn't crazy about the way I ran this investigation."

"I gathered as much."

"What do you think about it, James?"

His face darkened a little. "Your methods are a little different than I suppose I'm used to."

"Different good, different bad?"

"Both. To be honest."

"Shit is going to rain down on this place. You know that, right?"

"Maybe it won't."

"Until it does, are you still willing to work for me?"

"Yes, ma'am. I am."

"You can call me Hazel now, James. It's just us."

"Okay," he said, nodding nervously.

"So if you're still with me, then you'll take a direct order? Even if it seems a little ill-advised?"

"There's no reason to stop now," he said.

She laughed. "Good. I have a job for you."

It was well past dinnertime, but she had no appetite. She was hungry only for air. She put on her runners and headed toward the lake.

It was almost the end of November now, and the trees were utterly bare. Something about this month had always seemed contingent to her, as if it were a temporary bridge between places. They'd put November up with planks and pennynails at some distant point in the past to link autumn with Christmas, but then they'd forgotten it was supposed to be replaced with something sturdier, something more lasting.

What had she wanted out of this life, back when she was thinking about such things? Had Greene been right when he accused her of wanting an excuse to go it alone? She'd never detected the will in herself to be a hero, but that didn't mean it wasn't true. She cast her mind back to her time in the academy. She'd once been excited by the idea of playing a role in keeping *order*, but perhaps that meant she'd once believed in such a thing. Order. Now, after more than thirty years on the force, she knew it wasn't something worth waiting for. Order was not possible, but the dream of balance wasn't entirely vain.

A balance between what you could control and the chaos that surrounded it. A balance between good and evil. A balance between what was difficult to do, and what, through repetition, you could do in your sleep. Trying to strike a balance kept things interesting. Hadn't things, at least, always been interesting?

The truth was, though, that the police prayed for boredom. Not for order, not for balance, even, just regularity. Nothing out of the ordinary. And this year *had* started out looking like any other, she thought. Break-ins, car crashes, bar fights. If anyone had told her back in May when she was slapping cuffs on Mattie Barnstow for driving his VW Rabbit through his ex-wife's living-room window that it *wasn't* going to be the height of excitement for the year, she would never have believed them.

Murder, she thought. And not just murder, a lunatic murder. And God invoked. And the rest of the country tied to them in it, even if they didn't know it. This was the stuff of movies, of third-hand tales. Even as an end to it all (an unhappy end, it would appear) came closer, it seemed less and less real to her. A symptom, perhaps, of her experience with ordinary disasters. Divorce, pain, parenting an unhappy daughter. Nothing, not even a life in law enforcement, could prepare you for the wild imaginings some people, in their passionate madness, could unleash.

It was too cold to be outside with the sun going down. She returned to the house. Her mother had eaten and was reading in her room. It was fine with Hazel that there was no one to tell her day to. It was too awful a day to speak of. She sat in front of the television numbly watching bits and pieces of a bunch of different pro-grams. The picture and sounds seemed to reach her from far across the room.

Sunderland's editorial the previous Thursday had called her a "little general," and she'd realized that this was one of Greene's phrases. How could she have worked so closely with this man and never have sensed his exasperation? He'd always been capable of a sharp word here or there, but she'd always seen it as a form of camaraderie. What if she'd misread more of the people in her life as egregiously as she'd misread Ray Greene? In the last two weeks, she'd sensed the wheels coming off, but now she thought perhaps there'd never been any wheels at all. What if, for much longer than everyone but she had realized, sparks had been flying off the chassis?

She went to bed at nine, too exhausted to wait for Wingate's call any longer. The phone would wake her. When it rang at eleven, she shot up in bed and picked up the extension on the bedside table. "Wingate?"

"Yeah."

"Well?"

"The word 'unprofessional' was used," he said.

"I should have it put on my letterhead. Were you able to get past that?"

"Yeah," he said. "It's done."

] 20 [

Wednesday, November 24, 8 a.m.

He pushed on, through a second sleepless morning. He'd watched the sun come up over Mount Carleton, turning the hills a deep red. The road unfurled through the provincial park as he tacked north and then west, toward Saint Quentin. He turned on the radio to keep himself awake and heard music from his childhood, music his father had put on the turntable for him and Peter when they were children. The Benny Carter Orchestra. Jack Millman's All-Stars playing "A Stranger Called the Blues." This was music their father had loved. Simon could not remember his father's face. For a moment, he closed his eyes tight and tried to bring that beloved face back, but he could not. Their father had given Peter his frail heart, the heart that broke on him when he was thirty-nine. He listened to his father's music drifting up in this unspoiled place.

He drove aimlessly, waiting for the way to become clear. He told himself he was only being tested. Something would come to him. This far north in the province, there was almost nothing but the bad roads and forest. It occurred to him that he might run out of fuel up here and have nowhere to turn. His body, devoured to bone by animals, would be discovered by hunters in the spring. He checked the tank. From where he was, he thought he could make it back to Kedgwick to gas up, and then he could do another circle of the interior and think.

Ten kilometres outside of the town, as he drove on fumes, the radio sputtered back to life. He listened to the news. There was nothing about him. It occurred to him that he wasn't doing anything to protect himself except to run. He drove down the main street of Kedgwick and refuelled. Inside, he bought one of the national newspapers. The smell of candy in the kiosk made his stomach twist. He was so hungry now he thought he might pass out. The town had a café, and he went into it with the paper and ordered hot water with lemon. The waitress hovered over his table, looking down at him. "I can pay for it," he said.

"I'm not worried about you running out on me for a slice of lemon. I just think you should eat something."

"Just the water and lemon, please." He kept his face averted.

When she came back with the teapot, she brought him a plate of toast as well. "It's on the house," she said. "I have a thing about customers dying at my tables." He thanked her and poured the hot water.

What had exercised his exhausted mind over the preceding forty-eight hours was the question of where had
he slipped up. He realized his faith had kept his attention on the horizon, and he'd never really entertained
the idea that anything he'd had control over could go
awry. But now he considered it. Someone had gained
access to his list, which meant one of two things: Carl
Smotes had contacted the police or Jane Buck had been
found out. But Smotes, even if he'd had a change of
heart, could not have known where Simon was the night
before he was to be in Trinity Bay. So that meant
someone had gotten to Buck, and despite her commit-
ment to them, she had broken. Buck was fervent, but
she was fearful. Perhaps someone else's authority had
elided his own. And this meant they had his laptop,
and, worse, had desecrated the shrine. He pushed back
the sudden anger that was blooming in him with this
thought and forced himself to think rationally. If this
was true, then it meant that they had an idea of who he
was as well. They were wrong, but it wouldn't matter.
How had they got to Buck? He wondered if he should
call her, but if he was right, and they had any respect at
all for his intelligence, then they'd be expecting that.
He wondered if it was the Micallef woman who'd tracked
Buck down. He'd spent part of Tuesday in a library in
Edmundston collecting information on Micallef, and
judging from the size of her detachment, he couldn't
imagine she had the resources to mount an investigation
of any magnitude, never mind one that might have
turned up one of their most trusted congregants. But
he could not discount Micallef: maybe he had made the

mistake in Delia Chandler of killing someone too well-loved. He knew how motivating a deep love could be. And it had somehow been Hazel Micallef's voice on the other end of that call Sunday night.

In the one photograph he'd been able to find of DI Micallef online, he saw that she was an older woman with short grey hair tucked up under her police cap. Broadchested, like the matron of an orphanage, but her eyes were not cruel. They were bright and lively: clever eyes. He did not like the thought of those eyes trained on him. So somehow, she'd gotten into step with him, but he'd veered off and now he was just a figure in the trees. He had to assume those eyes were sweeping the forest for him. He would have to emerge at some point, but in what shape and with what purpose?

He tried to distract himself with the newspaper. Reports on federal politics and problems in the Middle East and the cost of oil. Someone had written a column advising the reader to eat less salmon and more mackerel. He had to laugh. No one knew anything. The ecology of the body did not matter at all: it was a machine that could be transformed if you knew what to do to it. The body was a barrier to its own becoming.

"You're allergic to toast," said the waitress, appearing beside him.

"I'm not hungry," said Simon.

"Suit yourself, honey."

He paid at the front and left a generous tip. He went over his options: drive or sit still. But stillness was torment, and he could think behind the wheel.

At four in the afternoon, he reached the Quebec

border. He'd changed cars twice while crossing the country, so he was not afraid that his licence plate would mean anything to the authorities. He'd traded down each time through used-car dealers; this third vehicle he'd picked up in Manitoba. Probably he'd been driving it too long, but as the urgency of his travels intensified, he'd run out of time to stay on top of all the smaller details. He drove with his brother's glistening eyes on him: he saw them hovering over the road, in the trees, in his mirrors. Especially in his mirrors.

He crossed into Quebec and drove down to one of the smaller highways where he might find somewhere to stop for the night. Outside of La Pocatière, he at last saw the dreaded evidence that his actions in the world were being noticed. The New Brunswick papers had not paid any heed, but here, on the cover of *Le Journal de Québec*, he saw a picture of the cruiser he'd found in Tamara Laurence's driveway, now with yellow tape around it, and the simple headline: Une Attaque Sauvage. And now, finally, he heard a clock ticking.

He pulled into the first motel along the highway outside of the town and bought a room. Once inside it, he turned on the television and flipped channels trying to learn how limited his time would be. There was nothing about him on the evening news in French or in English. A woman dead and a cop mutilated and it wasn't enough for the six o'clock news in eastern Canada.

He continued to surf. After the news, it was time for sports, edutainment, and current affairs. On one channel, a white lynx prowled for rabbit, springing at one sitting almost invisible against the snow. Another channel fuzzily showed a crime-stoppers program. There was also hockey and curling. He watched the curling for a couple of minutes, the slow, inexorable progress of the heavy rock down the white sheet of ice, curving gradually off its line. It was a sleepy sport. He tracked back down the channels. The lynx was nursing a blind, naked kitten. Did they procreate in the fall? He went up and down the short dial, the images blurring together but united by the image of cold and ice, and he began to feel hypnotized by it all, to the point that, beneath the snow of static on one of the channels, he even thought he saw himself. And then the mask of his consciousness snapped back down into place: it was him. He shot up straight in the bed. It was the crime-stoppers program. He leaped from the bed and adjusted the crooked aerial until he could see himself better. It was a drawing. A perfect rendition of himself in a dark coat. He'd gone from moving in utter silence through the houses of the dying and the dead to being an open secret in a childish drawing beamed to every television set in the country. He was undone. He turned up the volume. They'd cut away from the drawing and now they were showing the exterior of a house he knew. He'd been in this house.

"On the morning of November fourteenth," a voice was saying through the buzz of the bad reception, "Grace MacDonald brought a visitor to her sister's house." They cut away to the inside of the house. The mother of Rose Batten was sitting at her kitchen table.

"I was scared of him," she said. "He came into the house and he wanted to see my daughter."

"Terry Batten's daughter, Rose," said a woman standing on the street now, talking into a microphone. "An eight-year-old girl with brain cancer. In her desperation, Terry agreed to let this stranger, a man claiming to be a naturopath, examine her child. To this day, neither sister knows exactly what the man gave Rose Batten, but at first it seemed to work."

Back on Terry Batten. He watched with dumbstruck horror. "She was her old self for a few days. Bright, energetic. Happy. We couldn't believe our luck," she said. "I wanted to find this guy and thank him. I would have given him everything I owned."

"But Miss Batten's joy was to be short-lived. By the middle of last week, her daughter began to decline again, steeply."

Now the girl was on camera, looking into the lens. Her face was pallid, her skin almost see-through. She seemed logy, as if roused from sleep. An off-camera voice spoke to her. "What did he do to you, Rose?"

"He didn't mean to hurt me," the girl said. "He was a nice man." She looked away from the camera, then up again, away from it, her eyes distant. "He wanted to help me. But nothing can help me."

Simon felt the heat returning to his limbs.

On the street again, the reporter said, "An innocent child and close call with a killer. Did he come here to help? Or has he taken another victim, here in the quiet hamlet of Humber Cottage?" They showed the drawing again. "If you see this man, do not approach him. It's believed he is somewhere in Nova Scotia or Newfoundland at this

moment. If you see him, or this car" – now a drawing of
his battered Chevy Cavalier: they had no licence plate,
but they had the make now; Grace MacDonald had seen
it of course – "call the police."

The reporter was staring beseechingly into the
camera. "With your help, Crime Stoppers can catch this
man before he kills again. Damian?"

They switched to a man at a desk in a studio. Simon
had seen enough. He turned the television off. There was
only one thing to do now. He was going to need his sleep.

He would have to eat to regain his strength. There
was a café across from the motel, but when he sat down
he became aware that others were looking at him. If
others had marked his wretchedness before he'd turned
up on television he hadn't noticed. He ordered a large
salad and an order of bacon to go and waited with his
back turned on the dining room. He hadn't eaten pig in
almost twenty years, but he needed the fat. People
came and went from the front cash to pay for their
meals, and he could sense their curiosity. He should
have shaved; he should have bought some better
clothes, but it had never occurred to him until this
moment that he would ever walk among people again.
He felt dangerously exposed. His order came and he
went to the front to pay. He asked the woman for
twenty dollars in dollar coins.

An hour later, fed and feeling like his strength was
coming back, Simon stopped at a bar and used the pay
phone. His tongue felt slick with fat and salt. An operator gave him the number he requested, and Simon put

two dollars into the phone and dialled. Terry Batten answered, and he hung up. Five towns and two hours later, he tried again, got Terry again, and hung up. Finally, three efforts later, in a gas station in the middle of the province, he heard the voice he wanted to hear.

"It's you," she said.

He cupped the mouthpiece in his hand and spoke as quietly as he could. "Why did you do that, Rose? I never harmed you."

She was silent, and he trained his ears on the background noise. There was nothing. "I'm sorry," she said.

"How sick are you?"

"I feel like there's a fire in my brain. And I throw up when I eat. I'm scared."

"I'm sorry I failed you," he said. "There's more art involved in what I do than I like to admit. I truly had faith that you'd be all right. Do you believe me?"

"I do," said the girl.

"I'm calling to apologize. It seems nothing I do right now is turning out the way I'd hoped. You must think some very bad things of me."

She let out a long, terrible sigh. "Can I ask you something?"

"Yes."

"Is it true? What they say you've done?"

He leaned against the wall looking out toward the pumps. "In a way it is."

"Are they going to catch you?"

"Probably," he said. "But I've never taken anyone who said they didn't want to go. I'm not a murderer."

"They say you are."

"I hold the door open to another place. People choose to step through."

He heard the girl shifting around, like she was taking the phone somewhere and hiding with it. "So those people wanted to die?"

"Yes."

"And you were helping them."

"Their deaths have changed them."

He heard her crying softly. "Would you do for me what you did for them? If I asked you?"

"Are you asking me?"

She was silent a long time. He listened to her breathe. "You never told me your name."

"You can call me Simon."

21

Friday, November 26, 10 p.m.

They stood on the street watching the preparations.

A handful of local officers had arrived the day before, and their unmarked cars had been parked on the side streets near the Batten house since Thursday morning where Hazel had ordered them to go. Everything would be on foot now. She had seven men, five from Renfrew, and three of her own officers. Two of the local men – Constables Fairview and Glencoe – had once trained as sharpshooters, but they were so rusty (the lack of demand for sharpshooters in eastern Ontario being such that not one of them had ever been called on to use their training) that Hazel ordered them onto a firing range in Hawley Bridge to practise shooting tin cans from three hundred feet.

Once *Canadian Crime Stoppers* had agreed to Wingate's request for assistance, things had begun to happen quickly. The segment played three times a day on each of Tuesday and Wednesday and they were prepared to let it go in heavy rotation until something happened. They expected that someone would recognize him somewhere east of Ontario and they'd simply close in on him. He needed gas, he needed food. But they also held out the faint hope that he'd see the segment himself and react. They'd been lucky.

During the week, information about the Mallicks had finally begun to filter in. The two men had lived in Port Hardy for almost twenty years. Neither had a criminal record, nor did they turn up in any of the credit bureau, social service, or medical records they could get access to. Although many people they spoke to had heard of the Western Church of the Messiah, it was not registered as a charity in the province of British Columbia, and there was no information on the sect. A web search brought up nothing.

The remote shack was in both their names; they'd bought it outright for $9,800 in cash in 1996. Before then, they'd lived in Victoria, in a house on Asquith Street. In 1977, their first year at the address, provincial records showed both men had changed their names to "Mallick." Before then, Peter had been "Welland," and Simon "Kressman." Why had they done this, and were the two men, in fact, related? Wingate's digging found that the Welland and Kressman names were both adoptive ones: their father had died when Peter was five and Simon eleven and the brothers had been separated, Simon going to a family named Kressman in the Interior of B.C., Peter to the Welland family of Milk River, Alberta. His adoptive parents had been murdered in 1976, when Peter was sixteen. And then his brother had legally adopted him. Their father's name had been Gordon Mallick. There was no trace of the mother.

So the elder had taken in the younger, had brought him home as it were, after the death of his adoptive parents. Peter's vocational trail was almost impossible to follow: it appeared that he'd worked for the post office briefly in the eighties, but apart from that, his worklife must have been peripatetic, a hand-to-mouth cash-in-an-envelope existence. Simon was in no records they could find at all. The silence of his history seemed to be in keeping with the establishment of a church they also could find no record of. If Peter Mallick had lived a crazy-quilt life, the fabric of Simon Mallick's life was gossamer.

That morning, they'd found out what was in the packages that Jane Buck had been dropping off at the Mallick shed. Sevigny had packed them into his rental car in Port Hardy and itemized the contents before returning to Sudbury. Hazel couldn't think of the kind of trouble they'd all be in if it were ever discovered that one of her officers had removed evidence from a crime scene. But in her heart, she was glad for what he'd done. "Slippers, books, Delia's duvet cover, a Bible, muffin tins —"

"Muffin tins," said Hazel.

"I can't explain it."

"The kinds of things you might want to have around while you're getting over your death?"

"Some of them came with cards," said Wingate. "The cards are creepy." He passed Hazel some scans.

"Please accept this small token of gratitude from me. I look forward to meeting you." Hazel squinted to read the signature. "Elizabeth Reightmeyer. She was going to need a lot of makeup for that meeting."

"I beg your pardon?" said Wingate.

Hazel leaned back and pulled a red folder from the middle of a mesh basket and passed it over the table. "She's the one with the railroad spike through her brain," said Hazel. Wingate declined to open the woman's file.

Hazel flipped through the scans. One showed a sympathy card with the lines, *Sincerest regrets for your loss.* "Christ," she said, "you're right about creepy."

"Detective Spere says he thinks these were payments of a sort. Shows of goodwill."

"We just call him Howard," said Hazel.

"He asked me to call him detective."

She passed the sheaf of paper back to him. "Well, all of this is informative, but it's sort of moot now, isn't it?"

"It's good to know more about him."

"Once the dreams start, you'll regret what you already knew about him." She'd looked at her watch then. It was coming up on five o'clock. There was a skeleton crew in the station house. It was time to get ready. "Have you eaten?"

"I was just going to go home and make something. Clean the place up a bit."

"Good idea," she said. "I'm going to try to get some rest. It could be a long night in Humber Cottage."

"They've all been long nights. I'll see you back here in an hour?"

She'd driven home on the cell the whole time, checking in with Renfrew, with Terry Batten. For the last two days, she'd spoken to Rose's mother six or seven times, calling her to reassure her with details of how their plans were coming, or taking calls in which Terry's first words would often be tearfully unintelligible. "This time tomorrow," Hazel had told her after lunch that afternoon, "there'll be nothing in the world left to threaten you except the tantrums of an eight-year-old." A couple of times, she'd even taken Rose's calls. "Terry is absolutely hysterical," she said in one of them. "I don't know what I'm going to do with her." As she pulled onto her street, Hazel was saying to the girl's mother, "Six more hours, Terry. You've been braver than any of us."

At home she'd smelled proper food cooking and heard voices when she stepped through the door. When she poked her head around the corner from the kitchen, she saw her mother and four other women sitting at her dining-room table. Was it an intervention? No, Hazel realized, it was poker night. Her mother was hosting. She gestured to her furiously from the cover of the kitchen, and her mother, a displeased look on her face, got up and came over. "Why didn't you tell me you were doing this tonight!"

"It's on the calendar, Hazel," her mother said.

"I need this kind of noise tonight like . . ." She couldn't think of what she needed it like. A murderer visiting a little girl? "Look, can you maybe finish up and go to Clara's? I need *one* hour of peace and quiet."

"I am not asking my friends to pack up in the middle of their supper and move on. And anyway, Paula Spencer is late, as usual. Do you plan on giving her her supper when she shows up and then playing stud with her?" She stared her daughter in the eye. "I thought not. Go shower. You smell like a locker room."

"Fine," said Hazel, throwing her hands up. She stepped forward into the dining room. "Clara," she said, waving. "Grace. Margaret. Mrs. Eaton." Sally Eaton did not approve of Hazel calling her by her first name. "Sorry to interrupt. I just wanted to say hello."

The women called their greetings.

Hazel stepped back into the kitchen. "There. I was nice. Now you can repay me by keeping it to a dull roar. And by making me a plate of whatever it is you old ladies are eating."

"There's a salad in the fridge."

"Christ, Mother."

"Go shower and rest. I have to put the pie in the oven."

She leaned into her mother, her voice strained. "I'm catching a killer and you're baking pie and playing nickel poker? Do you think you might cut me just a little bit of slack?"

"We don't play for nickels, dear," her mother had said, and then switched the oven to 250 before walking back to her friends.

—

It was dark and snowing hard. Wingate had brought three trays of coffee from town, and she watched him passing them out. In her doorway, Terry Batten was refusing his offer. She'd been standing in her parka on her front step staring at all the activity around her house and occasionally shooting Hazel a look. "She's one angry lady," said Wingate.

"Do you blame her?"

"She wants to know how many men are going to be in the house."

"I'm thinking five guys in radio contact at all access points coming toward the house from the town itself and the highway" – she turned to look at a house behind her – "one of the shooters there and a second one on the neighbour's roof. That leaves three constables, not including you and me."

"So three in the house?"

"Four. I want you there, James."

"Where are you going to be?"

She beat her hands together for warmth. "It's not a good idea for me to be there. You've built some trust with her and if I'm around too much, she might change her mind."

He nodded. "You're going to have to go in there eventually. We can't hold a briefing out here on the lawn."

"I know," she said. She looked at her watch. It was nine-thirty now. "He told Rose midnight. But with the snow coming down and the roads the way they are, we might be here all night. I'm going to do a final briefing at ten-thirty, and then I want everyone in position and ready to go right after that. We're just going to have to deal with the cold."

"Should I tell Mrs. Batten all that then?"

Hazel looked toward the house. Terry was still standing on her front stoop. She was smoking a cigarette with her arms crossed. "No, I'll tell her."

She crossed the lawn to the girl's mother, who, when she saw Hazel coming, turned sideways and cast her gaze up the street.

"I don't suppose you have another one of those," she said.

Terry Batten took a deep drag and passed Hazel the pack without speaking. "I know this wasn't an easy decision for you."

Terry laughed bitterly. "You mean dangling my daughter in front of a killer?"

"She's been magnificent, you know. Perfect."

"Yeah, well, maybe we'll put that on her gravestone. *She was magnificent.*"

The cigarette tasted strange in the cold. "In about an hour, if it's okay with you, we're going to bring everyone into the house and go over what we're doing here one more time. There are going to be three constables with you in the house, including one in Rose's room. I'm leaving James Wingate with you too, so if there's anything you need, he can get it for you."

"Your bagman has a talent for the sweet talk."

Hazel put her hand on Terry's arm and gently turned her to face her. "I don't want you to change your mind, Terry, but I want you to know that one word from you and we can move both you and Rose to somewhere safe and we can try to take him without Rose here."

"You think he's that stupid? Don't forget, I met him. He'll probably smell you guys from a hundred kilometres out."

"That's not going to happen."

"It doesn't matter if I change my mind anyway. Rose has made hers up. She wants to see him again."

"He's not going to put a foot inside your house. I promise you."

Terry threw her cigarette out into the snow, where it briefly sizzled and went out. She set her eyes on Hazel's. They were burning with rage. "You shoot him dead, Inspector, you hear? I don't care about your due process. I won't ever be able to sleep again if I know he's alive and thinking about what we did to him."

"Where he's going, Terry, it doesn't matter what he thinks about."

"He tried to kill my child, you know."

"He saved your child."

"Yeah," she said, "but now he's coming back to put her out of her 'misery.'" She pushed past Hazel and put her hand on the doorknob. "You have children, don't you, Detective Inspector?"

"I do."

"Knowing what he can do, would you want him in jail or in the ground?"

"I hear you."

Terry paused at the door and stared at Hazel. "I want you to see her. You've been skulking around out here all day, but I think you need to see her. So you understand *fully* what you've asked us to do."

She held the door open for Hazel and followed her into the house.

During the day, they'd wanted Rose to take a nap to make it easier for her to stay up as late as the operation required. "The excitement will keep me up," she'd told Wingate. When Hazel walked into the kitchen, the girl was sitting at the table eating a plate of oatmeal cookies and drinking camomile tea. She looked as fresh as a daisy.

"Hazel!" she cried out in delight, and leaped up to hug her.

"Hello, Rose. It's wonderful to see you again."

"Cookie?"

"Thank you," said Hazel, and took one. She sat across the small table from her. "I wanted to tell you how very brave we all think you are."

"Brave means you're scared but not showing it. I'm not scared." Terry had taken the seat between them and was rubbing her nose with a tissue. "*Terry* is being brave," she said. "But I don't need to." She patted her mother's hand. "Do you want to see a drawing I made?"

"Yes, Sweetie," said Terry, and the girl bounded from the table to the hall. One of the Renfrew officers had to get out of her way. Hazel realized they would have to get someone to make up the girl, to take the colour out of her cheeks. Rose came back with a sheet of paper rolled up into a tube. It took the two women holding down both edges of the drawing to keep it open. It showed Rose walking a stairway that went high up into a night sky, a stairway that vanished among the stars. She was holding Simon in her arms. Terry let go of her half and the paper snapped shut like a blind rolling up into a ceiling. She rushed from the room.

"I want to do this," said Rose, taking the paper from Hazel.

"I know you do. But I want you to understand, Rose, that when we take Simon from here, it won't be to Heaven. He's going to jail."

"I can write to him though, can't I?"

Hazel blinked twice at the girl. "That's up to your mother," she said.

"You know what Terry's going to say about that."

She took Rose gently by the upper arm. "I bet Terry would love to be called 'Mummy.' I bet she'd really like that a lot."

She seemed to think about that for a moment, and then she said, "He's sad."

"Who?"

"Simon. His heart is broken."

Hazel leaned forward and took both of the girl's hands in hers. "Rose, I want you to listen to me. This man is very dangerous. No matter what he did for you, he's still a man who's done very bad things, and what we're doing here today is to make things right. For all the people he's harmed."

"He didn't harm me."

"I know. What he did for you was wondrous, Rose. But he's still a murderer." Rose was smiling at her, stroking the back of Hazel's hands with her thumbs. "You're a marvellous little girl, you know that? You're smarter than most of the adults I know. But don't make the mistake of thinking that Simon is a good man. Tell me you know what he's done is wrong."

"Of course I know that, silly."

"Good."

"But he's not a bad man, Hazel. He's just sad."

"Okay," said Hazel, and she released the girl's hands. "Go give your mother a hug, would you?"

The girl tilted her head at her, as if Hazel were from a different species, then skipped out of the room. Hazel watched her go, and for a moment, the thought appeared in her mind that the Belladonna and his intended victim had access to a dimension she could not begin to imagine. But it was a place where death was somehow equivalent to life, and the transition between the two was a holy space. Perhaps, having peered into that space herself, it seemed not so strange to Rose. Perhaps it was even welcoming. She wondered for a moment if they could trust the girl.

She left the house by the back door and stood in the denuded garden under the bare trees and got her cell-phone out. Its little screen reflected the sky. Spere was already on his way to the site when he answered. "Howard? We need someone who can make this girl look like she's on death's door."

"There's probably a funeral home in the town," he replied. "They know how to do that kind of thing."

"How fitting," she said. "Listen, what's the chance you can get Jack to call in a prescription for some mild sedatives to the local pharmacy here?"

"You out of whiskey?"

"For Mrs. Batten."

"Ah," he said.

She stood scuffing the dirt with her foot and looking at the cellphone in her hand for a moment, as if she might be able to discern Spere's facial expression in it. She put it back against her ear. "Howard?"

"Yeah."

"How chummy are *you* with Gord Sunderland?"

"What?"

"Or Ian Mason for that matter."

"If this is your way of asking me out on a date, Hazel, it's not going to work."

"I just want to know how some of my other loyal associates are going to air their grievances."

"Look, Hazel, you're a pain in the ass, but for the most part, you're good people. Everyone knows that." He paused for a second. "Almost everyone."

"Uh-huh."

"I'm sorry about Ray. I am. But what he did doesn't make any of the rest of us assholes. At least not for the same reasons. Okay?"

"Okay," she said.

"Good. Now you want me to call Jack?"

"Yeah."

"I can get you whiskey, too."

"Fuck off, Howard," she said, but he'd made her smile. She erased it from her face immediately, worried that someone might see her.

"I'll catch you there," he said, his voice lifting at the end, as if he wasn't sure if he actually would. She hung up, feeling anew the stab of disbelief that Ray had betrayed her. It came at her like that raw sensation that visits you at unexpected times after someone dies. When, for a moment, you've stopped thinking about it and then suddenly it comes at you, fresh and terrible, and you realize it's still true. Someone you loved is gone for good.

She put the phone away and leaned backward to stretch out the tightness in her lower back. This almost never worked, but on a night when she was determined not to indulge in any of her regular painkillers, it was all she had.

At ten-thirty, she called muster in the house and the ten men and women who made up her team gathered in Terry Batten's living room and stood around its perimeter. Hazel invited Terry to listen in, but she would have none of it and stayed in the kitchen. Hazel went over the final details. Wingate would give the sign to the shooters to move into their positions on the two rooftops near the Batten house as soon as muster was over. The officers assigned to the interior were not to leave the house; the five rovers were to be in their cars doing their circuits as of eleven o'clock.

Wingate was point man inside the house. Hazel would take up a post one street over, listening on an open channel for progress reports. She wanted radio silence as of eleven o'clock; they were to go fully dark unless something unexpected came up.

"Like what?" said Terry from the kitchen.

"We're going to be prepared for anything," said Hazel.

"Like if he's early?"

"No," said Hazel. "He's never early."

Terry's gaze lingered on her a moment. "Well, I guess you have the plan."

Wingate stepped forward. "Mrs. Batten, this is the largest police presence I've ever seen at a stakeout, and I worked for eight years out of a station house in downtown Toronto. Every one of us has your safety and Rose's safety at the front of our minds."

"Are your guns loaded?"

He looked at Hazel, whose mouth twitched. "Yes, they are."

She looked around the room at the police officers, and Hazel braced herself for another angry outburst from Terry Batten. But instead she headed back toward the kitchen. At the swinging door that led into it, she turned to the gathered force in her living room. "I've got a pot of stew on and a couple loaves of garlic bread. I want you people to eat and then do your job and get out of my house."

On her way out, Hazel took Wingate aside. "Look. Get the rovers moving now."

"It's only ten-forty."

"Just in case," she said.

At 10:55 p.m., standing out in the street again, Hazel could see curls of steam coming from the rooftops as the officers kept warm with flasks of soup or coffee, but as soon as the clock struck eleven, they were in lockdown. Hazel's cruiser was at its post one street over. She'd said her goodbyes after muster and sat with the child one more time, to go over what Simon expected her to do and what the Port Dundas PD needed her to do. Terry had stood in the doorway to the girl's bedroom and added her comments to Hazel's instructions when she thought there was any chance that Rose might forget who was really in charge under this roof.

"You don't say anything, Rose," said Hazel. "You just do as he's asked you to do: you're to stand here looking out. Your voice might give away that you're not as sick as you've told him."

"And you don't put any part of your body outside of this house!" said Terry Batten.

"I won't," said the girl. It had seemed to Hazel that Rose was getting nervous as the time approached. She wondered if she shouldn't dose her with a little of what was keeping her mother level.

"I want to stay here with her until the last possible moment," Terry said.

"You can be in this room until midnight, Terry. But after that, we have to clear the area. We don't want him seeing shadows in Rose's room. He's got to be certain that everything is as he's asked. Or he could be gone before we even see him."

"I'll lie in the bed with her. We'll be as still as the grave."

"I can't, Terry. The instant it's over, the two of you will be together, I promise."

Rose reached out and took her mother's hand. "Mummy?" she said, and both of the women looked at her with their eyes wide.

"Sweetie?"

"I'm going to be fine. I'm not scared at all."

Terry scooped her daughter up in her arms and pressed the girl's face against her shoulder. She wept, holding Rose tightly against her. This is it, thought Hazel. She's going to ask us to get out of her house. But instead, Terry said, "You're such a big girl now, aren't you?"

"Do what the police officers say, okay, Mummy? Tomorrow morning, this'll all be over and people will thank us."

"We thank you now," said Hazel. "But she's right. There's no turning back."

Hazel was in the car one block over, and the look on Terry's face when she'd at last let go of the little girl and agreed to leave the room was still branded on her mind. They'd closed the door on Rose's somewhat uneasy smile, and one of the Renfrew cops led her lightly by the arm away from the room. There were three officers in the house, two set up on rooftops with clear views of the street, the front of the house, and Rose's window. Hazel had linkup on a single frequency, but it was radio silence after eleven, and no one was to break silence unless it was an emergency, or Simon Mallick was captured, incapacitated, or dead.

At ten after eleven, Spere startled her by appearing at the passenger door. He opened it and stepped in. "Forgot I was here?" he said.

"I thought you'd gone back to Mayfair."

"Wouldn't miss this for anything. Plus, it sounds like you need all the friends you can get these days."

"We're friends?"

"You've made my life interesting again," he said. "I'm totally renaming all my goldfish 'Hazel.'" He settled back in the passenger seat and rubbed the tops of his legs. He eyed the ham sandwich wrapped in wax paper that she'd brought from home after making it secretly in the kitchen. After staring at it five seconds too long, he looked up to see her watching him. "What?"

"Friends share?" she asked.

"If they're not going to eat it they do."

"Go ahead," she said, and he unwrapped it and ate it in five bites. Spere ate like a camel, his mouth slewing side to side. Hazel wondered how anyone could stand him outside of a professional context, and then she remembered that he was married and had three kids, and that at the summer fund-raising picnics, he was often the only cop in the place whose family looked like they were enjoying themselves. The whole world was stuffed with crazy imbalances like this. Spere: a happily married man.

"How's the back?" he said, making her jump a little. She had to remind herself she'd only been thinking her thoughts, not saying them.

"I'm ignoring it," she said.

He crumpled up the wax paper and stuffed it into the little plastic tub that was the garbage can. Then he dug in his coat pocket and took out a single white pill. He offered it to her. "Jack's script was for three pills. I held one back, thinking you might want it."

She looked at it, a single Valium. "I bet Gord Sunderland would love to have a photographer here right about now."

"I told you, I didn't —"

"I know you didn't," she said. "And this is very kind of you, Howard, but I think I'd better live with the discomfort tonight."

He nodded at her, closing his fingers over the pill. He was putting it back into his pocket when he opened his hand in his lap and pushed a fingernail into the pill. It snapped in half. He looked at the two pieces lying there in his palm like he was expecting them to do something magical.

Hazel reached over and took one of the halves. "This'll just take the edge off."

"That's what I'm thinking," he said.

She swallowed it with a dry mouth. "After this night is over, Howard, you're going to go back to being a thorn in my side, right?"

"I promise," he said.

"Because too much has changed in my life lately to take you transforming into a gentleman."

"It won't happen," he said. He settled back into his seat and stared out the windshield.

She looked at the digital display on the dashboard. It said 11:13. She looked at it ten minutes later and it said 11:16. Howard had closed his eyes. The wait was going to kill her. She got out her cell and dialled the house.

"Paula?" said her mother.

"No, Mum, it's just me. I wanted to call and see how you were."

"Very full, a little drunk, and up sixteen dollars." She lowered her voice to a whisper. "Sally Eaton will call *anything*."

"I'm sorry I lost my temper with you before."

"You're under a lot of pressure, Hazel. You need a vacation."

"I do."

There was laughter in the background. "How's your stakeout? Are you having fun?"

"You *are* drunk, aren't you?"

"Just a moment, dear." Her mother held the phone away from her mouth. "Clara, will you get that? It's Paula." She came back to Hazel. "Stupid woman. She's owes us twelve dollars in antes. I better go. But if you catch your man, you can have the last piece of pie, okay?"

"Thank you."

"Don't wake me before ten tomorrow!"

Her mother hung up, and Hazel put the phone down on the console between the seats. Her mother, drunk with her pals on a Friday night. When am I going to learn how to live? she thought.

The cold wind outside the car drove the snow into the headlights and went rustling through the tops of the trees. The branches whipped in sudden frenzies and gusts of snow exploded off the branches where it had settled. Then everything would come to stillness briefly. They'd sat silently for nearly another hour watching the occasional traffic move past slowly as well as a few nightbirds taking their dogs out for a last walk before turning in. It was nearly midnight; there had been no word from inside the house nor from the roving cars nor the men stationed on the rooftops since eleven. The radio silence was spooky. Even with a half a Valium inside her, Hazel Micallef was wide awake. She kept as still as she could in the driver's seat; any shifting sent shivers of pain down into her leg. The Valium made it feel as if it didn't matter, but she knew from experience that as soon as she stood up, she'd get a full dose of something else. In a matter of minutes this would all be over and she could move on to the next part of her life. In three weeks' time, she'd undergo a test even her GP warned her was "unpleasant." A CT myelogram. A spinal tap to fill her spine with ink, followed by a scan. Nothing else would be as definitive: after the test, they'd know if it was the knife for her or not.

Midnight came and went. "Christ," said Spere, rousing himself. "What if he doesn't show?"

"He'll show," she said. "He's going to prove to us he can do it." She keyed the radio quietly. "Maintain positions." She got a "copy" from Wingate and from Fairview across the road from the Batten house.

"What's the chance he's changed cars?" said Spere. "Are we sure the officers on point are going to see him coming?"

"They're just the first line of defence. He'll probably get through. But when he does, he won't be out of the car long before we're on top of him."

"Are you shooting?"

"If he so much as tilts his head, yes."

They sat in the cold for another forty minutes and watched the snow coming down. It was blowing past in more than two directions, a soft chaos. At one-fifteen, Wingate radioed her. "I'm sorry, Skip. But the mother's getting pretty anxious in here."

"Did she take a pill?"

"I think we'd need an elephant tranquilizer at this point."

"Keep her calm," said Hazel, but as she was speaking another voice broke in, saying *please advise*. "Who is this?" she called. "I *do not* copy —"

"A car —" came Fairview's voice, breaking up, over the radio.

"God, he's there," said Spere.

"— in front of the house —"

"Who has him?" There was a flurry of voices: Glencoe and one of the officers inside the house by the name of Shepherd.

"Shepherd, if you're at a window, get away from it. Glencoe?"

"Here —"

"You have a clear shot?"

"It's not the right car —"

"He could have changed cars!" shouted Spere into the handset.

"He's getting out," said Glencoe. "I repeat, I have a suspect going up the walk. Rick, you got him?"

The other shooter came on. "I can see him, but he's yours, Glencoe."

Spere was already out of the car, shouting toward the houses. "Take a shot, goddammit!"

"Howard!" she called after him, but he was already in the street, the snow closing around him. "Goddammit! I need an ID!" hissed Hazel into her radio. "You know what this guy is supposed to look like —"

"Shoot your fucking guns!" shouted Spere from the road.

"It's not him — it's a kid," said Fairview, "a teenager. He's carrying something." They listened to the officer scrabbling across the roof to a new location. "Positions inside the house —"

"We're ready," came Wingate's voice.

"This isn't our guy —"

They heard a shot fired, and Hazel threw the car door open and sprang from the car. "Man down!" shouted Glencoe, and she was in the road, sprinting. She hit the verge on the other side and something low in her back twanged and she went to the ground as if she'd been shot. Spere heard her shout and rushed back to her. "Help me up —"

"Can you walk?"

"Goddammit," she roared as he lifted her from the road. "Is this fucking week ever going to end? Go! Let's go!"

He took off ahead of her and, willing herself to move through the pain, Hazel took off after them. They rounded the corner and already they could hear shouts from the house. Wingate and the three other officers were flying out of the house and three of the roving cruisers had fishtailed onto the street from two different directions. There was a pile of three men on top of the suspect, and he was screaming in agony. They all arrived at the same instant, and Hazel dragged the cops off the kid. He'd been shot through the thigh and he was roiling on the ground, a star of dark-red blood soaking the snow. She could see all the porchlights going on up and down the street. "Who are you?" she shouted, falling on him and turning him face-up. "Who are you!"

"Oh God! God!"

"Who are you!"

"Danny! My name's Danny!"

A frightened thought rushed across her mind, and Hazel lifted herself off their suspect. "Is anyone still watching the house?" The men looked back and forth over her. "For Christ's sake, someone get into that bedroom!" There was a sudden shudder and the small crowd of officers flew apart. She returned her attention to the kid on the ground beneath her. "What are you doing here? Who sent you?"

"I come from Bond Head," he said. The tears were pouring down his cheeks. "I been five hours in shitty weather, lady."

"*Why.*"

"A guy paid me a hundred dollars to deliver a letter." The thing he'd been holding was lying in the snow ten feet away, where it had landed after the kid had been knocked flying by the officers in the house. It was a small, white envelope. She could see from where she was that her name was on it, in a tight, black script. "I swear to God!"

She pushed up, willing herself to stand. The kid rolled into a ball, moaning. One of the men inside the house returned to the front door with both Rose and Terry. "I want the whole perimeter of the house staked out. You've shown your faces now, so just make sure no one gets within five hundred metres of this place." She'd been hearing doors opening and closing; in a matter of moments, they'd have a crowd. "Keep people away from here!" she shouted to the officers in the cruisers.

"What's happening?" said Terry.

Hazel limped across the lawn, waving Wingate's hand off, and leaned down to pick up the small envelope. It weighed almost nothing. She'd left her gloves in the car and already her hands were beginning to freeze.

"Don't touch that, Hazel," Howard Spere said.

"It's for me," she said, panting for air. She put a fingertip under the edge of the flap and tore the envelope open. Her heart was pounding. She pinched the sides of the envelope and looked inside. There was a single, stiff piece of paper within. She drew it out and instantly dropped it into the snow, as if it had burst into flame at her touch.

"*My God*—"

"What is it!" called Spere from ten feet away.

She fell to her knees. Instantly, her people were around her, their voices rising in fear. In the snow, a plasticized little square lay on its face, its black back shining up like a piece of slate. Wingate knelt beside her, his arm around her shoulders, but she couldn't speak. "Skip? Hazel . . . what is it?"

"A Polaroid," she murmured.

He reached down in front of her and turned it over. A wave of light moved over its surface.

"That's my house," she said, taking it out of his hand. "That's a picture of my house."

—

She said goodbye to her daughter, put the phone back on its hook, and came out cradling three glasses between her hands. Clara came down the hall with a strange look on her face.

"It's not Paula," she said.

"Oh for God's sake."

"It's a man looking for Hazel."

"All right, just a moment everyone," Emily said, and she put down the last glass and wiped her fingertips on the front of her pants. "I'll go see what he –" she started to say, but before she could finish, Clara Lyon's face had disappeared in a spray of blood and bone. Clara fell back as if in a faint and, stepping around her, holding up a steel mallet drenched in gore, was a man in a long black coat. The whites of his eyes glowed a pale yellow and his skin hung from his skull as if it were dripping from the bone.

"Emily Micallef?" he said. She stared at him in mute terror. The man stepped to her. "I am Simon of Aramea."

22

Saturday, November 27, 4 a.m.

At the age of six, she'd lost her mother in a supermarket. Once a month, her mother would drive down to Mayfair to the big grocery store and Hazel would be allowed to push the cart up and down the aisles. She was old enough to read the prices on the little red stickers and already quick with numbers, and Emily gave her the task of choosing the least expensive brand of julienned green beans, or to calculate how much two sirloin steaks would cost. In her head, Hazel could see the numbers coming together, could hold the ones apart in her mind as she added the tens first. If, during this monthly outing, she was particularly useful or clever, her mother would buy her a barley-sugar sucker at the checkout, or even allow her to choose a cake for after supper.

They'd been in the aisle with the rice and dry beans and at the end of the aisle, turning toward the dairy section, Hazel realized that she had been following a woman wearing the same coat as her mother. She turned and went back down the direction she'd come, but her mother was not there. Neither was she in either of the aisles on either side, nor in the frozen foods section, nor at the meat counter. Hazel stopped at the front of the store, where the pyramids of tuna and washing powder stood before the cashiers, and she recalled (now, as her entire complement of officers assembled at the station house in the middle of the night) that it was dark through the high windows at the front of the store, storm clouds had gathered, and she was afraid. But she did not want to call out or ask an adult for help because she thought if she did her mother would never reappear. What she feared most would become real. She clutched the cart's handle and began to search up and down the aisles in an orderly fashion even as a grip of terror tightened in her belly. At last she found her, at the very back of the store, inspecting a carton of eggs. She was picking each one out, turning it over, and replacing it in its cardboard cup. Hazel rolled the cart up to her. "How many eggs is a dozen and a half?" her mother had asked her, and Hazel told her eighteen. "Did you find what you were looking for?"

"Yes," said Hazel.

"Then let's pay," said her mother. To her, Hazel had not been missing at all, and perhaps the entire episode had lasted less than two minutes. But Hazel had never forgotten the terror of thinking her mother had vanished.

—

The overnight duty officers were Sergeant MacDonald, and constables Forbes and Windemere. Wingate had called the station house from the road, roaring back along the 121 with Hazel paralyzed in the passenger seat, telling the three officers that all hands were needed immediately, and when they arrived, all but PC Jenner and Sergeant Costamides were there. The moment Hazel passed through the doors, Forbes, Ashton, and Windemere were given orders to hit the major highways west, north, and south, and MacDonald and Wilton were to take unmarked cars and scour the side streets for suspicious activity of any kind in Port Dundas, Hoxley, and Hillschurch.

She stood in the pen in front of the rest of them and she knew her fear was naked. She could not muster at this moment what it would take to hide her torment from these people. Clara Lyon's body was on its way down to Mayfair. They had called Clara's daughter in Toronto, who was beginning the long drive north in a state of choking horror. Simon had herded Emily's three remaining guests – Grace Hughes, Margaret Entwhistle, and Sally Eaton – into the garden shed and locked them there in their evening clothes. All three were in hospital suffering from hypothermia and there was some doubt that Mrs. Entwhistle, already fragile with rheumatoid arthritis, was going to make it to morning.

By the time the sun was coming up, they'd heard from all of the officers on patrol and there was nothing. In each of their voices, Hazel could hear the exhausted panic of having no time to succeed. There were no sightings of the car they believed Simon was driving, or reports of accidents, or untoward incidents of any kind. A call to Equifax established that Simon Mallick had two credit cards and a savings account, but he'd not made use of any of it in the preceding twelve hours. In fact, there had been no activity at all in any of his accounts since before the spring. In the station house, five constables had ceaselessly been dialling motels, inns, gas stations, and all-night variety stores within three hundred kilometres to collect fax numbers; a hastily thrown-together description of Simon, Emily Micallef, and the car was faxed out. If there was no fax machine, verbals were given. The entire place was roiling, but Hazel knew in the deepest part of herself that the Belladonna would not be tripped up now. It was possible her mother was already dead, and that her killer had gone to ground. Grace Hughes was the only one of the three elderly ladies who was capable of talking to them: Kraut Fraser had gone to the hospital to interview her. She'd given the description of a man of skin and bone. She'd heard the vertebrae in his back grinding when he moved. He'd smelled to her of Juicy Fruit gum, she'd said, but underneath the sweetness, there was a scent of rotting meat. She told Fraser she was certain he was going to kill them all, but when he'd closed the shed door on them, he'd looked upon them all kindly and wished them a good night.

"Juicy Fruit is ketones," said Spere. He'd asked if he could speak to her in her office. "He's starving himself. It comes from the breakdown of fat reserves. And if he wasn't crazy when he left Vancouver Island, you can bet he is now. If an old lady can smell ketones on this guy, then he's practically digesting his own body, including his brain."

"So this means my mother's dead or alive, Howard?" she snapped.

"I'm just trying to give you a picture of the guy," said Spere. "What his state of mind might be."

Some of the overnighters had gone home at 6 a.m. to sleep for a few hours, and now they were coming back in, and some of the others were heading out, but reluctantly. All night long, it had felt to her like the place was shaking, as if they were on a ship in rough seas. It was no calmer now that daylight had come.

She'd tried to avoid being in her office since arriving back in Port Dundas at 3 a.m. She hadn't wanted to see her desk, her phone, her chair, or any part of this room in which she'd failed to foresee the kind of upending Simon Mallick had plotted for them all. The room stank of her disastrous lack of foresight. She'd known he wasn't stupid, and yet she'd proceeded, in the thrall of what she thought of as her last hope, to try to trap him. And he had mocked her by striking at her very heart.

She was aware that Howard Spere was staring at her with a tilted head. "You okay?" he asked.

"What?"

"We were talking and you sort of zoned out. Maybe you should let one of your people take you home for a couple of hours."

"No," she said. "I won't be going home until this is . . . settled." She drew the palm of her hand down over her face, as if to scour herself awake. "Whatever you might think of this man's state of mind, Howard, it's at least as sharp as ours, and we've only been up one night. This guy's been living rough for two months, and from the sound of him, he's firing on all cylinders with no fuel at all. So we're not going to use the word *crazy* about him to anyone."

"Okay," he said, looking down.

"Why did you ask me in here, Howard?"

"Oh. Well, I thought you'd want to know that Margaret Entwhistle has died."

"Give me something, people! Who has news? Who knows anything?" She was standing, hands on her hips, and she'd startled them by flying into the pen already shouting. Some of them put down their phone receivers or pens and turned to her, flicking glances at one another. They were already doing everything they could. "Come on!" Hazel shouted. "We don't have a week to put a god-damned case together!"

Sergeant Renald took a chance and stood to read something from his daybook. "Report of a break-in at a pharmacy at Seymour Lake."

"Okay!" she said, stepping forward. Seymour Lake was ninety minutes southwest of Port Dundas. "Any surveillance tape?"

"Chief, this is a town of fourteen hundred people. There's probably a single camcorder there, you know?"

"Fine," she said. She was faintly aware of Wingate's presence beside her. "What was taken?"

Renald consulted his notes again. "Uh, a shelf of adult diapers and also some chewable vitamins."

She was nodding. "Great. That's our lead? He's incontinent and fighting *fucking scurvy!?*"

"Hazel," said Wingate quietly.

"This is the ex-mayor of our town. This is my mother. Can you people get your heads on straight and figure out where this guy is? Who haven't you called? Where does he think we won't be looking? Look *there!* Have you thought of that?"

"Skip," said Wingate.

"What?" He walked back into the hallway and her guts flipped. "What is it!"

"It's nothing," he said, "nothing about anything."

"Then what?"

"Don't you think you should go home? Rest up a bit? This could go on for a while."

"Did Spere send you over to tell me that?"

"No," he said. "I don't need Detective Spere to tell me you need a break."

"What am I going to do at home, James?"

"These people need to focus."

She pushed past him, a caged animal. "Would *you* go home, James?"

He had to admit he wouldn't. But he wanted to give her a chance to decide for herself to leave. An officer driving Ian Mason up from Barrie had radioed from the road: they'd be there in half an hour.

By mid-morning Terry Batten had filed suit against the OPS for reckless endangerment. She and Rose were in Mayfair, having insisted that Central put them up somewhere safe while she thought about their options. She had already decided that the house in Humber Cottage would have to be sold: they would not live in that town, she'd told Mason, not in a house marked by a killer. She'd filed a second suit for mental anguish naming just Hazel. She and her lawyer were working on other charges.

Mason parked in the rear and sent in one of his men to ask Hazel to come talk to him outside. He told her he was sorry about her mother and that all the resources of OPS Central Division were being brought to bear on finding her. He reassured her that the abduction of her mother was *not* being treated as any other missing persons case: all available personnel as far south as Barrie were on it. Mason spoke to her with more respect and warmth than she'd ever seen coming from him, so she knew it was going to be bad. He asked for her badge.

"I can't do that," she said.

He turned his gaze to the two large police constables standing beside the car they'd driven him up in. "You can have a radio," he said. "You'll hear what we hear in real time. But you can't be at the station house now, Hazel."

"You're going to need a judge."

He produced an envelope and held it up. "I thought you might say something like that. I don't actually need anyone to take you off the job. But I've got a warrant for your arrest if I need it. You want to open it?"

"Arrest for what? I'm being sued. It's not illegal to be sued."

"Trespass is illegal, Hazel. You're relieved of duty, and so as of this moment, you're trespassing."

"You're a piece of work, Ian." He noticed the men and women standing in the hallway behind the glass door that led to the parking lot. She turned and looked. "Do you really think they're going to let your two drug-squad bruisers jam me into the back of a car and drive me home?"

Mason gestured to the small mob to come join them, and they pushed through the door into the cold sunshine of midmorning. He pushed up on his toes to see to the back of the crowd. "Which one of you is Jim Windgate?"

He stepped forward under Hazel's steady gaze. "Et tu, Wingate?"

He offered her a miserable look. "He's going to move the investigation to Mayfair and put Spere in charge of it if you don't go." Mason offered the young detective his hand. Wingate looked at it as if he were being asked to sign on the dotted line.

"Take it," said Mason, and Wingate did. "Congrats, you're the new interim CO."

"Um," said Wingate.

"Look everyone," Mason said to the officers, "Detective Inspector Micallef has to take a break from active duty, but I know you'll all be reassuring her that you're going to carry on in her *temporary* absence under the capable direction of Sergeant Windgate –"

"Detective Constable Wingate," said Wingate.

"Yes," said Mason, "and that everything here will proceed as per the instructions you've been given."

An unhappy murmur from the gathered officers. Wingate turned to them. "I'm sorry, everyone, I don't like it any more than you do. Anyone who can't work under this arrangement should say so now, no prejudice. Otherwise, everyone back to their desks. There's a woman's life at stake."

"There you go," said Mason, and he was grinning at her. "It's like you were never here."

"I'll take my own car, you son of a bitch."

Her people were filing inside with backward glances. "It's not *your* car, Hazel. It's the detatchment's." One of his men opened the back door of Mason's cruiser. "Constables Erwitt and Atget will be more than happy to get you home."

She began to move to the car. Mason made a sound behind her, and she turned to him.

"Your badge," he said.

"You want my gun too?"

"Wingate will hold on to it for now."

"Why can't Wingate hold on to my badge."

"He can reassign the gun."

"That's not what I asked you."

"Just give me the goddamned ID, Hazel, and get into the car."

She tried to stare him down, but the man was an obelisk. He just stared back at her as if thinking of something else entirely. She'd never settled for herself whether Mason's sangfroid was a result of not caring or having seen it all. "There's nothing you can do to me, Ian, that's any worse than what I've done to myself."

He shook his head slowly, and she realized to her regret that he was pitying her. "After all this time, you still don't know me at all, do you, Hazel?"

It was a long, silent drive back to Pember Lake.

She cleaned the house for the rest of the day, furiously mopping, spraying the windows and washing them with newspaper in wide, wild circles, swabbing out various basins and tubs with mad application, and called in to the station every half hour for updates. She spoke only to Cartwright, standing in front of one of the clean windows with sweat pouring down her. There was no progress at all. She went back to cleaning, but in the middle of the afternoon when there wasn't a single unscoured surface, she broke down and threw a scrub brush into the hall mirror. It exploded like a window shattered by a rock, but revealed, instead of the unmediated background, a dark, featureless wall.

She recalled a theory from one of Martha's high-school science classes. She couldn't bring to mind all of the details, but the basic idea was that if you put a cat in a windowless box and subjected it to a random process that could cause the cat's death at any given moment, then you had to say that the cat was both dead and alive until you were able to observe what was actually happening. This was how she felt about her mother. Her mother was equally dead and alive at this moment in time, and their investigation was the box. Simon Mallick was the random element, the radioactive isotope (as she now recalled) that might, at any moment, break down and cause her mother's death. The feeling of helplessness that suffused her now combined with the urgency in her muscles and she felt a kind of sick thrill in her veins, as if she were dying and being born all at once.

Night fell. She lay on the bed with the phone on her chest. She dialled Melanie every half hour until her shift ended at eight o'clock. Then she dialled Staff Sergeant Wilton. He said, *There's nothing* in her ear all night long. He stopped saying *I'm sorry, Hazel*, at three in the morning. She could hear the voices of her people in the background. Somewhere, in the deeper background, was her mother, and Hazel didn't know if there was still a voice to be heard.

The house seemed like a museum where all the artifacts from her life had been carefully reproduced and placed in attitudes that recalled to her that she had once lived there and had, at times, been happy. She had led a married life here, as a wife and a mother, with no awareness of what her future held. She would leave everything behind now, she told herself, this house, this town, this body even, if her final thoughts could contain the knowledge that her pride and her stupidity had not cost her mother her life. But what was there to hope for now? Her mother had not had her calcium supplement in two days, nor her blood thinners, her painkillers for her arthritis, nor her manganese, her B vitamin, or her iron. The Fosamax she took for her osteoporosis lay powerless in its bottle. And it was so cold outside now, with the snow falling and falling, accumulating – where was she? She had been taken in indoor shoes and without her coat. Was she outside? Was she walking in this? Was she alive?

The Toronto *Sunday Star*: "Maverick Smalltown Police Chief Puts Eight-Year-Old in Line of Fire."

She took her pills early and kept to her bed and the living room. Her heart kept pounding. She took Ativan. Daytime television seemed especially sinister, like some kind of alternative reality in which lonely women were being trained for a violent takeover of the world's kitchens. She would watch the various shows with their strange codes and drowse off with the sound up. When the credits music woke her, she called the station house. Melanie was back on as of ten. There was still nothing to report. Hazel was dying. "I never thought I'd be saying this," said her mother standing in the big picture window, the light a corona around her head, "but I think you should eat something."

"I'm not hungry."

Emily Micallef came and sat on the coffee table, pushed the jumble of the day's newspapers aside. "Public life has its risks, Hazel. We think we'll be commended for serving, but really, the only thing that gets noticed is failure. You just had a longer run than most."

"You can shake off a political mess, Mother. But if you let a murderer go, it's something else."

"It's just a different level of public relations," said Emily.

What she wouldn't have done to be twelve again, in tears, her face against her mother's chest, willing, at last, to listen to the soothing platitudes mothers are so good with when their children's tempests threaten to overflow their teacups.

Except this wasn't a tempest, it was an earthquake. She realized that she could see the television through her mother's chest and she sat up on the couch, fear rippling through her. "Where are you?"

Her mother was fading. "Somewhere cold," came the reply, and then Hazel was alone in the room.

] 23 [

She woke and lifted her head off her chest. Her eyes fell on an expanse of darkness broken only by a thin yellow flame clinging to the wick of an oil lamp on the other side of the room. It illuminated only the space of the lamp itself, four glass panes enclosing a square of dim light. She was in a hardbacked chair staring out onto nothing, but the staleness of the air suggested an enclosed space. A back room or a shack of some kind. She moved a foot over the floor and felt her shoe rumbling over grit. She swept to the right and then, with the other foot, to the left – semicircles to the sides of the chair. Nothing. She was not bound in any way. It meant she was free to move and it also meant that he was in complete control, that he did not fear she could somehow turn the situation to her advantage. It was risible, anyway, to think of herself sitting there, in the cold, looking for an angle. But what person who wanted to live would not?

What must Hazel be going through, she wondered. She thinks I'm dead. And they must know about poor Clara by now. She clenched her eyes. We who survive our widowhoods, our cancers, the benighted mates our children choose, the many small insults of old age . . . and then to die like that, in sudden pain and horror. She tried to push back the image of her dear friend's mild eyes, that unassuming smile. And the sudden savagery of it, those features she knew so well vanishing in a moment of unthinkable violence. Her friend's blood was still on her clothing. And then this man had stepped over Clara's body as if it were nothing more than a spot on the floor and herded them out of the back of the house, the remaining four of them steeped in a terrible silence full of knowledge. At the last moment, he'd held her back and put the others into the garden shed. The screech of the steel door closing on them. "They'll die of cold," she'd said to him, and she'd felt a sharp pain in her upper arm. She thought he'd cut her. But then a strange warmth filled her and she was falling through space and the next thing she knew, she was in a chair in the dark.

He was using her for bait.

She tried to imagine all the mechanisms that were already in place to find her, and she dreaded what it meant for Hazel. Because if she was alive, it was Hazel he wanted. Although Emily could not imagine what difference her being alive or dead could make to this man. She hoped that they would never find her. It was the only hope she had now.

Her eyes had adjusted somewhat to the poor light, and although she could not see her own body, ten feet away there were a few inches of lit wall behind the oil lamp. There might be a door in that wall, she thought. She decided to try standing, and she leaned forward to get up, but as she did, she heard a flutter of movement from the other side of the room and she slowly lowered herself back into the seat. A bandaged hand floated up in the space between lamp and wall, and the flame climbed the wick. Its light crept along an arm to a shoulder and stopped there, holding the disembodied limb in its glow, and then the man who had called himself Simon leaned into the light and it picked his eyes out of the darkness like two dying stars. She thought her heart would stop.

"You're awake," he said. "How are you?"

She wondered if he could see her, if she was yet safely enclosed in her own darkness, and she felt like shrinking into it, pushing away from the threat of that light on the other side of the room. But when he'd spoken, she knew from how the sound of his voice had travelled that there was not far to run.

"You may feel a little logy. Be careful if you get up. I wanted to keep the light low in case you needed to rest longer. Are you rested? Do you feel all right?"

"Do you care how I feel?"

"I do." He turned the lamp up higher and a yolky, pulsating light bloomed into the space. Now she saw what she had intuited: a small cabin with nothing in it but a table and two chairs, a woodstove in the corner where he sat, and a window beside it looking out on a moonless night. He was dressed exactly as he had been (earlier in the night? How long had she been out?) his coat flowing over his legs. There was a single door to the shack, directly in front of her. He saw her looking at it. "Do you want to go outside? Take the air?"

"No," she said quietly.

"Ask yourself if you'd be alive right now if I did not will it."

"I would have come with you. You didn't have to do what you . . . what you did."

"Words would not have been enough to express the urgency of my situation."

"I would have come if you'd only asked."

"I apologize then. If I was too forceful." He rose on *forceful* and her chairlegs squealed beneath her: she'd instinctively pushed herself away from him. He picked up both the lamp and the small table it had been sitting on and came toward her. The ball of light went with him as he moved through the room and she saw his body in full again: he was like a sliver of black soap, as if the very air had been wearing him away to nothing. When she'd first seen him, in the briefness of her fear he'd seemed immense. Now it was as if he were made up of incommensurate parts: the heavy, bony hands, one of them wound with a bloodied cloth wrap, at the end of the seemingly powerless arms; the starved skull over broad shoulders. She had a strange thought: he was not the man in charge. He was the forward scout, the messenger. She expected a man with more life in him to come through the door. Although she knew in her heart it was only this man, just this man, and whatever unnameable thing he carried with him she was never going to see nor understand. He put the table and the lamp down in front of her and then retrieved his seat and gingerly lowered his body into it. A sweetly sour odour emanated from him, like stale sweat, and something else, something she couldn't identify. He seemed exhausted with the effort of crossing the room three times and she could hear the air whistling thinly in his chest when he sat in front of her. She took him in: the sallow, parchment-coloured skin, the putty-pale eyes. She looked at his hand. "What on earth happened to you?" she said.

"I hurt myself." He blinked as slow as a tortoise. "Tell me . . . did you choose your life, Emily Micallef?"

"Yes, I did."

"Could you have said no to any of the things you were called upon to do? Any of the things you were meant to be?"

"I could have."

"If you could have, you would have learned your calling was false," he said. He laid his hands on his knees — long, thin hands her mother would have called piano-playing hands — and straightened his back. "Else you did what you were meant to do."

"I was in politics my whole life," she said. "Meaning never came into it. People who claimed to have a calling were usually people who couldn't justify their actions any other way."

He turned his chin minutely to the left, as if to look at her more closely. The light of the lantern hit his right eye and turned it a blinding white. "I'm not in politics."

"No. You help others by murdering them."

"We pass into others' care," he said. "And they pass into ours."

"If that's what you want to call it."

"You were once mother to a helpless child, and now she houses you. Soon she'll feed and bathe you. You brought her into life, and she'll . . ." He breathed in and out deeply. "She'll play the role nature gave her."

"So you're an agent of nature."

"A different nature."

"And whose child are you, then?"

"No one's," he said, and his eyes moved off her.

"You're someone's child."

"No," he said. "I am not child, parent, or brother. I am not even I. Simon has survived himself. And he guides those who are willing to survive their deaths to another way of being." He brought his gaze back and his eyes were dead now, flat like a dried stone. "So much as a loyal child guides her mother to death."

She made eye contact with him. His hair lay down along his forehead and the sides of his skull. "I don't need Hazel to die," she said. "All you need to do is keep me here another day or two without my medications, and I'll be quite capable of dying on my own."

"I'll minister to you."

"I'm sure you will," she said. She'd placed the other scent now. It was the odour that came off a steak that had gone grey in the fridge. Fleshrot.

"Your daughter and I will have much in common," he said. "I wonder if she will give of herself as I have."

"We'll see what she has to give when she finds you. I think you might be surprised."

"She won't find me," said Simon. "But yes, I'm sure it will be a surprise." He scraped his chair closer over the grit until his knees were almost touching hers. The scent of decay washed over her. "Have you accepted my apology?"

"For what?"

"For your friend. I don't want there to be bad feelings between us."

"What does it matter to you what I feel?"

He wiped his hands over the tops of his legs, as if sweeping crumbs away. "You're right. It doesn't matter. But there's no need for me to be rude." He put one hand, his fingers splayed, against his chest and smiled with a mouth full of loose teeth. "I'm your *host*," he said. He stood again. "Why don't we have some tea?"

"No, thank you."

He got up and moved back to where she'd first seen him, where there was less light, and she heard metal scrape and sparks flew up from the inside of the stove. He put a kettle over the fire. She looked toward the door across from her again. He'd invited her to "take the air," and she wondered what would happen if she did. She got up from her chair, being sure to make enough noise that he wouldn't think she was trying to be careful. Her legs had fallen asleep from sitting as long as she had and her knees buckled as she stood. The table was close enough to steady herself on. "Don't get up too quickly," he said from the stove.

She turned around and looked at what was behind her. There was another window above a low, single bed. It glowed in the dimcast starlight like something seen at the bottom of a pond. She could also make out a line of small, shiny squares on the wall above the bed, but could not figure out what they were, beyond the fact that they were of identical shape and size. There were at least twenty of them. As she stared at them, trying to see clearly, they began to brighten as if imbued with their own light and the skin on the back of her neck prickled. Simon was coming up behind her with the lamp. "Can you hear them?" he asked her.

The objects were Polaroids and the light was beginning to pick up details. Faces. Mouths. The blood was roaring in her ears. "My God," she gasped. She heard the chair she'd been sitting in clatter to the side before she was even aware she'd burst for the door. She opened it and was through it and immediately she felt the sudden, too-bracing cold around her like a noose and the snow was beneath her feet and all around her the naked limbs of birch and alders stood against the predawn sky, vertical bars of treetrunks lining the world on all sides. She turned in a circle once, twice, the air piercing her, and she fell to the ground. He stood in the door to the cabin, the gauzy orange light bleeding out from behind him, the only sign of life anywhere and he called to her. "Do you need some help?"

"Go to hell," she cried.

"Hell?" he said, stepping down from the doorway. "Do you mean where there's fire and it's warm?" He laughed softly and returned to the cabin, closing the door behind him. Emily pushed herself up to sitting and stared at it. He would not let her die. He needed her. Even though Hazel would come anyway. She would come for her whether she was alive or dead. But Emily wanted to live.

She could barely get herself to standing; it felt as if she weighed a thousand pounds, dragging herself back to the promise of the cabin's meagre warmth. The door was locked. He would humiliate her now, make her beg for his murderous succour. "Let me in!" she shouted, and banged on the door. After a moment, he did, and he stepped aside as she entered. Steam rose from the mouth of the kettle. "Take the blanket from the bed," he instructed her, and, quaking, she did, pulling it around herself and sitting on the edge of the mattress. She felt powerless now, and for the first time, her fear gave way to grief and she felt her eyes fill. "Now for something to warm you up," he said.

"Just kill me," she pleaded. "I want it over with."

He was removing objects from a kitbag she hadn't seen before now and placing them on the stovetop. Glass vials. "Are you offering your life?"

"Will you leave my daughter alone?"

"Do you offer it freely?"

The tears were coursing down her face now. "Yes," she said. "I do."

He put the vial he was holding back down on the stove and came toward her. "Shake my hand," he said. She looked at him bewildered. Her life would end on a deal sealed with a handshake, like a business transaction or a bet. He held his hand out, palm up. After a moment, her heart breaking, she laid her hand in his. But he didn't close his fingers over the back of her hand as she expected, only moved his forearm up and down minutely in the space between them. "Just as I thought," he said, moving back toward the stove.

"Just as you thought?"

"One hundred and fifteen pounds," he said, reaching for one of the vials. "Now, let's see what you'll take in your tea."

] 24 [

Monday, November 29, 5 p.m.

One of the sinister benefits of a life in policework was
the context it gave one's own troubles. Many times,
Hazel had reflected on a lost child, a life being ruined by
drugs, those who died by their own hands. The suicides
both haunted and reassured her: they were object
lessons in how bad it *hadn't* been in her own life, even
when she and Andrew were splitting up, even when one
of Marty's depressions felt like thunder in the distance
of her own life. In the midst of the joy-occluding pain
she sometimes felt in her body, she could still take
inventory in comparison and know how good her life
was. So it was a revelation of the darkest kind when she
realized there was nothing that could contrast with this
moment in her life now. That there wasn't someone
else's shoes she could be grateful for not being in.

There had been no news for the rest of Sunday. She felt as if she were standing over a huge body of water into which someone had vanished and she was telling herself not to give up hope. Maybe a person can hold their breath for this long. Maybe they can tread water for this long.

Monday morning, nothing. They'd expanded the road-to-road sweep into the smaller towns lining the 121 to the west, and all of the towns and villages within fifty kilometres of Highway 41 all the way to Fort Leonard. No one who listened to the radio, watched the television, or read the *Westmuir Record* could not be aware that the largest manhunt in the county's history was unfolding over every inch of it. Sunderland had, for the second time in as many weeks, spent the entire weekend resetting his front section. It was now dedicated to Emily Micallef's abduction and Clara Lyon's murder. His introduction to Adjutor Sevigny had inspired in the editor a certain new caution: the paper reported the latest tragedies to hit Port Dundas with something approaching sobriety. The bodily insult done, in various forms, to another five of the town's elderly population did not result in any woolly speculation on how safe it may or may not be to enjoy one's retirement in Port Dundas. However, sitting with nothing in front of her at the kitchen table but the paper, Hazel could not bring herself to feel grateful for the *Record*'s newfound discipline. She was looking at a picture of her mother standing in front of Micallef's in 1952, her chin high, eyes bright, with that self-possessed smile of hers. Most children think of themselves as immortal, but as a child, Hazel had always looked into this confident face and believed that her mother was the immortal one. She lowered her head into her hands and wept.

At his supper break, Wingate showed up at the house with food. He stood in her doorway, willing her to say or do anything to him she felt she had to, but after a moment of staring into her red-rimmed eyes, he simply put down his bags, stepped into the foyer, and held her. She turned and led him down the hall and into the kitchen, where she put the kettle on for coffee. "I know you haven't eaten," he said.

"Not hungry."

"You could need your strength at any moment," he said.

She leaned against the counter. "You mean to help me bear up when the bad news comes?"

"I mean to lead."

She laughed, a dry, clicking sound in her throat. "Sure, James. From my empty living room in Pember Lake."

"You have no idea how many of us have personally made our opposition to Mason's decision known to both him as well as anyone they can get through to at the OPS head office in Toronto. You have everyone on your side."

"Have you spoken to Mason to oppose his decision?"

He hefted his bags onto the kitchen table and without looking up, he said, "I'm not Ray Greene."

"I know that," she said. "Ray would have brought me whiskey." She watched as he expressionlessly removed a sixteen-ouncer from one of the bags and put it on the table. "Ah," she said.

He sat down awkwardly at the small table and arranged the rest of his purchases. Cheese, deli meat, bread, a large bar of dark chocolate. She saw the chocolate and felt hungry for the first time in two days. She poured the hot water into a mug and put it and a jar of coffee grains in front of him, but didn't give him a spoon. He said nothing; it seemed a lot to ask for a spoon at this moment. At the station house, there had been a lot of whispering about Hazel having been under a doctor's supervision for some time. If she hadn't been, he hoped she was now, or would be soon. He knew what intractable grief could do to a person. He looked at her carefully as she reached into her cupboards for a couple of plates. He saw she was sockless in slacks and a freshly ironed blue dress shirt. It was as if she'd dressed the role to the 60 per cent mark and stopped. He half expected to see an empty holster on her hip.

"You want me to make you a sandwich, or are you skipping right to the chocolate?" he asked.

"I'm going to be positive and say that sometime soon there's going to be someone back in this house telling me what to eat. So yes, I'll have the chocolate now."

He passed it to her and she unwrapped it. The smell of the dark bar caused her mouth to fill with saliva. She imagined she might look like a starving dog. When she bit into the chocolate, the glands at the back of her jaw clenched with such force that she thought she was going to cry out in pain.

"To answer your question, yes, I did tell Mason how I felt. He gave me a choice to wait and hear the outcome of the investigation in Barrie or to lead it here in Port Dundas."

"Did you call him 'sir'?"

"I didn't call him what I wanted to call him." He tore a chunk from the baguette with his bare hands and then split it open. "I did tell him that if Simon Mallick had shown up at Humber Cottage three days ago that Mason would be having his picture taken beside you right now."

"The thing you should be asking yourself right now, James, is whether or not a bottle of Scotch and a loaf of bread is enough to make you a codefendant in the eyes of the magistrates of Renfrew and Westmuir counties."

"I'd sit at that table with you, Hazel."

"Let's hope it doesn't come to that."

She put a full carton of milk and the sugar bowl on the table, and then finally noticed he didn't have a spoon, and she placed one in front of him wordlessly. "Look," he said, "there's something I have to say."

"Go ahead."

"I get why Ray quit. I understand why he did what he did."

"I see."

"They told us when we were cadets that nothing was personal when it came to the world outside the stationhouse door. But that inside the doors, we're family."

"And I got that wrong?"

"You saw a killing in your own town as a personal affront. You were willing to do anything to get this guy. You crossed all kinds of lines."

It hurt to hear him talk this way, more perhaps than the way Greene had spoken to her. Wingate bore her no ill-will. He was telling her the truth. "Well, I've been punished then."

"I'm not saying I wouldn't have done the same thing, maybe. In your shoes. I know a little about what it feels like to want to avenge something."

"Tell me about that."

"Another time," he said. He tore off a piece of bread and chewed it thoughtfully for a moment, looking down at the table. "I just want to say that we should have all gone down together. You're the skip. You lead, we follow. But we shouldn't have been that far in back of you, Hazel. Ray Greene was better than that. I'm better than that."

She felt sodden, sinking into the floor. "I wish I was going to have the chance to make it up to you, James, I really do."

"You might. When the dust settles they're going to take a long look at this place and try to decide how they want it to run."

"They're going to amalgamate us. Everything that just happened here is catnip to Ian Mason. Greene was right. God knows Mason'll probably tap him to take over." She looked over at Wingate and the colour had drained out of his face. "You're kidding me."

"I was going to circle around it a while longer. Get a sense of how hard you were willing to fight before I told you."

"God."

"They haven't asked him yet. They wanted to test it out on us."

"I don't think it's going to matter what you want, James. That's not how they work."

"I said I understood why Ray did what he did. But I never said I agreed with it. Nobody wants to work for Ray Greene. We want to work for you."

She reached for the instant and turned to stir a spoonful of it into her cup. "You people shouldn't be wasting your energy trying to save my bacon."

She heard his chair slide back suddenly and she turned and he was leaning over his fists on the table. "Do you see? Do you see what you said? We're not trying to save just *your* goddamned bacon, Hazel!" His arms were shaking.

"I'm sorry, James."

"Family *inside*, the rest of the world *outside*. That's how I was trained to see it. If we fight for you, will you try to see it that way?"

"Yes," she said, thoroughly ashamed. "I'll try."

He slowly sat back in his seat, his eyes sliding away from her. Who was this young man, she wondered? This ferocious young man? Would she survive all of this to be permitted to return to that world he lived in?

"I heard from Sevigny this morning."

"You did, eh."

"He called from some back room in the courthouse in Sudbury."

"What's going to happen to him?"

"Nothing good." He made eye contact with her again. "Hazel, he searched Jane Buck's house before he left Port Hardy."

"What?"

"Told me she wanted to help our investigation. I think it might have been a euphemism."

"Christ, James! Why didn't you say that as soon as you walked in?"

"I had more important things to say first." She came to the table, drew a chair out, and sat. He watched her process what he'd just said. He wondered if his treatment of her here today would come back to haunt him. "He said he'd had an intuition about Buck when they were out at the cabin. She flinched when he took the Lord's name in vain. So he took her home and 'motivated her' was how he put it."

"I don't want to know."

"He spared me the details. He had the right instinct about her though: turns out she was the church secretary. She'd been in it right from the beginning; she had all kinds of paraphernalia." He reached into his jacket pocket and withdrew a couple of folded sheets. "He talked some clerk at the Sudbury courthouse into faxing this for him. It's the back and front of a pamphlet advertising the church. It's from 1988."

She unfolded it and began to read. The pamphlet invited those who were dissatisfied with their own churches to consider one that understood the conditions under which the True Christ would return. "Will the Christ," she read aloud, "who suffered in the wilderness, come to deliver those who wear furs and whose breath stinks of blood? In whose veins unnatural abominations run?" She looked up at Wingate.

"Keep going," he said.

The pamphlet asked the reader to consider whether the Son of God would descend to deliver the venal from their false gods. The church proposed a return to severe purity. Its touchstones were extreme hygiene, a diet based in local and natural foods, and an obsessive belief that it was only to a wilderness imbued with this kind of propriety and integrity that Christ would return. Modern medicine of any description was forbidden. It was a short argument, intended to attract only those who were already halfway there. The leader of the group was Simon Mallick.

"There's a picture of him at the bottom of the second page," Wingate said, and he folded back the page she was reading. There was a picture of a man at the bottom of the last section. He sported a huge, black beard and was as stout as a Viking.

"*That's* Simon Mallick?" said Hazel, looking at Wingate.

"Exactly."

There was no doubt in her mind that the man pictured in the pamphlet was the same man whose body Detective Sevigny had discovered in the Port Hardy cabin. The Simon drawn by Rose Batten was a different man: a wiry, rat-eyed creature. Pinched, angry, desperate. The one in the pamphlet was a Buddha: soft, calm, with laughlines around his eyes. The charisma of one who could draw in the lost and needy.

"Jane Buck called the man in the cabin *Peter*," said Wingate. "So if the dead man is actually Simon Mallick . . ."

"Then the man in Rose's drawing —?"

"— has taken his brother's name."

"And he's stalking the countryside rebuilding his brother's church." She refolded the faxed sheets and handed them back to her new CO. "Well, there's the reason there's been no activity in any of Simon Mallick's accounts. We've plugged the wrong name into the database."

"Costamides is already on it."

"Wow. When they let Sevigny out of jail they should give him a promotion." She sat thinking for a moment. "If you guys are prepared to fight for me, we might as well start now."

"I was hoping you'd say that." He stood and picked his cap off the table.

She poured the coffees into the sink. "Bring the chocolate," she said.

No one attempted to stop her.

Hazel, in full uniform, went through the front doors of the station house and into the pen. Everyone stood as she passed and a few saluted. She had never been saluted inside her building. She went to the back of the room. "Anyone who feels they can't work under me can leave with no fear of consequence," she said. "If you stay, you're in direct violation of an order from the commander of the Ontario Police Services. So make up your mind right now."

There was no movement in the room.

"I want to apologize to you all for the chaos you've been operating under. Obviously nothing could have

prepared us for this. You've all been consummate pro-
fessionals, and no matter what Mason tries to do to us as
a team, your grace under pressure these last few days,
and your dedication, will be the stuff of legend in this
town." She scanned the men and women standing before
her, and Cassie Jenner, standing closest to her, passed her
a tissue. She'd spoken with force, her voice unwavering,
but she'd wept steadily. She refused the tissue and stood
before them all, her face red and streaked and stared at
them. "I hope you understand what it means to me, to
have your support."

"All due respect to Detective Wingate," came the
voice of PC Peter MacTier, "but welcome back, Skip."
Under any other circumstance, she could imagine the
room breaking into applause, but instead, she felt every
eye on her, and she knew there was not a dissenter
among them. She imagined their unity might have a
salutary effect on Mason when it came time to decide
what to do with her. Although she doubted it.

Wingate said, "I've briefed the skip on what Detective
Sevigny learned, and although it isn't exactly a break in
the case, at least we know now who we're dealing with.
Have we heard back from the credit card companies?"

"I've got it all," said Sergeant Costamides. "He
hasn't used a credit card since May. I guess he thought
better of taking it with him. But the last thing he used
it for was heavy-duty painkillers and sedatives."

"Broke his own rules," said Hazel. "Things must
have been getting bad at home."

"He took out eight hundred dollars from a bank
machine in Norway House, and since then there's only

been one more withdrawal, in Pictou, for three hundred. There's only two hundred left in the account."

"Let's hope he needs it soon," said Wingate.

Her people, her mother's only hope, returned to their desks. Phone tips had been coming in since Saturday afternoon, but nothing had led anywhere. Peter Mallick was not going to be caught by a stray sighting. As the evening wore on, few of her people spoke to her directly, but they would touch her as they passed, keeping their hands on her for slightly longer than necessary, to let her know they were there, they were with her.

She stayed out of view as much as she could, in her office or in the rear hallways. At shift change, Wingate passed her in the hall, and in answer to her unspoken question, shook his head.

"Every minute that passes could be her last one on this earth. And we don't know."

"Is there anything at all that I can do?" he asked.

"I need something to keep my mind occupied."

He gestured with his chin to the pen. "You want a desk out there?"

"No. It'll distract them. How far behind are we on reports?"

"I'm sure they're piling up."

"Will you bring me some? I'm sure they'll have to be redone, but it's better than pacing."

She waited for him in her office, and he came in with a cup of coffee and a white file folder. She took both from him silently, and he stood in front of her desk with his hands folded in front of him. "It wasn't worth it," she said. "I ran him right into my own house."

"You don't know yet if it was worth it, Hazel. Everyone out there is ready for when the next thing happens, and you need to be ready too. Be what it's hard to be right now."

She filled her chest with air and let it out heavily. "Thank you, James."

He left, and she pulled the incident reports toward her. The folder contained the usual passel of complaints, disputes, petty thefts, and vandalism that made for an average month in Port Dundas. Hazel scanned the reports for names she knew and came across three familiar last names, all sons or grandsons of respectable people from the town and environs. What would Percy Adamsen think of his sweet grandson Arthur driving off with a full tank from the Beaver gas station on Bethune Road? Or Temperance McMurtry, dead now almost forty years, what would she make of her great-grandson Nicholas Grant, who'd been caught smoking a bong in the shape of a breast in Centennial Park on the previous Saturday night? Perhaps they wouldn't be surprised at all: the younger generation always appears to be headed for disaster anyway, doesn't it?

She wrote her notes in the files, setting aside a couple for follow-up in an unimaginable future when everything would be normal again. She felt amazed at herself that she was even capable of such an activity. She recalled that Nick Grant had hot-wired a car out in Kenniston two years earlier and made a mental note to visit him and speak to him personally about the direction he was heading in. It was hard to scare kids these days, though, and she imagined if she did give him a talking-to that she'd be fodder for comedy at Gilman High the very next day. As she was plotting what she should do with this young man, a swooping wave of terror suddenly passed through her and she realized that, for the first time in three days, she was not thinking about her mother. The switch out of those thoughts and then back into them came with a sensation like an electrical shock.

Wingate knocked and came in. "I thought you'd like to see this one too," he said. She reached across for the folder he was holding and cast her eyes down on it. "You're kidding."

"No."

"After all this time, she files a report? She must have been pretty upset to find out what happened to her kitty."

"It's not legal to keep a cougar as a housepet," said Wingate. "She was hoping it would come home on its own."

Hazel closed the file. "I guess that's not going to happen."

"I'm supposed to ask you what we did with the body."

"Ah," she said. "It went to the Metro Zoo for study purposes. She'll have to call them."

"One case closed."

"Next," she said.

At three-thirty in the morning, feeling her lower back seize and unseize, she got up to walk through the building. She went through the pen like a ghost, unmarked, and passed into the back hallway that led into the cells below, cells that were almost permanently empty. Even their so-called worst criminals (how she longed for those men and women now: purse snatchers, drunk drivers, speeders) were reasonable people: there was rarely a reason to lock someone up. The first time the Central OPS had tried to cut the size of the Port Dundas force, her mother had been mayor, and she'd shown her disapproval by insisting she be locked in one of the cells. Hazel had been a cadet at the time and had not been terribly impressed by the stunt. But it worked: Central hadn't cut anyone. That was 1973. Hazel recalled standing where she was right now, watching her mother sitting in the cell making a salad for her supper. She was sitting on that very bench, cutting a tomato in her hand into a wooden bowl. That's how she always cut a tomato, Hazel thought in a wonder of heartache, never with a cutting board, but in the palm of her hand.

She walked back to the stairs gingerly, turning to face them once to stretch out the back of her leg. In the basement, the lights were off, and it was cool and dark. She had the thought of letting herself into one of the cells and curling up for a couple of hours, but thought better of it and went back to the ground floor. When she got there Wingate was standing in the back hallway, his arms at his sides and his irises as small as pinheads. He said nothing but turned and began walking, and she knew to follow him.

In the pen, they were all standing, as if to show their respect. But they had their backs to her, and two of them near the front of the room had their guns drawn and trained on Staff Sergeant Wilton's counter. The man who called himself Simon Mallick was standing calmly in the waiting area in front of the counter, his hands at his sides. She stared at him as if she had in fact gone to sleep in the cells and dreamed him. But he saw her and stepped forward. "Detective Inspector," he said, and she could hear two officers holding their guns on him take their safeties off.

The small, silent group of men and women parted as Hazel walked through them. The air felt as if it had turned to syrup. She was worried that Peter Mallick would vanish if she took her eyes off him. "Lower your weapons," she said to her officers as she walked past them, and then she was face-to-face with him. His starving eyes were set in his head like yellow jewels. He regarded her almost expressionlessly, although (so the thought went through her mind) he seemed faintly relieved to see her.

"What have you done with my mother, Peter?"

He blinked slowly. "My name is Simon."

"What have you done with her?"

"I've brought my car," he said. "If you'd like to come with me, I'd be grateful if you'd allow one of your officers to handcuff you."

"Handcuffing me isn't going to stop me from killing you."

"It would be unsafe for us both if we had an altercation while I was driving."

"Where is she?"

He folded his hands in front of himself. She saw now

that his left hand was wrapped tightly in discoloured gauze the colour of a bruise. He looked like a dying crow, his wings tattered, his stubbled, piebald skull. "I am as unhappy at this turn of events as you must be, Hazel Micallef, but we need each other right now, and time is not on your mother's side, so please do allow one of your men to prepare you for your trip."

She heard Wingate's voice behind her. "We can't let you take her, sir. I'm sure you understand that. But I'll be happy to accompany you and hear you out. It's in everyone's best interest to ensure no one else is hurt."

"James –" Hazel began, but Mallick held his hand up.

"James what?" he asked.

"Wingate."

"Ah. Detective or Officer Wingate?"

"Detective Constable," James said, coming closer to the front counter.

"Were you part of the grand plan to draw me back to Humber Cottage?"

"That's not important right now."

"No, of course not," said Peter Mallick. "But you must have had high hopes. I picture you squatting in wait behind a juniper bush at three in the morning, tasting your victory. Now look where we are."

"We underestimated you," said Wingate in a conciliatory tone. "We did. But you haven't made a single mistake in your entire journey. So why make one now? Take my gun. Cuff me. I'll go with you willingly."

"Is that really what you want, Detective Constable Wingate?"

"It's the best solution."

"Well, Detective Constable," said the Belladonna, his voice as soft and comforting as a priest's, "this is what I'd like to do. I'd like to slice you from hip to hip and collect your steaming bowels in a sack as you watched. And then, to put the images out of your mind, I'll press your eyeballs through the back of their sockets with my thumbs until I feel them embed in your brain like candles in a birthday cake." He offered Wingate a very small smile. "I don't suppose you have any handcuffs on you?"

Wingate turned away from the force of Mallick's eyes. "Skip, you put me in charge of this, you said —"

"Give me your handcuffs, James," Hazel said.

"I can't let you go with this man."

Like a mechanized toy, Peter Mallick suddenly stepped forward and flung open the countertop. Wingate leapt back and Hazel held her hand up to warn the others to hold their fire. "If anyone follows us, I'll kill us both," said Peter. "Do you doubt me?"

"No," said Wingate, his voice clenched in dread.

Hazel turned her wrists to him. Wingate unhooked his cuffs from his belt and locked them on her, put the key into Peter's hand. She saw from the look in the detective's eyes that he wanted some kind of permission from her, and she shook her head deliberately from side to side. His face fell.

Peter Mallick pocketed the key and held his ruined hand out to her. She went to him. "Good evening, one and all," he said.

] 25 [

She'd been on these roads since she was a child. Even with her eyes closed, she could have told the distances, the sideroads, the feel of the asphalt or the dirt beneath the tires. He could have driven for half a day in any direction and she would still know where she was.

He'd put her in the back seat, strapping her into the middle seat belt, where he'd be able to see her in the rearview mirror. There had been no point in hooding her: he knew nothing would escape her notice, seen or unseen. They drove north out of town, onto the main highway, and he'd kept to the main road for almost two hours. She'd seen signs for North Bay, but he'd turned off east onto one of the rural sideroads, and she imagined he was making for Algonquin Park. It had been pitch-dark when he left Port Dundas, but now the sunrise was beginning to glow greyly on the empty fields, most of them shorn of anything like life, and a few with bare, snow-covered raw cornstalks lying in them like a huge rabbit pelt. Then they'd passed into the provincial park and the road narrowed. A canopy of bare branches covered them.

He drove at exactly the speed limit. She noted his movements were spare, concise. When he lifted his good hand to clasp the turn signal, he held it in his fist like a bar. The flesh over his knuckles was the yellow of uncooked chicken skin. The pointed bones in the back of his neck rose up like nailheads beneath worn wood. She was being driven to her fate by a skeleton.

She didn't know what was waiting for her at their destination. There was no reason to think her mother was still alive; Mallick knew Hazel had no choice but to go with him. But whether her mother was alive or not, she also knew she was going to die tonight, and she told herself whether it was in payment for her mother's freedom or in penance for her death, it was an acceptable exchange. An inevitable one.

It was fitting that she was here, that her life had come to this moment. That she was sitting in a car with a man whose plans, like hers, had come to nothing. They'd set off on separate journeys with entirely different goals in mind, but here they were, their two paths become one, both broken in body and mind. It was as if she'd become Peter Mallick's twin. And now he would kill her as well, but not out of love. She wondered how much of what was left of the Belladonna could be measured in love and how much in grief and rage.

She shifted quietly in her seat, her hands in her lap, small thrills of terror horripillating her arms and legs, and bent a finger into one of the handcuff rings, thinking perhaps Wingate would have had the presence of mind to leave one of the cuffs unlocked. But he'd done it under Mallick's cold glare, and she recalled the sharp, racheting *snick* that signified that she was properly restrained. At least her hands weren't behind her back. There was nothing to do but wait.

He'd spoken to her only a little on the way, asking her if she was cold, asking her if she was thirsty. She had answered no both times. He'd looked at her in the rearview mirror when asking her these questions, his eyes like marbles gleaming in a cup, but other than that, he did not bother with her. He had nothing to fear from her.

As the highway narrowed leading into the provincial park, he'd said, "It's a big country."

His voice had come from the front seat as casual as a cabbie's. Small talk. She decided to prod him. "It would have been faster to fly."

He said nothing more for fifteen minutes, and she wondered if she'd only imagined the short exchange. But then he said, "If more people travelled and saw the vastness of this country and the people in it, it would humble them, I think."

"Are you humbled, Peter?"

"You will call me Simon."

"But Simon is dead, Peter."

She saw the corners of his mouth turn up a little. "To answer your question, all servants are humble. But it humbled me more to meet so many friends in so many different circumstances and to be of service to them."

She laughed, a short hiss between her teeth. "You took the deaths of these people from their families. You made the end of their lives even more difficult. How is that a service?"

She saw his eyes slide over her in the rearview mirror and she saw in them the quick warmth she knew he had shown his victims, a flicker of tenderness he must have learned from his brother. Peter's nature was colder; as a child he had lived too many years without hope before being rescued and had never truly come to live among people. She knew this nature, had encountered it before in the few men and fewer women she'd come across in her policing work whom she would have called psychopaths, people with no moral compass, whose lives were guided by internal drives only. Being a member of a church would have been very difficult for Peter. She considered the effort it must have taken for him to wear his brother's face and wondered if she would see cracks in it. The murder of Clara Lyon had been a tremor along that faultline. "You think I have a misplaced sense of compassion," he said.

"If that's what you would call it."

"But I don't. It's not compassion at all. *Compassion* means to 'suffer together.' It's an inactive state."

"I see."

"*Prayer* is active. You must participate. What I have done is offered communion. It's a very different thing."

"You've just been murdering people willy-nilly, Peter. Sorry to cut through the crap, but you can feel free to tell yourself whatever you want." Outside, she watched a burnt farmhouse track past in her window. She wondered if she could recall the case, if anyone had been hurt or killed. But like many of the cases that crossed through her station house, she could not bring any particulars to mind.

"Your observances are just different than mine," he was saying. "We both have our faiths."

"God," she murmured, "to talk to you, you seem sane."

He turned in his seat, twisting his head back over his shoulder, and she was eye-to-eye with him. "I *seem* sane."

"Watch the road –"

"Why don't you tell me what I am, Hazel?" He'd begun to speed up. "Since you've been studying me for so long. I must be mad! Surely you think me mad! Who am I? Say my name!"

"You're a brother-killer, Peter Mallick. And a wife-killer, a mother-killer –"

He wrenched the car over to the side of the road and her head smashed into the door. The next moment, the door was open and he was wrenching her out of the back seat. Where did his strength come from? Her hips hit the snow-covered gravel shoulder and there was a shattering deep inside her and he dragged her into the middle of the road. She twisted onto her side and brought her knees up to her chest. He stood over her and she saw the last of the star-filled night in the gloaming beyond him. "Peter Mallick is dead," he hissed. "His small life is over." She spat a mouthful of blood onto his shoe. "Now, shall I make you part of my great work?"

"I don't care what you do to me."

"Do you care about your mother?"

"My mother's already dead."

"If you believe that, then why are you here?"

"Fuck you, Peter."

He kneeled down in front of her and pushed her over onto her back. He put a knee on her chest. She could barely feel the cold. The blood was flooding her limbs. "How do you think your bravery sounds to me, Hazel? When I've witnessed true courage over and over again? You believe you're willing to die, but you don't *need* to die. That's the difference between you and them. They let go so beautifully because they needed to. I gave them their quiet, beautiful deaths and they accepted them like benedictions."

"I deserve to die."

"I predict you'll do it screaming, meddler." He leaned into her and grabbed the front of her shirt, pulled her to sitting. It felt to her as if her legs had been cut off. "You don't know what I am," he said.

"I do, though," she said. "You're the same as me." He glared into her eyes. "You're pride masquerading as justice."

He pulled her to standing. She heard his knees crack. She let him put her back into the car. "Your mother is alive," he said.

They drove deep into the dark, pine-thick forest, the snow spiralling in the headlights. Her head was pounding and she could still taste blood. It felt as if her pelvis had been replaced by a block of ice, but she felt almost no pain at all. As he took a series of smaller and smaller roads, she began to wonder if she knew any longer where she was. They were somewhere in the northwestern corner of the park, but Peter was pushing off-road now, driving the narrow spaces between trees, crossing roads perpendicularly, taking their thin pathways and then cutting back into trees. Branches lashed the car, the shadows of snow-bent branches flickered by in dark stripings. She wanted to ask him where they were going and when they would get there, but her tongue was thick with fear now, her words boiled dry. Her cold bowels roiled.

At last, he hit a pebbled path and stayed on it. It was almost seven in the morning now. Somewhere in this world, people were sitting down to their breakfasts in houses warmed by little fires. She could not be farther from the comfort and safety of anything she held dear.

In the distance, a small shack appeared as a dark square against the base of the trees. He slowed as he approached it, and then stopped at the door. He pulled her to standing outside of the car. Smoke rose up from the chimney. She believed now that neither she nor her mother would ever be heard from again, and the grief of knowing how her children would suffer went through her like a blade.

He stepped forward onto some flagstones leading to the door, and Hazel knew her only chance was now. She exploded forward, twisting and driving her shoulder into his back, her whole weight behind the blow, and it was like breaking down a door that was already open: his body offered no resistance. She felt herself propelled through the air with him beneath her and when they hit the ground, it was as if there'd been nothing to break her fall. She felt a nauseating crunch under her and the breath shot out of him. Silence beneath her, a spasm in his legs. She smashed her forehead into the back of his skull for insurance. She leaped up, fell, scrambled to her feet again and looked around frantically for something to smash her cuffs on. There was a huge hunk of grey-and-white stone beside the cabin and she ran to it and heaved her wrists at it again and again, smelling the sparks as they flickered up like tiny approximations of the night sky she'd stared into the first time she thought she was going to die this day. The cuffs warped and bent, gouging her flesh, and there was blood all over the rock. Finally, one of the clasps sprang open and she pulled her swollen wrist free of it and spun to see Peter trying to push himself off the ground. She was to him in an instant, kicking him in the ear with the tip of her boot, and then she was at the door in a single movement, crying for her mother and pounding the heavy door again and again with the full force of her body. At last, she stood back and kicked it in and there was a darkness before her filling with dust from which no sound emerged.

"Mum!" She rushed into the lightless cabin, the air swirling with particles. It smelled bitter, like boiled mustard greens. As her eyes adjusted, she could make out a single table in the middle of the room with one chair tucked under it, and dark curtains over two windows, one to her right, beside a stove, the other across from her. Beneath it, in deeper shadow, there was a square shape, a bed, she saw now, and on it a form. A slow, sweet reek was making itself known.

She rushed to her mother's side and the smell intensified. Insensate, Emily Micallef lay on her back, her cheeks sunken, and Hazel saw her mother's face slicked in stinking, black blood. She slipped to her knees and heard her own voice quietly crying out, the voice of a lost child. "No no no —"

"Get up."

She saw him standing in the doorway, a solid black shape, legs slightly akimbo. A needle of light danced off the tang of a long, curving knife. She'd seen her father use such a knife to gut fish when she was a child. "Go to hell," she said.

"If you want her to live, you'll do as I say."

Her mother's cold hand in hers. The dead hand. She stood and faced him in the door. "If I believed what you believed, I'd make whatever deal you asked for, Peter. But I don't. And whatever it is you want from me now, you're going to have to take it because I'm not offering it. You told me she was alive."

He'd stepped forward into the body of the room and she heard a match scraping and saw the tiny flare of a fire, then he lit a small oil lamp and the room shimmered into being. His forehead was matted with blood, his nose smashed against his face. He showed no sign of being in pain. He was otherworldly, calm, in utter possession of himself. On the walls to her right, she could see a line of pictures, pictures she knew from a cursory glance were his victims. His own pictures of them. His trophies. "I did bring you here to make a trade, Hazel. She's not dead."

In the light, Hazel looked at her mother again. Beneath the thin, closed eyelids, she saw a faint strobing.

"She dreams," said Simon. "Feverfew for her pain, enough to keep her asleep."

"You drugged her? You *fucking* —"

"She is balanced on a line. The tincture of licorice root to thin the blood, the feverfew for the pain. But a dangerous combination. It can stop the heart. An injection of oil of thyme will bring her back, though."

"She's eighty-seven! You couldn't have just tied her to a chair like a regular lunatic, could you?"

He remained behind the table. The lamplight was pale and yet his white face shone in it like a coin. He kept the knife in his hand, but pointed it to the floor. "What you said about pride was right. But in the Bible, 'pride' means blind arrogance; it is not a dignified thing. But I *am* proud. I have a right to be. My pride is just." He tilted his head at her. "Is yours?"

He walked toward her, his broken face catching the stray light as if its facets were the folds in a crumpled piece of aluminum foil. "Time is of the essence," he said. "I'm going to give you this knife, Hazel." He stood in front of her, the knife held out to her in the palm of his hand.

"I'm not going to kill myself for you," she said, trembling.

"Christ did."

"You've been reading a different book than the rest of us."

"And the night before, he bled in the Garden of Gethsemane." He felt his face with his fingertips and held his stained hand up for her to see. "As it is written. *He was heavily pressed.* He kneeled in the Garden and his awareness of what he must bear weighed on him." He took another step toward her, the knife laid across his two palms. "His messenger is lashed to you. You are anointed."

"Neither of us is Christ, Peter. You're just a grief-struck —" and she felt the point of the knife against her bottom lip.

"Call me Peter again and I'll bind your lips with steel. What is my name?" She said nothing. He withdrew the blade. "I've got something more efficient than a knife. If you'd rather die like a coward."

"Let us go," she said, trembling. A thin rivulet of blood ran down over her chin. "Think of all the people you've shown love to, and let us go. You know how to vanish. You can do that."

He flung his arm out behind him and the knife flew to the door and stuck in it with a bang. She jumped. He stepped back to a bag on the floor behind one of the chairs and drew a gun out of it. She stared at it. The knife had been a test, but she knew the gun was for real. "I'll take her somewhere where your people can find her," he said. "I'll let her say a prayer over your grave before I drive her out of here. It'll be daylight when we go so she'll be able to find her way back. To lay flowers if she likes."

"Please," she said. "Wake her up. Prove to me she'll make it out of here alive." He stared at her flatly, the gun hanging from his fingertip. "Simon, please."

"Ah, now I'm Simon. Now that you want something from me."

"Just let me say goodbye."

"You want your mother to watch your death? Is that the kind of child you want to be to her in your last moments?" Without warning, he brought the gun up, aimed at her head, and pulled the trigger. She heard the empty click of the hammer and felt the power go out of her legs. She collapsed to the floor, her arm out, searching wildly for purchase. The broken handcuffs clinked on the floor. "Go ahead and wake her then," he said behind her. "Leave her with that fine memory of you." Hazel found her mother's arm and gripped it, pressed her face into that beloved flesh. The scent of her mother entered her, fugitive beneath the scent of rotting blood but still insistently alive, and it was that same scent that was woven into her memory, the whole record of her beingness: it was limned by this, the source of her life. She wanted to go on. It was a bright, clear thing now, this need to live. After losing everything that she thought had mattered to her, after loneliness and humiliation, after pain and failure, she still wanted to live. She dug her fingers into her mother's arm, but Emily Micallef did not wake. Hazel rose and faced her killer.

"All right," she said. "I agree to your terms."

He was searching for something in one of his pockets and brought out a single bullet, which he loaded into the chamber of the gun. "Terms? There are no terms here. Your *agreement* doesn't mean anything."

"No. Just like it was never truly a condition of what you offered your victims. You took advantage of their desperation, like you'll take advantage of mine." She could hear the rattle in his chest. Exhaustion, starvation, sickness: death was as close to him as it was to her, like the shadow of a cloud racing across a valley. "You broke His first commandment," she said. "Do you think He'll let you come to Him with all of these stains on you?"

"No one who has died is truly dead."

"One of my officers found your brother in the cabin you shared, his body surrounded by dust, stinking and full of maggots, abandoned with no one to bury him. The one who brought you out of the hell you once lived in. And that was how you showed your love?"

"It doesn't matter how I show my love, only how He shows his. And now, how you show yours."

"Just know this: I don't give myself freely."

"You said it yourself. You deserve to die."

"I do," she said. "But it doesn't mean I want to. I agree to your terms because I don't have a choice."

His jaw tightened and then he made himself release it, and he smiled at her. "You should be careful. You don't want me to believe you're false. It may incline me to be false as well. And you do want your mother to live, don't you?"

"I do," she said. "But if I'm to die here today, I won't do it as a liar. She wouldn't want me to tell a lie just to save her. The truth is, in my heart I don't want to die. I can't pretend that, even to save my mother." She took a careful step toward him. "If I give myself to you and you bring your brother back from where he's gone, what is he going to say to you? What will he think of your great work when it's cost the lives of so many people? Would he have saved himself at any cost?"

"Every second you talk, Hazel, your mother moves closer to death. Tell me you want her to live."

"Put a bullet in me." He lifted the gun and she looked down the dark eye of it. "But first show me how you want my mouth."

"You needn't worry about that."

"I want to, though. If you're going to make me a liar, I want to tell the lie myself."

He watched her, motionless. She thought that if she could keep him here, that the last of his strength would ebb from him and he would vanish like smoke before her. For weeks she had feared him, hated him, but standing before him now, feeling the force of his broken heart, she felt for him for the first time. To get back what is gone no matter the cost. Who could not understand that? Anyone who has lost hope is in that wilderness, she thought. And there is only prayer in the wilderness.

"I can tell the whole lie," she said, "I memorized it."

"Make your peace, Hazel."

"*Libera eos de vinculis* —"

"Don't you —"

"We've both lost the one who loved us most," she said.

"Your mother still lives."

"My husband left me. Your brother is gone. Simon is gone."

"He stands before you."

"No, his broken-hearted baby brother stands before me. Simon is gone forever. So you tell me: who is going to save Peter now?"

She saw his eyes flicker backward and there was a shudder in his body. And then there was nothing. There was stillness and quiet and all the desolate, broken dead were in their graves. She saw him know it. "*Mortis*," she said.

He opened his mouth as if to sing and put the gun in it.

] 26 [

Saturday, January 1

New Year's Eve had seen its share of disturbances, misdemeanours, drunken behaviour. Sam Roth had driven his brand new Skylark clear across Howard Tyler's field at two in the morning and through the side of a barn. The car was a writeoff, but Tyler declined to press charges: the barn needed rebuilding anyway and Roth had saved him the trouble of demolishing it.

There were nine fights, a bottle thrown through a window in Kehoe Glen, and an ambulance dispatched to Clifton right after midnight to assess a black eye caused by a champagne cork.

It had begun to warm up since Christmas and on New Year's Day, the temperature would reach six degrees by noon. The *Westmuir Record* would report the following week that it was the highest temperature ever for a

January first. In the morning, the usual garbage blew across the streets and it rained. A quieter Sunday than many she'd recently passed.

The hospital had sent Emily Micallef home on the Thursday morning, after almost a month in hospital, in time to mark the new year in the comfort of her own home. Hazel had transformed the living room into a bedroom: her mother could walk again, but the stairs winded her, and her doctor's advice was to preserve her energy as much as possible. The same went for Hazel. She'd driven out of the park with Peter Mallick's body in the trunk of his car and her mother reclined in the front seat, and the whole time she had been forced to hover over the driver's seat with her elbow braced against the door to keep from fainting from the pain. She'd not felt the disc in her back finally rupture when Mallick had dragged her out of the car – adrenalin had kept her attention away from it. As soon as she had her mother in the car, though, it announced itself, and Hazel had to make the drive in agony. It was more than an hour before she saw a sign for a hospital and when she turned into the curving emergency driveway, she leaned on the horn and blacked out. When she woke, they'd operated on her back and her mother had been airlifted to Mayfair, where she remained in a coma until the week before Christmas. In two separate hospitals they were hooked up to identical machines, their vital signs translated into electronic code, as if they'd both finally been plugged into the same ethereal grid that Peter Mallick had hunted his victims in. Hazel, not capable of much more than hobbling on a walker at first, spent her entire recuperation in her mother's Mayfair hospital room. She read her the yearly Christmas story from the *Record* when she woke up – the last part of it appeared on the day before Christmas Eve. Hazel could recall her father reading the conclusion of the Christmas tale to her and her brother, Alan, over the holiday turkey. Those hopeful stories. On December 30, her mother came home.

Emily Micallef would not talk about her ordeal. When she looked at Hazel, her eyes began to shine, and Hazel understood that the unspoken thoughts were too much to put to words, at least for now. They both hobbled back and forth through the house more or less avoiding each other, although there was no rancour between them. It was as if they had both been made aware of a grave new truth and its presence was enough to keep their minds occupied. The night of New Year's Eve, Hazel made them breakfast for supper: eggs, hash-brown potatoes, bacon, and toast. Comfort food, which they ate in silence.

Earlier that afternoon, Wingate had appeared at the door, his cap in his hand. She noted the absence of the traditional New Year's bottle, and for a moment she felt that he was being critical of her, but she knew in her heart that Wingate was kind. No bottle was a way of saying it might very well be a new year indeed. What he did have was coffee and a bag of pastries (one vice at a time), and the two of them sat in the front room. To his surprise, Hazel declined a cruller. Since coming home, she hadn't had any craving for sweets.

"How's your back?"

"I'm going to need another operation. There's no disc there now. They'll probably do a fusion when this heals up."

He grimaced. "And your mother?"

She peeled back the lid of her coffee cup and stuck the flap down. "Dr. Sumner says she made it by the skin of her teeth, but she's still weak. The only reason he let her come home is because she used to get his father off his parking tickets when she was mayor."

"Your people are made of stern stuff."

"I had no idea what I was made of until four weeks ago, James." She drank, staring down into the steam that rose up to obscure her face. "First, I was scared I was going to die, and then I knew I was going to die. And that was a completely new thought, you know? A feeling I'd never had before. Imagine getting to sixty-one and having a feeling for the first time in your life."

He was shaking his head slowly from side to side. "I can't. It must have been awful."

"But now, nothing feels like bad news. You could tell me I had six months to live and my thought would be, *How am I going to fill six whole months?*"

He was smiling at her and he reached across the back of the couch and gripped her shoulder. "Well, there's no bad news this week. I heard yesterday that Terry Batten is going to drop the charges."

"Yeah, I heard that too."

"I guess she doesn't want to be the one to add insult to injury."

"That's Ian Mason's job."

"We'll see," he said. "I doubt he wants his last official act to be canning the person who brought down Peter Mallick."

"Peter Mallick brought himself down. I just survived it."

Wingate pressed his lips together. He'd been around enough now to know when it was time to stop reassuring her. He tried to imagine what the lay of the land would be when he marked a year in Port Dundas, and he had to admit, he could not picture it.

"Did you speak to Sevigny?" she asked.

"Yeah," he said. "They gave him four months' suspension, no pay."

"Christ."

"He'll be okay. We took up a little collection and sent it to him."

"Put me down for five hundred," she said. "Tell me something." He held his coffee halfway to his mouth. "Did you like him?"

He lowered the cup to his lap. "What do you mean?"

"I mean did you like him? He's back on the job in four months, but I can't imagine he's going to be the most popular guy in his detachment. We could use another body here."

"Sure," Wingate said quickly. "He'd be a good addition. He's disciplined."

"He's crazy, James."

"That too."

"He'd fit in," she said, and he laughed.

She pushed herself off the couch with some difficulty and went into the kitchen, where she poured the rest of her coffee into the sink. Her stomach couldn't take much excitement right now: even a cup of coffee was a challenge. She braced herself against the sink to let the pain from standing discharge itself down her leg. She was aware of Wingate in the doorway to the kitchen, watching her.

"Here's the question that keeps going through my mind, James."

"What?"

"Zemba or Tonga?"

"Sorry?" he said, smiling.

"The cougar, James, what was its name?"

The smile widened into a huge grin. "Dave," he said.

Sleep was difficult. She was afraid to turn off her light and berated herself for being foolish, but still, she could not bring herself to be alone in the dark. On New Year's Eve, long after her mother had fallen asleep in the makeshift bedroom downstairs, Hazel had sat alone in her bedroom with the lights burning and listened to the faint sounds of celebration reverberating from down the street, from over the treetops. At midnight, there was a tiny roar from everywhere. A communion, she thought ruefully.

On New Year's Day they watched the Rose Bowl Parade first thing in the morning and then the football game. They ate no meals, just snacked out of bowls all day: chips, garlic bread, popcorn. By five o'clock, when night fell, Hazel felt as if she'd eaten the contents of a vending machine. Her mother announced that she wanted to spend the first night of the new year in her own bed, and between the two of them, they got her up the stairs. Her mother was in bed by seven. "Happy New Year, Hazel," she said, her thin hands along the top of the sheet.

"Many more," Hazel had replied.

Later that night, she lay in her own bed with her eyes open, staring at the yellowy lamplight blooming across the ceiling. She saw, again and again, the back of Peter Mallick's head opening in that terrible room, his wasted body falling away from her, and she felt anew the strange sensation that her life was going to continue. But all of those people, in their faith, who had given themselves to him: what had they died for? If you are the only person left to hold a belief and you're right, then you're a prophet. If you're wrong, you're a fool. But who had died in that cabin in the trees? The prophet or the fool? And who had survived? Her limbs buzzed. An hour later, she was still awake. She walked down the hall and pushed her mother's door open. The radio played quietly beside the bed. Emily opened her eyes. "Hazel?"

"Can you move over?"

"What?"

"I want to get in."

Emily Micallef stared at her daughter standing at the side of the bed, then slid aside with some difficulty, and Hazel pulled the sheet back. "I'm okay, Hazel."

"I know you're okay. But I don't feel like letting you out of my sight right now."

She saw her mother smiling faintly in the near dark. "You mean you don't want to be alone."

"Sure," she said. "That too."

"I won't be able to stay awake with you, Hazel. I'm too tired."

"That's okay."

"You can turn the radio off if you want."

"No, I like it." An orchestra was playing softly, something from another time. She couldn't identify the music – she had perhaps never developed her listening abilities very well – but it was peaceful and she could picture the roomful of people who had made this music, all of them working together to produce something that sounded like a single voice.

"Mum."

"I know, Hazel."

They lay there listening to the music. "We're not a little town any more, are we?"

"No," replied her mother. "Those days are gone forever."

When she opened her eyes again, she wondered if she had fallen asleep. She listened to the house. Under the quiet music, her mother's breathing, slow and deep. The old wood beams crying in the walls. This was their home. Outside, the bare branches tapped hollow in the dark ravine and beyond the trees it was the middle of the night in the town where she'd been born.